THROUGH THE FLAMES
CAME THE MOORISH PHYSICIAN'S VISION:

"Your destiny, O woman, is to journey through darkness
towards the sun, like our mother, the Earth.
But the night is dark and the sun is far away.
In order to reach it—for you will reach it—
you will need more courage than has hitherto
been demanded of you.
I see many trials, and blood—much blood.
The dead line your path as the altars of fire
line the mountain roads of Persia.
Lovers too . . . but still you move on and on.
You might almost be queen,
but you will have to give up everything
if you wish to find real happiness . . ."

Catherine
Royal Mistress

Juliette Benzoni

translated by
<small>JOCASTA GOODWIN</small>

AN AVON BOOK

AVON BOOKS
A division of
The Hearst Corporation
959 Eighth Avenue
New York, New York 10019

Originally published as *Il Suffit d'un Amour*, Vol. II.
© Opera Mundi, Paris, 1964

Published in Great Britain by William Heinemann, Ltd.
as *Catherine*.
Translation © Opera Mundi, Paris, 1965.

First Printing, November, 1968
Third Printing, July, 1969

Cover design by Milton Charles

AVON TRADEMARK REG. U.S. PAT. OFF. AND
FOREIGN COUNTRIES, REGISTERED TRADEMARK—
MARCA REGISTRADA, HECHO EN CHICAGO, U.S.A.

Printed in the U.S.A.

Prologue

On 27 April 1413, during a day of rioting, the people of Paris, led by the butcher Caboche and the university teacher, Pierre Cauchon, have stormed the Palais de Saint-Pol. Catherine Legoix, daughter of a goldsmith on the Pont-au-Change, and her friend, Landry Pigasse, are among the crowd. Young Catherine, who is only thirteen, becomes passionately interested in a young nobleman, whom the mob are dragging off to the gallows. Michel de Montsalvy is handsome, he is seventeen years old; that is enough to make Catherine risk her life in an effort to rescue him. With the help of Landry and Barnaby the Cockleshell Man, a strange old beggar, she succeeds in getting him away from his guards and hides him in the cellar of her father's house. But the hiding-place is discovered and Michel is cut down before Catherine's horrified eyes by her cousin, butcher Legoix, in the presence of both Caboche and Cauchon. In reprisal Catherine's father is hung, and his house destroyed. Catherine and her mother take refuge with Barnaby, in the Cour des Miracles, the Parisian beggars' own quarter of the city. Meanwhile Loyse, Catherine's sister, is kidnapped by Caboche who has taken a fancy to her. Before leaving Paris for Dijon, where the Legoix family have an uncle, Barnaby, Landry, and Black Sara, a mysterious gipsy woman who has become very attached to Catherine, successfully plan to snatch Loyse back from her captor. The whole party then travel by boat along the Loire to Dijon. Among the many memories of this time Catherine treasures the unforgettable image of the handsome Michel de Montsalvy.

All around them the civil war continues. King Charles VI is mad, his wife Ysabeau has auctioned the kingdom to the highest bidder and two rival factions, Armagnacs and Burgundians, are fighting for power.

Nine years later we take up the thread of the story again in Bruges: Catherine has become a ravishing young girl and with her uncle Mathieu Gautherin, a cloth-merchant, is in Bruges to make some purchases. During the Procession of the Sacred Blood, a certain merchant becomes over familiar with Catherine, who slaps his face and starts a noisy scene. She is arrested and taken before the Duke of Burgundy, Philippe the Good, a notorious womanizer. The girl's beauty excites the prince, but he sets her free, assuring her that he will not forget her.

Now, on the journey back to Dijon, Catherine and her uncle find a wounded knight by the wayside and the sight of him throws Catherine into a panic; he is the living image of Michel de Montsalvy. They take the knight to an inn, where he is tended by a Moorish doctor, Abou-al-Khayr, who is travelling to acquire new skills, and there the mystery is cleared up: he is Michel's brother Arnaud de Montsalvy, and Catherine is instantly attracted to him, so much so in fact that she is about to give herself to him when Arnaud discovers her name and rebuffs her harshly. He has sworn undying hatred of the whole Legoix breed, for it was a butcher called Legoix, a cousin of Catherine's, who killed Michel. . . .

Catherine is forced to leave him in despair and follow her uncle. At Dijon she soon finds herself the object of the attention of a certain very important personage: Garin de Brazey, Lord Treasurer of Burgundy, and to her amazement finds that she has been ordered by Philippe to marry him. Catherine rebels against the decree and tries to have her old friend Barnaby kill Garin before the marriage can take place. But Garin is only wounded and Barnaby meets his death as a result. Catherine has to marry Garin.

As it turns out, however, he proves a very strange husband. The marriage is never consummated despite all Catherine's efforts, aided and abetted by Sara, who is still her confidante and has now become her chief maid. There seems to be only one possible explanation: Garin has been ordered to keep his wife intact for the Duke. Meanwhile he surrounds her with every luxury and, on becoming lady-in-waiting to the Dowager Duchess Marguerite, Catherine enters the brilliant Court of Burgundy.

During the betrothal feasts of the Duke's sister, at Amiens, one of King Charles VII's knights comes to challenge the Duke on behalf of his master. Although a French prince, Philippe is just about to marry his sister off to the English invader and refuses to pay homage to his legitimate sovereign. The knight is none other than Arnaud de Montsalvy. . . . The

6

challenge is accepted. Montsalvy meets the Burgundian champion, Lionel de Vendôme, in the lists. He is victor, but is wounded, and Catherine takes the opportunity to see him in his tent.

Arnaud treats her harshly at first but soon succumbs to the irresistible beauty of the woman he secretly loves, even while believing her to be the mistress of the Duke of Burgundy. He is on the point of making love to her when he finds that he has fallen into a trap set by Jean de Luxembourg, commander-in-chief of the Burgundian armies. He is arrested, in defiance of the laws of chivalry, with his friend Xaintrailles, and holds Catherine responsible for the whole thing. Appalled by this turn of events, and convinced that the Duke knows nothing of Luxembourg's hasty action, Catherine goes to see him to explain what has happened. Philippe is harsh and suspicious. He demands that she become his mistress there and then and Catherine is even prepared to go through with this to save Arnaud. However, to her great surprise Philippe does not come to her at all that night, reappearing only the following morning after a great banquet for the ladies of the city.

He embraces her tenderly but passionately and then, before Catherine can get out of bed, has Arnaud and Xaintrailles brought into the room to apologize to them for the way they have been treated. Catherine realizes that she has been outwitted. Arnaud, seeing her in the Duke's own bed, will be convinced that she is the Duke's mistress. He goes off full of contempt, without a backward glance. This is the end for Catherine. What does it matter now whether she gives in to Philippe's entreaties or not?

"I shall send for you tonight," he says, as he sends her home.

Why not? Catherine leaves the palace and returns to the home which she is sharing, during her stay at Amiens, with her friend, Countess Ermengarde de Châteauvilain. . . .

7

Part I

PHILIPPE

1423

CHAPTER ONE

Ermengarde

It was nearly midday by the time Catherine reached the wool-merchant's house in the litter which Jacques de Roussay had had brought into the inner courtyard of the palace. It was closed in by heavy leather curtains, thus protecting the young woman from inquisitive stares. As they drew near to the lodgings Catherine sent up a silent prayer that there should be no one but Ermengarde in the house. She feared the sharp, malicious eyes of the young Vaugrigneuse girl and, above all, she wished to be alone with her friend, whose advice she had come to value and respect. The house seemed strangely silent. In the entrance hall she ran into a servantgirl carrying a plate of steaming cabbage soup. The girl dropped her a hurried curtsey and flashed her a look which she vaguely registered as nervous but without troubling to inquire why. She must simply be a timid, easily overawed girl. . . . Shrugging slightly she picked up her skirt in both hands and ran quickly up the dark, steep stairs. On the first small landing a ray of sunshine shone through the red glass of a narrow pointed window, casting a glowing pool of color on the white flagstones which gave a touch of life to the otherwise sepulchral house. She could hear a faint murmur of conversation coming from the ground floor, where the wool-merchant and his family must be at their midday meal, but up here there was silence.

Thinking that all the ladies-in-waiting had gone out, Catherine lifted the latch and went into her room. It was in fact empty except for Garin, who was standing near the window facing the door, his hands behind his back.

"You! What a surprise!" Catherine exclaimed and went

9

towards him. She was smiling, but as she drew nearer to him her smile gradually faded. She had never before seen her husband in such a towering rage. His whole face was contorted out of recognition. A nervous tic kept twitching up the corner of his mouth below the sombre black eye-patch. For the first time she was frightened of him; there was something almost Satanic about Garin's face.

"Where have you been?" he asked. The words whistled through his gritted teeth. Catherine clenched her fists under the folds of her dress to calm herself and help ward off the icy terror which was gripping her.

"I thought you would know," she said clearly. "I've come from the Duke."

"From the Duke? Really?"

Deciding that confidence was the best approach in dealing with an angry man, and strong in the knowledge that she was only speaking the truth, Catherine gave an impatient little shrug.

"Ask him, and see what he says."

She went across to the chest where her headdresses were kept to put away the little velvet hat she had been wearing and which she had just taken off. But she had no sooner turned her back on her husband when she gave a shrill cry of pain. Garin had seized her by the hair and dragged her savagely towards him. She fell heavily to the ground and lay there at his feet, instinctively raising an arm to protect her face. Garin let go of her hair and grabbed her arm so brutally that Catherine screamed again. He bent over her, his face swollen and crimson with rage. Catherine saw with terror that he held a dog-whip in his free hand.

"From the Duke? So you come from the Duke do you, you little slut? As if the entire court did not see you go into Montsalvy's tent and Luxembourg had not found you practically in his arms! Do you think I don't know that that accursed Armagnac did not return to Guise last night? So you spent the night rolling with him in some hovel, did you? I don't expect to get the truth out of you, but one thing I can do, and that's cure you of lying for the rest of your life!"

He seemed to have lost all control of himself. Before Catherine could utter a single word he cracked the whip viciously down across her back. She screamed and huddled against the floor, covering her head with her arms and trying to make herself as small as possible a target for his blows. Garin was striking at her like a madman. The whip whistled through the air, slashing across Catherine's back, shoulders and buttocks. She no longer cried out for fear of exasperating

10

him further. But her very silence seemed to drive Garin into a further paroxysm of fury. He suddenly bent over her prostrate form and seized her gown, ripping it and her chemise open with a dry tearing sound. Catherine's back and hips were now quite bare, and still the whip cracked down. But now it bit so cruelly into her tender flesh that it cut the skin. Catherine screamed in agony as the fiery lash seared her back. The blows began raining down upon her now, faster and more viciously than ever, and Garin's fury showed no signs of abating. Catherine dragged herself across the floor, groping for somewhere to hide and protect herself, a piece of furniture, a chest, behind the bed. But each time Garin got there first and flung her back into the middle of the room. Her tattered dress no longer protected her body, which writhed and twisted in agony under the lashes. She had no feelings left but pain, searing animal pain. Like a terrified beast she searched for some shelter from this rain of fire which was falling upon her. Would Garin never stop beating her? Through a red mist she dimly made out an immense black shape, an arm which rose and fell again and again. . . . He was panting like a blacksmith at his bellows. He would kill her. . . . Catherine could no longer feel the blood flowing from her lacerated flesh. She had stopped screaming. . . . She felt herself losing consciousness. The blows seemed to reach her through a sort of padding. . . .

She made one last effort, glimpsing the door opening before her. If she could just reach it . . . crawl through it . . . escape this torture. . . . But then something blocked the escape hole . . . something red which moved. With a little moan Catherine collapsed at Ermengarde's feet. . . .

The Mistress of the Robes' scream of horror pierced even the wretched girl's half-conscious stupor. She sensed that rescue had come and clung to her saviour's feet.

"By the Pope's intestines!" Ermengarde bellowed. "I have never seen anything like it!"

Freeing her feet from Catherine's clutching hands, the massive Dame hurled her whole two-hundred-pound frame into the attack. Anger and indignation redoubled her already formidable strength. With a push that sent him flying she flung Garin to the other end of the room, snatched the bloody whip from his hands and threw it into a corner. Then she seized Garin by the collar of his doublet and began shaking him vigorously while she gave vent to a stream of oaths, insults, and curses which would have done credit to a trooper. He offered no resistance whatsoever and allowed himself to be dragged, almost carried, towards the landing, like a rag doll. His passion of rage seemed to have exhausted his strength

11

completely. Ermengarde flung him down the stairs, shouting after him:

"Get out of this house ... and don't let me catch you putting your nose in here again!" Then she closed the door, and returning, knelt beside Catherine's inert body, her broad face stricken with pity. The unfortunate girl was certainly in a pitiable state. Her bloodsmeared body, striped with long black and blue marks where the whip had struck her, was almost naked except for a few rags of black velvet which she was still clutching to her bosom. Her long tousled hair clung to her face, which was wet with tears and sweat. Ermengarde gently smoothed it back with her white hand. She was almost weeping as she spoke. "Gentle Jesus, what has that brute done to you, my poor lamb! I am going to carry you to your bed ... put your arms round my neck."

Catherine raised her arms to put them round the Countess's neck, but her torn shoulder hurt her so much that, with one last cry, she fainted away.

When she regained consciousness it was night, and she realized she was in her bed, and so tightly swathed in dressings from head to foot that she could scarcely move. As she opened her eyes she saw Sara sitting near the fire cooking something in a little iron pot. The sight took her back several years. When she woke in Barnaby's cave in the Cour des Miracles she often used to see Sara sitting there by the fire with that same thoughtful expression on her handsome face. This childhood recollection made her feel better. She tried to move her arm to pull back the covers, which had crept up round her eyes. Her arm felt as if it were weighted with lead and her shoulder hurt so much that she moaned faintly. Instantly Ermengarde's impressive bulk loomed up between the bed and the fire. The Countess leant over the bed and placed a cool, strangely gentle hand on her burning forehead.

"Are you in much pain, my child?"

Catherine forced herself to smile, but it cost her a painful effort. There did not seem to be a single muscle, or particle of flesh even, which did not ache terribly.

"I am hot," she whispered, "and my body hurts all over. It feels as though I were lying on a bed of thorns. Everything burns and smarts. ..."

Ermengarde nodded compassionately, and then moved aside to let Sara approach the bed. As she bent over her the gipsy's face wore a fierce and determined expression.

"That brute would have killed you, my love, if Dame Ermengarde had not arrived in time. I suspected something

12

was brewing when I saw him appear this morning. He looked mad. . . ."

"Where were you when I came in?" Catherine asked weakly. Ermengarde explained.

"He locked her into the closet under the stairs. That's where I found her when I got in. She could hear your screams from there and she was kicking up the devil of a row to try and make them release her. But the people who live here did not dare. Garin had threatened to throw them into a dungeon if they so much as lifted a little finger to help. When I went to see them to get some lint and bandages I found them almost dead with fright hiding behind their cabbage soup."

"I hope you reassured the poor things?"

"Certainly not!" the Countess replied with a roar of laughter. "I scared them right out of their wits by telling them that there was a good chance the Duke would have them skinned alive when he found out what they had allowed to happen. They instantly insisted that we should have the use of their own apartments and I wouldn't be surprised if they weren't packing their bags right now. . . !"

Catherine looked around more carefully and realized that it was in fact a different room from the one where she and Ermengarde had been originally. This was larger, more comfortably furnished and hung with two fine tapestries. . . . It did not open into another room like the one they had been sharing, and the thought of being shielded from the prying eyes of Marie de Vaugrigneuse gave her considerable satisfaction. Sara then returned to the hearth and began ladling the contents of her little cooking pot into an earthenware bowl, while Ermengarde settled herself at the foot of the bed and described to the invalid how she and Sara had had to anoint her entire body with soothing balm before completely swathing her in linen bandages.

"You are swollen and cut all over," she announced cheerfully, "but fortunately none of the cuts has gone very deep. Sara seems to think that you will only have a few, very faint scars and none on the face at all. I have the impression, may God forgive me, that your husband must have gone clean out of his mind! What did you do to him?"

Ermengarde was evidently consumed by curiosity, but Catherine felt as weak as a kitten and had no immediate desire to begin describing everything that had happened the day before. She held up her bandaged hands and gazed at them with a kind of bewildered amusement. The balm with which she was covered from head to foot had seeped through her fine bandages, leaving large greasy yellow patches. She felt as though

13

she had been turned into a big rag doll. Only her hair, which had been neatly plaited and lay on the coverlet in front of her, seemed to be alive and really part of her body. She sighed, and Ermengarde, who was more sensitive than she looked, instantly understood.

"You are quite right," she said. "You had better not talk now. You are too tired. You shall tell me all about it later on. . . ."

She herself however launched into animated conversation. Garin had not dared show his face again but his friend Nicolas Rolin had called a little earlier to ask how she was. Ermengarde had greeted him coldly and told him that she had assumed full responsibility for the nursing and care of the Dame de Brazey, and meantime the less she heard of Garin and his friends the better. Rolin had left without another word. Catherine's self-appointed guardian had said something similar, though in a slightly more amiable tone, to the page whom Monseigneur had sent round half an hour ago. Catherine raised her eyebrows under the mask of bandages.

"The Duke sent a page, did he?"

"Yes. His favorite page, young Lannoy. I got the impression that His Highness was expecting your company this evening. Naturally I made your excuses."

"What did you tell him, dear Ermengarde?"

"I simply told him the truth. I said that your charming husband had whipped you like a dog and left you half dead. That ought to earn that brute Garin a reprimand he won't forget in a hurry. With luck it may even stop him ever trying again."

"God help me," the young woman groaned despairingly. "The whole town will be laughing at me now. I shan't dare look anyone in the face when they hear that I've been thrashed like a slave."

"Young Lannoy is a gentleman, my dear. He knows very well that what is confided to him for his master's ears alone is not to be whispered into any others. He won't breathe a word of this to a soul. He was genuinely shocked and indignant too, I might add. The lad entertains a great admiration for you, my pretty. It wouldn't surprise me to find that he was even a little in love with you. Now drink this."

Sara arrived at that moment with a bowl of vervain into which she had stirred a number of potent and mysterious drugs. Assisted by the stout Ermengarde, Catherine managed to struggle to a sitting position in the bed. Leaning against her friend's arm she drank the brew. It had a slightly acid

14

taste, but was not disagreeable. And it was hot and comforting inside her.

"I've mixed an herb into it which will put you to sleep at once," said Sara. "While you are asleep the pain will disappear...."

Catherine had no time to reply, for just then the door opened and a man dressed in black, wearing a black mask, appeared.

The women started back in alarm. He remained framed in the doorway, motionless as a statue. Only his gray eyes could be seen glittering through the slits in his mask.

"Who are you?" cried Ermengarde, instantly on the defensive. "What do you want?"

But then she sank into a deep, hurried curtsey, for the newcomer had just removed his mask. It was the Duke Philippe. The gesture, however, must have been quite automatic. Philippe, no doubt hypnotized by the scene that met his eyes, seemed frozen by shock.

"It can't be you, Catherine," he exclaimed incredulously. "It *can't* be!"

The young woman started to giggle. She could well imagine the effect that her mass of bandages would have on Philippe, the devoted slave of beauty. He must have rushed round expecting to find her ailing, a little bruised perhaps, but certainly not in the state in which he now discovered her. Perhaps young Lannoy had not repeated Ermengarde's message word for word. At any rate the Duke still stood transfixed in the doorway. Then he stammered:

"Is it as bad as that?"

"Worse!" Ermengarde answered, rising from her curtsey. "Dame Catherine is black and blue from head to foot, and somewhat cut about into the bargain. She is in considerable pain... and finds it hard to speak."

Philippe clenched his fists and swore that he would have Garin flung into a dungeon and summarily executed. He ranted and raged, a veritable fire-breathing dragon in his wrath, while his cheeks were wet with tears of emotion. Ermengarde was so used to this habit of his that she paid no attention, but Catherine looked on curiously as the Duke wept. The Countess finally managed to calm him down. She pointed out that only Madame de Brazey had the right to lodge a complaint against her husband, and that while Garin might be a brutal husband, he was nonetheless a loyal and valuable subject.... Philippe was finally forced to agree that it would be unwise to unleash a scandal by arresting Garin.

15

He sat down on the edge of the bed and took one of the bandaged hands in his own with infinite gentleness.

"It breaks my heart to see you in this state, my sweet. Just when I was waiting for you to come, with my mind aflame with your dazzling beauty. . . . You must be cared for and cared for well. . . ." He turned towards Ermengarde de Châteauvilain, and added. "My mother has sent for you, has she not, Madame de Châteauvilain?"

"That is so, Monseigneur. Madame the Duchess has not been at all well and now her condition seems to be deteriorating she wishes me to hasten my return."

"Stay here a few days longer and take Madame de Brazey back to Dijon with you. I want to separate her from her husband for a time. She will recover more quickly in Dijon and I shall feel easier about her, knowing that she is under your protection. May I entrust her to you? She is . . . infinitely precious to me."

"It would be an honor," the Countess replied, curtseying again. Catherine felt obliged to thank Philippe, in a faint voice, for his solicitude on her behalf. The idea of departing with Ermengarde for company was a pleasant one. She would be happy to leave Garin—and Philippe too if it came to that! This way she would at least have a period of respite in which to think about her own problems. While Philippe took his leave of her with many sighs and a fresh outbreak of tears, visibly more and more moved by the pathos of her condition, Catherine suddenly reflected that she quite forgave Garin the appalling beating because, thanks to it, the event she feared still more was postponed again, this time indefinitely. She would not become Philippe's mistress tonight after all. It was battered but still virginal, this body she wanted to keep untouched for the man she loved.

But though she might forgive, she could not understand. Why should Garin have half killed her because he believed her to have spent the night with another man? He did not love her, he did not want her himself, and he knew she was destined for Philippe. So what difference could it make?

Catherine finally had to abandon the whole subject as incomprehensible. Anyway her head and body ached too much to concentrate for long. Gradually Sara's sedative drug began to take effect. Philippe, whom Ermengarde had escorted to the front door, had been barely five minutes out of the room before she fell asleep. Sara was seated by the fire once more, her black eyes studying the flames as though they could decipher strange mysteries in them. Outside the

16

street was silent. The only sound to be heard was the clatter of Philippe's horse's hooves receding into the distance....

CHAPTER TWO

Jacques de Roussay's Mission

They left Arras several days later. Catherine was by no means completely recovered, but she did not wish to delay her friend Ermengarde too long. Besides, she was in a hurry to return home and put as much distance as possible between herself and this town of painful memories. Thanks to the devoted care of the Countess and Sara and the many balms which had been applied to her wounds twice a day, Catherine was now able to dispense with most of her bandages. By the time of their departure she had only four dressings left, one on her shoulder, two on the thighs and one across the small of her back. Sara said that the fresh air would help efface the marks, and speed up the healing of the rest. On the morning of their departure she dressed her mistress warmly because the weather was chilly for early May. She made her wear gloves lined with fine leather which had been smeared with some softening oil. To hide the bruises which still showed on her face, including a dramatically blackened left eye, she wrapped Catherine's head in a thick veil which hid the worst of her disfigurements.

In view of Catherine's still delicate state of health, the journey had to be undertaken in a sort of large, mule-drawn litter in which she could travel lying down. Ermengarde de Châteauvilain was to travel with her to keep her company. This, as she frequently reminded Catherine, was a great sacrifice, because there was nothing she liked so much as riding on horseback. Sara and the two ladies' remaining servants would follow on mules. An armed escort was to be provided because of the state of unrest prevailing through most of the country through which they would be traveling. When the escort and litter turned up on the morning they were to leave, Catherine had to suppress a smile. The litter was emblazoned with the ducal arms and the escort was under the command of a beaming Jacques de Roussay, overjoyed at the prospect of such an agreeable mission.

"This will be our second journey together," he exclaimed, when he came to pay his respects to Catherine, whose muffled appearance seemed to astonish him. "The first was so delightful that I am eagerly looking forward to this one."

But he had reckoned without Ermengarde, who swept out of her room just then, drawing on her gloves.

"You had better curb your raptures a little, young man," she rapped out. "Madame de Brazey is my responsibility, and I feel perfectly equal to coping with it. You will have quite enough on your hands seeing to our lodgings and your men along the route."

At this rebuff Jacques de Roussay's shoulders drooped. But then Catherine held out her hand to him.

"You mustn't be too severe, Ermengarde. Messire de Roussay is a loyal friend of mine, and we shall be quite safe in his care. Are we ready?"

With his high spirits quite restored by these kind words, de Roussay went off to order his men their stirrup-cup for the road while the mules were loaded and the ladies took their places in their litter. Both of them had their jewel-chests with them for fear of thieves. Catherine's collection, which contained the celebrated black diamond among other things, was itself worth a small fortune.

The little party finally set off towards mid-morning. The weather was bitter and a chill wind swept cuttingly across the flat countryside. In accordance with his orders Jacques de Roussay took the road towards Cambrai instead of heading due south. The plan was to avoid Péronne and the Vermandois country, which was in the hands of Charles VII's supporters. De Roussay had no intention of allowing a hostage as valuable as Catherine to fall into their hands.

In spite of her assertions to the contrary, Ermengarde did not prove to be the most entertaining of traveling companions. No sooner had she settled herself among the cushions beside her friend than, as was her wont, she fell fast asleep. Her conversation was confined to loud snores, and she regained her accustomed vitality and gargantuan appetite only when the litter halted at an inn or a convent, for meals or the night.

Catherine was therefore thrown upon her own company and had plenty of time to mull over her recent experiences. She had not seen Garin again. He had sent for news of her progress every day, usually by a servant but once or twice by his friend Nicolas Rolin. The proud Chancellor, however, did not enjoy these errands much, as they brought him into overly close contact with the far from friendly

Ermengarde. Other than this daily inquiry after her health, Garin had done nothing which might have been construed as an attempt at a reconciliation. A few days earlier Catherine had learnt that he was intending to leave for Ghent and Bruges on business, and he left Arras the day before his wife's departure without bidding her farewell—not that this mattered to Catherine, who had no desire to find herself face to face with her husband until it was strictly necessary. She had often thought over Garin's outburst of fury against her, and what might have provoked it, and she had finally decided that he must have been afraid that his wife had angered the Duke by visiting Montsalvy in his tent. There seemed no other possible explanation. Jealousy was unthinkable in Garin's case.

Their journey continued uneventfully. As before, crossing through war-devastated Champagne proved nightmarish. There were the dead villages, famished faces, and bands of refugees, with the few animals and possessions they had managed to save from the wreck, plodding along the roads towards the frontiers of Burgundy where they hoped to find refuge. Catherine and Ermengarde dispensed as much charity as they could along the way, but from time to time de Roussay had to intervene to push back the hungry crowds who pressed too close to the litter. Catherine's heart ached at the sight of so much stark and abject misery.

As the little group of travelers were approaching the frontiers of the Duchy of Burgundy they fell in with a strange looking cavalcade one evening. They had just left Troyes and were beginning to look about for an inn where they might stay the night. The procession in question consisted of a long procession of swarthy-skinned men and women, who from a distance looked as though they might be refugees from some sacked village. As they came nearer, however, the travelers noticed that there was something distinctly out of the ordinary about these people. The women all wore linen turbans, one end of which passed under their chins, and clothes of striped wool over a rough-spun linen petticoat cut very low at the neck. They carried their small, brown, half-naked babies either in slings suspended from the shoulder, or in baskets which jogged soothingly against the flanks of their mules as they rode along. They all wore coin necklaces and had coal-black eyes and dazzlingly white teeth. Their menfolk sported bushy black beards which left little of their faces visible, faded felt hats and colorful but ragged clothes, and they all had both sword and dagger hanging at their sides. These people were followed by a motley collection of horses, dogs and poultry and the language they spoke to one another was foreign. They were singing as they walked, or rather chanting a slow, harsh lament which instantly struck Catherine as familiar. She drew back the leather curtains round the litter to look out just in time to see Sara's mule speed by like an arrow loosed from the bow. Sara galloped towards the strange procession of travelers with her hair streaming behind her in the wind and her eyes shining. She called out to them joyfully at the top of her voice.

"What has come over her?" Ermengarde asked querulously, waking up with a start. "Has she gone mad? Or does she know these folk?"

As Sara drew level with the man who appeared to be their leader, a young fellow, lean as a vine-shoot but with the bearing of a king in his ragged clothes, she reined in her mule and began speaking volubly to him. Catherine had never seen her looking so happy before. Ordinarily Sara rarely laughed and spoke very little. She was above all active, efficient and silent. She disliked wasting speech or time. Only once before, in Jacquot-de-la-Mer's tavern, Catherine had seen through the window into Sara's innermost, secret soul. Now, watching her as she chattered animatedly to the swarthy-skinned man, the light of some inner fire blazing in her excited face, Catherine felt a twinge of apprehension.

"She may know these people," she told Ermengarde. "But I think it more likely that they are blood-brothers or members of the same tribe, whom she has just recognized."

"What? You mean that these ragged people with their black eyes and their knives—?"

"—are gipsies like Sara," Catherine finished for her. "As I may have told you, I believe the tales my kind and faithful foster-mother tells me. . . ."

At a sign from Catherine, de Roussay ordered their party to halt and they all stood staring at Sara. Catherine's sadness deepened with every passing minute, for Sara seemed to have forgotten everything except this dark-skinned youth. Suddenly she turned and caught sight of Catherine, lying in her litter propped up on one elbow. She ran towards her.

"These are my own people!" she cried, suddenly communicative in her joy. "As you know I had resigned myself to never seeing them again. And now, suddenly, here they are, just as the old woman prophesied so many years ago. The tribes have taken to the roads and gone a-wandering. These people come from Moden, at the foot of Mount

Gype, and I come from Cyprus, the island of Aphrodite—isn't that extraordinary?"

"Quite extraordinary!" Ermengarde cut in. "But must we stay here all night discussing this?"

Sara did not deign to reply to this. She looked at Catherine with imploring eyes.

"Let me spend the night with them," she begged. "They are going to pitch camp at the next village, the one where we are going to stay the night too."

"Would this give you such pleasure, then?"

"You cannot know how much! If only I could explain. . . ."

Catherine silenced her with a gentle smile, and said, "You don't have to. I think I understand. Go to your people . . . but don't forget me altogether."

Sara stopped swiftly, still as agile as any girl, and pressed her lips to Catherine's hand. Then she ran excitedly towards the gipsies. She had left her mule with the armed escort. Catherine watched her swinging along beside the dark-skinned youth, who had shortened his mule's step to fit in with hers. You might have thought that Sara had just met her lover from the sparkle in her eyes and the brilliance of her smile. Ermengarde looked at her and shook her head.

"I wonder whether she will return to you tomorrow after all," she said.

Catherine whirled round to face her friend, with a look of dismay on her face.

"But why shouldn't she come back?" she asked. "Her place is here with me."

"*Was* here with you! Till now she has always been an exile, cut off from her own people without any hope of ever seeing them again—you were her port in a storm. But now she has found her own folk again. . . . Come, come, you mustn't cry my dear," she added hastily, seeing Catherine's eyes mist over. "She loves you, I know . . . and she may well return one day. Meanwhile let us make haste to find shelter for the night. I am hungry and it is beginning to rain."

The little caravan set off once more in the direction of the village, whose square church tower and spire could just be seen in the distance.

The gipsies pitched camp in a field behind the inn where Catherine and Ermengarde stopped for the night. The window of the room they were sharing overlooked the camp site, and Catherine amused herself watching the wanderers settle down for the night. Huge bonfires were built on which to cook the cauldrons of stew for the evening meal, and while the children ran to and fro as they pleased, the womenfolk

21

sat themselves down to pluck chickens and prepare the few vegetables they had managed to collect. All these people, barefoot and ragged as they were, had something strikingly dignified about their appearance, and many of the young women, with their black hair and eyes, were real beauties. Catherine caught sight of Sara sitting next to the young chief on a sawn-off tree stump. The gipsies seemed to be treating her with great respect, and when the meal was ready she was served first after the chief. The children's happy cries rose, clear and sometimes ear-splittingly shrill in the pearly spring twilight. Their parents sat quietly chatting, slowly and thoughtfully eating in the way of people to whom the next mouthful is a serious business. From time to time the sound of laughter reached the window and Catherine felt a sudden urge to join the charmed circle round the fire. A large piece of canvas had been fixed to three trees in one corner of the field, and this was to serve as shelter during the night for the women and children. The latter, however, seemed to be in no hurry to go to sleep. Some of them played hide-and-seek around the bonfires, and others stood holding hands listening while one of the older boys strummed a lute in the shelter of the trees. Most of the children were only half clad, and a few were quite naked, with comic little pot-bellies. A group of girls stood close at hand, shaking and rattling their tambourines restlessly, evidently impatient for the dancing to begin.

At last there came a rousing series of chords from the lute and a dozen or so girls sprang forward, forming a wild spinning circle round the highest blazing fire. As the rhythm of the dance grew faster and more frenzied, their brown nimble feet flashed over the ground and their full striped skirts flew higher and higher round their long bare legs. . . .

As the tempo of the dance quickened the tambourines clashed in the lean brown hands and long dark plaits unraveled, spinning loose over bare shoulders as the dresses slipped lower and lower in the frenzy of the dance. The moon shone down suddenly through a gap in the clouds, adding its soft brilliance to the brazier's ruddy glow and the gipsy girls went wild. Their feet sped through the intricate steps faster than the eye could follow. They were like living flames soaring and flashing in the darkness around the fire. They twisted and turned and swooped in the middle of the ring of hypnotized eyes. Catherine herself was enthralled by the wild beauty of the scene. They were like priestesses of some dark, unknown cult, those lithe girls dancing in the moonlight. They lifted their faces with closed

22

eyes as if offering them to the silvery light streaming down. ... The gipsy tribe was infected by a sudden feverish gaiety and they clapped their hands faster and faster in time to the music. A few villagers had gathered rather nervously to watch what was going on. They were standing in the shadow of the inn walls and Catherine could just make out their faces—at once eager and mistrustful—beneath her windows. Suddenly a voice soared like an arrow above the harsh, staccato throbbing of tambourines and hands, a vibrant passionate voice which effortlessly dominated the eerie melody of lute and violin. The mysterious words of the song lent it a spell-binding quality which Catherine knew of old.

"What's that?" Ermengarde whispered, coming up behind her friend.

"It's Sara! She's singing!"

"So I perceive ... but what an astonishing voice! Strange ... but magnificent!"

Sara had never sung before as she did that night. In Jacquot-de-la-Mer's smoky tavern she had sung out of nostalgia and regret, but now she sang of the wild joys of a nomadic life, its infinite spaces and wild rides. Catherine could see her sitting there with her hands clasped round her knees, hurling her strange song towards the star-studded sky. Suddenly she stood up, throwing her arms towards the great full moon as if she wanted to embrace it. The dancing and singing blended, faster and faster, wilder and wilder. The whole tribe had joined in the singing now and their song rolled across the sleeping countryside like the rumble of thunder.... With a wild yell the dancers tore off their dresses revealing slim brown bodies naked and gleaming with sweat. There was a scuffle from somewhere beneath Catherine's windows. The peasant women were trying to force their reluctant husbands to go home.

"Oh!" Ermengarde exclaimed, half admiring, half scandalized.

Catherine smiled. She had seen too much in the Cour des Miracles and Jacquot-de-la-Mer's tavern to be shocked. She found nothing objectionable in the nakedness of these young, beautiful girls. Their well-formed bodies moved with supple grace, beautiful as statues magically come to life; the gipsy men's eyes were glowing like hot coals. Then the moon slipped behind a bank of cloud once more and the fire sank to a dim red glow. Little by little darkness engulfed the countryside. A man who had been crouching near the fire sprang up and seized one of the girls, carrying her off in his arms towards a clump of bushes. Another followed

23

suit ... and another.... Sara still sang on, but now the night air was murmurous with sighs and whispers. Ermengarde pulled Catherine firmly away from the window and closed it. Catherine saw that her face was crimson with embarrassment and could not help laughing.

"Oh, Ermengarde! They have shocked you!"

"No, I'm not shocked ... but I've every intention of getting a good night's sleep and sights like that aren't good for a woman of my age ... or yours, when your husband is far away."

Catherine did not answer. She felt that the Countess was right and that it was wiser to turn her back on the bacchanal outside. But she lay awake for a long time that night with eyes open, listening. From time to time she heard Sara's voice humming rather than singing, accompanied by the soft chords of the lute. Then, little by little everything grew silent.

Catherine's first action, when she woke the following morning, was to run to the window. She flung back the wooden shutters and leaned out into the fresh morning air. An exclamation of dismay escaped her. There wasn't a trace of the gipsy camp ... except for a few blackened rings on the grass where the fires had been. They must have left very early, before dawn even, melting into the pearly light like figures from a dream. The countryside was peaceful and serene. The bacchanal of the night before had been dissipated as completely as the smoke from the camp fires. Someone was whistling under Catherine's window, which was opposite the stable doors. Catherine saw that it was one of the soldiers in the escort party and called out to him.

"Tell Messire de Roussay that I wish to speak to him."

The man smiled, bowed and disappeared at a run round the corner of the building. A few minutes later Jacques de Roussay knocked at the door of the room which the two women shared. Catherine stood waiting to receive him by the window, dressed in a flowing wrapper. Ermengarde, however, was still in bed. She kept the covers pulled up round her nose and fixed a fierce and unmistakably disapproving eye on the scene before her. But the young captain ignored her—he was far too preoccupied by the anxious look on Catherine's face.

"Have you seen Sara this morning?" she asked, too agitated even to reply to the young man's respectful greeting.

"No, but one of my men saw her just after daybreak. She left with the gipsies, riding pillion behind the chief."

"Left?"

24

A great pang of grief stabbed at Catherine and she felt like bursting into tears, like a little lost girl. Ermengarde was right. The old ties of affection and tenderness had meant little to Sara when she found herself tempted by the charm of her old free vagabond way of life. Catherine was forced to recognize what she had been so reluctant to face up to the night before. Her head drooped and Jacques saw a tear roll down her cheek.

"What? You are crying?" he asked, astonished.

"Yes. . . . I'll be all right in a moment. Thank you, Jacques. We will be ready to leave again within the hour. Please see that everything is prepared."

She turned to the window to hide her tears and in his embarrassment Jacques dared not try to console her. Ermengarde shrugged and, from the depths of her comfortable bed, signed to him to go. As soon as the door closed behind him she got out of bed, padded barefoot across to Catherine and threw her arms around her.

"You have a good cry, my dear. . . . I never imagined that what I said last night would be proved right so quickly! You musn't think that this means that Sara didn't love you— it's just that she belongs to a race of migrant birds. There are certain signs they cannot resist. They go—but they always come back."

Catherine shook her head, swallowing back a sob.

"She will never come back! She has found her own people again, her rightful element . . . but what really hurts me is that she should have left like this . . . without even saying goodbye."

"She probably thought she might not have the courage to leave you if she had. . . . Get dressed now, Catherine, and let's be on our way. It's too depressing here!"

An hour later the litter in which the two women were traveling was on the road again. The sun was already high in the sky. Jacques de Roussay sang little snatches of song to himself as he rode along beside them, not daring to look at Catherine. She kept dabbing at her eyes with her lace handkerchief and the young man was depressed by his inability to comfort her. They went on in silence. Towards midday they had crossed the frontier into Burgundy without a single trace of Sara and her gipsy troupe. They seemed to have vanished into the morning air.

Catherine was genuinely glad to be back in her house in the rue de la Parcheminerie and to find Abou-al-Khayr, busy but amiable as ever, waiting there to receive her. The

25

little doctor now scarcely ever left his laboratory, where, thanks to Garin's liberality, he now had everything he could possibly need for his experiments. Messengers kept arriving from Bruges and Venice with plants, herbs, metals and spices for him from which he prepared his balms and medicines. Catherine's appearance swathed in veils and bandages provoked the same horrified reaction from him as an attack on some work of art would have done. He flew into such a towering rage that she did not dare admit that it was Garin who was responsible for this outrage. Besides, she had no wish to undermine the genuine gratitude and esteem which the Moorish doctor entertained towards his host and protector. She told him some vague story about falling from her horse while crossing some particularly rough, thorny countryside, which did not fool Abou-al-Khayr for a minute, but he pretended to believe her out of politeness.

He did, however, insist on looking at her injuries despite her scandalized protests. He carefully inspected her scars and weals but made no comment, much to her relief. As he ran a gentle finger down her back he permitted himself one wry comment.

"Odd, the way these thorns lacerated the skin... ! I shall have to make a special journey up north to see them for myself ..." he remarked, with only a hint of irony and so much kindliness that Catherine merely smiled in reply.

He was full of praise for Sara's use of his Matarea balm. It was the sovereign remedy for all wounds, he claimed. He suggested, however, that she should use a different ointment on her face composed of sweet almonds, rose water, myrrh, camphor and the finest pork fat, and gave her a large pot of it with instructions to use it morning and evening.

He also did his best to soften the cruel blow of Sara's departure. Catherine had not yet recovered from its effects and she flinched from this brutal abandonment as from an insult. Little by little, however, anger took the place of sorrow. Since Sara's flight the young woman's character had altered and she had become defiant and rebellious. She was tired of being the plaything of fate, tossed this way and that by events beyond her control. It seemed to her as though everyone made a point of exploiting her and using her without even troubling to think whether this might or might not be acceptable to her. First Philippe, calmly according himself the right to marry her off against her wishes in order to gain access to her more easily himself. Then Garin, who had married her in name only and did not even seek to explain his cold treatment of her. Catherine had

never been able to decide whether he thought of her principally as an *objet d'art* to be adorned and paraded, or as a
slave over whom he exercised rights of life and death. Since
his terrible chastisement of her she had inclined towards the
latter view, for if Ermengarde had not appeared on the
scene he would almost certainly have killed or severely mutilated her. And she was at a loss to know what to make
of Arnaud, who rejected or accepted her according to his
changeable moods. He took advantage of her overpowering
love for him to heap scorn upon her. He took it upon
himself to judge her life, conduct and even her friendships
while affecting to consider her as an inferior being. Finally
there was Sara, whom she had trusted completely, who had
been her friend, and who had now abandoned her without
a word of farewell to follow a nomad tribe whom she had
never clapped eyes on before but who just happened to be
of the same blood!

Sara's flight was the drop which had filled her cup of
bitterness to overflowing. Catherine decided that the days of
concessions and meekly bowed heads were finished and done
with and that from now on she alone would be responsible
for her own destiny. She would do as she pleased without
worrying whether it pleased everyone else as well. Everyone else seemed to think they had a perfect right to do as
they liked with her so she could not see why she shouldn't
behave in exactly the same way herself. . . . Abou-al-Khayr
had been watching her expressive face since he let drop his
remark about Sara, and he could follow her thoughts as
clearly as if they had been spelled out there.

Now, as he renewed the dressing on her right hand, he
smiled and said:

"You rely too much on people and circumstances. Life is
like a battle where there are no rules, a savage jungle where
the strong devour the weak and batten on their flesh."

"I have no doubt," Catherine said with a smile, "that
some poet or philosopher in your country has noted down
some reflections on the subject."

"Indeed there are many—for this is philosophy's least pal-
atable truth. The poet reminds us:

> "Seek no friend at the feast,
> Hear but do not heed my words,
> Accept my pain without seeking to cure it,
> Endure evil but seek no consolation. . . ."

"That's beautiful," Catherine said dreamily. "Who wrote it? Was it Hafiz?"

"No, Omar Khayyam ... a drunkard, but he knew what he was writing about. Your servant's desertion of you has hurt you, naturally, but there is nothing you can do about it so why go on tormenting yourself? Life goes on. ..."

As he said, life goes on, and soon Catherine took up the thread of her old familiar existence once again. She divided her time between the Dowager Duchess, whose health was failing fast, and the running of her home and countless visits to her mother and Uncle Mathieu.

By June Catherine had recovered completely and there was not a trace of her injuries to be seen except for a fine pink scar on the lower part of her back, fortunately too far down to mar her magnificent shoulders. However, she had not the slightest desire to return either to Philippe or Garin. They were both at Troyes at that point, attending the wedding of the Princess Anne and the Duke of Bedford. Ermengarde was not attending the wedding because nothing in the world would have made her leave the Dowager Duchess in her weakened condition.

After Anne's marriage Marguerite de Guyenne returned to her mother while Philippe accompanied the new Duchess of Bedford to Paris, where she was to take up residence in the sumptuous Hotel des Tournelles. The marriage between Marguerite and Richemont was to take place that October, in Dijon itself. The young woman had insisted upon this so that she could be certain of her mother's presence, bedridden though she might be. Catherine herself was delighted by this arrangement because this made it almost certain that she would not have to see Garin before October. Philippe had business to attend to in Paris and Flanders. He would not be returning until the wedding and Garin would remain with him as he usually did.

In truth, Catherine was not so preoccupied by Garin and his activities because she had other things with which to occupy herself. He left her severely alone and this was all she wanted. Philippe, on the other hand, made quite certain that she did not forget him. About twice a week a dust-spattered messenger would dismount or, rather, tumble from his horse in the courtyard of the Brazey house. Sometimes the horse would collapse as well as the rider ... but the ceremony was invariable; the messenger would kneel and proffer a letter with one hand, and a parcel with the other.

The letters were generally brief. Philippe le Bon was not

a great letter writer. A few tender words or, more often, some verses borrowed from a poet. But his gifts were always of a rare beauty. ... The Duke's riders never brought jewels, for Philippe held that this would have been insulting to Catherine. Only a husband or lover might give jewelry, Instead he sent her ravishing *objets d'art,* statuettes of amber, jade, crystal or ivory, or richly enamelled gold reliquaries, the patient work of Limousin craftsmen, whose colors echoed the brilliance of the gems with which they were studded; or there might be lace, furs, perfumes, or a clockwork toy; a juggler dressed in red satin who threw and caught gilded balls. Everything, in short, which could flatter the vanity of a pretty woman or arouse her interest. Catherine accepted everything with a gracious word of thanks ... and at once thought about something else.

For some time past she had been aware of an unusual agitation surrounding her wherever she went. Idling figures were always strolling up and down the street outside her house and, on her excursions into the town, she could be sure of finding one of these figures dogging her heels. The costume varied. Sometimes it might be a soldier in the uniform of a ducal guard, or an apparently innocent-looking citizen, a student, one of the copyists employed by the neighboring parchment sellers, or even a monk.

These attentions began by annoying and ended by infuriating the young woman, particularly as she had no idea who was behind them. The likeliest person seemed to be Garin. Who but a suspicious husband would have taken it into his head to have her watched? But how did he suppose she would find occasion to misbehave in a town where she was as well known as in Dijon? Perhaps he was merely trying to make sure that she did not receive messages from Montsalvy? Whatever the explanation it was a highly disagreeable situation and Catherine was sorry she did not know her husband's exact whereabouts so that she could let him know just what she thought of him. She hesitated to accost any of the people who followed her for fear of appearing ridiculous. But as the days went by her irritation was becoming uncontrollable.

Then one afternoon as she was returning from a luncheon with the Champdivers she recognized one of the soldiers of the ducal guard which had escorted her back from Arras disguised as a burgess. In spite of the huge, floppybrimmed hat which made a sort of tunnel round his head, the man's face was too extraordinary to go unremarked. He had a drunkard's strawberry nose and a large purple birthmark covering half one cheek. He was pacing casually up and down the Bourg at the moment when Catherine rode out of the rue Tâtepoire. And later, when she had dismounted with the help of the steward, Tiercelin, and gone up to her room, she could still see the man with the hat from her little tower window, pacing to and fro in the street. He always kept to the same route: from the corner of the Brazey mansion as far as the shop of Maître Aubin, the famous parchment seller from whom Garin got all his supplies, where he would stand for a moment innocently studying the elaborately prepared and illuminated white sheets of vellum which decorated the shop front. Then he would go back and start the whole pantomime again. Catherine stood there thoughtfully considering what action she should take. If Sara had been there she would have sent her out after the fellow and solved the mystery in a moment. No one was more skilful than the gipsy at wheedling facts out of people. But Sara was no longer there and she realized anew how sorely she missed her. Abou-al-Khayr was too conspicuous and picturesque to be entrusted with a mission of this sort and Catherine could not quite visualize going out into the street herself to question the man.

The man's appearance inevitably directed her thoughts towards the charming young Captain of the Guard who always betrayed such agitation in her presence. "I must get to the bottom of this," she thought to herself.

Towards midday she set off for the Ducal Palace to take up her duties as lady-in-waiting to the Duchess Marguerite. This time it was a dirty ragged beggar who attached himself to her. He followed her almost as far as the guard-post, but she took no notice of him. She went into the palace without letting him know that she had seen him and went straight up to the Duchess's apartments. The Duchess had only that moment fallen asleep, overcome by the drowsy summer heat and Catherine found no one there but Ermengarde who seemed about to follow suit. The Grande Maîtresse was having the utmost difficulty keeping her eyes open.

"If you feel like taking a nap in our august company," she remarked to Catherine, stifling a yawn behind a shapely white hand, "I see no reason why you should not do so. If the idea does not appeal to you I should make the most of the sunshine and come back later. Her Highness will sleep till well after three."

Delighted by this chance of carrying out her plan at once, Catherine thanked her and said that in that case she would go out into the garden to rest in the fresh air. She strolled for a while along the paved paths surrounding the fish pond, and through the formal garden, smelled the Duchess's favorite roses clambering over the pergolas and then headed towards the part of the palace where the Captain of the Guard was lodged.

The heat was intense. The air buzzed with wasps and flies. Helmets awry, the palace guards stood leaning on their lances, half asleep. Catherine had no difficulty reaching the staircase which led to Jacques de Roussay's room. It was as hot as an oven up there because of the lead roofing which made the place an inferno. The young woman felt the sweat trickling down her body, though she was only wearing a light summery dress of apple-green gauze striped in silver, a color as fresh and sharp as spring water. Her hair was simply coiled over her ears and held in place by two silver nets joined by a fine band from which a pear-shaped pearl hung down in the middle of her forehead.

The sound of voices as she was climbing the stairs made her pause. She recognized de Roussay's voice. He must have left the door of his room open because of the heat.

"We'll leave that for the moment," the Captain was saying. "I want to dictate a letter to Monseigneur. I should have written two days ago and I can't put it off any longer because a rider is leaving for Ghent this very evening. Not that there is anything to tell him!" he added, sighing. "Are you ready?"

"Quite ready," said a voice which Catherine did not recognize.

She had paused on the top step, where the angle of the wall just hid her from view. Something told her that she was about to hear something of interest.

"Illustrious and mighty Lord," Jacques dictated, "I crave Your Highness's pardon for not having written more often, but I would also like to draw Your Highness's attention to the fact that happily, or unhappily, I have very little news to communicate. The discreet surveillance under which I have placed the Dame de Brazey . . . am I going too fast?"

From where she was standing Catherine felt her throat tighten with anger and at the same time a sense of satisfaction stirred her at having guessed so accurately. "So it *was* he after all!" she thought to herself. "Oh, the little wretch! As for discreet surveillance I should be surprised if the whole street hasn't noticed that I am being watched! Let's see how this charming letter goes on!"

". . . placed the Dame de Brazey," came the voice of the invisible scribe.

31

". . . seems unjustified to me. She leads the most orderly and peaceful existence, seeing no one but her mother and uncle and the Champdivers family. She neither sends nor accepts any invitations, and aside from her visits to the aforementioned persons only leaves her house to attend Mass at the Notre-Dame church. . . ."

The Captain was well into the customary long and elaborate compliments by the time Catherine recovered from her fury. But gradually an idea was taking shape in her mind and a smile replaced the angry set of her mouth. For once she was going to have a bit of fun.

She stole down the stairs again without making a sound, holding her silk skirts with both hands to stop them rustling. Then she heard Jacques's secretary ask him if he had any further need of his services. At this, she let go of her skirts, coughed, and turned back up the stairs again, making as much noise this time as she could, with the result that by the time she reached the top of the stairs she found Jacques standing framed in the open doorway.

"What?" he cried, flushing to the roots of his disheveled fair hair. "You mustn't come here!"

Catherine flashed her most charming smile at him and held out her hand for him to kiss.

"Why not?" she asked archly. "Since you won't come to see me I must perforce come and visit you! I ought to be quite cross with you! We were traveling companions for days on end, you never left my side for an instant and yet the moment we reach Dijon you vanish out of my life! I never so much as clap eyes on you! It really is unkind of you. . . ."

Scarlet with embarrassment Jacques did not know where to look. Behind him the little clerk, a pair of spectacles perched on his immense nose, was straining to see over the young man's broad shoulders.

"I hope I haven't disturbed you," Catherine added, taking a step forward to make it quite clear that she intended to enter his room. Jacques made way for her and the little clerk fell back, bowing and scraping and murmuring that he was just about to leave.

"You aren't disturbing me in the least," the poor young man finally managed to stammer. "I . . . I was just writing a letter to my mother and Father Augustine here was kindly helping me with the penning of it, because I am not much of a scribe myself."

"Ah, I know," said Catherine, smiling again. "As a man

32

of action, you naturally prefer the sword to the pen. But your room is charming . . . quite charming!"

In fact, the place was in a state of chaotic untidiness. The furniture was handsome and the hangings colorful, but everywhere there were untidy heaps of clothes, weapons and bottles. On the table where the scribe had been at work, papers and empty goblets stood next to a pitcher of wine whose moisture-beaded surface showed that it had only recently been to the cellar to be filled. The bed was rumpled and unmade and Catherine virtuously averted her eyes from so scandalous a sight. In spite of the little window which opened out into the stable yard it was stiflingly hot.

"It is quite unfit to receive you in," the young man cried. "And my appearance. . . ."

"Don't worry about that! You look perfect. In this heat. . . ."

The Captain wore nothing but green slippers, tight hose and a fine-spun linen shirt opened in front to the waist. Catherine thought to herself that she preferred him like this, rather than in his uniforms and armor. In this casual attire he looked as healthy and vigorous as a young peasant, and if he did smell a little of wine and sweat it was not disagreeable. Catherine pointed to the pitcher of wine.

"You must give me a drink," she said, seating herself gaily on the foot of his bed. "I'm dying of thirst and that looks so cool and refreshing!"

"It's some Meursault wine. . . ."

"Give me some Meursault wine, then," she said, with an enchanting smile. He rushed to obey, almost kneeling as he handed her the brimming goblet. She sipped at it daintily without taking her eyes off him. He seemed to have recovered from his initial surprise, but his marveling expression told Catherine that he was still dazed at his good fortune.

"Why are you looking at me like that?"

"I find it hard to believe I'm not dreaming! Is it really you . . . here . . . with me?"

"Why not? We are such good friends, after all, you and I. Mmmm . . . this wine is *delicious!* A little heady, perhaps. I feel quite giddy. I'd really better go now. . . ."

She stood up but almost at once she gave a little cry and put her hand to her forehead, swaying slightly as she did so.

"Oh . . . what can be the matter with me? I feel so strange!"

She seemed about to fall, but just then Jacques bounded up and put his arms round her, ostensibly to help her to a seat.

33

"It's nothing," he said, reassuringly. "Just the heat . . . and the wine! It's very cold and I expect that took you by surprise. You may have drunk it a little too fast. . . ."

"I was thirsty! Oh, dear, I feel quite dreadful . . . I can't breathe. . . ."

She raised trembling hands to her bodice, as if implying that this frail silk carapace, low-cut and sheer though it was, were suffocating her. Her meaning was not lost on the young man. Jacques was only too anxious to be of assistance. He began untying the laces which fastened up her bodice while Catherine allowed herself to sink back, as if in a swoon, among the cushions. As she did so, two deliciously rounded breasts slipped out of their sea-green nest right under the young man's nose, and their fragrance went to his head even more speedily than the Meursault wine. At this, the unfortunate young man lost all control of himself. Quite forgetting his anxiety over Catherine's indisposition, he clasped her tightly to him and began raining ardent kisses on her bared bosom and murmuring incoherent endearments.

Catherine lay back with her eyes apparently closed and watched him intoxicating himself with her charms for a moment or two. But she had to cut short the experience before there was any danger of getting carried away herself, which was by no means out of the question, for Jacques was young and attractive, if not actually handsome, and as lusty and strong as a young oak. She gave a deep sigh and pushed the young man away with a strength which would doubtless have astonished him in a swooning woman had he been capable of coherent thought. But Jacques was far beyond that! He was almost out of his mind with joy!

When Catherine sat up he tried to take her back into his arms, but she gently pushed him away, with a pretty show of confusion at the disarray of her clothes.

"What happened to me? . . . Heavens . . . I remember now, I must have passed out. The heat . . . and this wine on top of it! Forgive me, my *friend*" (she maliciously emphasized the word "friend") "I seem to have behaved outrageously. I don't usually faint like this. . . ."

But he was scarcely listening to her. He knelt before her with her free hand clasped passionately between his and his eyes fixed on hers beseechingly.

"Don't go yet . . . stay awhile. . . . Rest for a moment. If you knew how happy it makes me to have you here. . . ."

But she gently withdrew her hand and pushed him away. Then she got up and took a few steps across the room.

"Yes, yes, Jacques," she said in a faint voice. "You are

34

the most considerate of friends. You must have looked after me wonderfully well just now because I declare I feel better already!"

He was still kneeling beside the bed. But then, unable to endure the thought of her going, leaving him just when he had been so near to realizing a sweet, long-cherished dream, he stood up and came over to her with outstretched hands.

"You mustn't go just yet," he said, smiling. "You are still weak and the heat is overpowering."

Catherine shook her head.

"Don't tempt me. I must go back now. I don't even know what time it is."

"It's early yet. Drink a little more wine," Jacques suggested treacherously. "It will make you feel better. Anyway, you still haven't told me to what I owe the pleasure of such an enchanting visitor."

Catherine, who was almost at the door by now, turned back.

"I'm not thirsty any more. Anyway, your wine is dangerous, my dear Jacques. As for the purpose of my visit. . . ."

She paused for a moment and flashed him a mocking smile. Then, suddenly dropping the languishing tone she had been using and speaking in her normal voice, she added in the gentlest, most ironical way:

"I simply wanted to give you something to write to the Duke concerning the Dame de Brazey. You should have all the material you need now to write the Duke a long and interesting letter about your views on friendship . . . and the best way to revive unconscious ladies! If I were you, I should send for Father Augustine again. Or would you rather I wrote your letter for you? I write a fine hand, you know. My Uncle Mathieu says it might easily be mistaken for a Benedictine monk's."

Then, delighted with the success of her trick, she raced towards the stairs and ran down them at breakneck speed, laughing mockingly as she heard the young Captain calling after her. She didn't stop running till she reached the palace garden.

In the days that followed Burgundy had need of all the Dowager Duchess's failing strength. Taking advantage of Philippe's stay in Flanders, King Charles's men attacked all along the northern boundaries of the Duchy. The Armagnac troops of the Bastard of La Baume held the Auxerrois country and a part of Avallonais. But, in their eagerness to open up champagne to the King, the Constable, John Stuart Buchan,

35

and Maréchal Séverac laid seige to Cravant. The danger had to be met with prompt action. Marguerite summoned up her courage, dispatched troops under the command of Maréchal Toulongeon, and wrote a letter to her son-in-law, the Duke of Bedford, asking him to send help.

The departure of the Duchess's letter for Paris gave rise to a tragic scene between Marguerite and Ermengarde at which Catherine was a stricken witness. Ermengarde was bitterly reproaching the sick woman for having appealed for help to the Englishman. Marguerite turned a pain-wracked face towards her and dragged herself up on her pillows with Catherine's help. Then she held out her hand to her old friend.

"Burgundy is in danger, Ermengarde ... my son, the reigning Duke, has placed the Duchy under my care. In order to safeguard it and keep it whole, intact and undamaged, I would be prepared to sell my soul to the Devil himself in return for his assistance. If the Englishman who married my daughter can save it for me he will have earned my gratitude."

Marguerite fell back on the pillows again quite drained of strength. Ermengarde did not answer, but it was the first time since she had known her that Catherine saw this indomitable woman weep.

On 30 July the Battle of Cravant was fought, with disastrous results for the King of France, thanks to the troops sent by the Duke of Bedford under Lord Suffolk's command. Catherine listened in despair as Nicolas Rolin, who had been the instigator of Marguerite's appeal to the Duke, gave the Duchess a detailed account of the battle. The Constable Buchan had lost an eye, the battle field was strewn with dead and many valuable prisoners had been taken. It was then that Catherine first learnt of the capture of Arnaud and Xaintrailles.

She had never liked Nicolas Rolin, but from this moment on she actively hated him. She was disgusted by the boastful, arrogant way he ascribed the successful outcome of the battle to the intervention of the English. Ermengarde was obliged to leave the room to stop herself attacking the Chancellor in a fury. As for Catherine, she was so enraged that the incident wrought a significant change in her attitude to many important things and affected her behavior in the months to come. She now regarded Nicolas Rolin as one of her personal enemies.

Each morning Catherine attended Mass at Notre-Dame as she had done regularly since she was a young girl. After

36

Mass she often went to visit her mother and uncle. She liked strolling through the town in the cool of the early morning before the fierce August heat made the streets unendurable. Wearing a light linen dress with a Missal in her hand and a fine veil thrown about her head, Catherine would take her place in the darkened church, her maid beside her, and follow the ceremony as fervently now as she had once been absent-minded. God in His omnipotence alone seemed to hold a solution to the warring emotions within her and day after day she implored Heaven for the help she so urgently needed.

Since Sara's departure, Catherine had promoted one of her former tiring-women to the position of personal maid. Perrine was eighteen years old, fresh-faced, good-humored and utterly devoted to her mistress. She would have unhesitatingly jumped into flames for her if it had been necessary. She was simple and placid and incurious and Catherine appreciated these qualities.

One morning as the two of them knelt in their usual places not far from the Black Madonna's Chapel a monk came up and knelt down beside Catherine. He wore a dusty brown habit, girdled by a thick cord, and its hood all but hid his face. What remained to be seen of it was pleasant enough. Everything about it seemed to be round—nose, mouth, even the full cheeks. But when he raised his head to look at his neighbor Catherine was startled by the sharpness and liveliness of his glance. He bent towards her and whispered:

"Forgive my intrusion, but you are the Dame de Brazey, are you not?"

"Yes, but. . . ."

The monk hastily put his finger to his lips:

"Sssh! Not so loud. You are the lady I have been looking for. Mme de Champdivers sent me to you. I come from Saint-Jean-de-Losne and I would have gone to your house if I had not been afraid of arousing too much curiosity among your servants . . . or possibly being turned away altogether. So I made inquiries."

Catherine darted a quick glance at him.

"No one sent by my friend Odette need have any fear of being turned away, Father. What can I do for you?"

"I wish to speak to you . . . privately."

"Then follow me out after Mass has ended, which will be any minute now. The best place to talk would be my own home."

"It's just that . . . Dame Odette warned me to avoid meeting Messire de Brazey."

37

"My husband is away, you need have no fear of meeting him."

The Mass was nearly ended. At the altar the priest turned towards the faithful for the final blessing. As soon as he had disappeared into the shadows round the High Altar Catherine stood up, genuflected reverently, and went towards the door followed by Perrine and the monk. In a moment all three of them found themselves out in the bright sunshine of the street. For once Catherine denied herself the pleasure of a visit to the rue Griffon and hurried home instead. She was curious to know why Odette had sent this strange messenger to her, and what it was he wanted to say.

When she reached the Hotel de Brazey she dismissed Perrine and received the friar in her own apartments.

"Sit down," she said, pointing at a chair. "We are alone now, and no one can hear us. You may speak freely. What can I do for you?"

"Help us. But first I must explain who I am. My name is Étienne Charlot and, as you see from my habit, I belong to the Order of St. Francis of Assisi. I have come from Mont Beuvray where I live with others of my order."

He described how he had been summoned to the unfortunate King Charles VI on the strength of his reputed skill with herbs and simples and how he had become the friend of Odette de Champdivers, the mad king's devoted nurse. The "little queen" had at once responded to the solid Burgundian good sense of this gentle but forceful monk. The tisanes he brewed had more than once soothed the poor King's slumber. When the King died he had returned to Mont Beuvray while Odette herself returned to her native Burgundy. But, as Catherine was soon to hear, this did not prevent them both from pursuing a secret, unswerving aim—to serve King Charles VII as devotedly as they had served and loved his father.

"We both felt," the monk finished, "that we could best serve our master in the enemy camp rather than by praying for his success in battle from the safety of the King's own territory. Dame Odette and I would have been assured of a welcome from the King, but we chose to return here. The geographical situation of Mont Beuvray is quite exceptional, standing as it does within the enclave of the Château of Chinon. It is a narrow wedge of land belonging to Duke Jean de Bourbon driven between the Duchy of Burgundy and the County of Nevers. . . ."

"I see," said Catherine, smiling. "The perfect espionage post!"

"Let us say, the perfect observation post," Brother Étienne amended. "And an excellent escape route."

Catherine studied her visitor attentively. With the sun full on his face he appeared older than she had thought him in the dark church. His face was fresh-complexioned and his cheeks round and rosy and plump, but there were crowsfeet at the corners of his eyes and his cropped hair was going grey. He was not handsome as men go, his face was too round for that, but the intelligence and kindness of his face appealed to Catherine. She interrupted his lecture on political geography with a smile.

"I quite understand all this. But I am at a loss to see what role I am expected to play. . . ."

Brother Étienne looked at her with sudden gravity.

"Your role will be to help us, as I said before. Dame Odette believes that your sympathies are secretly with King Charles VII . . . and you have considerable influence at the Burgundian Court. You could prove an invaluable source of information to us. . . . No, don't frown, I know what you are about to say: that you aren't a spy; isn't that so?"

"Thank you for expressing my feelings so clearly."

"Nevertheless, I must ask you to reflect—the cause of King Charles is just and legitimate because it is also the cause of France, but the Duke Philippe does not hesitate to extend the hand of friendship to the invader, with the sole object of increasing his own power and the extent of his lands."

Catherine was familiar with these arguments. How often had Ermengarde spoken likewise! And they were almost identical, word for word, with the remarks which Arnaud had flung in Philippe's face at Amiens. But Brother Étienne was still speaking.

"The end justifies the means. The King's cause is a sacred one—he is the Lord's Anointed, and whoever serves him serves God Himself. And in the hour of triumph he will not be found wanting in gratitude towards those who have helped him . . . although," he added with a sweet smile, "you do not strike me as one of those people who expect to be rewarded for what they do."

"But they say that King Charles is frivolous and fickle, and interested only in women and entertainments. . . ."

"I must confess that I am sorry I cannot take you to his Court. He would lose his heart to you. I hope you will forgive such wordly sentiments in a monk. But if the King himself is weak, there is an angel standing guard over him—

39

the power and wisdom are all in the hands of one woman, his mother-in-law, a very great and noble lady, Yolande d'Aragon, Queen of Sicily and Jerusalem, Comtesse d'Anjou and Comtesse de Provence, the highest and most valiant princess of our time. It is she, above all, whom I serve and she honors me with her confidence. I can assure you that her memory is reliable, her head sound, and her political genius quite extraordinary ... and that she is a good person to serve. Well? ..."

Catherine stopped short. An idea had come to her suddenly, a brilliant flash of inspiration, an idea so appealing that she could not help smiling with pleasure. Brother Étienne leaned across impatiently.

"Well?"

"Supposing I were to ask your Queen a favor before agreeing to help her. Do you suppose she would agree to it?"

"I don't see why not if it is within her power to do so. Yolande is no haggler. She is a generous woman. There can be no harm in asking."

"At the Battle of Cravant many nobles were taken prisoner by the Earl of Suffolk. Some ... friends of mine among them. I would like the King to ransom Arnaud de Montsalvy and Jean de Xaintrailles. Let them be set free ... and you may make use of me as you wish. Odette was speaking the truth—I believe the King's cause is just and should be upheld."

A joyful gleam appeared in the monk's eyes. He got up and bowed.

"You have earned our gratitude, Madame. This evening I shall leave for Bourges where I shall see the Queen and pass on your message. And unless I am much mistaken, your wishes will speedily be granted. It so happens that Her Majesty sets great store by the courage and loyalty of these two particular captains. I trust I shall soon be able to bring you good news. ..."

"Bring it to Saint-Jean-de-Losne where I shall be visiting my friend. Meanwhile, you shall be my guest till this evening. Shall we go in to dinner now? We still have much to say to each other. ..."

Taking her new friend by the hand Catherine led him towards the dining-room where the midday meal was about to be served.

That evening Brother Étienne left Dijon. The following day Catherine herself followed suit on her way to stay with

Odette at Saint-Jean-de-Losne. The Duchess Marguerite had graciously permitted her to take a short holiday. The short journey of some seven or eight leagues delighted Catherine as much as a schoolboy escapade. Leaving the Hotel de Brazey in the charge of Tiercelin and Abou-al-Khayr, she set out on horseback in the morning, accompanied only by Perrine and two servants who were in charge of her baggage. The weather was brilliant. The sun beat down on huge tracts of wheat standing ready for harvesting, and, remembering the desolation of the countryside round Champagne, Catherine found much to admire in this somewhat monotonous countryside which undulated gently, interspersed with woods, towards the Saône.

Catherine found Odette by the river. The former King's favorite was supervising her servants as they did the household washing. She wore a linen dress with the sleeves pushed up. Her neck and throat were bare and her hair was caught back by a simple ribbon. Though she was over thirty, she looked like a young girl; it was something to do with the slenderness of her waist, the liveliness of her movements and her gay smile.

The two young women fell into each other's arms and embraced warmly.

"What a delightful surprise!" Odette kept exclaiming. "How nice of you to come and visit me in my hermitage."

"I've been meaning to come ever since your mother told me that your daughter was ill. And then yesterday I had a visit which finally made up my mind for me. From another hermit, believe it or not!"

Odette glanced round her hurriedly and signed to Catherine to be quiet. Then she slipped her arm through her friend's and they set off together towards her house after giving the servants instructions to carry on without her. The two young women passed through an open postern gate in the wall and climbed a short steep lane at the end of which stood a high tower which could only be entered via a Gothic doorway surmounted by a coat of arms.

"I'm afraid you will find my home very spartan," Odette said with a sigh. "I am living in the town commander's castle and he has installed himself in other quarters in the main street. It's cold, not very comfortable and far from gay, but it's not too bad in the summer."

Catherine's holidays began very happily. She and Odette had a great deal to talk about. Catherine, above all, for the fair recluse of Saint-Jean-de-Losne was eager to hear about all the parties and banquets her friend had attended.

Catherine set herself to gratify this wish, and when midnight came she was still talking. . . .

The next day it was Odette's turn to take up the story, rather more thoroughly than she had done before now. She talked about King Charles and his Court, which she knew so well. When Catherine ventured to mention Arnaud, it transpired that Odette had often seen him at Court, in the Duke of Orleans' entourage.

"You will find it very hard to make him go back on his word," she warned her friend. "He is the sort of person who throws himself heart and soul into everything he does and he is devilishly proud. He hates and detests everything Burgundian and if you want him to love you, you will have to give up everything—husband, fortune, position, everything. . . ."

"You seem to think I would do better to give him up," Catherine sighed. "But I can't. One can't stop one's heart beating."

"I didn't say you should give him up. I merely said that it would be difficult, and might take a long time . . . and the patience of an angel. I think you might succeed. Besides . . . you are so beautiful that he will find it hard to hold out against you, however much he tries. . . ."

Odette watched as Catherine stepped out of the water, wringing out her dripping hair, and wrapped herself in a large white towel. It was so hot that the two young women had gone down to the river to bathe. As it passed under the town walls the Saône widened to form a little creek where one could bathe unseen, except by the occasional passer-by on the opposite bank. Odette and Catherine had lingered for a long time in the water, which was transparently clear just here. Then they had slipped out, screened by the reeds and tall grasses which grew so high that they concealed them almost up to the neck. Odette had already wrapped herself in a length of soft stuff and she sat on the grass combing her hair while Catherine dried herself.

"Does . . ." Catherine asked timidly, "does . . . Messire de Montsalvy have much success with women?"

Odette burst out laughing, amused as much by her friend's nervous manner as by the naïveté of the question.

"Much success? That would be putting it mildly, my sweet. It would be truer to say that there isn't a single woman or girl at Court who doesn't languish after him to some degree or other. You need only look at him, after all—I don't believe there can be a more attractive man in the whole of Europe. He harvests hearts as easily as a peasant cuts through wheat with his scythe."

"In that case," Catherine went on, trying to sound casual, "he must have lots of mistresses. . . ."

Odette lolled back against the bank with a blade of grass between her teeth and smiled as she watched her friend trying to hide the jealousy written all over her expressive face. She laughed again and pulled Catherine down beside her on the grass.

"What a ninny you are! Of course Arnaud de Montsalvy isn't a virgin—far from it! He takes women the way he drinks a cup of wine—when he feels the urge. But when the urge is satisfied he forgets about the empty goblet on the table. I don't believe there is a woman alive who can boast of spending more than one night with him, and I know many whose hearts he has broken, yet he never seems to fall in love himself. I really believe that he despises women in general, with the one exception of his mother, for whom he cherishes a deep and tender love. Now if you want to know what I think—I think that if there is one woman in the world who might have a chance of capturing that elusive heart, it's the one sitting right beside me. The difficult thing will be getting him to admit it ... but the services you render the Queen of Aragon may be of assistance to you there. The Queen of Sicily is honored, if not with the love, at least with the profound respect and devotion of Messire Arnaud. . . ."

And so the days passed peacefully and happily for the two friends. They had decided not to discuss politics till Brother Étienne's return and gave love the pride of place in their conversations. They would rise late and go down to the river to bathe, lazing in the clear water before returning to their midday meal. After that they took a short siesta and then either returned to bathe once more or went riding through the neighboring countryside. In the evening, after supper, a page would sing for them, or they would listen to the tales of some wandering minstrel. In this way, three weeks slipped by without any more notable event taking place than the arrival of a letter from Ermengarde recounting all the Court gossip and the latest news:

"The most extraordinary thing, my dear Catherine! The Duke Philippe has been obliged to travel to Ghent with all possible haste because some woman there was posing as his own sister, our beloved little Duchess de Guyenne, and creating a scandal after having been welcomed and received like a princess. It turned out to be some poor madwoman,

43

a nun who had escaped from a convent at Cologne. The Duke handed her over to the Bishop and it only remained for that worthy prelate to send her back to the abbess. These events, however, have delayed Monseigneur's arrival in Paris. They say that his purpose there is to make Bedford pay over what was still owing to him on the dowry of the late Duchess Michelle, God rest her soul, which has led to some pretty haggling going on between the French prince—because he *is* French, whatever he may say—and the English regent, who has already been forced to hand over Péronne, Roye and Montdidier, plus two thousand écus, plus the Château d'Andrevic and the toll-gate of Saint-Jean-de-Losne, an item of news which ought to interest your friend. Philippe hasn't actually got the three towns in his possession yet, however, as they must first be prized away from the royal troops who have occupied them...."

The letter rattled on for several pages in this vein. Ermengarde was not a prolific letter-writer, but when she did take up her pen, she would cover leagues of parchment without drawing breath. Odette listened to the letter being read aloud with a bitter smile.

"I am touched by the Regent's generosity in rewarding his allies with lands which do not belong to him in the first place ... He gives away Saint-Jean-de-Losne and Philippe graciously accepts it—doesn't it even occur to him that I shall be ruined?"

"It may never happen. I'm sure you will keep your town, Odette," Catherine said.

But the young woman shrugged contemptuously.

"You don't know your Philippe of Burgundy. His father had this town given to me because I was useful to him with King Charles, but now that Charles is dead, my usefulness is at an end and everything I was given will be taken back again. Philippe is like his father, my dear; a rapacious soul beneath an elegant exterior. He gives nothing away without good reason and the certainty of making a handsome profit...."

"There's me, though," Catherine suggested. "Philippe is always saying he loves me. He'll have to listen to me...."

That same evening, Brother Étienne Charlot presented himself at the drawbridge and demanded entrance. He was quite grey with dust and his feet, in their light sandals, were torn and bleeding. But his smile was radiant.

"I am so pleased to see you both together," he exclaimed as he greeted the two women. "God be with you both!"

"And with you, too, Brother Étienne," Odette replied.

"What news do you bring us? But first, sit down and rest. I will order some refreshment to be brought to you."

"Thank you. It's a long journey from Bruges, and a dangerous one just now. A Burgundian mercenary, Captain Perrinet Gressard, has captured the country areas and is now marching on La Charité-sur-Loire. I was hard put to it to give him the slip. But I bring good news, particularly where Mme. de Brazey is concerned. The King has paid the ransom demanded for Messire Jean Poton de Xaintrailles and the Seigneur de Montsalvy and they should both be back at their posts in the Vermandois by now. But what news have you?"

By way of answer, Catherine handed him Ermengarde's letter. This was her first open act of rebellion against Philippe of Burgundy. She had made up her mind. By paying for Arnaud's release, Yolande d'Aragon had earned Catherine's undying loyalty.

The monk rapidly scanned the sheet of parchment covered with Ermengarde's flamboyant scrawl and shook his head.

"Bedford is making some handsome concessions. He needs Philippe . . . and the King will need your help."

"What do you mean?" Catherine asked with an unconscious touch of hauteur.

Brother Étienne's voice was as gentle as ever as he replied:

"The Duke Philippe has left Paris and is now heading for Dijon to prepare for the wedding of Madame de Guyenne . . . the holidays have come to an end for the wife of the Lord Treasurer of Burgundy."

His meaning was transparently clear. Catherine looked away, smiling.

"Very well," she said, quietly. "I shall return to Dijon tomorrow."

"I shall stay here," Odette said. "If the Duke wants my town he will have to come and take it from me—over my dead body!"

"Don't imagine that would worry him!" the monk said with a sly smile. "And with the Saône so close, he would have no trouble in disposing of your remains. You cannot possibly hold out against him, so why try?"

"Because. . . ."

Odette blushed, bit her lip and finally burst out laughing.

"You are right, Brother Étienne, there is nothing heroic about me and I am not the type for big speeches. The reason I am remaining here is that I am expecting a messenger from the Duke of Savoy who still has hopes of making peace

45

between the enemy princes. Once he has come, I shall also return to my parents in Dijon."

Catherine spent most of that night sitting by her bedroom window looking out; the moon was full and brilliant and the river glided past beneath the walls, its waters like liquid mercury. The whole Saône valley slumbered, wrapped in nocturnal peace. The only sounds to be heard were the barking of a dog, or a small bird calling from some tree. Catherine had a premonition that these fleeting tranquil moments would not return for a long time. A time of strife was coming, a time of anguish and fear. She was now a spy in the service of the King of France. Where else would her love for Arnaud take her?

CHAPTER THREE

Garin's Return

Garin de Brazey arrived home on the feast of St. Michel. It was very early when he dismounted in the courtyard of the Hotel de Brazey, but Catherine had already gone out to attend early Mass. She had abandoned Notre-Dame for once in favor of the Church of St. Michel, it being the Archangel's feast day. In spite of her hopeless passion for Arnaud, she had not forgotten Michel de Montsalvy, her first and purest love. Unfailingly, every 29 September, she would kneel before the altar and pray for the soul of the young man who had been so unjustly butchered. She found some respite from her tormenting passion in praying for Arnaud's beloved brother.

The Church of St. Michel, which stood at the far end of the town under the ramparts, was an unpretentious building, consisting of a square tower above an ancient nave, with wooden side aisles. It had been clumsily repaired after the last fire, but Catherine found it much easier to pray there. She lingered on for a while after Mass with Perrine and the morning was far advanced by the time she returned home. The stir and bustle in the street outside, now crowded with horses and baggage mules, the wide open gates into the house, and the gaggle of young apprentice clerks from the nearby parchment vendors watching open-mouthed as the luggage was unloaded, all warned her of her husband's return. She was not surprised, for she had been expecting him daily, but she was a little dismayed. She would have preferred him to return later in the day so as to have more time to prepare herself for a meeting whose consequences were, to say the least, unpredictable.

She saw Tiercelin in the hall, supervising the carrying of a large, iron-studded chest.

"Has my husband asked for me?" she inquired as she removed her veil. The steward bowed respectfully and shook his head.

"Not as far as I know, Madame. Monsieur Garin went straight up to his apartments. I have not seen him since."

"Has he been here long?"

"About an hour. Would Madame like me to inform him of her return?"

"No, don't bother. First I must change out of these clothes. Monsieur Garin doesn't like very simple things," she said with a smile and nod towards the plain white silk dress she wore over a leaf-green underskirt. She hurried up the stone staircase leading to her room, with Perrine at her heels.

"Quick, come and help me dress. . . ."

As they entered Catherine's room both women gave a cry of astonishment. The room had been transformed into something magical and unreal, a kind of Ali Baba's cave. The furniture had completely disappeared, buried under a heap of fabulous, glittering, shimmering stuffs. Chairs, stools, credences were hidden beneath cascades of colored brocades, some shot with gold and silver, or encrusted with sparkling jewels. There was a positive riot of color spread before her. From the top of the bed tester hung a great torrent of snowy laces, lace from Bruges, Malines, Brussels, whose frothy whiteness set off the brilliant colors of the other cloths. A large silver coffer stood open in the middle of the room and from it protruded bottles and flagons of gold, crystal, jade and cornaline filling the air with their medley of rich scents and perfumes. . . .

Catherine stood staring at this astonishing silken explosion. Perrine, meanwhile, was riveted to the threshold, openmouthed and wide-eyed. As Catherine turned towards her the maid suddenly sank to the ground in a deep curtsey and Catherine realized that Garin must be approaching. She felt herself trembling inwardly, but with a great effort she controlled herself, swallowed, gripped her gilded Missal tightly between both hands and turned to face the door, a slender, gallant figure.

The next moment Perrine had vanished and Garin was

standing there in the doorway. Catherine had not even heard his footsteps in the gallery. As was his wont he stood staring at his wife from the doorway without making any sign or gesture of greeting. He was dressed, unusually for him, in dark purple with a fine silver border embroidered round the bottom of his doublet and sleeves. He was hatless, revealing his short-cropped helmet of black hair lightly touched with silver round the temples. He had not yet had time to change his clothes. His thin face was so expressionless that it might have been carved from stone as he stood there looking at Catherine.

Then, suddenly, a faint smile lightened his sombre countenance. With a sweeping gesture he indicated the dazzling array of precious stuffs.

"Do you like your room like this?"

"It's . . . it's beautiful! But Garin, why have you done all this?"

He stepped forward and placed his hands on the young woman's shoulders.

"Something told me that I ought to make amends . . . this is the tribute of a repentant conscience . . . and it proves that I, too, was thinking of you. . . ."

Calmly, and apparently unemotionally, he came closer and dropped a kiss on her forehead.

"Repentant?" said Catherine. "That word sounds strange on your lips."

"I don't see why. It is the correct word in the circumstances. I accused you wrongly and I regret having done so. I have since learned that you spent that night in Monseigneur's room . . . and quite alone, so it would appear."

His calm, aloof tone annoyed Catherine.

"May I ask who gave you all this information?"

"Why, the Duke himself! He told me that he had offered you his hospitality. . . . My anger was unjustified. I thought you were with someone else. So, once more, I crave your pardon."

"Nevertheless, I *was* going to visit that other man wasn't I? What makes you so sure you were wrong?" Catherine asked irritably. She was growing angrier each minute. She felt horribly humiliated, reduced to the status of a mere pretty toy by the calmness with which Philippe and his treasurer discussed the deal they had made over her. Garin laughed and shrugged.

"Nothing, except common sense, perhaps . . . and the latest news. I somehow doubt whether the Seigneur de Montsalvy

48

would carry on the way he is at present if he were truly a prisoner to your charms."

"What do you mean? I heard that he had been captured by the English at the battle of Cravant. The Duchess Marguerite read out the list of prisoners to us."

"He was, indeed, taken prisoner, but King Charles ransomed him, together with another knight . . . that red-headed Auvergnat with the abominable accent. No, it's his forthcoming marriage I was thinking of. . . ."

"What?"

Garin pretended not to have noticed the force with which Catherine uttered the word. He had picked up a length of satin striped in almond green and pale mauve and was admiring its sheen in the light from the window. Without looking at his wife he went on smoothly.

". . . to Isabelle de Séverac, the maréchal's daughter. It seems the match has been arranged for some time . . . the parties concerned are very much in love, so they tell me."

Catherine dug her nails into the palms of her hands to stop herself crying out. The pang of misery which shot through her was unbearable. But not for anything would she have given Garin the satisfaction of seeing how deeply his news had hurt her. In a tone void of emotion she inquired:

"How did you come by all this news? I had no idea that the people in Paris and Burgundy were so interested in King Charles's Court."

"But of course . . . when it's a case of such an important match! When two such old and celebrated families are united the fact is of interest to the entire nobility. Anyway, I heard the news from our bailiff at Amiens, Louis de Scorailles, who is related to the Montsalvy family. The marriage was to have taken place in December . . . like our own. But it appears that the betrothed couple are too impatient to wait that long and now the wedding is arranged for a month hence, in Bourges. Well, I dare say the news has delighted you as much as it did me. It is always pleasant to be able to share in a friend's happiness, not to mention the fact that it set my previous fears at rest, and proved just how wrong I had been in my suspicions of you. Have you forgiven me?"

He drew closer to his wife and took her hand between his as he bent forward to look at her face more closely. Catherine forced a pale smile to her lips.

"Yes, of course I have . . . forgiven you. Don't worry. And I cannot thank you enough for all these beautiful gifts."

"It occurred to me," said Garin, dropping a light kiss on the cold hand he was holding, "that you would be needing new dresses for the wedding celebrations. I want you to make yourself beautiful . . . divinely beautiful! It makes me proud to know you are being admired."

From Garin, such compliments were rare. Catherine forced herself to smile again. She was numbed by the news, but pride made her keep up the semblance of normality. She must not let Garin notice her distress. She suspected that he had been awaiting some such reaction when his sharp eyes scanned her face a moment before. . . . To give herself time to compose her face she pretended to examine the lace he had brought her. This allowed her to keep her eyes lowered —eyes which were wet with unshed tears.

Catherine heard Garin sigh. He went towards the door, but turned back to her on the threshold and said softly:

"I was forgetting—Monseigneur the Duke does you the honor of remembering you with favor. He asked me to be sure to tell you that he hopes to see you again before long. . . ."

The implication hidden in Garin's words effectively destroyed Catherine's last shreds of self-control. Nothing could have more blatantly underlined her wretched status as a piece of human merchandise. After all, what could a simple commoner like herself amount to compared with someone like Isabelle de Séverac? She could be bought and sold, her body and her maidenhood disposed of in a squalid business deal. What humiliation! What an indignity! How dared two men treat an innocent woman in such a fashion!

The face she turned to Garin was white with anger and her eyes glittered.

"I do not intend to see the Duke," she retorted, her voice low and hoarse with indignation. "You and your master can say farewell to all the pretty schemes you have hatched out between you. You are quite free to neglect your husbandly duties, to dishonor yourself and make yourself a figure of fun, but I, who am not noble, but merely a common little bourgeoise, I forbid you to treat me like something to be bartered and sold. . . ."

The tears suddenly overflowed and poured down her face, but her fury was far from appeased. She snatched up a great handful of precious stuffs, hurled them on the ground and trampled on them in her rage.

"That's what I think of your gifts! I don't need your stuffs or new dresses. I will never return to the Court again . . . *never,* do you hear!"

Cold, rigid as a block of ice, Garin watched Catherine's display of temper unmoved. He shrugged.

"No one chooses their own destiny, my dear . . . and yours does not strike me as being as wretched as you would have me believe. . . ."

"Not you, perhaps, but what about me? . . . What right have you to deprive me of all the things which make up a woman's real happiness—love, children. . . ?"

"The Duke offers you his love. . . ."

"An adulterous love which I repudiate. I don't love him and he will never have me. As for *you* . . . get out! . . . Leave me alone! Haven't you realized yet that I can't even stand the sight of you? Get out of here!"

Garin opened his mouth to speak but shut it again almost at once and went out with a final shrug, closing the door behind him. His departure gave her the chance to abandon herself to grief. Catherine flung herself face down on her bed and began sobbing brokenheartedly. The cascade of lace slipped down from the canopy and fell upon her, burying her in its snowy folds. . . .

This really was the end. Nothing made sense any more in this stupid life of hers. Arnaud was to be married. . . . Arnaud was lost to her for ever because he loved another woman, a woman who was young, beautiful, worthy of him; a woman he could respect, whose children he would be proud of, whereas he could never have felt anything but contempt for the daughter of the Legoix family, wife of an upstart, unprincipled Treasurer, the sorry creature he had found in Philippe's own bed! Catherine felt desperately alone. She had been abandoned in a vast desert with no star to guide her to safety or point the way to salvation. She had nothing . . . not even Sara's shoulder to weep on. Sara had abandoned her and scorned her, just as Garin and Arnaud despised her, and as Philippe himself would cast her aside once he had slaked the desire he felt for her.

Her bosom was heaving with hysterical sobs. The tears scalded her eyes so that she could hardly see. . . . She sat up a little and, finding herself entangled in the skeins of lace, seized them in both hands to tear herself free. Then she stood up. The room seemed to be spinning around her. She clutched at one of the bed posts. It was like that day when she had drunk too much sweet wine at Uncle Mathieu's. She had been dreadfully sick afterwards, but at the time, the wine had made her feverishly gay, whereas now she was drunk with pain and grief. Before her, on the dresser, stood a little chest in the shape of a cask decorated with blue and green enamel. She snatched up this chest with both hands, clutched it to her heart and then collapsed to the ground. Her heart was beating

51

as though it would burst inside her. This last action of hers seemed to have drained all her strength. She opened the chest and took out a little crystal bottle enclosed in a gold cover.

Abou-al-Khayr had given her the poison after arriving at her house as ceremoniously as if it had been a precious treasure.

"It kills instantly and painlessly," he told her. "It is my masterpiece and I feel that you should have it, because in these dreadful times, every woman should have a way to escape from the appalling fate which could befall her at any moment. If I had a wife whom I loved, I would have given her the flask as I now give it to you . . . who are dear to my heart."

It was the first and last time that the little doctor had ever alluded to his feelings for her and Catherine had been touched and also proud, for she was well aware of his sentiments toward women in general. Now, thanks to the friendship of the Moorish doctor, she possessed the means of escape from a fate which she rejected and a future which had ceased to interest her. She took the phial from its gold case. The liquid it contained was as colorless and inoffensive-looking as plain water. She crossed herself hastily and her eyes wandered towards the great ivory crucifix hanging on the wall between the two windows.

"Forgive me, oh Lord . . ." she whispered. Then she raised her hand to put the flask to her lips. In a moment all would be over. Her eyes would be closed, her memory extinguished and her heart would have stopped its stricken beating.

The crystal was just about to touch her lips when the phial was snatched from her hands.

"I didn't give it to you so you could use it now," Abou-al-Khayr scolded her. "What is the terrible danger threatening you now?"

"The danger of living! I can't go on!"

"Idiot! Madwoman! Haven't you everything a woman could desire?"

"Everything. . . . Except the things that matter—love, friendship. Arnaud is getting married . . . and Sara has deserted me."

"You have my friendship, worthless though it may be to you. You have a mother, a sister, an uncle. You are beautiful, young, rich, and you have the effrontery to say that you are alone in the world!"

"What does anything matter now that I have lost him for ever?"

Suddenly pensive and frowning, Abou-al-Khayr stretched

out a hand to help the young woman up. Her reddened, wild eyes and grief-striken face were pitiful.

"Now I understand why your husband sent me to you saying that you were in danger. Come with me."

"Where?"

"Come. We are not going far; only to my room."

The sea of pain in which she had been floundering since Garin's return had destroyed Catherine's powers of resistance completely. She allowed herself to be led from the room like a little child.

The Griffon Room had changed a great deal since the Moorish doctor had installed himself in it. The luxurious décor had, if anything, become even more opulent: a mass of cushions and rugs was scattered about in a dazzling riot of color. But most of the furniture had disappeared. The only Western-looking object left was a large, low table which stood in the center of the room, and not much of that was visible under a pile of immense books, packets of goose quills and jars of ink. On every available surface—mantelpiece, shelves —were arranged an immense collection of phials, jars, retorts and bottles. The neighboring room which one entered via a door which Garin had had made expressly for the little doctor's convenience, was similarly furnished and the air in there was fragrant with the sacks of spices and packets of herbs of which Abou-al-Khayr always kept a large stock. It also contained a large, black stove on which strange concoctions were constantly simmering.

But the doctor did not take Catherine into that room, where the two black slaves were busying themselves. Instead, he carefully shut the intercommunicating door, made the young woman sit down on a cushion near the fireplace, and threw a handful of firewood on the embers. The fire instantly blazed up again. Then he took a pair of scissors off a shelf and went over to Catherine who sat musing, staring into the flames.

"Allow me to snip one curl from this magnificent head of hair," he asked.

She signed to him to do as he wished, and he cut off a golden lock behind one ear and held it for a moment, gazing up towards the roof beams and murmuring some incomprehensible words in an undertone. Intrigued, despite herself, Catherine watched him. . . .

Suddenly he threw the hair into the fire together with a pinch of powder from a tin box. He stretched out his hands to the flames which soared high, now, with flashing greeny-blue lights in them, and recited what sounded like a spell.

53

Then he bent forward and stared intently into the flames. The only sound in the large, quiet room was the fire crackling. . . . Abou-al-Khayr's voice rose up in prophesy, sounding strange and foreign:

"The spirit of Zoroaster, Lord of the past and future, speaks to me through these tongues of fire. Your destiny, O woman, is to journey through darkness towards the sun, like our mother, the Earth. But the night is dark and the sun is far away. In order to reach it—for you will reach it—you will need more courage than has hitherto been demanded of you. I see many trials, and blood . . . much blood. The dead line your path as the altars of fire line the mountain roads of Persia. Lovers, too . . . but still you move on and on. You might almost be queen, but you will have to give up everything if you wish to enjoy real happiness. . . ."

Catherine coughed. The sulphurous smoke billowing from the fire was beginning to choke her. In a low, awed voice she asked:

"Is there really any hope of happiness for me, then?"

"The supreme, absolute happiness . . . but . . . how strange! Listen: you will attain this happiness only when the great fire is lit. . . ."

"A fire?"

Abou-al-Khayr emerged from the rigid, hieratic attitude of the seer and wiped off the sweat which was streaming down his face with the back of his wide sleeve.

"I cannot tell you any more. I saw the sun above a furnace in which a human being was burning. You must be patient and forge your own destiny. Death can only bring you nothingness, and you have no need of that. . . ."

He went across to the window and threw it open to allow the sulphurous smoke to escape. Catherine stood up and shook out her skirts with an automatic gesture. Her face was still drawn and her eyes were sad.

"I hate this house and everything it stands for."

"Go and spend a few days with your mother. Yes, that's it! Go back to that house to which those brutish laborers brought me trussed like a fowl on that unforgettable occasion! Return to your own people—your mother and my old friend, Mathieu, for a few days."

"My husband will never allow me to leave the house."

"Alone, possibly not. But I will accompany you. I have long wanted to know how the grape is harvested in this country. We shall depart this evening . . . but first, you will return to me that phial I so foolishly gave you."

Catherine shook her head and smiled wanly at her friend.

"No need. I shall never use it now. I give you my word! But I insist that you let me keep it."

That afternoon, while Garin was visiting Nicolas Rolin, Catherine left the house in the company of Abou-al-Khayr, leaving a letter with Tiercelin for her husband. Some hours later the two of them reached Marsannay where Mathieu and Jacquette welcomed them warmly.

Marsannay, during the wine harvest, was not the ideal place in which to mend a broken heart. From all about the nearby Morvan hill district gay bands of youths and girls flocked down to help in the harvesting, as they did at Gevrey, Nuits, Meursault, Beaune and all along the Côte. They were everywhere, sleeping in the barns and haylofts during the still clement nights. From dawn to dusk the harvesters, stooping under their bursting sacks of black, juicy grapes, sang at the tops of their voices:

> "Off to the harvest
> To earn myself a sou,
> Sleeping in the straw
> As fleas and lice do, too. . . ."

But this was a song of mock-protest, because the tune was a cheerful, rousing one. And in the background some lively boy or girl was always to be heard proclaiming that:

> "Wine is necessary,
> God grants it should be so,
> Else he would have made the black grapes bitter. . . ."

But Catherine kept herself resolutely aloof from all this somewhat rowdy hurly-burly. She spent the whole day in one of the upper rooms of the house, seated beside her mother, spinning yarn as she used to do, or weaving linen cloths while her eyes occasionally wandered over the russet-colored expanse of the vineyards. She liked watching the sun stabbing through the wraiths of mist in the early morning, and the ruddy flames which the sunset lit over the vineyards in the evening. As the evening wore on they gradually turned from molten gold to deep crimson.

Jacquette Legoix had refrained from putting any questions to her daughter when she arrived at the house looking pale and drawn. A mother can always sense a child's suffering even when it is well concealed. She contented herself with fussing over Catherine as though she were an invalid and avoided all mention of Garin, whom she had never grown to like, and Sara, whose strange behavior had greatly disappointed her. Catherine had come back in search of the tranquillity of family life and a complete change from the milieu into which

55

her strange marriage had thrown her, and it was this which Jacquette was bent on giving her. . . . As for Uncle Mathieu and his Arab friend, they were rarely to be seen from one day's end to the next. As long as it was light enough to see, Uncle Mathieu would be out in the vineyards with his sleeves rolled up, helping where he could, filling a basket here and emptying one there. And Abou-al-Khayr, his fantastic turban abandoned for once in favor of a knitted cap, his legs encased as far as the knees in laced boots, and a home-spun smock pulled over his silk robes, trotted happily all day behind his friend, with his hands behind his back and a look of intense interest on his face, chatting incessantly. At nightfall the pair would return exhausted, filthy beyond belief, red-faced, and happy as kings.

Catherine, meanwhile, was under no illusions as to how long this blessedly peaceful interlude would last. It was sufficiently strange that a week should have elapsed without bringing word from Dijon. Sooner or later Garin would come to claim her, because she was the stake in the most profitable deal he had ever undertaken. Every evening, as she went to bed, she wondered anew that another day should have passed without bringing his tall sombre figure back into her life.

But it was not Garin, after all, but Brother Étienne who was destined to be the first in the succession of visitors to Marsannay. Catherine's absence had worried the monk. He had paid two or three abortive visits to the Hotel de Brazey. His interview with Catherine in Uncle Mathieu's vegetable garden was almost fruitless. The young woman announced firmly that she had absolutely no intention of returning to Dijon, that she did not want to hear another word about the Court or the Duke, and still less about politics. She had come to regret bitterly having Arnaud released from the Earl of Suffolk's dungeons, because this had only served to precipitate the young man into the waiting arms of Isabelle de Séverac. And she was very angry with Brother Étienne for having been instrumental in arranging this release and having, in short, made a complete fool of her.

"I have no talent for that sort of intrigue," she told him. "I would only bring disaster to you all."

To her surprise, the monk did not try to make her change her mind. He apologized for having disturbed her and was about to leave when he added, gently:

"Your friend, Odette, will soon be forced to leave her château at Saint-Jean-de-Losne—the Duke is taking it back from her. She will have to go back to her mother's house,

56

and the last time I saw her, she seemed greatly distressed at the prospect. Must I tell her, as well as Queen Yolande, that you no longer care about her fate?"

Catherine felt a pang of remorse. She was ashamed of having shown herself so capricious and selfish, and realized that she had no right to abandon the people who trusted her because of a mere disappointment in love, however bitter.

"Don't say anything to her," she said, after a pause. "Not to her, or to the Queen. I have just suffered a grievous blow, and I need peace and quiet in which to recover. Give me a little time."

A smile replaced the anxious lines which had appeared on Brother Étienne's normally sanguine face.

"I understand," he said, sympathetically. "Forgive me for having been so importunate . . . but do not stay away for too long. . . ."

Catherine had no wish to tie herself to a precise date. She would not commit herself beyond an evasive promise to return soon, quite soon, and Brother Étienne had to be content with that.

The following day it was Ermengarde who put in an appearance. Her arrival was accompanied by all the usual excitement and commotion. She soundly kissed Catherine and her mother, complimented Uncle Mathieu on his domestic arrangements and robust good health, made a round of the cellars as a connoisseur, sampled the sweet wine as it gushed from the press from a ladle as large as a soup bowl and promptly invited herself to dinner.

While Uncle Mathieu and Jacquette bustled about, crimson with pride at being asked to entertain so distinguished a figure, and anxious to provide a fitting repast for the occasion, Ermengarde sat herself down beside Catherine in the vine arbor and reprimanded her sharply.

"Your country retreat is charming," she said, "but you are behaving like a fool. You do not seem to realize that life in the ducal palace has grown quite impossible since you left. The Duke is in a perpetual rage. . . ."

"That's all I need to know," Catherine interrupted. "He sent you here to see me. . . ."

"What do you take me for? No one sends me. I send myself when I think the occasion warrants it. Would you mind telling me what your plans are? The wine harvest is a delightful season, but it doesn't last for ever. I take it you do not intend to spend the winter in the country?"

"Why not? I prefer it to the town."

Ermengarde let out a shattering sigh. She had rarely had to deal with a more obstinate person.

"At first I set your behavior down to a coquettish ruse on your part. What could be more delightful than to keep a man waiting, especially when the man in question is a prince? But it doesn't do to push matters too far. Patience is not Monseigneur's most outstanding quality."

"Why doesn't he lose patience, then? Nothing would suit me better. I only want him to forget about me and leave me alone. . . ."

"You don't know what you are saying. When we left Arras you were very nearly ready to give yourself to him, and now you say you don't want to see him again. What's happened? Why won't you tell me about it? Why?"

"Because it's all so ridiculous, and I'm afraid you won't understand."

"I can understand anything from a woman," Ermengarde said sharply. "Even the most lunatic behavior. I suppose all this has something to do with that Montsalvy of yours?"

Catherine flashed her an awkward smile and, to hide her embarrassment, began toying with a green vine shoot which hung down above her head.

"You always guess right, my friend. I have lost him for ever this time . . . he is getting married!"

The young woman's tone was melancholy, almost tragic, but Ermengarde burst into a great roar of laughter which went on for several minutes. Watched by an indignant Catherine, the Mistress of the Robes sat there holding her sides, her face as red as her dress, and her cheeks wet with tears of merriment. She seemed to be suffocating with mirth.

"Ermengarde!" Catherine cried in an offended voice. "You are making fun of me!"

"Quite so, my child!" Ermengarde puffed, as soon as she had recovered her breath. "The whole thing is too absurd. So it's our hero's forthcoming marriage which has sent you into the back of beyond with that martyred look on your face, is it? It's to *that* we owe those pale cheeks and sunken eyes! You must be out of your mind, my dear! It's perfectly normal for a boy of his rank and ancestry to marry! Indeed, he owes it to himself and his family to carry on the family name. He needs a son, an heir. And who can give him one except a woman?"

"But I love him! I was keeping myself for him, for no one but him!" cried Catherine, bursting into a flood of tears which left Ermengarde quite unmoved.

"And a great mistake on your part it was, too!" she declared. "A woman like you is *made* for love. I've been trying

58

to din that into you for months now. So Arnaud is getting married, is he? So much for that! You can take him as a lover the moment this imbecile war is over . . . and be as happy as you like. What were you hoping for, anyway? Did you think you would be able to marry him yourself? Your own husband is very much alive, my pretty, and unlikely to depart this world for very many years to come. Well, then, let young Montsalvy find himself a little white goose of a girl, a nice, rich, titled bride who will bear him a whole string of heirs in years to come . . . and let yourself be the one who dispenses the joys of forbidden love—so much more exciting than the conjugal stew-pot!"

This rather curious piece of advice left Catherine nonplussed, but somewhat comforted. The terrible Ermengarde had a realistic attitude to things which not only had a certain charm, but was also oddly effective. She wound up her sermon with these words:

"Don't spoil your life because of a ninny who takes himself a wife, however handsome he may be. Philippe loves you, and desires you, and he will make you his, you mark my words. Why not try to get some enjoyment from the situation? He is young, handsome in his own way, charming when he wishes, and powerful enough to flatter the woman of his choice . . . and not one of his mistresses has ever had anything to complain about! He usually has the utmost trouble shaking them off. And that's partly why I've come to see you now. . . ."

So Dame Ermengarde's visit had a purpose, after all! Catherine suppressed a mocking smile. The apparently casual way she had brought out that last remark of hers was a *tour de force* of diplomacy in itself. Catherine did not have much trouble getting to the bottom of the story now. It seemed that Ermengarde—who "only sent herself"—was in reality a messenger from the Duchess Marguerite who was perturbed by the reappearance of Philippe's official mistress, the Dame de Presles, in Dijon, a woman whose ambitious scheming was common knowledge.

"I daresay you remember that blonde creature who gave that idiot, Lionel de Vendôme, her scarf at the joust?" Ermengarde added. "That's the woman I mean. And the Dowager Duchess is in a dreadful state. This woman is determined to become the next duchess. She is clever and unscrupulous and she knows Philippe inside out. Heaven knows what she may not wheedle out of him if she is given the opportunity. She is completely won over to the English cause, and if she gets her way there is no knowing what catastrophes may follow. France and Burgundy will never be united again. In short. . . ."

The Countess got up and stood over her friend. Suddenly solemn, she laid her fine white hand on Catherine's shoulder and added, in an unusually gentle voice:

"Your Duchess is appealing to you for help, Catherine de Brazey. You must not disappoint her. She is so frail!"

Catherine bowed her head without speaking. She was torn by conflicting feelings. She realized now that she stood at the center of a tangled web of intrigue whose possible repercussions extended far beyond her own fair person. Great and important personages were seeking her help, using her personal friends as intermediaries. The Queen of Sicily, through Odette and Brother Étienne, and the Duchess Marguerite, via Ermengarde . . . and both appealed to her in the name of duty, in the name of a cause which in both cases boiled down to the same thing—putting a stop to the bitter feud between Philippe and the King.

The appearance of Uncle Mathieu rushing in to announce that dinner was ready saved her from having to give Ermengarde an immediate answer. Throughout the meal which she attacked with all her customary gusto, Ermengarde refrained from mentioning politics. Instead, she won Mathieu's admiration with her wide knowledge of commerce. When the time came for her to make her departure everyone present joined in entreating her to pay another visit.

"Ah, that all depends . . ." she said, flashing a meaningful look in Catherine's direction. Catherine simply smiled.

"I promise I'll think it over, Ermengarde," she said.

And the Countess, like Brother Étienne, was obliged to be content with this half-promise. After her departure, however, Catherine remained deep in thought. Ermengarde's words, with their rather blunt positivism, seemed to map out her future destiny for her. She had advised her to accept Philippe's love, and, for once, in the midst of this soft, golden autumn, the idea appeared to Catherine in a more pleasing light than it ever had before.

She went back to the garden where she could think without fear of interruption. It was her favorite spot in the entire estate. With its neat, clipped borders and sprawling vine, it was pleasant and unremarkable, but the rural landscape in which it was set lent it a peculiar charm. A row of tall black pines sheltered it on one side, planted close by the low walls covered with rambling roses which separated the garden from the vineyard. Catherine strolled for a while under the pines which cast deep shadows in the sunset glow. Her skirts rustled as she passed over the first fallen leaves. With her head bent, she wandered over towards the great, round well, dating from Roman times, so they said, and leant against it deep in thought. The extraordinary mildness of the autumn evening soothed the turmoil in the depths of her being. Serene, almost smiling, she let her eyes wander beyond the garden walls . . . and gave a sudden jump of surprise: she had just caught sight of a black plume moving along past the stone walls, a plume which could only belong to a man's bonnet. The plume moved the length of the wall and then retraced its steps again. Catherine shrank back into the shadow of the honeysuckle which garlanded the wrought-iron well canopy and held her breath as she watched these strange manoeuvres. The plume halted and appeared to rise up before her. A gray bonnet appeared first, then a forehead, then a pair of eyes whose color Catherine was unable to distinguish in the fading light. The unknown visitor made a thorough inspection of the garden without revealing himself further. He did not see Catherine, who was completely hidden by the honeysuckle. Then the head vanished, and there was nothing to be seen but the black plume waving and nodding as its wearer skirted the wall.

Catherine rushed out of her hiding-place and ran towards the wall which she climbed without much difficulty, with the help of creepers and some uneven stones. But all she could see when she reached the top was a masculine figure wrapped in a dark cloak disappearing in the direction of a clump of trees where a horse stood waiting. The unknown man leapt into the saddle, spurred his horse vigorously without turning back for another look at Mathieu Gautherin's house, and galloped off in the direction of Dijon.

Catherine stayed for a moment where she was, perched on top of the wall, looking after the retreating figure and reflecting on what this curious visit might mean. In all likelihood this cautious figure was another of Jacques de Roussay's spies. The young Captain, doubtless acting on his master's orders, was still having her watched. Decidedly, she was not much trusted in high places, for this notion of keeping her under surveillance at her own home could not have originated with Garin. A brief, impersonal note had arrived from her husband only that morning in which he informed her of the exact date of the forthcoming princely marriage, which was to take place at the end of October, and added that he had taken the precaution, in her absence, of having various gowns made for her which he felt she would require for the festivities. Dame Gauberte knew her measurements and tastes, and would be able to execute his designs almost as satisfactorily as if Catherine were there in person ... in other words, it was a calm and colorless letter with nothing in it to suggest that Garin saw his wife's absence as anything more than a routine family visit. No, Garin could have nothing to do with this evening's visitor. ...

Her mother's voice calling to her from the house sent Catherine hurrying back. But she promised herself that in future she would keep her eyes open. She intended to spend a few more days at Marsannay, in any case, from pride if nothing else, so that it would not look as if she were giving way too tamely to Ermengarde's arguments.

She spent the whole of the following day, after early Mass in the village church, which she had got into the habit of attending, working on a piece of embroidery in the garden. However, the white silk chasuble destined for the Curé of Marsannay did not progress very far because Catherine was quite unable to concentrate. She kept glancing up from the wheat sheaf she was embroidering in gold thread in the hope of surprising a shadow against the wall, or a bobbing plume. But nothing happened. Nothing disturbed the tranquillity of this serene autumn day except the occasional faraway singing of the wine pickers. Almost unconsciously, Catherine was savoring the beauty of the scene in every fibre of her body. The Burgundian autumn, the most opulent, and possibly the most beautiful, throughout the whole of France, unfolded its majestic splendor before her. Nature seemed to show herself at her most fertile and prodigal there.

When the evening meal was announced, Catherine put away her needlework and returned to the house with regret. She felt that the garden still reserved some secret surprise for her and decided to return there at nightfall. Towards the end of the meal, she heard muffled hoof-beats. It must be the unknown visitor of the previous night returning . . . On the pretext of a sudden attack of giddiness, she left the table hurriedly, without waiting for Uncle Mathieu to say Grace, determined to get to the bottom of these nocturnal events. No one noticed her leave. Jacquette, wearied by a day spent washing tub after tub of soiled sheets and clothes with the servants, was dozing in her chair. As for Uncle Mathieu, he and Abou-al-Khayr were deep in discussion of the wine which they had pressed that day from grapes which grew on the furthermost confines of his estate, and its probable quality when matured. . . . Neither of them noticed the young woman slip from the room.

As she crossed the hall, her eye fell upon the stout stick Uncle Mathieu carried with him during his tour of the vine-

62

yards standing in a corner and she decided to take it with her. It was made from a straight oak branch with a knot at one end forming a stout knob. Her Uncle's hand had smoothed and polished the rough wood over the years, but the stick was still a heavy weapon to carry. In the hand of a powerful man it could become a formidable weapon.

Thus armed, Catherine went back into the garden, her mouth set in a purposeful line. If that intruder returned, he would find he had someone to reckon with. . . . However, there was not a sound to be heard. The countryside seemed to be fast asleep. It was almost pitch dark. Catherine took several cautious steps towards the pine copse, keeping within the shadow of the wall. The silence alarmed her, because she could have sworn she had heard the sound of a galloping horse . . . though it was true it had come from a long way off. Perhaps it had just been a traveler hastening back along the road to Dijon before the town gates were closed. . . . All the same, she stayed where she was, listening and watchful.

She had been there about ten minutes when she heard a loose stone clattering and a light footstep crunching over the pebble path on the other side of the wall. Someone was stealthily approaching. Catherine held her breath and took a firmer grip on her knobkerry. . . .

Very cautiously, taking care not to make a sound as she crossed the gravel path, she went up close to the wall and pulled herself up till she was astride the top of the wall, screened by a bush. Catherine could hear the man breathing as he searched about for a foothold. It was difficult to see him clearly in the murky darkness, but little by little the young woman made out the familiar outline of the plume rising slowly above the wall. This time, the visitor seemed bent on climbing over the wall and entering Uncle Mathieu's garden.

Keeping her eyes firmly fixed on the black silhouette, Catherine raised her stick with a feeling akin to enjoyment, like a cat watching a mouse run within reach of her claws. When the intruder's head seemed to be within range, she struck out with all her strength. There was a muffled cry, a scattering of loose masonry, and the nocturnal visitor crashed down onto the road. Elated by the success of her plan, Catherine tucked the stick under her arm and, after making sure that the man had not moved, returned to the house to fetch a lantern.

When she returned, two or three minutes later, her victim was stirring. Catherine, still holding onto her stick, knelt down to have a closer look. She whipped off the black plumed hat and held the lantern close to the man's face. No sooner had she done so than she started back with an exclamation of surprise. The man she had knocked unconscious was none other than the Duke Philippe in person.

CHAPTER FOUR

The Arguments of Philippe le Bon

It was a moment or two before Catherine could take in the full enormity of her action. She frantically invoked the protection of every saint whose name she could call to mind. Luckily, Philippe was showing signs of returning to consciousness. Otherwise, she might have thought she had killed him. . . . But, still, how was she to know that the all-powerful Duke of Burgundy would roam the countryside disguised as one of his own soldiers? As her presence of mind returned to her, she laid a hand on his forehead. It was hot, but not excessively so, and there was no sign of a wound. Philippe might thank the stout material of his bonnet for that, as it had undoubtedly softened the force of Catherine's blow.

She felt she dare not return to the house for help. If Philippe had gone to such trouble to disguise himself, it could only be because he did not want his presence there known. Then, remembering the garden well, she ran to bring up a bucket of water, in which she dipped her handkerchief to lay on Philippe's brow. The remedy worked wonders. The well was deep and the water very fresh. A moment later the Duke opened his eyes and smiled as he recognized the young woman.

"So I've found you again at last, my fair vagabond?" he exclaimed with a chuckle. "Where have you been hiding yourself? Well, you are certainly well guarded. . . . Ouch! My head!" he cried. "What happened?"

"Someone struck you on the head, Monseigneur. . . ."

"And none too gently, either, so it seems. Who must I thank for this experience?"

Catherine looked away to hide her confusion, and picked up the stick which she had let drop in her astonishment.

"It was this stick, here, Monseigneur, and me! Please forgive me. . . ."

Philippe remained speechless for a moment, then he gave way to a sudden burst of laughter; an uproarious, boyish laugh with nothing regal about it.

"This was not the kind of souvenir I had expected to take away with me, my sweet. . . . It looks as if it will be the biggest bump on the head I have ever had . . . the only one I shall cherish, at all events!"

He sat up and seized Catherine's hand and kissed it. She tried to pull it away, but he held it fast.

"Ah, no, you won't escape so easily! You owe me that, at least! But when are you going to settle down and become a law-abiding citizen, my dear? The first time I saw you, you were starting a public riot right in the path of a religious procession. The next time, you burst into my room, uninvited, to steal some prisoners away from under my very nose. . . . And, now, here you are laying about you with a knobkerry! Don't you think you are a little in my debt after all this?"

"I grant you that, Monseigneur, but I don't know how I can settle it. . . ."

"By telling me the truth. Why did you run away and hide yourself down here in the country? When we parted at Arras I thought everything had been smoothed out between us . . . that we would have an understanding in future . . . and that you had finally decided to stop being difficult."

Catherine gently withdrew her hand and stood up, clasping her hands together behind her back.

"I thought so, too, Monseigneur. But then I realized that we didn't really look at things from the same point of view. There are the terms of the . . . agreement which Your Highness reached with my husband. . . ."

Philippe had also risen to his feet, but he was no sooner standing up right than his legs buckled under him and he had to clutch at Catherine's shoulder for support.

"I would prefer to continue this conversation sitting down . . ." he said, smiling faintly. ". . . if you don't object, that is. Let me have your arm to lean on and let us go and sit down in some quiet corner. No, not here in your garden. I don't want to be found here on any account. But, if you wouldn't mind accompanying me to that thicket of trees where I have left my horse. . . ."

Slowly and cautiously they made their way towards the place Philippe had chosen. Catherine was so anxious to make amends that she did not notice that the Duke's strength seemed to be returning with every step he took, and that he

65

no longer had need of her supporting arm. He continued to lean on her as heavily as before, but this was because he could better appreciate the scent of her hair that way. When they reached the spot where the tethered horse stood quietly grazing, he sat down on the grass and pulled Catherine down beside him. The trees hid the sky, and their trunks walled them in almost as solidly as the walls of a house. . . . There was no wind and it was as warm as a summer's night and only a little darker. Catherine's face and neck were a pale blur in the darkness on which the Prince feasted his eyes longingly. He still held her hand clasped in his, but, sensing that her mood was troubled, with his strange skill in understanding feminine reactions, he took care not to upset her.

"Let us talk now," he said gently, "and straighten things out between us. We are quite alone. There is no one to spy on us, no Court etiquette or protocol to come between us. It's not the Duke and his subject now, but a man and a woman. I am Philippe and you are Catherine. Now tell me, frankly, what it is you have against me."

For the moment, Catherine found she could think of nothing to say. It is always the same when one has been storing up grudges for weeks—when you are asked to explain, you can never think of a single good reason. How could one possibly be angry with a man who spoke so sweetly and took such pains to minimize the distance between them. Finding her still silent, Philippe spoke to her again:

"Is my love so offensive to you, then? Or do you just find me repulsive?"

"Neither," she said. "I have no doubt that I should have been gratified by your attentions if I had not felt that I had no choice in the matter. Ever since I heard that I was to marry Garin de Brazey I knew that I was also expected to . . ."

She paused, not daring to go on. Once again the Duke came to her assistance, smiling.

"To come to my bed? May I remind you that you spent an entire night in my bed on one occasion . . . without coming to any harm?"

"That is true, Monseigneur, and I must admit that I was a little puzzled by the episode. . . ."

"Nothing strange about it, really. I was simply testing your—shall we say—loyalty as a faithful vassal that evening. You obeyed. But I would have been truly despicable if I had taken advantage of you, helpless as you were. If I seemed brutal in my behavior, it is because I was jealous. But sweetheart, what I want you to know is that I shall never force you

66

into anything. I want you to choose me of your own free will."

He bent closer to her and his warm breath caressed the nape of her neck. His voice in the darkness took on a vibrant warmth and seductiveness which Catherine had never heard in it before. He sounded completely sincere and Catherine found difficulty in shaking off the spell of these murmured endearments in the soft darkness. She tried to dispel their charm by stirring up her old grudge against him again.

"But what about this . . . arrangement of yours with Garin?"

"What arrangement?" Philippe asked, with a touch of unconscious arrogance. "This is the second time you have mentioned it. I have made no such agreement with Garin de Brazey. What a low opinion you must have of us both! I merely ordered one of my most loyal servants to marry an admirably beautiful girl whom I did, indeed, entertain hopes of wooing one day, but I did not confide these particular hopes to him, you may rest assured of that. I ordered him to marry you, as I said. And like the loyal subject he is, he obeyed without argument. That is the whole story! Was it a crime on my part to wish to see you rich, noble, living in the style which you deserved?"

Catherine shook her head and shivered, at which Philippe took it upon himself to put his arm round her shoulders on the pretext that she must be feeling the cold. She no longer resisted. Aware only of the pressure of his arm about her, her anger quite forgotten, she gazed dreamily into the darkness and murmured:

"A loyal subject, to be sure . . . of an inviolable loyalty. You may not have exacted any promises from him, Monseigneur, but let me assure you that he must have read your secret wishes. For surely, when you made me his wife, Monseigneur, you must have supposed that he would exercise his marital rights? And yet he has not. He violently refuses even to touch me."

"Have you asked him to?"

Catherine turned towards him in an attempt to make out his face in the darkness. When she spoke again, her voice was defiant.

"I offered myself to him one evening in such a way that no other man could have spurned me. And he was on the point of yielding, when he suddenly pulled himself up and said that it was impossible, and that he had no right to touch me. So you see that he clearly thinks of me as belonging to you."

She felt a certain malicious delight as Philippe's arm tightened round her. But when he spoke again his voice was quite even.

"I told you that this subject was never mentioned by either of us. After all, he may not have been thinking of me when he said that. . . ."

"What could he have been thinking of, then? Or whom?"

Philippe did not answer immediately. Perhaps he was thinking. Finally he said:

"I don't know."

There was silence between them. A dog barked a long way off, and an owl hooted, but this only served to emphasize Catherine's feeling that she and the Duke were alone in the world. He held her against him now.

As he spoke, he put both arms round her, and she allowed her head to rest on his shoulder. It was a tender moment and Catherine had had her fill of sterile conflicts. Arnaud had forgotten her in another woman's arms, so why should she refuse so passionate and sincere a love, a love which only sought to ensure her greater happiness? A faint scent of irises arose from Philippe's garments of coarsely woven cloth. He rocked her gently like a little child and she was grateful to him for not pressing his suit more bluntly. She felt his breath against her hair and neck. With her eyes closed, she asked softly:

"Does your head still hurt, Monseigneur?"

"Stop calling me 'Monseigneur.' I am 'Philippe' to you. I want to forget about everything else. Nothing hurts me now. . . . I'm happy, happier than I have been for a long, long time. You are here; I'm holding you in my arms and you are not saying harsh things to me any more. You let me speak to you, and no longer spurn my advances. Catherine . . . my beautiful, adorable Catherine . . . may I have one kiss?"

Catherine smiled into the darkness. His humble, almost childlike tone touched her more than she would admit. She remembered the proud seigneur who behaved with such superb confidence, ordered everyone about, addressed her in the familiar "tu" the first time they met, as though she already belonged to him. Tonight, he was just a man passionately in love. . . .

She lifted her head a little so that her lips were close to his.

"Kiss me," she said simply, unhesitatingly; everything seemed simple all of a sudden. She still remembered the passionate kiss at Arras and when his lips touched hers she closed her eyes and gave a small sigh. She knew instinctively that with this man who was both cold and passionate the pleasures of love were guaranteed. He knew how to make his

68

partner forget everything, politics, people, everything, because he had learned to control his own impulses. His kiss was extraordinarily gentle, a masterpiece of passion and restraint. Where love-making was concerned, he was the master whom all women are unconsciously waiting for and Catherine, suddenly submissive, allowed herself to be carried away on a sea of pleasure and caresses which soon broke down all resistance. For Philippe, finding her at his mercy at last, did not stop at the one kiss he had demanded from her. Soon the fresh breeze which stole through the trees carried sighs and loving endearments away to disperse over the sleeping countryside. The only witness of his master's final triumph was the Prince's horse.

At the moment Catherine experienced the reality of physical love for the first time, her eyes widened and she gazed up at the still leafy branches criss-crossing overhead. The silvery light of a new moon stole through the glade and lit up her lover's grave, tense face. He seemed almost supernaturally beautiful to her at that moment. She did not know that her own face was illuminated by passion. Philippe silenced her brief cry of pain with a kiss and a moment later it became a long moan of pleasure.

When at length they drew apart, Philippe hid his face in her silky mass of hair and covered it with kisses. Catherine stroked his face with her hands and found his cheeks were wet with tears.

"You are weeping?"

"From happiness, my darling . . . and gratitude. I had never imagined that when you gave yourself to me it would be so complete, so wonderful . . . that I should be the very first. . . ."

She put her hand over his mouth to silence him.

"I told you my husband had never touched me. What did you expect?"

"You are so beautiful . . . there must have been so many temptations. . . ."

"I can protect myself," said Catherine, with such an enchanting grimace that it won her another kiss. Then, as a stray moonbeam fell upon her naked body, Philippe went to fetch a roll of blanket attached to his saddle and wrapped her up in it before taking her into his arms once more. He began to laugh.

"When I think that I had planned that our first night together should be adorned with every splendor that my palace can offer, the most exotic flowers, the most sumptuous setting . . . and when it came to the point, all I could offer you, my poor darling, was damp grass and a night wind which will give you a dreadful chill. What a sorry lover I must appear!"

"What nonsense!" Catherine exclaimed, pressing closer to him. "First of all, I'm not cold and secondly, what better setting could you have than nature herself? Anyway, you weren't to know that I would hit you over the head when you set out."

They burst out laughing like a couple of children and the horse began whinnying gently so as not to feel left out. Then silence fell once more in the glade beside the road which led to Mathieu Gautherin's house.

Despite Philippe's impatience for her return to Dijon, Catherine had to spend three or four days longer at Marsannay because of the dreadful cold she had indeed caught.

"What a ridiculous idea to stay out so late in the garden and then fall asleep out there!" Uncle Mathieu trumpeted as he watched her swallowing a bowl of hot tisane. "It was so late I didn't even hear you coming in!"

As for Abou-al-Khayr, he bent his head discreetly so that Catherine should not notice the amused twinkle in his eyes. The little doctor had seen a rider set off along the road to Dijon very late that night, and a white figure standing at the end of the path watching after him till he was well out of sight.

Several days later, Catherine de Brazey, looking dazzlingly beautiful, attended the marriage of Marguerite de Guyenne and Arthur de Richemont in the Sainte-Chapelle of the Duke's palace. Dressed in a green velvet gown embroidered with golden stars and trimmed with white ermine, she presented a radiant image of youthful beauty and grace. Her complexion glowed with an inner radiance, her eyes shone under their long, curling fringe of lashes, so bright they dimmed even the brilliance of the matchless emeralds at her throat and ears, a gift from Philippe, who no longer made any secret of his love for her.

The Dame de Presles, Philippe's official mistress, had been despatched to Flanders in a fury, and Marie de Vaugrigneuse had been asked to retire to her property in the country for a while. A malicious remark about Catherine which the latter had made had come to the Duke's ears, and not even her position as the Dowager Duchess's god-daughter had been able to save her. Everyone could draw what deductions they pleased from Catherine's position in the chapel. It was noticeably more elevated than her rank entitled her to. Finally, it would have been difficult not to notice how frequently Philippe's eyes sought hers and the burning glances which passed between them.

Garin, standing among the men, on the other side of the church, did not look at his wife once. Since her return from Marsannay, his behavior towards her had been perfectly courteous, but cold. He only saw her at meals, and when the Moorish doctor was not with them, his conversation to her consisted of a string of banalities. When he was with Abou-al-Khayr he discussed scientific topics which meant nothing to his wife. These were the only moments when he seemed to come alive. Occasionally, Catherine met his eyes, but she found it impossible to gauge the expression in them as he always looked away immediately.

The day before the marriage Philippe's page, young Lannoy, had come to the Hotel de Brazey to bring Catherine the famous set of emeralds. Garin had been crossing the hall at the very moment his wife was coming down the stairs. He had thus been present as she received the gift, but he had not shown the slightest astonishment. He had merely nodded in reply to the boy's respectful greeting and gone on his way without speaking.

Towards the end of the nuptial Mass, however, as the guests turned to face each other, Catherine met Garin's eyes at last fixed full upon her and, in spite of herself, she gave a start of fear. Not even when he had assaulted and beaten her so savagely had his face been so contorted with fury. He was white with rage and a nervous tic convulsed the scarred side of his face. He looked so dreadful that Catherine had to turn away. The gleam in his solitary, glittering eye was unmistakably a gleam of hatred. But just then, the new Countess of Richemont, quite rosy with emotion beneath her veil, passed by on her husband's arm and Catherine sank into a deep curtsey which momentarily released her from this brief nightmare. When she stood up again, Garin had vanished into the crowd and the guests were streaming towards the chapel doors accompanied by the loudly pealing organ. It had been a protracted ceremony and everyone was hungry; they were hurrying to launch themselves on the banquet which awaited them.

Catherine was not feeling hungry. She strolled slowly in the direction of the great hall, idling a little as she passed through the long gallery and gazing out at the last roses in the garden. She had no particular wish to take her seat at the banquet because her lower rank kept her at a considerable distance from Philippe, Ermengarde would not be leaving

71

the bedside of the failing Dowager Duchess and her husband's terrifying glare had robbed her of any desire to see him again for the present.

The long gallery was emptying rapidly. As the various courtiers drew level with Catherine they bowed and then hurried on. As the young woman passed one of the doors leading to the ducal family's private apartments, each door guarded by two archers, one of them opened and a robust young man, dressed entirely in green, came out. It was one of the riders of the Duke's Horse and he appeared to be on his way somewhere with a message from the Duchess, as Catherine saw him slipping a folded parchment into the front of his armored tunic. He did not look at anyone in the Long Gallery. He was merely intent on crossing it to reach the great staircase in the New Tower, or beyond that, the one which led to the stables. But Catherine's face had brightened and she instantly forgot about the banqueting hall and its festivities and hurried after him—it was her old childhood friend, Landry. Since the first time she had seen him, on the day of her presentation to the Duchess, she had never found an opportunity, despite all her efforts, to see the Duke's horseman again. This time he was not going to escape! She caught up with him just as he was about to start down the great stone staircase. There was no one else within earshot. She called to him:

"Landry . . . wait for me!"

He stopped at once, and turned to look at her, but without any apparent eagerness. His face was impassive, unsmiling; he gave no sign of recognition.

"What do you want . . . Madame?"

With her face sparkling animatedly and eyes shining, she placed herself between Landry and the staircase window so he could see her with the light full upon her. Then she laughed.

" 'Madame?' Now come, Landry, don't pretend you don't know who I am. Have I changed so much in ten years? Or have you lost your memory? You look just the same as you ever did . . . except that you are a bit taller and stronger. But you look as surly as ever. . . ."

To her astonishment, Landry did not raise his eyebrows at this. He merely shook his head.

"You do me too much honor, noble lady. I have, I believe, an excellent memory, but I have no recollection of our ever having met. . . ."

"Ah, well that must mean I really have changed a great deal," said Catherine, good-humoredly. "Very well then, I

72

shall have to refresh your memory. Have you forgotten the Pont-au-Change and the Cour des Miracles and the riot in the Hotel de Saint-Pol? Have you forgotten Catherine Legoix, your little friend from those days?"

"I remember all that very well, Madame. . . . And I did know a little girl of that name, but I am afraid I do not see the connection. . . ."

"Ah, what a blockhead! Oh, no, you certainly haven't changed! . . . But *I* am Catherine, you idiot! Wake up! Take a closer look at me!"

She was expecting an exclamation, even cries of delight. The old Landry would have danced with joy, played the fool. But the Duke's horseman might have been carved from ice. His eyes remained perfectly indifferent.

"Please do not mock me, Madame. I know very well who you are: the Dame de Brazey, the richest woman in the town . . . and Monseigneur's most valued friend. I beg you to finish this game."

"This game? Oh, Landry!" Catherine cried, hurt. "Why do you persist in not recognizing me? If you know who I am, and my name, you must know that I am called Catherine, and that before marrying Garin de Brazey at Monseigneur's orders, I was simply the niece of Mathieu Gautherin, the cloth-merchant in the rue du Griffon. A niece called Catherine Legoix!"

"No, Madame, I did not know all this."

"Well, go and see my uncle then. You will find my mother there. I daresay you would recognize her, at any rate?"

As Catherine stepped closer to him in order to persuade him the better, the young man moved away down the stairs. He bowed slightly.

"There would be no point, Madame. This visit could not tell me anything. I did once know a Catherine Legoix, but you are not that Catherine. . . . Now I must ask you to excuse me. I have a mission to complete, and no time to waste. . . . Forgive me. . . ."

He would have run on down the stairs, but she detained him for a moment longer.

"Who would have believed that the day would come when Landry failed to recognize Catherine? For *you* are Landry Pigasse, are you not?"

"At your service, Madame. . . ."

"At my service?" she echoed sadly. "There was a time when we shared everything, sweetmeats as well as clouts. We were friends, almost brother and sister to each other, and if I remember right, we even risked our lives together.

73

And yet you persist in denying all this only ten years later, and without any reason that I can see."

But she had the impression that she was running up against a brick wall. Landry had retreated behind an invisible armor of indifference, or perhaps deliberate forgetfulness, and she seemed to be searching in vain for a chink in it. It was incomprehensible. She made one last effort, and murmured bitterly:

"If only Barnaby were here . . . he would know how to make you recognize me! Even if it meant giving you a good thrashing!"

He had turned away from her a few seconds earlier, but when she mentioned Barnaby he wheeled round and glared at her angrily.

"Barnaby died under torture for having attacked your husband, Madame! At least that's what I was told when I returned from a mission in Flanders. And you still insist that you are Catherine Legoix? You? No . . . you are not Catherine . . . and I forbid you to use her name. Anyway, you don't even look like her! Your servant, Madame."

Before Catherine could recover from her astonishment at this unexpected burst of speech, Landry was hurtling down the stairs at breakneck speed. She heard the metallic clatter of his armed shoes gradually receding out of ear-shot. Soon silence had once more fallen over the great staircase. The sounds of the banquet were faint and faraway. The young woman stayed where she was for a long time, motionless. The scene in which she had just taken part was painful and incomprehensible. Why did Landry refuse to recognize her? For that was what he had done: he bluntly refused to do so, even when the evidence stared him in the face. Could it be because of Barnaby? His anger when she had mentioned him would be an understandable reason for his refusing to enter into friendly relations with the Dame de Brazey. But he had not seemed surprised when she gave him her maiden name. Obviously, like everyone else in the town, he knew all about her curiously unconventional marriage. He must have known for some time that she was the Catherine he used to know . . . but he no longer loved her! More than that, he hated her, holding her responsible, like Garin, for Barnaby's death. Responsible she undoubtedly was, and even more so than he realized. It was not the first time that Catherine was seized with remorse and grief as she remembered the Coquillart who had gone to a terrible death for no reason at all.

But something else puzzled Catherine. If Barnaby and Landry had renewed their old friendship again, why had Barnaby never mentioned the fact to her? And why had Landry never called round at Uncle Mathieu's to see his old childhood friend before she married? Catherine sighed heavily; these questions must all remain unanswered for the moment. She was torturing herself pointlessly.

A cold voice broke into her reflections, startling her.

"May I inquire what you are doing here? You are expected at the banquet."

Garin was standing there looking at her. Without moving Catherine raised a wan face towards him.

"I don't want to go, Garin. It doesn't amuse me and I'm not hungry. I would rather go and see Madame de Châteauvilain and the Duchess."

A sarcastic smile cast a disagreeable light over the Lord Treasurer's face.

"Whether it amuses you or not is quite beside the point," he said harshly. "This is not the moment to play at preferences. I have told you that you are expected at the banquet. At least have the courage to accept the rank you have been assigned and the consequences for your actions."

He held out his arm to her, to escort her to the banqueting hall. With a weary sigh, Catherine climbed the flight of stairs she had run down in pursuit of Landry and laid her hand over her husband's.

"What do you mean?"

"I mean just what I said: that your place at this moment is not out here on the stairs."

He conducted her to the banqueting hall which was brilliantly illuminated because of the dull gray weather outside. The din in there was staggering. The wedding feast was uproariously gay, and a good number of the guests were already drunk. Laughter, shouts and jests flew from one to another of the three immensely long tables arranged in a U-shape on three sides of the hall. An army of footmen served the food, arranged on immense platters which the scullions brought up from the kitchens below. The squires trenchant and cup-bearers busied themselves on all sides . . . only the newly married pair and the Duke Philippe remained silent. Richemont and Marguerite sat holding hands gazing at each other, oblivious of the food pressed upon them and everything else. Philippe sat staring in front of him, a brooding look on his face. He was the only person who observed Catherine entering and being escorted to her place by Garin. Instantly, his face brightened. He smiled tenderly at her.

"Didn't I tell you that you were expected?" Garin whispered in her ear. "Your presence works miracles, upon my

75

word! Look how gracious Monseigneur has become all of a sudden! A moment ago he looked quite dangerous."

Her husband's bantering tone irritated the already over-wrought Catherine.

"Under the circumstances, you should be feeling quite overjoyed yourself. At last you've got what you wanted!"

She smiled back at Philippe as she took her place at the table. The meal seemed interminable. Never in her whole life had she felt so bored. Nevertheless, this wedding day still held surprises in store for her. One might have thought that all the figures out of her past had taken it upon themselves to reappear before her all at once. At the reception after the banquet, which was attended by a great press of nobles from the ducal provinces, a good number of English, Bretons, and even a few French, Catherine noticed a prelate surrounded by a great throng of people. His clothes were ostentatiously rich—a blaze of purple brocade, lace and gold embroidery. A magnificent diamond pectoral cross glittered on his swelling paunch. He must have been somewhere between fifty and sixty years old. His whole person exuded pride and prosperity. He was tall and strongly built though inclined to stoutness, and would have been an impressive figure but for the dis-agreeably cunning expression on his long flat face. This per-sonage was conversing loudly in a strong Rheims accent which struck Catherine as vaguely familiar. She had seen that face before somewhere. But where?

Leaning toward her neighbor, Mme. de Vergy, she pointed to the bishop and asked:

"Who is that?"

Alix de Vergy turned a surprised, faintly patronizing stare upon her.

"You mean to say you don't know the Bishop of Beauvais? It's true you haven't been at Court very long."

"I may not know the Bishop of Beauvais," Catherine re-torted, "but I know that man. What is his name?"

"Why, Pierre Cauchon! One of the leading lights of our age and one of the most ardent supporters of the English alliance. He was much talked about at the Council of Con-stance a few years back, and some months ago the Regent, Bedford, conferred the title of Almoner of France upon him. A remarkable man. . . ."

Catherine repressed a grimace of disgust. Caboche the Skinner's confederate Almoner of France? It was ludicrous! Her red lips set in a scornful curl which surprised Mme. de Vergy.

"He was talked about a lot in Paris, too, a few years

76

back. He enthralled the butchers and had every poor wretch who disagreed with him hanged without mercy. And now he's a bishop! Ah, it's a worthy recruit Our Lord has made there! Would you mind introducing me to him?"

Somewhat astonished, Alix de Vergy complied. The self-assurance of this recently ennobled little bourgeoise took her breath away. And still more, the fact that she dared to speak in so disdainful a fashion of Monseigneur de Beauvais who enjoyed the Duke's favor. A few minutes later, Catherine was graciously permitted to kiss the episcopal ring. She did so with a faint *moue* of distaste because the said ring decorated a hand which was fat and dimpled. But a feeling of defiance drove her to pursue this interview with Cauchon.

"Madame de Brazey," the Bishop said suavely, "I am delighted to make your acquaintance. We have a very high opinion of your husband at the Council—a remarkable financier! But I have not yet had the honor of meeting you— for I should certainly have remembered. Apart from the fact that I never forget a face, yours is not the sort of face a man is ever likely to forget . . . even when he is a priest."

"You are too kind, Your Worship!" Catherine fluttered, with an air of pretty confusion. "But you have seen me before, nonetheless . . . a long time ago, it's quite true."

"Really? You surprise me!"

The two of them had moved forward a few paces as they talked and, sensing that the prelate wished to have a moment's conversation alone with the fair Catherine, his entourage moved aside, taking Alix de Vergy with them. Catherine decided to take advantage of this momentary isolation. Cauchon was saying:

"Could your father have been one of the servitors of the late Duke Jean, God rest his soul? He was a dear friend of mine! I would be obliged if you would remind me of your maiden name. . . ."

Catherine shook her head, laughing softly.

"Messire, my father, was not one of the members of Jean-sans-Peur's entourage, and I can assure Your Worship that if you ever did meet him, it could not have been in circumstances remotely like the ones you are imagining. You had him hanged . . . Monseigneur!"

Cauchon started back in astonishment.

"Hanged? A gentleman? Madame, if I had played a part in such a thing, I would certainly remember!"

"Ah, but he was not a gentleman," Catherine went on, quietly, with a disturbingly gentle note in her voice. "He was only a humble bourgeois . . . a modest goldsmith from

77

the Pont-au-Change in Paris. It was ten years ago. His name was Gaucher Legoix, a name which ought to mean something to you. You and your friend, Caboche, had him hung because I, poor fool, had hidden a young man in the cellar of our house . . . another innocent wretch who was murdered in front of my eyes."

At the mention of Caboche, two red spots appeared on the fat pale cheeks of the Bishop of Beauvais. He disliked being reminded, in all his new-found episcopal dignity, of old and hardly flattering associations. But his little yellow eyes fastened upon Catherine's face.

"So that's why your face reminded me of something! You are the little Catherine, isn't that so? But I may be excused for having failed to recognize you because you have changed a great deal. Who could have imagined. . . ."

". . . that the daughter of a humble craftsman would finish up at the Court of the Duke of Burgundy? Neither yourself nor I, certainly. But it has happened, nevertheless. Destiny is a strange thing, is it not, Monseigneur?"

"Exceedingly strange! You remind me of things which I prefer to forget. I speak plainly, as you perceive. I will now speak more plainly still. I had no personal animosity towards your father. I might even have saved him if it had been possible, but it was not."

"Are you quite sure you did everything you could to spare him the rope? You were inclined to make short work of people who annoyed you in those days . . . and he annoyed you."

Cauchon did not flinch. His heavy face remained expressionless. His stare was as hard as though his eyes had been pale, amber-colored stones.

"As you say, he annoyed me. It was not a time for half-measures. You may be right, after all—the reason I didn't try to save him was because I didn't see the point."

"Well, that *is* frank!"

They had been standing in a deep window embrasure. The Bishop placed his hand on one of the colored panes, his finger absently following the meandering lead outline.

"There is something I would like to know. Why did you arrange to meet me? You must hate me."

"Yes, I hate you," Catherine replied imperturbably. "I just wanted to take a closer look at you . . . and remind you of my existence. Anyway, I have some cause to be grateful to you, because, when you hanged my father, you did at least spare him what would have been an equally painful, but much slower death. . . ."

78

"What was that?"

"Dying of a broken heart. He loved his country and King and the city of Paris too much to be able to see them in English hands without suffering."

A flash of anger momentarily lit up the Bishop's cold eyes.

"The Englishman is entitled to rule by birth and royal heritage! He is our legitimate sovereign, son of a Princess of France and the heir designate chosen by his grandparents, while the bastard of Bourges is . . . an adventurer!"

His speech was cut short by a little, insolent laugh from Catherine.

"Who are you hoping to convince? Not me, surely . . . or yourself! Your Worship must be aware that King Charles VII would never have chosen you to be High Almoner of France. The Englishman is not so fussy . . . he can't be, he has no choice in the matter! But allow me to say that, for a priest of God, you are not making much effort to fall in with His wishes and recognize the elected King of France. . . ."

"Henry VI is the rightful King of France. . . ."

The Bishop seemed to be on the verge of apoplectic fit. Catherine smiled her sweetest smile.

"The trouble with you, Monseigneur, is that you would almost certainly die rather than admit you were wrong! Smile, Your Worship! We are being looked at . . . by the Duke, in particular. Someone must have told him that we are great friends."

With an almost superhuman effort, Pierre Cauchon managed to compose his face. He even smiled, but it was a forced smile and he hissed at her between clenched teeth:

"Be sure that I shall not forget you, Madame!"

Catherine bowed slightly, then murmured smoothly:

"You are too kind. For my part, I have never been able to forget Your Grace. I shall follow your career with interest."

And with this parting shot, Catherine walked off, a slender, graceful figure, her green and white dress swirling out behind her like a wave, to rejoin Philippe who had observed her little aside with the High Almoner with evident astonishment. Seeing her approach, he came towards her and gave her his hand. No one ventured to follow them. The Court was too versed in these matters not to have divined that from now on Catherine de Brazey was to be the center of attraction and the sole object of the Duke's affections.

"What were you talking so earnestly about to the Bishop of Beauvais?" he asked, with a smile. "You looked as solemn as prelates in Council. Were you debating a point from

Saint Augustine? I was not even aware that you knew each other. . . ."

"We were debating a point of French history, Monseigneur. I have known His Excellency for a long time now, over ten years to be exact. We met quite often in Paris at one time . . . that was what I was reminding him about. . . ."

She broke off and suddenly turned a pair of tear-filled eyes on the Duke and asked him in a voice which shook with suppressed anger:

". . . How can you employ . . . and respect such a man? A priest who has waded through baths of blood before reaching his episcopal throne? You, the Great Duke of the West? . . . He is a miserable wretch!"

Philippe loved to be addressed by this flattering title, and Catherine's emotion stirred him deeply. He bent towards her so as to make sure he was not overheard.

"I know, sweetheart. I employ him because he is useful to me. But there is no question of respecting him! You must understand that a ruling prince must make use of instruments of all kinds. Now . . . give me a smile and let us open the ball together!" In an undertone he added:

"I love you more than anything in the world!"

A faint smile returned to Catherine's lips and eyes. The musicians in the gallery were striking up the opening chords of a pavane. She allowed the Duke to lead her into the middle of the huge ring formed by the guests who stood watching with admiring and envious faces.

CHAPTER FIVE

Nunc Dimittis

The day on which Marguerite of Bavaria's funeral took place was one on which Catherine thought she would die of both cold and misery. The Dowager Duchess had died suddenly three months after her daughter's marriage, on 23 January 1424, in Ermengarde's arms. Philippe, who was staying at Montbard at that time with Arthur de Richemont, had returned too late to see his mother alive, and since his return a dark desolation had fallen over both the palace and the town where the dead woman was widely and sincerely mourned. A few days later, on a bitterly cold day, the mortal remains of the Duchess were conducted to their last resting place beneath the handsome vaults of the Chartreuse de Champmol, near the city gates. Other members of her family were already buried here: her husband, Jean-sans-Peur, her father-in-law, Philippe the Bold, and her daughter-in-law, the gentle Michelle de France.

That morning, when Perrine had been dressing her mistress for the long day of ceremonies ahead, she had exclaimed in horror over Catherine's pallor.

"Madame ought to stay at home, make her excuses. . . ."

"Impossible! Only those who were present at the deathbed can excuse themselves from attending the funeral. It would simply offend the Duke in his bereavement," Catherine replied.

"But, Madame . . . in your condition!"

"Yes, Perrine," Catherine had smiled sadly. "Even so."

Only two people in Catherine's entourage knew that she was pregnant—her little maidservant and Abou-al-Khayr, who had been the first to diagnose the reason for the young woman's sudden fainting fit a little while before Christmas. Since then, Catherine's health, though she made every effort to hide the fact, had been fragile in the extreme. Her pregnancy was a difficult one and she was tortured by sickness and giddy spells. She could not endure the smell of cooking, and the odors from the tripe-sellers' cauldrons made her writhe with revulsion every time she was obliged to cross the town. But she struggled courageously to hide the truth from her husband for as long as possible.

Since the wedding festivities, her relations with Garin had shown a marked deterioration. The Lord Treasurer treated her with icy politeness in public, and in private, on the rare occasions when they met, avoided speaking at all unless it were to address some cutting remark to her. Catherine did not understand his attitude. He clearly knew, like the rest of Dijon, the nature of her relationship with the Duke. But that he should behave in this outraged fashion was something Catherine could not comprehend. Had he not done everything possible to create this very situation? Why did he adopt this contemptuous attitude towards her, then? Catherine found his contempt hard to endure, especially since she had scarcely even seen Philippe for the past month and a half, occupied as he was with State business and endless traveling. His passionate tenderness, and the vigilant protection he mounted over her were gradually becoming indispensable. And then it was he who had awakened her body to the delights of love

81

and Catherine had to admit to herself that she had known moments of unforgettable ecstasy with him . . . moments she would not be reluctant to live through again.

Perrine finished wrapping her mistress up as warmly as possible. Like the rest of the Court, she was in deep mourning, which meant she was dressed in black from head to toe, but a king's ransom-worth of sables lined her heavy velvet garments. A thick black veil hung from her round, fur-trimmed hat. Short furlined boots, hidden under her dress and cape, and black gloves, completed this ensemble whose austerity was unrelieved by a single jewel. Catherine was well protected, but the cold outside was bitter. The young maid shook her head doubtfully as she looked out of the window. A thick layer of snow covered the rooftops and gradually turned to icy mud as it was trampled underfoot in the streets, or dangerously slippery puddles. Catherine would have to cover a large part of the journey to the Chapel on foot.

The Requiem Mass at the black-draped Sainte-Chapelle seemed to last for an eternity. Despite the forest of candles around the altar and catafalque it was bitterly cold in there. Everyone's breath smoked. But the worst part was the interminable funeral cortège, which wound slowly on foot through the town. It had been a real calvary for Catherine.

The procession had passed between black-draped houses under a leaden sky to the sound of funeral trumpet calls and the incessant tolling of all the city's bells. The only touch of color in this sombre procession was the bier itself, which Philippe had insisted should be identical with his father's. It was drawn by six black horses and the Duchess's embalmed body was covered by a great square of gold cloth on which a large crimson velvet cross had been sewn. Pennants of blue silk embroidered with gold thread fluttered at all four corners of the bier, and sixty torch-carriers and a vertible army of weeping, psalm-chanting monks walked in procession around it. Philippe followed just behind, bare-headed despite the freezing cold, his face deathly pale and his eyes devoid of all expression. The entire Court followed behind, together with the townspeople and the banners of the various city Guilds.

When she first caught sight of the Duke, Catherine's heart stopped. He looked like a robot. Remote in his grief, Philippe appeared before her once more as the haughty, intimidating ruler . . . just when she had this particularly delicate and difficult favor to ask of him! The night before, Marie de Champdivers' old maid, Colette, had come running to find Catherine to tell her the awful news—a few hours earlier, Odette and Brother Étienne had been arrested at the Franciscan monastery, and the young woman's parents sent into immediate exile. Colette, alone, had remained behind to inform Catherine, whom Marie de Champdivers saw as her last hope.

The case was a serious one. The Duke of Savoy had managed to engineer a new truce between the enemy princes. But at Odette's instigation, the unruly bandit chieftain known as the Bastard of Baume had violated the terms of the treaty by attacking a Burgundian village. He had been captured and had confessed everything, being loath to lose his skin for such a trivial enterprise. Retribution had fallen swiftly: Odette, Étienne Charlot and a merchant from Geneva who was said to have been their accomplice had been cast into prison where torture and death awaited them.

Catherine was at a loss to understand what could have led Odette to such folly. There were rumors that the plot even encompassed the assassination of the Duke himself. Was it the annexation of Odette's town, or simply a desire to speed the rule of King Charles VII to whom God had sent a son and heir on 3 July 1423? In any case, Catherine had no intention of leaving her friend in such danger, whatever the personal risk to herself.

The Chartreuse de Champmol stood outside the town walls, between the road to the west and the River Ouche. It was still fairly new, having been built by Philippe's grandfather, Philippe the Bold, from plans conceived by the architect Drouet de Dammartin. Catherine had often heard the praises of this Abbey sung, and it was renowned as one of the glories of the age, but she had never before had occasion to enter it. Only men were allowed to enter the Abbey proper, and women were only admitted to the Chapel on occasions like this. This chapel had replaced that of Cîteaux as a burial place for the Dukes of Burgundy.

By the time they had passed through the Ouche gate, the willow plantation with its trees twisted and blackened by the frost, the Abbey's extensive enclosures and garden, it was almost night and Catherine had difficulty keeping upright. She kept taking the little tablets and sniffing the salts which Abou-al-Khayr had given her, but, in spite of her heavy clothes, the deadly cold had seeped into her body. The smoke of the torches made her cough. On entering the Chapel, she stumbled and nearly fell. Ermengarde's hand came to her assistance in the nick of time as they passed by the stone effigy of Philippe the Bold, praying arrogantly before the façade of the Chapel, opposite his wife. Catherine flashed her a grateful look. She had not dared to ask her friend to come to her assistance. Ermengarde, like Philippe himself, seemed to have changed into a strange, black ghost with unseeing, expressionless eyes. The death of her Duchess had been a bitter blow to the Mistress of the Robes. She was a different woman in her black veils, but her hand remained warm and comforting. Catherine drew courage from it; courage which she had much need of.

She scarcely noticed the interior of the Chapel, the master-work of the Flemish sculptor, Claus Sluter, with its windows of emblazoned pearly glass, the carved stone jewel which was the tomb of Philippe the Bold, the angels bearing candelabra around the altar, or the golden figure of the archangel carrying the Ducal banner at the point of the apse. She saw only Philippe, his expressionless face which did not look at her, his grey, unblinking eyes. She seemed to be surrounded by stone faces, and black statues, and all of them were starting to spin fantastically. . . . The voices of the invisible monastery choir overhead began to chant a requiem, the work of Jacques Vide, one of Philippe's body servants. The words seemed charged with menace and doom as they fell on Catherine's ears.

"Nunc dimittis servum tuum, Domine, secundum verbum tuum in pace. Quia viderunt oculi mei salutare tuum. . . ." Now lettest Thou Thy servant, Lord, depart in peace according to Thy word, for mine eyes have seen Thy Salvation.

And just then, Catherine suddenly felt that she was in danger of going, too. . . . She swayed. Ermengarde hurriedly slipped an arm round her waist to stop her falling to the floor in the middle of the ceremony, and held her firmly upright.

"Silly little fool!" she whispered roughly but fondly. "You might have told me!"

"What?" Catherine murmured weakly.

"That you were pregnant! It's written all over your face! And here was I not noticing a thing! . . . Courage, it's almost over and I won't let go of you."

Ermengarde seemed quite human again and Catherine reflected that, but for her, she might well have died on the spot . . . the ceremony did at last appear to be drawing to an end. The Duke Philippe, who had been standing all this time in the family's private chapel to the left of the altar, was delivering over his mother's body to the prior of the Abbey. Soon Marguerite of Bavaria would be rejoining her husband beneath the black marble slab which marked their temporary tomb. . . . But Catherine had felt his eyes upon her for a brief instant, and the tender, anxious expression in them had reassured her. Her sick feeling was wearing off, as though Ermengarde's own strength were being transferred to herself. The suffocating weight on her chest seemed to be lifting. . . . Why did it have to be just then that she should chance to catch Garin's eye? It glittered with hatred, and she gave a long shudder. The Treasurer's face was that of a madman. Catherine could have sworn she heard him grinding his teeth. . . . Luckily the moment of terror soon passed. . . .

A few seconds later, still with Ermengarde's strong arm around her, she found herself out in the fresh air again. It was a night of Siberian cold and blackness, but out there the air was at least free of the smoke of burning tapers, and the heavy clouds of incense which hung about the Chapel.

"Are you feeling better?" Ermengarde asked.

She gave her a grateful smile.

"Much better. I'm so grateful to you. If you hadn't been there, I should have made a laughing stock of myself."

"Bah! Nonsense! But you should have told me what the matter was. Does the . . . Duke know?"

"Not yet!"

The two of them were going towards the Abbey buildings which lay south and west of the Chapel. There were torches blazing in the iron sconces in front of the prior's dwelling, but the rest of the huge monastery was plunged in darkness and silence.

"It's a sinister place!" Ermengarde said, shivering, "Let's go. Thank heavens I had the sense to order my people to bring a litter here to wait for me. I couldn't possibly have gone back along this road on foot, in the snow. Shall I send word to your husband that I am taking you with me?"

"It's not necessary," said Catherine, shaking her head. "My husband is not interested in what I do."

"He must be heartless or a complete fool, then! But then, I've never been able to understand the workings of Messire Garin's mind. Come, my dear!"

The two women walked towards the Abbey gateway, greeting the friends and acquaintances whom they passed. They were just about to enter their rather cumbersome vehicle when a page came up. He had a note in one hand which he held out to Catherine.

"From Monseigneur," he whispered.

The young woman recognized Jean de Lannoy. The youth smiled at her, made a low obeisance, and then hurried back to join his master's escort. The two women climbed into the litter and sank down among the cushions. Ermengarde slipped a footwarmer under Catherine's feet while she hurriedly unfolded the little note and began deciphering it by the wavering light of a candle fastened to the wall of the litter by a gold ring. The leather curtains were a stout defense against the cutting wind outside, but Catherine was frozen to the marrow and her teeth chattered for several minutes. However she was delighted by Philippe's note.

"Come to me tonight," the Duke wrote. "I implore you! I long to see you and I shall only be here three days. Forgive me for importuning you. I love you too much, you see! Lannoy will wait for you by the garden gate till midnight. . . ."

The note was unsigned, but Catherine did not need a signature. She crumpled the paper into a ball and hid it in her rosary case. All at once, she felt she could breathe more freely. The distress which had been oppressing her since the previous day seemed to be lessening. She felt a sudden hope that she might soon be able to save her friend. The thought of the frail and sensitive Odette chained and flung into a dungeon in this bitter weather tormented her. But, thank God, she would have an opportunity of imploring Philippe's mercy and her friend's release this very night! All at once her giddiness and cold melted away as she thought about it. And tonight there would be Philippe . . . his love, his gentle hands and tender words!

By the time Ermengarde's litter set her down in the rue de la Parcheminerie Catherine was almost gay again.

Young Lannoy was keeping vigilant watch at his post when Catherine knocked three times on the little door let into the wall of the Duke's premises. It was long past the curfew, but the night was a little warmer than the day had been thanks to a heavy fall of snow just after Compline. Since that time at Marsannay, Catherine had become used to these nocturnal expeditions. She wasn't frightened—in fact, she found it all rather fun, like playing truant from school. She had nothing to fear from drunken soldiers, Jacquot-de-la-Mer's cut-throats, or any other dangers which infested the streets and alleys after dark, because Abou-al-Khayr had thoughtfully placed his two Nubian slaves at her disposal, and their gigantic presence, together with their stygian blackness, even blacker than the night itself, soon put to flight any rascals who might have been tempted to attack an unescorted woman. Well fed and warmly dressed, the two dumb negroes were as good as a whole troop of men-at-arms. Knowing this, Catherine could set out for her assignation with

Philippe without a qualm. It was by far the most practical arrangement.

Jean de Lannoy hopped from foot to foot in the snow and slapped his thighs vigorously to try and keep warm. He flung the gate open eagerly to admit the visitor.

"It's kind of you to have come so quickly, Dame Catherine!" he whispered slyly. "It's devilish cold. . . ."

"It was because of you that I hurried—I was afraid you might catch a chill."

"Monseigneur has reason to be grateful to me, then!" the page finished up, laughing. "Particularly as he can hardly contain his impatience to see you."

"How is he?"

Lannoy made a face which meant "so-so," and took Catherine's hand to lead her across the garden. The snow was so heavy that one had to be familiar with the lay-out of the place not to fall into ditches or stumble over stones and other obstacles. Once inside the palace itself, Catherine consigned Omar and Ali, her two bodyguards, into the page's care, and then ran up the little spiral stairway which climbed inside a windowless turret and led directly to the Duke's apartments. Scented wax candles lit this velvet-hung spiral. A few moments later, Catherine fell into Philippe's arms. Without a word, he clasped her and embraced her passionately, covering her face with kisses. A long moment later he released her, then took her face between his hands to kiss her again.

"How beautiful you are!" he whispered, his voice choked by emotion. "And how I have missed you! Forty-five whole days without you, without your smile or your lips! What an eternity it has been, my darling!"

"Now that I'm here," said Catherine, smiling as she returned his kiss, "you can forget all that."

"Do you forget the bad times so quickly? I don't. . . . I was a little nervous of subjecting you to this nocturnal sortie just now, in spite of desperately wanting to see you again. You looked so pale in the Chapel! I could tell that you were feeling ill. . . ."

"It was so cold! *You* looked pale, too!"

He still did. Catherine could feel the long, thin frame tremble as he held her against him. She did not want to tell him about the child yet, because then he might not have dared to touch her. And she knew that he desired her, imperiously, urgently. It was a physical hunger. . . . His face was still marked by recent tears. He had wept torrents of tears over his mother's body and the emotional strain had exhausted him. But his tragic air only made him dearer to

87

Catherine. She still did not know the exact nature of the strange bond which linked her to Philippe. Did she love him? If love were this mental agony and piercing hunger she felt every time she thought of Arnaud, then it was clear she didn't love Philippe. But if it were simply tenderness, powerful physical attraction, then perhaps Philippe had really stolen a corner of her heart.

He helped her off with her thick, heavy coat and, lifting her up in his arms, carried her over and laid her on the enormous bed. Then he knelt before her to take off her shoes. Very gently, he slipped off her little black leather boots, then the fine silk stockings which came as high as the knee. He held her slim bare feet for a moment in his hands, dropping a kiss on each of their rosy nails.

"You are cold," he said, tenderly. "I will make the fire hotter."

There were already three entire tree trunks blazing in the fireplace, but, to make the flames still hotter and fiercer, Philippe went and gathered up an armful of branches from a near-by basket and piled them on top of the logs. The fire leapt higher. Then he came back to Catherine and began to undress her. He always brought the greatest delicacy and care to the slow ritual of taking off her clothes. His movements were soft and caressing, almost adoring. It was a rite they both enjoyed because it exacerbated desire and added fuel to the wild storm of passion which followed. Philippe humbled himself only to dominate the more completely afterwards.

A long time later Catherine roused herself from the delicious torpor which enfolded her. Her cheek rested against Philippe's breast. He was awake, leaning on one elbow as he played with his mistress's silky mane of hair. Spread out on the pillow, it looked like a cloth of gold, and reflected back the dancing flames in the hearth. He smiled when he saw that her eyes were open and his long, haughty, rather severe face took on an unexpected charm.

"Why do I love you so much, I wonder? You fire my blood as no other woman has ever done. What is your secret? Are you a witch?"

"I'm just myself," Catherine said, laughing.

But Philippe was suddenly grave. He was studying her thoughtfully, with a sort of awe.

"Just yourself ... and yet that's the whole secret of your magic. Yourself ... a rare creature, half woman, half goddess ... an incomparable, precious being whom entire armies would do battle for. There was a woman like that, once ...

two countries slaughtered each other for ten long years merely because she decided to leave one of them for the other. A capital city was burnt to the ground, and men died in the thousands so that the abandoned husband might get back his wife. Her name was Helen ... she was blonde, like you ... though not so fair, I daresay ... What woman, including our mother Eve herself, can ever have had a mane to rival yours? ... My golden fleece!"

"What a pretty name!" Catherine exclaimed. "What does it mean?"

Philippe took her into his arms again, drawing her close to him and silencing her with a kiss.

"Another legend from antiquity. I'll tell it to you one day...."

"Why not now?"

"Guess!" he said, laughing.

And once again, the fire crackling was the only sound to be heard in the room as Philippe and Catherine became oblivious to the world around them.

When she told him she was pregnant he was speechless with astonishment for a moment. Then a jubilant delight took possession of him and he thanked Catherine as though she had made him a rare gift.

"You have quite banished my guilty feelings!" he cried. "I was feeling ashamed of myself for sending for you tonight ... the very night my mother ... but now this new life on the way cancels out my sin. A child ... a son, naturally!"

"I'll do what I can," Catherine said demurely. "Are you pleased?"

"Need you ask?"

He leapt out of the bed and went to fill two golden goblets which were standing on a chest. Then he handed one to Catherine.

"Wine from Malvoisie! Let's drink the health of our child!"

He raised his cup, drained it at a gulp and then got back into bed again and watched while Catherine drank hers in little sips.

"You look like the cat who's got the cream," he said, leaning across to catch a drop of wine rolling down Catherine's bosom with his lips. "Now tell me how I can give you back a little of the happiness you have brought me."

He held her against his breast again. Catherine could hear her lover's heart beating close to her ear. But hers was beating the faster of the two.... The moment had come ... she reproached herself for having put it off so long. In the joys of

89

this night of love, she had almost forgotten Odette's plight. She murmured:

"I . . . I have a favor to ask you."

"Quick, tell me what it is. I grant it in advance."

She sat up and laid her hand over the Duke's mouth, shaking her head mournfully.

"Don't make any rash promises. You won't be pleased when you hear what I am going to ask . . . you will probably be angry!"

She waited to see how he would react to this and to her alarm, Philippe began to laugh.

"It isn't a laughing matter," she said, feeling slightly hurt.

"Oh, yes, it is! I already know what you are going to ask me. Let's wager . . . I know, we'll wager a kiss that I know what it is!"

"You can't possibly!"

"Really? It's quite simple if one knows you. You always have some impossible 'favor' to ask me up your sleeve, even when you aren't wearing sleeves. Do you suppose I don't know about your friendship with that stupid Odette de Champdivers? My police are not such fools, my beauty."

"Well then?" Catherine asked, her throat constricted with anxiety. "What *does* the Duke of Burgundy propose to do with the conspirators?"

"The Duke of Burgundy intends to do precisely nothing, so as not to bring tears to those pretty eyes of yours. The girl and the monk and the merchant can go and get themselves hanged somewhere else. . . . They are all to be set free. But I am afraid they will have to be banished from Burgundy. Your Odette can go to Savoy where she will be sure to find refuge somewhere. The monk can go back to his Mont Beuvray—on the understanding that he never crosses our frontiers again, and the merchant can go back to Geneva. Well, are you satisfied?"

"Oh, yes!" Catherine cried rapturously, her eyes shining. "Oh, yes!"

"Well, now let me remind you that you owe me a forfeit because I guessed right . . . so pay up. . . ."

Catherine paid up so fervently and enthusiastically that it wasn't long before the lovers were once more lost to the world.

It was long past Matins in the neighboring Saint Étienne convent by the time Catherine and her two mute escorts reached home. The night was inky black and the frosty air chapped her face under the voluminous hood but Catherine

90

was too happy to notice. Odette was to be set free that very morning and would spend the next twenty-fours hours with her before setting out, under armed escort, for the frontiers of Burgundy. And the prospect of exile need not be too alarming—Catherine promised herself to do everything possible to ensure that her friend and the monk lacked for nothing.

She was desperately tired. The funeral ceremonies had been exhausting, and then a night of love ... enough to tax the strength of someone twice as robust. As she hurried back to her warm house, Catherine found herself thinking pleasurably of her soft, warm, comfortable bed. She felt extraordinarily well, in spite of her condition ... she had not felt so relaxed and happy since Christmas. She knew she would sleep like a child.

Back in her own room she undressed quickly and slipped into the bed which Perrine had hastily warmed for her while she was getting undressed. The house was still and quiet. She couldn't hear a sound.

"Don't let me sleep too late," Catherine told her maid. "I have to go to the prison in the morning to fetch Dame Odette and I'm so tired now I feel I could sleep till the evening."

Perrine promised, curtseyed, and left the room. In a moment Catherine was asleep behind her silk curtains.

She was awakened from this state of happy unconsciousness by a strangely brutal occurrence. She felt herself being snatched up, hands seizing her by the shoulders and thighs, and swung into the air. Her sleep-swollen eyes vaguely registered dark, darting figures around her in the pallid dawn light. Her room, which suddenly seemed quite unrecognizable, seemed to be full of phantoms. They moved without a sound and this silence only added to the nightmarishness of the scene.

Catherine tried to scream—like a sleeper waking from a bad dream—but the sound died away on her lips, stifled, not by that strange paralysis which follows a particularly terrifying dream, but by a large and unmistakably solid hand which had been clapped over her mouth. She realized then that this was not a dream at all, but that she was being kidnapped. But by whom? The shadowy figures all wore masks. ... Now more hands were swiftly wrapping her in a blanket, one end of which was pulled up over her head. Terrified, Catherine found herself in total suffocating darkness.

She heard whispering and then felt herself being carried along. They were moving along the gallery now, and now, slowly, down the stairs ... step by step. The two men who

91

were carrying her swung her about as unceremoniously as if she were an old basket. She couldn't scream because her head was muffled in the blanket. . . . A sudden shock of icy air told her that they must now be in the courtyard. It was all happening, all unmistakably real, but the sensation of being caught up in a strange dream persisted. How could she be spirited away from a house full of people? There were Perrine, Garin, Abou and the two mutes. . . . There was Tiercelin, too . . . and yet here she was being carted away like a sack without a voice being raised in protest.

She was being thrown down roughly into something which must have been some sort of cart because it started to move almost at once. Catherine struggled so wildly that she managed to get one arm free in spite of the ropes lashed round the blanket.

"Quick," whispered a muffled voice.

Catherine took the advice as meant for her and managed to half uncover her head. She was lying in a cart on a layer of straw. . . . Day was breaking. She could just discern a street corner . . . someone was blocking her view—a man's figure . . . The man was Landry Pigasse. With one last frantic effort, she managed to get her mouth free of the blanket and screamed:

"Landry . . . help!"

The cry sounded strangely weak as it burst from her throat. Her kidnappers must have noticed that she had succeeded in struggling free. A heavy blow crashed down on her head and Catherine subsided, unconscious, into the straw.

She did not know that the cart had passed through the Ouche gate and was now rattling along the road to the west.

CHAPTER SIX

The Room in the Tower

Catherine recovered consciousness to find herself stiff with cold, with a painfully aching head. She was too tightly bound even to move, but at least her face was uncovered. This did not help much, since the gag had been replaced in her mouth. She was almost buried in the straw and could see nothing but the sky and the two men sitting nearby. Her head was just about level with their feet.

She had never seen either of them before. They wore rough sheepskin jerkins and felt hats pulled down over their eyes, and they sat with their red, square-fingered hands splayed out over their knees. They looked like peasants, and they seemed to have about as much human feeling as stones. They were swaying to and fro with the motion of the cart, and when Catherine groaned, they did not even glance round at her. If their breath had not hung smoking in the icy air one might have mistaken them for a couple of wooden statues. But Catherine soon forgot them in her own distress. The bumps and jolts of the cart were making themselves painfully felt along every inch of her body. Her hands and feet were icy and her stomach convulsed by violent cramps. Waves of nausea swept through her. The gag was suffocating, and the cords which bound her were so tight that they cut into her flesh even through the thick blanket in which she was wrapped.

A moment later a voice called out:

"Faster, Rustaud! Whip them up!"

The voice was unrecognizable—not that Catherine was making much effort to identify it. The pain and distress into which she was suddenly plunged made her previous discomfort seem almost pleasant by comparison. The rickety cart bounced and shook as it rattled along the deeply rutted road and Catherine's poor aching body was flung mercilessly about with only a little straw between her and the wooden floor of the cart. Fiery arrows shot through her stomach, back and thighs. Each bump in the road sent her jolting about like a sack of dried peas. The tears she was too weak to repress rolled down her cheeks. Her two guards were now contemplating her sufferings with a sort of bestial glee, and they met her groans with coarse shouts of laughter.... She was tortured, racked with pain, all she longed for was to die.... What was behind this appalling experience she was being forced to undergo? Who could be responsible for making her suffer so cruelly?

These thoughts were brought to a sudden stop as the cart lurched over a particularly large stone and Catherine's head was flung so hard against the wooden side that she lapsed into merciful unconsciousness.

When she recovered consciousness for the second time, she found herself lying in what looked like a cellar. She still had a sort of straw bed under her, but the place was so dark she could not make out much of her surroundings. A vaulted stone roof receded into the shadows far overhead. As she turned her head to get a better look, she was conscious of something cold, hard, and constricting, something which clanged metallically as she moved. Her hands flew up to her neck—there was a great iron collar round it, attached to a chain whose other end was bolted to the wall. The chain was just long enough to give her a little freedom of movement. Catherine gave a cry of horror, sat up and started wrenching at the chain in a pathetic attempt to free herself. This pitiful move was answered by a sneering laugh.

"It's a stout chain, and well anchored. I fancy you will find it difficult to take it off," said a cold voice. "Well, what do you think of your new palace?"

Catherine sprang to her feet, oblivious of the pain tearing at her battered body. The chain dropped, clanking, to her feet. To her amazement she found Garin standing there before her.

"You! So it's *you* who had me brought here! But where are we?"

"I don't really think there is much point in your knowing, my dear. All you need to know about this place is that it is no use your screaming or hoping to be rescued—no one will hear you. And this tower is high, solidly built, and not a little isolated. . . ."

As he spoke, Catherine stared round at the immense circular room which was, presumably, the only one in the building. The only light came from a narrow slit window, criss-crossed by heavy iron bars. There was no furniture whatever except for a stool near the immense chimney where one of the two men in sheepskins was trying to get a pathetic fire going. That, and the straw litter on which Catherine was lying! After looking round her prison, for such it was clearly destined to be, Catherine's eyes fell with a shock of surprise upon herself. She was dressed in a coarse linen shift, a dress of some thick brown material, woollen stockings and wooden clogs!

"What is the meaning of all this?" she asked, amazed. "Why have you brought me here?"

"To punish you!"

Garin started to speak and, as the words came pouring out, his features grew ugly and contorted with anger and a wild hatred.

"You have made a fool of me and covered me with shame . . . you and your lover! If I hadn't already guessed from your face and your sunken eyes that you were breeding like a bitch I should have known from your behavior yesterday in the chapel. You are pregnant by your lover, isn't that so?"

"Who else could it be?" Catherine asked in astonishment.

"Not by you, that's certain! But why should you object? Isn't that what you have always wanted to do—throw me into the Duke's arms? Well, you succeeded. And now I am carrying his child. . . ."

Her voice was cold and disdainful. She was shivering in her thick dress so she went over to the chimney where the man was still puffing at the fire. The chain clanked behind her as she moved, echoing hollowly round the grim room. The man who was leaning over the fire moved away and grinned at her unpleasantly.

"Who is this?" she asked.

Garin answered:

"His name is Fagot . . . and he is my slave in everything. I am afraid he is not very refined. You may find him a little less delicately scented than the Duke. But he is just the man for my purposes. . . ."

Catherine hardly recognized Garin. His one eye was fixed and staring and his hands shook convulsively. From time to time his rasping voice rose to a high note of hysteria. A chill of fear crept over Catherine. She had not quite finished with him, however.

"What do you want with me?" she asked, turning her back on Fagot.

"I want to make you lose that child you are carrying—I have no desire to give my name to a bastard. I had thought that little trip here might have been enough to make you miscarry, but I forgot that you are as strong as a mule. It is possible that we may not succeed in getting rid of it in time, in which case I shall be obliged to attend the birth . . . and dispose of the tiresome little creature when it appears. Meanwhile, you will remain here with Fagot. And believe me, you will find him more than a match for you. I have told him to do as he likes with you. . . ."

The Treasurer's face was twisted by nervous spasms. He looked like a man possessed by the devil. The sneer on his thin lips, his pinched nostrils and the occasional note of hysteria told Catherine, who was beginning to feel quite sick with terror, that to all intents and purposes, the man before her was a stranger—Garin was mad, or little short of it. Only a madman could have thought up this diabolic plan of handing her over to this bestial lout of a man so as to make her lose the child. Would he really kill the baby if it came to the point? She made a last attempt to reason with him.

"Come to your senses, Garin. You are out of your mind! Have you thought what the consequences of such an action might be? Do you suppose no one will wonder what has happened to me? Or try to find me? The Duke. . . ."

"The Duke leaves for Paris tomorrow, as you well know. I shall simply mention your weakened state of health . . . and later I can let it be known that there has been an accident. . . ."

"You can't believe that I would remain silent about all this once I'd been set free!"

"I can't help feeling that after a few months of Fagot's treatment no one will be very interested in your plight, my dear . . . least of all the Duke. As you know, he only likes beauty . . . and you will no longer be beautiful then. He will soon forget you, believe me. . . ."

Catherine was beginning to panic. Mad he might be, but he seemed to have thought of everything. She made one last appeal.

"What about my friends and my family? They will look for me. . . ."

"Not if I tell them that Philippe of Burgundy has taken you with him. . . . Everyone would think that quite natural after his only too obvious display of interest in you. . . ."

Catherine felt as though the ground were sliding away beneath her feet. The world seemed to be rocking around her. Tears of impotent rage sprang to her eyes. But she still could not believe that Garin was quite heartless. She stretched out her hands in supplication.

"Why do you treat me so? What have I done to you? It was you, you remember, who spurned me when I tried to give myself to you. We might have been happy together if you had wanted it that way. But you had to go and throw me into Philippe's arms . . . and now you are punishing me for that. Why? Why? Do you hate me so much?"

Garin seized her by her slender wrists. He started shaking her ferociously.

"I hate you. . . . Oh, yes, I hate you! Ever since I was forced to marry you I have died a thousand deaths on your account. . . . And now am I to watch while you parade your belly insolently about my house? Must I be father to a bastard? No! . . . a hundred, thousand times, no! I was forced to marry you, I couldn't refuse! But I have reached the limits of my endurance. . . . I can't go on. . . ."

"Then let me go to my mother . . . at Marsannay."

He gave her a brutal push which flung her to the ground. She fell painfully onto her knees, trying to free her neck from the painful iron collar, and imploring him:

"Have pity on me. . . ."

"No! No one had pity on me! You will expiate your sins here . . . and then you can go and hide yourself in a convent . . . when you have grown ugly. Then it will be my turn to laugh. I shan't be forced to gaze at that insolent beauty of yours . . . that shameless body which you were happy to display anywhere, even in my own bed. . . . Ugly! Loathsome! That's what you will be by the time Fagot has finished with you!"

Catherine lay on the ground, with her arms crossed protectively over her head, sobbing without restraint. Her whole body ached and she felt herself giving way to despair. "You aren't a man . . . you are a sick creature . . . a madman," she cried. "No man worthy of the name would behave like this."

A grunt was her only answer. Lifting up her head, she saw that Garin had gone. She was alone with Fagot. He was standing in front of the fire which he had at last managed to get alight, staring at her with his tiny black eyes which looked like two black nails driven into his puffy, red-veined face. He was shaking with imbecile laughter from head to toe, shifting from foot to foot with his hands hanging by his fat sides, like a performing bear. A wave of terror swept through Catherine, leaving her faint and sick. She stood up, backing away as the hideous man drew nearer and nearer, not daring to take her eyes off him for an instant. Never before, in her whole life, had she been stricken by such desperate, abject terror. She was helpless before this monster . . . and then there was the chain—this dreadful chain which fastened her to the wall! It was not even long enough for her to reach the window. . . . Like a frightened child, she shrank back against the wall, shielding herself with her arms. Fagot was still advancing towards her with his arms outstretched as though he meant to throttle her. Catherine believed her last hour had come. The man had been hired to murder her and Garin's diatribe had only been intended to prolong her suffering.

When Fagot's clumsy hands fell upon her, however, Catherine realized that it was not her life he wanted. He pushed her back into the straw with one hand while he tried to lift up her skirt with the other. A hideous reek of sweat, rancid fat and sour wine met the girl's nostrils and she all but fainted away. But the consciousness of imminent danger saved her. A strangled scream broke from her.

"Garin! Help. . . ."

But the scream froze in her throat. If Garin were there, he would only enjoy her terror. He knew perfectly well what he was doing in abandoning her to this brute. Catherine gritted her teeth. Fagot's calloused hand fumbled at her thighs and

97

left her almost paralyzed with fright, but she just managed to struggle against the heavy weight crushing down upon her hungrily, like a beast upon its prey. The man was surprised by her resistance, and he tried to clap his hand over her face so as to pin her down to the floor. She bit him so hard that he howled with pain and lurched away. Now that she was freed from his weight, Catherine was able to spring to her feet. She gathered up a loop of chain in one hand. It might make a handy impromptu weapon.

"If you come any nearer," she hissed at him, "I'll kill you."

The man fell back, alarmed by the murderous glint in his prisoner's eyes. He went over to the door, out of Catherine's reach and paused for a moment. Then he shrugged, and sneered:

"Naughty! . . . No food, then! No food till Fagot's had his fun. . . ."

Then he went out, sucking his injured hand on which a thin trickle of blood had appeared. Catherine heard the sound of heavy bolts being pushed into place. Heavy footsteps went down the stairs, and Catherine fell back into her straw litter, suddenly drained of the nervous energy which had sustained her during this appalling scene. She buried her head in her hands and began to sob convulsively. Truly, Garin had condemned her to the cruellest death when he handed her over to this bestial creature. If she did not yield to him, he would starve her to death. . . . Her empty stomach was already beginning to torture her. The meagre fire which Fagot had lit had burned down to a few glowing embers and the poor girl crept across and knelt beside it, trying to warm her icy hands. Night had fallen and the window was a faintly paler rectangle in the oppressive darkness of the tower. When the last embers had burnt out, Catherine would be alone in the darkness and the cold, at the mercy of the terrible gaoler Garin had chosen for her.

She spent the whole night hunched up against the wall, her eyes straining into the darkness and ears pricked for the slightest sound, not daring to sleep. She had pulled the straw up round her as much as she could to try and keep warm. But when dawn came, Catherine was trembling with cold.

The next three days were torture. She was weak from hunger and chilled to the bone because the wretched little fires Fagot lit each morning gave out no heat, and she still had to summon up enough strength to withstand her jailer's assaults. She suffered agonies from the cramps which racked her starving stomach, and the icy, brackish water which was all Fagot

98

allowed her brought no relief. She took the risk of going to sleep at last, after she had noticed that the bolts made enough noise to awaken the dead when anyone drew them. At last she was spared the fear of a surprise attack. But each time the monster threw himself upon her, she found it harder and harder to defend herself . . . the struggle grew more and more painful. Her arms and hands were terribly weak. It was only thanks to her solid constitution and magnificent health that she was able to hold out at all and muster the desperate strength needed to defend herself. But hunger was wreaking havoc in her, undermining her will and courage. The time was not far off when she would put up with anything for the sake of survival . . . even Fagot!

The morning of the fourth day Catherine was too weak even to raise an arm. When Fagot came into her prison she stayed where she was, lying in the straw, inert, unable to move. She had exhausted her reserves of strength. When she closed her eyes red stars exploded in front of them, and when she reopened them there were black butterflies dancing about all over her field of vision. . . . She was vaguely aware of Fagot kneeling down beside her. . . . When he laid his hand on her stomach to see how she would react, a feeling of despair overpowered her, but she was too feeble to resist. Instead, she felt a sort of detachment. Nothing mattered any more. . . . She would soon be dead. Tomorrow . . . or the next day, or possibly that very night. . . . What did it matter what that wretch did with her body? It had suffered so much already that it had almost no feeling left now. The only aching point of consciousness in her whole body was her neck, chafed and rubbed raw by the iron collar. . . . Catherine closed her eyes again and drifted into the welcome torpor which kept taking hold of her now at shorter and shorter intervals. She was vaguely conscious of Fagot undoing her dress, tearing at the laces in his impatience, ripping her chemise. The cold struck at her bare skin as her gaoler's heavy, greedy hands felt and fumbled at her body. He was grunting like a pig, lying on top of her. . . .

Catherine tried feebly to defend herself against the last profanation, but it was like trying to move through clouds of cottonwool. A heavy weight was crushing her . . . then suddenly, something happened. Fagot got up abruptly, leaving Catherine shuddering on her straw litter. Through a mist she dimly discerned Garin standing there with a whip in his hand. . . . It was this which had made Fagot get up.

He knelt down beside her and placed one hand over her

left breast. In spite of the buzzing in Catherine's ears, she perfectly understood what he said.

"She's half dead! What have you been doing to her?"

She heard the idiot's answer, too.

"No food. . . . She wasn't nice to Fagot. . . ."

"Do you mean she hasn't eaten for four days? Confounded imbecile! I told you to punish her—but not to kill her! She will be dead in a day or two. . . . Fetch me some soup . . . at once. . . ."

Garin bent over her and pulled her dress and chemise back into place over her wasted body. His hands were gentle and Catherine felt a faint stirring of hope. Was he beginning to regret what he had done to her? She thought she might even bring herself to forgive him if he took her out of this hell now.

A few minutes later Fagot returned, carrying a steaming bowl. Garin lifted Catherine up to make her drink.

"Gently, now . . . first drink a little soup. . . ."

Catherine's dry lips reached eagerly for the hot soup. One, two mouthfuls. . . . Little by little the life flowed back into her aching body. When she had drained the bowl to the last drop, Catherine felt better and she gave a deep sigh. She opened her mouth to thank Garin for taking pity on her, but as soon as he saw that she had recovered he sneered:

"If you could only see yourself! No prince would cast covetous eyes on you now! Your hair is lank and dirty, your skin is gray . . . and you'd put up with anything for a scrap of food . . . like a hungry animal! 'Struth, I'm quite sorry I prevented Fagot from taking you then. You're just right for him now. . . ."

Along with her strength, Catherine had recovered some of her pride. She did not open her eyes, but murmured:

"Get out! You are a miserable wretch . . . I hate you!"

"So I should hope," Garin cried, in that curious falsetto voice which he seemed to have acquired recently. "I only regret that your lover can't see you as you are now! He'd be hard put to recognize you! What's happened to the ravishing Dame de Brazey? The Fairy with the Black Diamond? She's nothing but a skinny mare with a swollen belly. . . . It's a gratifying sight to me, let me tell you . . . now I can sleep untroubled by recollections of your beauty. . . ."

He went on in this vein for some time, but Catherine had stopped listening. All she wanted was for him to go away and leave her to die in peace. She kept her eyes closed and wished she could do the same to her ears. At last, Garin wearied of this sport . . . there was silence, then the banging of a door. She opened her eyes again and found that she was alone . . .

Garin and Fagot had gone out. . . . An armful of branches was blazing in the hearth and a plate had been set down beside the young woman with a piece of meat and a few vegetables. She devoured them ravenously . . . but managed to force herself not to eat too fast, chewing each mouthful before swallowing it. The icy water in her earthenware pitcher tasted delicious after this slender meal. Her hunger was far from sated, but she felt much stronger, strong enough to sit up and readjust her dress and even to drag herself across to the hearth and stretch herself out upon the hearthstone. The warmth of the flames seeped into every corner of her body. Alas, this could not last for long, because there were no large logs among the armful of fuel which her jailer had thrown onto the fire. But meanwhile, the warmth stole back into Catherine's frozen, aching limbs. The hearth was a safe harbor, a corner of paradise. . . . Finally Catherine tore a strip off the bottom of her chemise and wound it round the iron collar. The cloth rasped her neck, but it did not hurt her as much as the ring of newly forged iron. She lay back with a sigh, resting her head on her arms, and drifted off to sleep. She would have liked to enjoy this fine blaze for a little longer, since it would be burnt out by the time she waked, but she was too weary. Sleep dragged at her eyelids. . . .

Almost at once, her eyes flew open again. She heard a loud coughing somewhere above her head. Something heavy dropped among the flames, sending up a shower of sparks. Catherine flung herself backwards so as not to be set alight and clapped her hand over her mouth to stop herself screaming. The object which had just crashed down among the flames was a man, and he was now extricating himself with a volley of hideous oaths.

In the darkness of the tower, Catherine could just make out a powerful form laying about itself to extinguish some little blazing twigs which had got caught up in his clothes.

"It was the only way!" this figure grunted. "But, 'sdeath! What a filthy way to enter a room!"

Thinking at first that she must be feverish and suffering from hallucinations, Catherine stayed where she was, not daring to speak. But then the strange apparition came over towards her and she instantly recognized the merry face with its crest of stiff black hair, in spite of the heavy layer of soot covering it.

"Landry!" she exclaimed faintly. "Is it really you? Or am I dreaming?"

"It's me, all right!" the young man cried gaily. "But what a

101

time I have had trying to find you! That madman of a husband of yours planned his stroke cunningly!"

Catherine still could not believe the evidence of her eyes and ears.

"I can't believe it's really you!" she faltered "Landry refused to recognize me. Landry has forgotten Catherine."

He sat down beside her and put his arm round trembling shoulders.

"Landry had nothing to do with the wife of Garin de Brazey ... and the mistress of the all-powerful Duke. But you are a victim, you are suffering, you need me. You are Catherine again. ..."

The young woman smiled and let her head fall on her friend's shoulder. It was so unexpected, this help and friendship fallen, literally, from heaven.

"How did you find me? And where are we?"

"In the Château of Mâlain, which Garin must have borrowed from the Abbot of Saint-Seine. How I found you is another story. One morning, as I was on my way home after a night of roistering at the tavern, I saw a cart leaving the Hotel de Brazey. I heard a woman cry out in the cart—just once. I was drunk and on foot ... I let it pass, but when I sobered up, the incident stuck in my head. I went to your house and asked to speak to you. The only person I saw was a little maidservant, called Perrine, who was sobbing like a fountain. She said you had left, early one morning, without even waking her up. She said you were supposed to be joining the Duke in Paris ... but she didn't think that was very likely because all your clothes and things were still there. I couldn't find out any more from her because Garin was returning. But it all seemed a bit fishy to me. I watched your husband for days, and finally this morning I saw him set off on horseback and I followed him at a distance. He led me here and some instinct told me that this was the place I was looking for. They don't think very highly of this Château in the village at the foot of the ramparts. They told me at the inn that they heard screams and groans and a woman's voice calling out. The good people round here set it down to ghosts. They didn't bother to inquire further. At night they simply locked their doors and made the sign of the cross. ... I tried to find a way in here. The building is ruined and, mercifully, easy to climb into. Then I saw Garin's horse tied up in the inner courtyard and I also laid eyes on a sort of human bear who went into a hut to fetch a bowl of soup. No one took any notice of me. I climbed up the tower easily ... then I saw the chimney, and here I am. I always carry a rope attached to my saddle. Now

102

you know the whole story. Come, now, I am going to take you away. . . ."

He jumped up and held out his hand to help her to her feet. But she shook her head sadly.

"I can't, Landry, I'm too weak. That bowl of soup you saw was for me. My jailer hadn't given me any food for four days so as to make me give myself to him. Anyway . . . look! Garin thought of everything."

She showed him the chain hidden in the folds of her dress. The young man started back and changed color. Then he knelt and touched the chain and collar with a sort of fearful horror.

"The swine! How dare he let that monster touch you! Poor little thing! First he chains you, then he starves you and finally he exposes you to the attacks of that gross pig!"

"You see that I can't very well follow you."

"Wait!"

The young man examined the collar and chain carefully. The chain was immensely thick and it would have taken hours to file it through, but there was a lock on the collar.

"Where is the key?" Landry asked.

"I don't know. Perhaps Fagot has it."

"Fagot? That fat pig I saw?"

"Presumably. . . . But I am not certain that he has it. He is almost half-witted. . . . My fear is that this wretched key must be somewhere in one of Garin's pockets."

Landry's face darkened. He had worked out that the best solution would be to kill Catherine's warder, take the key from him and walk out through the door. But on reflection it seemed unlikely that he would have the key upon him, and as for taking Catherine with him the way he had come, as he had first blithely suggested, that was clearly out of the question. In her weakened condition, the young woman would be quite incapable of making the effort needed to pull herself up the chimney on the rope . . . not to mention climbing down the wall of the keep after that, or the ruined ramparts. What for him, with his hard muscles of the professional horseman, was just another form of exercise would represent a series of insurmountable obstacles to the unfortunate prisoner.

"Listen," he said at length. "I shall have to go out the way I came and leave you here for the moment. I could kill your jailer, but that would not really help because I haven't anything on me which I could use to free you from this chain. You will have to stay here till tomorrow evening. I shall come back with files to saw through that collar of yours and meanwhile I can arrange for somewhere for you to stay in hiding in the country. . . ."

"I feel brave enough for anything," said Catherine, "now that I know you're there and you're watching over me. You are right—Garin might return. He is probably not far away, and we don't know whether there are more men on guard down below or not. There were two men in the cart. One of them was Fagot and the other was someone just like him. . . . I can stand another day here. . . . The worst part is the cold. . . ."

Her teeth were chattering. The fire had gone out and the February night was far from clement. The pale light reflected in at the window showed that it might have been snowing outside.

"Wait," said Landry.

He rapidly unbuckled his belt and removed the heavy leather jacket he was wearing over his doublet and threw it, still warm, round Catherine's shivering shoulders. She snuggled into it gratefully.

"You won't feel so cold with this. All you have to do when you hear Fagot coming is hide it under the straw."

"But what about you? You will freeze. . . ."

Landry's grin was exactly as it had been in the old days when he was her boon companion and they roamed the streets of Paris together.

"Me? I'm in the pink of health—I'm not a poor frozen starving little girl. . . ."

"Pregnant little girl," Catherine added.

Landry froze. Catherine couldn't see him in the darkness which enveloped them both, but she sensed his reaction from his hurried breathing.

"Whose?" he asked curtly.

"Philippe's, of course! Garin is only my husband in name . . . he has never touched me."

"That's much better! And I'm beginning to understand. He brought you here because you were pregnant, did he? His pride couldn't stand any more. Well, all the more reason for taking you away from him. I'll come back tomorrow after nightfall with all the necessary tools to set you free. One thing, though—you will have to put your fire out, assuming your gaoler lights one for you. I thought I was going to suffocate in the smoke when I was coming down."

"Very well. I'll put out the fire at nightfall."

"Right. Now, take this . . . at least you'll have something to defend yourself with."

Catherine felt something cold being slipped into her

hand. . . . It was a dagger. She tried to refuse it at first, remembering that it was Landry's only weapon.

"What about you? Supposing you meet Fagot?"

Landry's laughter was decidedly reassuring.

"I've got my fists. . . . Anyway, I can't stand the idea of leaving you alone and defenseless with that brute. Now go to sleep. I'll be off now. Sleep as long as you can to build your strength up. I'll bring you something to eat when I come. . . ."

Catherine felt Landry's hands groping for her shoulders. They rested there for a moment and he dropped a quick kiss on her forehead.

"Courage!" Landry whispered. "Till tomorrow. . . ."

She heard him going over to the chimney, stepping on the crackling twigs and swearing under his breath as he groped about for the end of the rope which he had left hanging inside the chimney. Then there was a sort of grunt as he levered himself up, a soft rushing sound of falling soot dislodged on his way up the chimney, and then silence. . . . Once again, Catherine found herself alone in the dark and cold . . . quite alone. She wrapped herself up as well as she could in Landry's thick jacket and pulled the straw round herself before trying to sleep. But the heavy sleep which had been on the point of overpowering her when her friend made his dramatic appearance seemed to have deserted her. Catherine found she couldn't even close her eyes. As hope returned, it seemed to have excited her nerves unbearably. The hours before Landry's return suddenly seemed appallingly long . . . an eternity of minutes and seconds. And, quite suddenly and surprisingly, she found she was afraid again. . . .

Catherine's imagination began working feverishly. The risks Landry had to run suddenly seemed enormous and her excited brain pictured them as more terrible than they really were. He might slip on the way down, or run into the gigantic Fagot, or possibly some other men as well. . . . All her hopes, her life itself, depended on that one young man, a brave young man, to be sure, but he might easily find himself outnumbered. If Landry were to perish, either tonight or when he returned the next day, no one would ever know what had become of her. Catherine would be abandoned to the loathsome Fagot and to Garin's sadistic caprices, quite helpless, and no one would ever be able to come to her assistance. . . .

As if to add to her terrors, a sudden long drawn-out howl sounded somewhere outside in the murky depths of the night. Catherine barely suppressed a scream of terror. . . .

It was a moment or two before it dawned on her that the sound was only a wolf's hunting cry and not the scream of a

105

man in his death agony. The agonized pounding of her heart went on for several minutes. As she shrank fearfully against the wall, she felt Landry's dagger under her hand and slipped it quickly into the bodice of her dress. The feel of the cold leather sheath against her skin was reassuring. It was comforting to know it was there and that it gave her the means of finishing, once and for all, suffering and hunger ... should anything happen to Landry. The thought that she had some sort of safety exit to fall back on, however desperate, revived her spirits. Her tense, aching muscles relaxed and a little warmth stole back into her frozen fingers. With one hand on her bosom, as if to protect the dagger, she stretched herself out on the straw, arranged the collar into the least painful position and closed her eyes. She fell into a light, nervous slumber, interrupted by nightmares and starts of terror.

A ray of light under the door and the creaking of bolts being stealthily drawn back woke her in an instant from this fitful sleep and she flattened herself against the wall behind her. Her heart was pounding and the sweat trickled down her back. It was still pitch dark and Catherine had no idea what time of night it was. But she knew only too well what was going to happen next. It was clear that Fagot expected to find her asleep from the stealthy fashion in which he had entered the room.... The squeaking of the bolts still went on, so faint as to be almost inaudible.... If Catherine had not been sleeping so lightly, she might easily not have heard.

The door swung slowly open. Then Fagot's unlovely figure appeared, silhouetted in the doorway. He must have hung his torch up somewhere outside the door because it threw bizarre flickering shadows into the room.... Then he closed the door behind him. The room was plunged into thick darkness again, but Catherine could hear the monster's labored breathing. She felt about feverishly for the dagger Landry had given her, drew it from her bodice and held it clutched in her hand. She smelt Fagot's unmistakable, disgusting smell just as the man's huge, damp hands seized her.... One slid round her throat while the other groped for her waist....

In the first wild, unreasoning panic, Catherine was hardly aware of what she was doing.... Her hand rose and fell.... Fagot gave a howl of pain and released her.

"Go away," Catherine hissed at him. "Go away and leave me alone or I'll kill you. ..."

The pain of the blow seemed to have stirred something akin to fear in the idiot's slow brain because she could hear him whimpering like an animal in little short gasps.... But he was going. The door opened and Catherine saw him lurch out

106

through it with one hand on his shoulder. . . . His moans remained audible for some time and she realized that he must have failed to close the door completely in his haste. . . . She had not heard the bolts being pushed back. . . . The alarm seemed to be over, but Catherine decided to stay awake till it was light. She had been too frightened by the little episode to relax again that night.

After what seemed an eternity, a gray dawn arrived. With a sigh of relief, she watched the arrowhead window growing slowly paler. Suddenly it was bright daylight and the terrors of the night before seemed less alarming. Catherine felt her confidence returning. If all went well, the dreadful night which had just ended would be her last in this prison. . . . She felt dreadfully weak and ill. She was devoured by hunger again, but the faith that moves mountains kept her going. It would keep her going till the evening, but, if Landry failed to keep the appointed rendezvous, the blow would be all the more cruel. . . . That night would find her either free, or dead. . . .

The day dragged on, the more slowly because Fagot once more omitted to bring his captive anything to eat . . . either through fear or a desire for vengeance. Catherine had to make do with a sip or two of water. And she would have no difficulty putting out the nonexistent fire, she thought wryly. If anything, it seemed colder than the day before, but Landry's jacket protected her from the worst of it. When the brief winter's day began to sink towards night, Catherine was gnawed by anxiety once more. How long would it be before Landry came? Would he wait till it was quite dark to cut down the risk of being seen by someone in the countryside around? Catherine had no idea, but she was inclined to think that he would not appear till late at night. Landry would obviously want to wait till circumstances were as favorable as possible. She had watched the window growing paler that morning with relief, now she saw it darken again with a twinge of apprehension. The night had still not lost its power to dismay and alarm the captive.

The sound of steps on the tower made her jump. Someone was coming up . . . two people, at least, for she could make out two voices in conversation, one of which was Fagot's. Catherine was frightened almost out of her wits, and to her fear was added a shattering sense of disappointment. Perhaps it was Garin coming back . . . with a new idea to torture her. . . . Who could tell what abominable new whim might not have sprung up in that diseased brain of his? What if he had suddenly decided to change her prison and shut her up in some underground dungeon, without light or air? No one, not even

107

Landry, would be able to rescue her then. Catherine's heart was pounding so hard it hurt. She almost screamed when the door opened.

Two men entered, one of them carrying a torch and the other a rope. Wide-eyed with terror, Catherine recognized the torch-carrier as Fagot. The other man was not Garin, but the second man involved in the abduction, the one she had seen sitting next to Fagot in the cart. There was a curious similarity between them. But the newcomer was possibly even more repulsive looking, because where Fagot simply looked like a slow-witted oaf, the other man showed every sign of an evil, malicious disposition. Far from looking like a simpleton, there was a gleam in his eyes which announced a formidably cunning character.

Grinning and swinging his rope, he came over towards Catherine and bent over her.

"So here we are, my beauty! So we're showing our teeth, are we? Don't want to give poor Fagot his bit of fun, eh? A good lad like Fagot!"

Fagot, who was standing at a respectful distance holding the torch, pointed at the young woman with dislike.

"Knife!" was all he said.

Catherine saw now that he had one shoulder swathed in bandages, but the sight left her unmoved. She only regretted that her aim had not been surer. . . .

"A knife, eh?" the newcomer echoed with alarming gentleness. "Well, we'll just have to take it away from her, won't we?"

Before Catherine could guess what he was up to, he had seized the chain attached to her collar and hauled her brutally towards him. Catherine thought her head was going to be wrenched off. She screamed with pain, but her tormentor ignored this and tugged all the harder, trying to pull her out of her straw litter. She rolled out onto the floor and, in doing so, the dagger she had been holding slipped out of her hand to the floor.

"Pick it up, Fagot!" the second man ordered. "There's the knife we want. Now you have nothing to fear. Good luck to you! A pity I had to leave you alone with this sly puss! Messire Garin should have realized that you wouldn't get very far without your little brother to help. . . . Well, here he is now, the good Pochard in person . . . and we'll soon see who gives the orders around here. First we want to know how this little dear found herself a knife. And this nice leather jacket, too. It can't have walked in all by itself. Something tells me you're

108

going to be a nice girl and tell us all about it. Aren't you, my pretty?"

He gave the chain another brutal tug, half strangling poor Catherine.

"See!" he sneered, "how nice and gentle she is already? I can see that we're going to get on very well together. But first light the fire, Fagot. We're going to need it ... even if it's only to burn her feet to make her talk. Besides, it really is a little nippy in here, for me anyway, though Madame looks quite flushed. . . ."

Catherine was half strangled by the iron collar and she felt as if her head were going to burst. Pochard suddenly dropped the chain so she fell on the floor. Then he seized her hands and tied them behind her back.

"Now we don't have to keep out of the way of her talons," he exclaimed waggishly. "We'll give her a bit of a breather, now, eh? Come here, Fagot, and leave that fire of yours for a moment. Since the damsel pleases you so much I'm going to give you a treat. I'll hold her while you take your pleasure of her. And, if she's as tasty a morsel as you say, I may even take my turn after you. Wait ... while I pluck her. . . ."

He had begun tearing off Catherine's wretched, ragged dress when the ghastly babbling of a man in his death agony made him start back and roused Catherine from the swoon she had fallen into. Landry had sprung upon Fagot just as he was about to step out of the huge hearth, and stabbed him in the back without more ado. The idiot slumped among the ashes, face down, a jet of blood spurting from his mouth. . . .

Landry snatched his dagger out of the corpse and bounded forward, agile as a tiger. He stood there, arms outspread, crouching forward, his black eyes glittering with hatred in his sooty face, confronting Pochard.

"Now let's have you, you swine!" he exclaimed between gritted teeth. "I swear to you, you won't leave this place alive!"

"So?" Pochard sneered, pulling a long knife from his belt. "Two can play at that game, my fine friend! I'll have your hide for this ... I loved that brother of mine. . . ."

He had forgotten about Catherine, who dragged herself into a corner and struggled to free her hands. Luckily, Pochard had not tied his knots very tight. She felt so weak and battered that she did not know whether to thank heaven for having sent Landry at such an opportune moment, or to tremble for his safety. He was young, lithe, and doubtless skilled in the use of arms like all the men in the Duke's Horse. But Pochard was a head taller, and his whole massive frame exuded a dangerous and threatening strength. Landry did not look frightened, however, and by the light of the torch which Fagot had placed in an iron holder against the wall, Catherine saw his teeth flash white in his blackened face; he was smiling. . . . The two men watched each other, circling around in a bizarre dance. Then suddenly they fell upon each other. Catherine screamed as she realized that Landry was underneath his adversary. The two men had fallen together onto the dusty flagstones and were engaged in a desperate hand-to-hand struggle. Their furious grunts were like those of wild beasts fighting for their lives and they moved so swiftly that Catherine found it hard to follow their movements. They seemed inextricably entwined. . . . This went on for what seemed an eternity to the terrified onlooker. Then suddenly Pochard succeeded in pinning his opponent down. Catherine watched in horror as he knelt on Landry's chest. He took him by the throat; he was strangling him. . . .

Summing up the little strength which remained, Catherine picked up a loop of her chain and swung it with all her might down onto Pochard's head. He fell back, stunned. . . . With one bound Landry was on his feet. He kicked the prostrate Pochard over onto his back and then, quite cold-bloodedly, bent over him and cut his throat. The blood spurted onto the hem of Catherine's dress. She herself had collapsed on the floor in a swoon. . . .

"Well, that's that," Landry announced with satisfaction. "Now we must escape while the going is good. Cathy, you saved my life, you know. If it hadn't been for you that swine would have throttled me. . . ."

He stood there for a moment, taking deep breaths until he got his wind back. He pushed Pochard's bloody corpse away from Catherine with his foot and then knelt beside her and stroked her tangled, lank hair.

"Poor little one! You look quite worn out. Now, wait a minute while I get this collar off you. . . . Poor Cathy, he's made your neck bleed. . . ."

Her slender neck was bleeding in several places where it had been rubbed raw by Pochard's brutal tugs on the chain. Landry tore a strip off what remained of Catherine's chemise and made it into a thick pad which he placed between the collar and her neck. Then, with the help of a large file he had brought with him, he set about cutting through the collar. His search through Fagot's pockets had been useless. He was not carrying the key to the collar on him. The operation was a slow and unpleasant one for Catherine in spite of Landry's precautions. The shrill rasping of the file set her over-excited

110

nerves still more on edge. But at last the collar fell apart and Catherine was able to stand up—free. She wanted to fling her arms around Landry and embrace him, but he gently pushed her away.

"You can thank me later. First we must get away from here, and fast ... I don't think there are any other guards here, but we don't want to take any chances. ..."

He put his arms round Catherine's waist to support her, for the young woman was at the end of her strength, and led her towards the door. Just as they were about to cross the threshold, Catherine stumbled and fell against her friend. She was so weak!

"What a fool I am!" Landry cried. "Have you eaten anything today?"

"No ... I've had nothing, only a little water."

Landry took a flat flask out of his pocket and held it to Catherine's lips.

"Drink some of that! It's Beaune wine and it will make you feel better in a flash. And look, here's a cake for you. I brought it for you, but I quite forgot to give it to you."

The wine warmed Catherine's stomach at once, though it made her heart burn. She nibbled at the cake and felt so much stronger that she tried to take a few steps forward. But it was hopeless. She fell to the ground and vomited up what she had just eaten, swept by a wave of violent nausea.

"Well, it looks as if we shall have to find another way," said Landry. Without more ado, he leant over and swung her up in his arms as easily as if she had been a feather. Then he raced down the stairs. The stone staircase was lit here and there by brands dipped in pitch in iron holders. In a few moments Landry and his burden were in the courtyard of the keep.

"That's the worst over," Landry whispered with a chuckle. "The wall of this palace is in ruins—there's a gap over there we can get out by."

Catherine, who was barely conscious, was dimly aware of black walls standing out boldly against the snow. The snow lay in white sheets over the crumbling masonry down which Landry was climbing as surefootedly as a mountain goat. Soon they had crossed the wall, and Catherine saw the countryside lying all about them, pallid with snow under a dark sky. They were now standing on the hillside at whose foot a few small huts and cottages nestled, like chickens under a hen's wing. Still holding Catherine tightly against him, Landry whistled three times. A shadow glided out behind a tangle of shrubs and boulders.

"God be praised!" said a voice which trembled with emotion. "How is she?"

"Not too well," said Landry. "She needs to be put to bed at once."

"Everything is ready. Come. . . ."

Weak though she was, Catherine's eyes had flown open at the sound of this voice. She was too exhausted to feel surprise any more and the last few hellish days had set her mind wandering a little. She wanted to be certain that she was not the prey of some hallucination. But there was no mistaking the evidence of her eyes.—Sara had returned as unexpectedly as she had left her, gliding out of the darkness as though it were the most natural thing in the world. To make quite sure that she was real, Catherine put up a hand to touch the face bent over her.

"Sara, is it really you? Have you come back?"

Sara snatched her hand and covered it with tears and kisses. "If you knew how ashamed I feel, Catherine. . . ."

But Landry broke into these explanations.

"Later I'll explain how we came to meet up again," he said, taking a firmer hold on Catherine. "Meanwhile, we must be on our way. We can easily be seen against this white background of snow, even though it is dark. I'll hand Catherine over to you and then I'll come back and wipe out my footprints."

"Where are we going?" Catherine asked.

"Not far, don't worry. . . . Just to Mâlain. Garin would never think of searching for you so near your prison. . . ."

"There's no need to come back," said Sara. "I'll see to the footprints. Besides . . ." and she held a finger up, ". . . it's started snowing again. Our footmarks will soon be covered."

Great white flakes were floating down around them, slow and far apart at first, but thickening fast.

"The heavens are on our side," Landry exclaimed cheerfully. "Let's be off!"

He hastened down the steep slope whose summit was crowned by the grim old fortress. Total silence reigned. It looked as though the fortress had no other guards but the two cold corpses whose blood was already congealing on the stone-flagged floor.

Landry passed through the straggling village at a run. Sara followed at his heels. They were making for a cottage which stood at the edge of a wood on the slope of the hill, where a faint light glimmered. The little dwelling was buried under such a heavy fall of snow that it looked like a white bump, but there was something homely and reassuring about its tiny window all yellow from the light within. Happy and confident,

112

Catherine allowed her friends to take charge of her ... Landry's arms were strong and warm and purposeful. ... A dog barked near the house. Then the door opened and a woman's silhouette appeared black in the lighted doorway.

"It's us," Landry said. "All went well. ..."

"You rescued her?"

The voice was pleasant, well modulated with sombre inflections. The woman rolled her "r"s slightly, but her Burgundian accent was very faint.

"Come in quickly," she said, moving aside to let them enter.

CHAPTER SEVEN

Sara is Suspicious

The woman who had opened her door for Catherine to enter was called Pâquerette and was reputedly a witch, but a very unusual sort of witch with nothing at all in common with the hideous, filthy, toothless old crone of the legends. Her humble little cottage with its floor of beaten earth was as immaculate as a Flemish burgher's home, and the iron cooking pot hanging over the fire shone like silver. As for Pâquerette herself, she could not have been much more than twenty. She was one of those blonde Burgundian beauties, strong and straight as a young tree, with a wild-rose complexion and thick golden thatch for hair. Her hair was so springy and abundant that it threatened to dislodge the white linen cap perched precariously on top of it. Her body was magnificent, full and rounded without being heavy, and smooth-skinned. Her lips parted in a smile revealing the solid white gleam of a faultless set of teeth.

But Catherine did not take in all these details at once. She only noticed two things as she was carried into the house—a cheerful blaze dancing in the hearth and the bed, a snowy white nest behind its red serge curtains which had been drawn back to admit her. After drinking the soup which her hostess produced for her, Catherine succumbed to a leaden slumber, all the sufferings and terrors which had tormented her for the last few days obliterated in a flash. She was quite astonished when she woke up the following morning and found herself in this cosy rustic setting instead of the dark and sinister room

113

where she had been imprisoned in the fortress. She had to cudgel her brains to remember what had actually happened on that fateful night which had been so prodigal in its strange events—the death of her two warders, her escape, Sara's miraculous reappearance. . . . But Landry had been standing at the bedside watching for the moment when she woke and he smiled affectionately as he noticed the way she instinctively shrank back as she opened her eyes.

"Come now," he said gently, "there's no need to be afraid now. Everything's all right. You are quite safe here!"

Catherine looked as though she found this hard to believe. Her eyes roamed round the room, looking at everything in turn but always returning to the fire . . . the fire whose absence had been so cruel during her imprisonment. Outside, the snow had stopped falling and there was even a faint glimmer of sunshine. Its pale gleam was reflected back by the immaculate expanse of snow and the dazzle of it filled the little cottage.

"Sun . . . and a fire!" Catherine sighed, with a wan smile.

Just then Sara and Pâquerette, who had gone to the stable to milk the goat, returned carrying a bucket half full of milk and some cheeses. When she found that Catherine was awake, Sara ran over to embrace her tearfully, bewailing her thinness and haggard appearance. Pâquerette, meanwhile, stood gazing curiously at the fugitive from the fortress. Landry had told her that this was the Lord Treasurer's wife and the mistress of the all-powerful Duke of Burgundy, but looking at the poor wasted creature lying there with her muddy complexion and matted, lustreless hair she found this hard to believe. Sara herself, now that her first emotion had subsided, was contemplating Catherine with despair. Who would have connected this ravaged face and raw and bleeding neck with the ravishing Dame de Brazey?

"Oh, the pity of it!" she murmured. "What a state he's reduced you to, Holy Jesus!"

"The main trouble is that she is filthy dirty!" Landry said cheerfully. "If I were you, I should give her a little milk and then start cleaning her up. . . ."

"I'll heat up some water," Pâquerette said approvingly, and took a pan down from its hook to go and fill it at the well.

While Catherine sipped her milk and Sara got together everything she would need to wash and tidy her, they began to explain how she came to be there. Landry described how he had run into Sara at Jacquot-de-la-Mer's tavern on the eve of rescuing Catherine—it seemed that the Duke's horseman often spent an evening there. She had arrived there only that day

114

after leaving Stanko—the gipsy for whom she had abandoned Catherine—and his tribe in the forest of Pasques.

"She didn't dare to go to your house," the young man added.

"I was ashamed and sorry, too!" Sara admitted frankly. "I longed to see you again, but I was afraid of meeting your eye. Dijon drew me irresistibly, though, and so I went to Jacquot's to see what would happen. When I heard that you had disappeared, I thought I would go out of my mind, and that God must be punishing me for failing in my duty. So I begged Landry to let me come and help find you."

"We kept watch alternately," Landry said. "And you know what happened then. The night I left you at the fortress, I went back to Dijon to get Sara. As for Pâquerette . . ."

He drew the girl towards him, circling her waist familiarly with one arm, and pressed a smacking kiss on her lips.

". . . I met her at Jacquot's tavern, too, about a year ago. She had been living at Fontaine with her mother, but the old woman was taken and burned as a witch. Pâquerette had to run away. She took refuge at Jacquot's. But she couldn't breathe properly in Dijon—she needs fields, countryside. Jacquot had a cousin here who had just died, so he gave her the cottage and here we are! She has nothing to fear at Mâlain unless the Duke decides to send a troop and destroy the whole village."

"But why should he?" Catherine asked. "Is this a place of asylum, then? I suppose it is church land. Didn't you tell me the fortress belonged to the Abbot of Saint-Seine?"

"Yes, it does, though the holy man has virtuously declined to be associated with it," Landry said, laughing. "And it *is* a place of asylum, but scarcely in the sense you mean. In fact, rather the opposite. The reason nobody comes here is that the village is almost exclusively inhabited by witches. Everyone knows that. . . . So one more or less! Pâquerette lives here in peace and your husband knew what he was doing when he shut you up in the old fortress. The good folk in the countryside round about don't come near these parts unless they are forced to. The fortress is said to be haunted and the village is accursed. . . ."

While Landry was talking, Sara had filled a big tub with hot water and dragged it in front of the fire.

"That's enough of your talk," she cried, pushing Landry towards the door. "Now, out you go and take a walk. We don't need a man around to help give Catherine a bath."

Landry slipped on his old leather jacket with a sigh, slipped a dagger into his belt and whistled for Pâquerette's dog.

"Very well, then, I'll take a walk through the woods. I may find some game there. Meat is always scarce in winter. . . ."

When he had gone out, Sara helped Catherine on to her feet and off with the tattered chemise. Then she helped her into the tub of warm water. When she felt the water against her skin, Catherine gave a great sigh of contentment. Next to a night's sleep in a comfortable bed, a warm bath was what she had longed for most. She had never felt so dirty in her life. When she looked at her skin and hair she felt ashamed and disgusted. If she had had to spend several months in that dreadful prison her looks would certainly have suffered irreparably. . . . She sank gratefully into the water and watched Landry going off towards the woods with the dog at his heels while Sara tenderly bathed the raw places on her neck and anointed them with balm. Pâquerette had gone with him to keep him company and Catherine saw her leaning tenderly on the young man's shoulder.

"This Pâquerette," she asked Sara, "is she Landry's sweetheart, do you think?"

"She is his mistress, and I have the impression she is madly in love with him. But I couldn't tell you what Landry thinks about her. Does he love her? It's hard to say."

"Do you think she's really a witch? She doesn't look like one. . . ."

"It's a sickness which is passed on from mother to daughter so they say. Anyway, even if she weren't, no one would believe her because it would be contrary to the usual order of things."

"What about you, though? What do you think?"

Sara shrugged and worked up a lather on the piece of cotton cloth she was using to wash Catherine's body. It was gradually going back to its normal color, apart from the bruises and scratches which marbled her skin.

"I don't know, but I wouldn't put it past her. She's a strange girl, you know! I've often seen her at Jacquot's—the men there were afraid of her because of the way she looked at them."

Recalling Pâquerette's strange eyes, one blue and one brown, Catherine thought they might have a point there. But she soon forgot her hostess in the pleasure of finding herself clean again. Sara helped her out of the tub and made her sit by the fire to dry. Then she fetched some more water to wash her hair. Catherine did what she was told, docile as a child. It was so nice to abandon oneself to Sara's skillful hands like she used to in the days when she was just a little girl who had shot up too fast. The dirt and fatigue seemed to roll off her all at once. She felt reborn.

When Pâquerette returned a little later, she stood transfixed on the threshold for a moment with a faggot of wood in her arms, staring open-mouthed at the sight which met her eyes.

116

Catherine was sitting, eyes shut and apparently half asleep, on a stool by the fire which cast rosy lights over her skin, wrapped in a piece of cloth which revealed her slender legs and beautiful shoulders. Sara stood behind her combing and recombing the thick gold mass of her hair, still damp from its recent washing, but the finest and longest the girl had ever seen. Could this really be the same woman as the pathetic, derelict figure of the night before, that grey, blood-stained thing which had suddenly been transformed into this radiant creature?

"Be kind enough to close the door," Sara said, turning towards her. "It's cold."

Pâquerette pushed the door shut mechanically, but her odd-colored eyes had narrowed curiously and Sara noticed the way they looked at Catherine. The fugitive's newly revealed beauty had struck Pâquerette with the force of a whip-lash and Sara could feel the jealousy eating into the girl's soul as clearly as if it were her own. She decided not to place too much trust in her in the future, but to keep an unobtrusive eye on her.

Landry returned late that night, covered with blood and staggering under the weight of a young boar he had killed with his dagger. He was exhausted and delighted with himself, but when he saw Catherine, a fresh and charming figure once more in a plain blue woolen dress of Pâquerette's, his delight knew no bounds. He snatched her up round the waist and swung her into the air.

"Ah, that's more like it!" he cried. "How pretty you are, my Cathy! The prettiest girl that ever was! A bit too thin, perhaps . . . but that won't last. . . ."

He pressed a kiss on each of her cheeks and then set her down again. Then he turned towards Pâquerette.

"I'm hungry," he said.

"The soup is ready."

The girl's voice was as smooth and calm as a mill pond, but Sara had seen the anger flash through her eyes when Landry embraced Catherine. The girl was decidedly jealous and Sara doubted that any good would come of this!

After supper they had a council of war. There had not been a sign of life from the fortress yet, so it seemed unlikely that the two dead men had been discovered. But Garin would soon be returning and it would be rash to expose Catherine to the risk of an informer, supposing anyone were to notice her presence in Pâquerette's cottage.

"The best thing would be to warn Monseigneur Philippe," Landry said. "Only that will take time. He is in Paris at present."

117

"And Messire de Roussay?" Catherine asked. "Isn't he at Dijon?"

"I think so, but he can't do much for you. Garin is your husband still whether you like it or not. He has every right over you, and no one, not even the Captain of the Guard, can stop him taking you back again. The Duke is the only man whom Garin would not dare to defy. I shall leave for Paris tomorrow. . . ."

It was clearly the most sensible solution, but Catherine could not repress a twinge of alarm at the thought of Landry's departure. While the young man was there she was afraid of nothing. He was strong, brave and gay! Just like the old Landry she used to know.

"Why not wait here quietly till the Duke gets back? He may not be away for very long."

"One never knows with him," Landry said. "Besides, I have to return to my post soon. I shall have to go and find him in Paris. Then he can give the necessary orders to ensure your safety and prevent your husband doing you any harm. If you weren't . . . in this condition, I would take you with me, but it's a long journey from here to Paris and the roads are dangerous. I shall be able to travel alone without danger and return all the more quickly. Now, come, let's see you smile! You know very well that I am more anxious for your safety than anyone else's in the world!"

He put such warmth into this last remark that Sara found herself glancing involuntarily at Pâquerette. But Pâquerette's eyes were on the ground. She collected together the plates and cups to wash them, her face expressionless as a stone.

"I'll make you something for the road," she said, not looking at Landry.

That night Sara, who was sharing the bed Pâquerette had generously vacated with Catherine, woke suddenly, alerted by that sixth sense that nomadic tribes possess to a high degree. The fire was out, and the house in darkness, but the gypsy woman sensed rather than saw that someone was standing by the bed. She held her breath; Pâquerette should be asleep in the attic above them, and Landry was in the stable with his horse and the goats. But there was a faint rustling noise from the other side of the bed where Catherine was sleeping peacefully. Sara could have sworn that there was someone there. She was just about to jump out of bed and light a candle when she heard footsteps, light but distinct, moving towards the door. The door opened noiselessly and Sara saw a woman's figure profiled in the doorway. Then the door was hastily shut. Sara did not hesitate. She slipped on her shoes and stockings, threw a shawl

118

round her shoulders and went out herself, taking care not to wake Catherine. Just then, Pâquerette came from the direction of the hen run carrying something under her voluminous black cloak and Sara only just had time to conceal herself in the darkness of the doorway.

The witch was rapidly making towards the woods behind her cottage. A little way from the house she stopped and lit a lantern and then hurried on, heading deeper into the trees. Her behavior struck Sara as so strange that she decided to follow her. Where could Pâquerette be going on such a dark night? The temperature had risen considerably towards nightfall and the snow was melting on the ground and branches, so that slushy white blobs slid to the ground from time to time. Pâquerette was walking fast and Sara had to hurry to keep up, but she was guided by the lighted lantern bobbing along in front of her between the trees. The girl was following a faintly visible track which led around the flank of the hill, past great dripping boulders, heading towards the summit of the wooded outcrop. But suddenly the lantern light vanished as abruptly as if the earth had swallowed it up. Sara paused for a moment, lost in the engulfing darkness. Then she pressed on in the direction which the light had vanished. Her eyes were gradually growing accustomed to the darkness and she was able to find her way without too much difficulty. It was soon clear where the light had gone. The path ran alongside a massive rock in which there was a narrow cleft just large enough for one person to squeeze through. Sara was certain that Pâquerette must have gone through the gap and she listened for a moment, straining her ears till she thought she heard the murmur of voices from within. She cursed herself for not having provided herself with a weapon, but she stepped bravely into the aperture, and began feeling her way along the narrow passage which cut into the heart of the rock. A moment later the passage widened and a bright light could be seen flashing in the darkness, while the sound of voices grew louder. A strange wailing song came from somewhere in the bowels of the earth, at the far end of this strange corridor. Sara hurried on, more confident now that the way was lit up. The passage plunged deeper and deeper into the earth, and the ground here was damp and slippery, but the air seemed distinctly warmer. Then the passage turned a sharp corner and Sara found herself facing a brightly lit aperture, half screened by a fall of rock where she found a convenient boulder to hide behind while she watched what was going on within.

What she saw made her cross herself hurriedly. The gap in the rock opened into a large cavern where a fire was burning. Beyond the fire there was a sort of altar hewn from the rock

119

wall itself and on this there stood a crudely carved wooden statue with a man's body and a goat's head, between whose horns three black wax tapers burned. A dozen men and women, of all ages and wearing peasant clothes, squatted on the ground in a semi-circle on either side of the statue. They were utterly motionless, and Sara would have mistaken them for statues, too, had it not been for the monotonous chanting song issuing from their lips. An old man, with white hair as long as a woman's, stood leaning in front of the grinning idol. He stood leaning towards Pâquerette, both hands deep in the sleeves of the long black robe, painted with cabalistic symbols, which reached to the ground. The girl had slipped back her hood and knelt bare-headed in front of the old man. She was speaking to him, and he replied, but Sara was too far away to hear what they were saying. She guessed that she must have stumbled upon a convocation of the witches of Mâlain in the secret temple where they celebrated the rites of their master, Satan.

Sara suddenly saw Pâquerette handing something to the old man, something shining. It was a lock of golden hair and she realized that it must be Catherine's. The witch had been snipping it off earlier on, when Sara awakened with the feeling that someone was standing by the bed. The old man divided the lock in two, placing one half somewhere in his robes and burning the other, the ashes of which he carefully preserved. Pâquerette then held a black chicken out to him, thereby explaining her visit to the hen run earlier on. The sorcerer put the chicken on the altar and struck off its head with one blow of his knife. He collected the blood which spurted from the neck in a wooden bowl. Some of this he mixed with the ashes of the burnt lock of hair and, when he had added a little flour to the paste, he held up the grisly sort of cake he had made to the idol's grinning mouth. Pâquerette flung herself face downwards against the ground while the ring of witches chanted louder and louder, swaying rhythmically from the hips. Sara had to shake herself to be rid of the insidious, evil influence of this scene. She gathered that Pâquerette, feeling that her own magic might not be redoubtable enough, had come to invoke the aid of a stronger power than her own against her enemy.

The old man reached the end of his incantations and turned to Pâquerette. With one finger, he traced a cross on her face with the black chicken's blood. Then he bent over and kissed her on the lips and handed her a packet containing what looked to be a powder. He murmured something in her ear and pointed to the exit.

This gesture warned Sara: Pâquerette was about to leave. She must escape before she was discovered! She turned and

120

hurried as fast as her legs would carry her towards the exit, bumping and scraping herself against the rock walls in her haste. She felt better once she found herself back in the open air again. She felt rather as though she had just returned from hell. The unerring instinct of a girl born and bred in the wilds led her straight back to the path and she sped along it, anxious to return before Pâquerette got back. At last she came to the edge of the wood and the cottage appeared before her. Silence reigned. Catherine still slept peacefully, as Sara tore off her clothes and slipped into the bed. Feeling this chilly body next to her, Catherine half awoke. She mumbled a few indistinct words, rolled over and went to sleep again. A few seconds later, Pâquerette herself came in. Wide awake this time, with her eyes straining into the dark, Sara heard the creak of the ladder which Pâquerette used to climb up into her loft. A moment later, the little house was quiet again, but Sara found it hard to go back to sleep. The scenes she had just witnessed strengthened her belief that Pâquerette in her jealousy would be prepared to go to any lengths to harm Catherine. She did not believe in the magic practiced by these rural witches, and was not in the least worried about their possible effects on Catherine. It would simply mean keeping her eyes open. But she was worried about the little packet the old wizard had given the girl, and wondered whether it could contain poison.

But she was soon reassured about this. Towards dawn, as the cottage window was beginning to show grey, Sara saw Pâquerette climb down her ladder again. She took no notice of the two sleepers. She got out a bowl which she filled with white flour and a little water and began to knead the mixture into flat cakes which she cooked in a long-handled, iron pan. Sara, who was watching between half closed lids, saw her quite distinctly sprinkling the contents of the packet into the dough. When the griddle cakes were done, Pâquerette cut some thick slices of ham from a haunch which was hanging from a hook in the chimney, wrapped them all in a white napkin and slipped the bundle into the knapsack which Landry would be carrying when he set out a few hours later. Sara smiled ironically. So the powder had been destined for the picnic meal which Landry would be eating *en route*! In that case, it could only be a love philtre. The overly affectionate glances which the young man had bestowed on his childhood friend the evening before must have convinced his formidable mistress that she needed the aid of magic!

Two hours later, Landry embraced the three women and swung himself into the saddle with a cheery "Au revoir!" His horse's hooves sent the slush on the road splattering in all directions. Catherine watched a little sadly as he galloped off, passing by the mount crowned by the black and threatening fortress, before vanishing round the foot of the hill. He carried all her hopes with him. Suddenly Catherine found that she desperately longed to see Philippe again. He was the one being with whom life seemed both easy and sweet. . . .

The snow gave way to torrential rain which turned the ground into a quagmire, the roads into puddles and the light into a damp grey mist which hung like a dreary curtain outside the small windows of the cottage. The heavens reeked of despair and ennui and the three women, shut up together in the small cottage and kept indoors by the dreadful weather, found the isolation difficult to bear. Landry had barely left when the rains came, thundering down upon the countryside as though determined to cut off Catherine and her two companions from the rest of mankind. After a few days of this, the situation became almost unendurable.

Sara was jumpy, Pâquerette was taciturn and Catherine uneasy without knowing why. Every time she looked out of the window, her eyes would fall on the château looming bleakly against the horizon, a silent, brooding bulk, hugging to itself the secret of the two corpses within its walls. There had not been a sound or movement from the place since the night of her escape. Sara had kept watch discreetly, keeping a lookout for the Lord Treasurer's return. But he had not appeared. And there was not a sign of life from the fortress.

Catherine had regained her strength. Her pregnancy still left her feeling tired much of the time, but the bouts of sickness had stopped at the end of the third month, and on the whole, she felt better than she had for some time. She whiled away the time as best she could with household tasks and duties. She found a certain pleasure in kneading the dough for bread, or learning how to make goat cheeses, humble tasks which she had lost the knack of in the mansion in the rue de Parcheminerie.

The inhabitants of Mâlain might have been invisible. No one came to visit Pâquerette during the first four days after Landry's departure. The squat village houses huddled under their overhanging roofs of shining tiles or ragged thatch. One could imagine the peasants cosily hugging the fire within, casting an occasional eye out at the inclement weather through their tiny windows of thick glass or oiled parchment.

On the fifth day, however, a man entered Pâquerette's cottage at a time when Pâquerette herself had gone out into the wood to collect firewood. Sara was busily washing clothes by the hearth and was dismayed to recognize in the visitor the tall old man whom she had seen in the grotto in the forest. Instinctively, she placed herself between the newcomer and Catherine, who was sitting on the hearthstone, spinning a distaff of hemp.

"What do you want, my good man?" the gypsy asked.

"I am a friend of Pâquerette's. Isn't she here?"

Sara pointed towards the forest:

"She's out there, collecting firewood, but you may wait here for her, if you wish. . . ."

Her voice trembled a little as she observed that the warlock's eyes, which were a peculiar faded blue in color, were fixed insistently upon Catherine. The old man shrugged his shoulders under his great coat of coarse brown stuff lined with sheepskin.

"No, I'll come back. But . . ."

He turned back from the threshold:

"You might tell her for me that Gervais came, and that he has carried out the commission she gave him."

"What commission?" Sara asked boldly, her suspicions thoroughly aroused by now. The man made an evasive gesture.

"Oh, nothing important! She'll understand. Good evening to you both. . . ."

"Good evening."

When Pâquerette returned, Sara passed on the visitor's message, her face imperturbable. She noticed that the girl flushed in spite of her efforts at self-control, and this served to confirm the suspicions which had been growing in her since the witches' Sabbath. She remembered the old man's stealthy gesture as he hid part of the blonde lock Pâquerette had given him in his loose robes. Why had he done so? For some secret magic rite or spell? Sara doubted it. Gervais, like Pâquerette herself, for that matter, would rely for their black magic on the revolting cake they had placed in the idol's mouth. No, that lock of hair must certainly be intended for another purpose. But what? Sara hardly slept a wink that night as she lay there racking her brains for a plausible explanation of the riddle. Towards morning, however, she sank into a profound slumber like a bottomless pit into which neither light nor sounds could reach. This state of unconsciousness did not last long, but long enough for it to be bright daylight when she finally awoke. Catherine was already up and sat cutting up cabbage for the soup. Pâquerette was nowhere to be seen.

"Where is she?" Sara demanded.

"Who? Pâquerette? She went out a moment ago. She didn't say where she was going, but I saw her heading for the other end of the village."

She was worried about Sara, who did not seem at all her usual self. She was nervous and jumpy. Catherine watched her

123

get up and tumble on her clothes, her mind clearly on other matters, and then stand with her nose pressed to the window pane. She refused the cup of milk Catherine offered her.

"Now tell me, what *is* the matter with you?" Catherine finally burst out. "You're as jumpy as a cat on hot bricks. What is worrying you?"

Sara did not answer. She stared up at the sky, which was somewhat lighter than it had been. It was still partially clouded over, but the clouds were not as dark as they had been latterly; some of them even glowed faintly pink from the dawn light. The rain had stopped, but the countryside was still dotted with great pools of water, reflecting back the indeterminate colors of the sky. Acting on a sudden impulse which she would have been at a loss to explain, Sara threw on her enveloping black cape and snatched up a wicker tray on which she had placed the bread ready for baking the night before.

"I'm going to the village now," she told Catherine. "Pâquerette should have gone—I can't think why she didn't take the loaves since she was going to the village."

Before Catherine could question her further, Sara was out of the door and striding down the muddy track. The communal oven stood in the middle of the village, between the crumbling church and an ancient stone cross whose steps were green with moss and age. It commanded a view of the road which passed alongside the fortress and joined up with the road to the west, whose course ran along the Ouche river. There were several women there already waiting their turn, each with a basket on her arm. They were all heavily wrapped up in their capes and bonnets. They spoke very little on account of the chilly wind, but pressed up against the wall for shelter like black birds. Sara did not even look at them. Her keen eyes had caught sight of a figure in a familiar blue dress standing at the foot of the road leading up to the fortress. What could Pâquerette be doing sitting on the old Roman boundary stone? She seemed to be waiting. But for what?

Then Sara gave a sudden smothered exclamation. A band of riders had suddenly appeared in the bend of the road. There were about twenty or so of them, all wearing leather jerkins covered with metal plaques which shone faintly in the grey light. And in the foreground of them rode a thin black figure, the sight of which set Sara's heart racing. This man dressed all in black, so tall and thin. . . . Sara still hesitated, but when she saw the man stop to speak to Pâquerette and saw Pâquerette pointing in the direction of her house, she hesitated no longer. The man in black was Garin . . . Garin whom the accursed sorceress must have sent for! In spite of a violent longing to

124

seize Pâquerette and administer the thrashing her wicked be-
trayal deserved, Sara did not waste a second, deciding to leave
the punishment of their wicked hostess in Landry's capable
hands. Leaving the unbaked loaves beside a near-by well, she
wheeled round and raced back towards the cottage, her voluminous cape billowing out behind her like huge black wings.
Catherine was busy skimming the soup as Sara rushed, panting
and white-faced, into the cottage.

"Now, what's the matter?" she asked.

Without answering, Sara snatched a coat from a near-by peg,
threw it round Catherine's shoulders and dragged her out
through the little door which led directly into the stables.

"We must run away!" she panted. "Garin . . . he's on his way
here! Pâquerette must have told him . . . She's bringing him
here!"

Panic seized Catherine and she felt her legs give way beneath
her.

"Run away? But where?" she cried tearfully, appalled by the
thought of what awaited her at Garin's hands if he caught up
with her again. A series of dreadful pictures flashed before her
eyes—the fortress room where she was imprisoned, the straw
litter, the chain, the iron collar, the corpses of the two mon-
sters who guarded her. . . .

"This isn't the moment to give in," Sara scolded her. "We
must run for it, do you hear? There isn't a moment to lose! The
forest . . . come!"

She snatched at Catherine's hand and pulled her along after
her, not even daring to glance back along the road. Fear lent
Catherine renewed strength. In a few seconds, they had reached
the edge of the wood and vanished among the trees. Almost
without thinking, Sara struck out along the path which she had
followed the other night behind Pâquerette. She hoped to find
the secret cave where she was quite sure Pâquerette would never
take Garin and his men-at-arms for fear of the unpleasant
fate which would undoubtedly befall her if they discovered
the wooden idol with the goat's head. She must reach this
refuge at all costs. It would at least give them a breathing
space. Turning round briefly in their headlong flight, Catherine saw that the danger was still greater than she had imagined—beyond the tree trunks she could already dimly distinguish the shapes of men dismounting from their horses
outside Pâquerette's cottage. . . . She could hear the horses
whinnying. . . .

"Faster!" Sara whispered. "Faster!"

It was hard going for the two fugitives. The path climbed
uphill and the recent downpours had left it dangerously slip-

pery. The glimpse of the soldiers had left Catherine almost paralysed with terror. Then a spur of rock came between her and this terrifying sight and she redoubled her efforts. The threat was still near enough for them to hear the loud voices of the men-at-arms. A cry from Pâquerette made itself heard:

"In the woods . . . they must have hidden there!"

It was followed by another voice—Garin's this time:

"Off you go, then . . . split into several groups!"

"That Pâquerette!" Sara hissed. "I'll catch up with her one of these days and then she'll be sorry! We leave the path here—I think this is the place. . . ."

She had just caught sight of a heap of grey boulders which, if her calculations were correct, ought to be the ones where the underground cave was hidden. It was dangerous to stay on the path. . . . She made Catherine follow her through the trees over the dead leaves which left no trace of their footprints. But this route obliged them to scramble up several boulders and Catherine was growing tired. She slipped on a mossy rock, barking her shins painfully, and had to grit her teeth to stop herself crying out. Sara was beside her in a flash, and seized her under the arms to try and pull her up.

"Listen!" Sara whispered, hoping to rally her courage. "They are in the wood now—we shall be safe up there, but we have to get there first!"

Sara's fierce insistence, together with the terror Catherine felt as she heard the soldiers pushing deeper into the forest, drove her to make one last effort. One final obstacle lay before them—a large boulder above which the crevice in the rock face could just be seen. Catherine spreadeagled herself over the wet rock, snatched at a bramble which ripped her fingers and clawed her way to the top—only just in time. The soldiers' helmets could be seen gleaming dully through the bare branches. Sara pushed Catherine into the rocky corridor leading to the underground cave and then carefully obliterated their footmarks in the muddy ground outside with a branch. It was not as dark as the gypsy had feared in the tunnel of mud and rock. Little chinks overhead let in enough light for the two women to be able to push far underground. They reached the large cave safely. It was dimly lit by a bramble-covered hole far above in the vaulted roof. After one's eyes became accustomed to the gloom, it was possible to see quite clearly. When Catherine's eyes fell on the wooden idol, Sara just had time to clap a hand over her mouth to stop her crying out in alarm.

"Be quiet!" she whispered. "They aren't far away. I don't think Pâquerette would dare bring them down here, though! she would be risking too much. . . ."

Catherine's eyes were dilated with terror as she contemplated the hideous little god of evil. It was the first time she had ever seen anything of the sort and it was hard to say which frightened her more—the idol or her pursuers.

"What's that?" she asked, pointing at the statue with a shaking hand.

"Satan!" Sara said brutally. "And this cave is the place where the witches of Mâlain met. I followed our friend Pâquerette here the other night. But hush! I hear footsteps. . . . They must be very close."

The soldiers did indeed seem to be drawing closer. But placed as they were, at the heart of a mass of rocks, it was hard for the two fugitives to tell precisely where they were. They seemed very near one minute and far away the next. Sara and Catherine huddled against each other, holding their breath. Catherine could hear her heartbeats pounding in her ears as loudly as surf crashing on the shore.

"If he captures me again I shall kill myself. Sara . . . I'll kill myself, I swear," she murmured, with such wild despair that Sara squeezed her arm comfortingly. Sara could guess at the dreadful tension her friend must be suffering at that moment. If they had to spend much longer listening to these sounds from outside, she was afraid that Catherine might lose control completely and start howling like an animal cornered in its lair. Sara herself came within a hair's breadth of howling as a black shape suddenly rose up from behind the wooden statue.

"Don't stay there," the shape said calmly, "come with me. . . ." His face was not visible in the darkness.

The two women were too frightened to say a word. But, when the man came nearer and she could see him clearly, Sara recoiled involuntarily—she had just recognized the white beard and hooked nose of Gervais, the leader of the sorcerers. He must have guessed her reaction because he shook his head and took the gypsy woman by the hand.

"Don't be frightened! You can trust me; Gervais has never betrayed anyone who sought refuge under his roof."

"That's possible," Sara said coldly, recovering her self-possession all of a sudden. "But first, I should like to know something—what did you do with the lock of hair which Pâquerette gave you the other evening . . . the one you hid in your robes?"

"My nephew took it to Dijon. It was given to the Seigneur de Brazey as proof that his wife was hidden in the village," he added coolly.

"And you have the brazen effrontery to admit to it!" Sara

cried indignantly. "Do you really think I'd be so rash as to go with you now, and trust my life and my mistress's to you?"

"You haven't any choice. Besides, things are different now. Pâquerette was free to break the sacred laws of hospitality and betray the guest who had sought refuge under her roof. She came to ask my help against an enemy, and I gave it to her. But now it is under my roof that you are seeking asylum, for this is where I live. You are sacred to me and I shall do everything I can to save you. Are you coming? Pâquerette hates you so much that she would even be capable of bringing the soldiers down here."

Catherine had listened to the conversation between Sara and the old man without understanding much of it, but now she broke in.

"We must go with him! Nothing could be worse than what will happen if we are captured again!"

"And if he should betray you?"

Catherine's eyes met Gervais's, and what she saw there must have reassured her, because she sounded quite decisive when she next spoke:

"He won't betray me. I trust him. My life or death can be of no possible concern to a man of his age, especially one like himself, who has chosen to live here alone, close to nature."

"Thank you, young woman. You are wise," Gervais said gravely.

He took the two women behind the statue where there was another passage, a long narrow tunnel leading into another cavern which appeared to be where he lived. A curious dwelling place, scantily furnished with a straw mattress and a few stools set around a table piled high with an odd assortment of things. A heap of dusty books stood in one corner next to a glowing brazier. There was a curious smell of smoke mixed with sulphur fumes in this lair which was lit only by chinks in the rock and the flames of the brazier. Gervais made his two visitors sit down, and poured some thick soup into two bowls from a pot which was simmering over the fire.

"Eat this," he commanded. "Then you can rest here till nightfall. Once it is dark, I will take you away from Mâlain by a secret way to a place where the soldiers will never find you."

Catherine clasped the hand which was offering her the soup between hers for a moment.

"How can I ever thank you for what you have done?"

A thin smile lit up the old man's austere face.

"By getting the fire put out when the Duke finally takes it into his head to have me grilled alive! But I have great hopes of ending my days here, in the bosom of mother-earth. . . . Eat, little one, and then sleep. You have need of both."

Catherine asked nothing better. As soon as she had finished her soup, she stretched out on the straw mattress and was soon fast asleep. Gervais turned towards Sara.

"And you? Won't you go to sleep, too? Or don't you trust me?"

"I trust you," Sara said peacefully, "but I'm not sleepy. Let us talk, if you have nothing better to do."

When night had come and the moon risen high in the sky, Gervais woke Catherine and gave her a fresh bowl of soup while he and Sara supped in their turn. Then he enveloped himself in a black cape, seized a stout stick and threw some ashes onto the fire.

"Come, it is time."

Catherine remembered that night journey through the ancient forest for a long time to come. She was no longer afraid. The forest was so peaceful everywhere! She could see the moon through the branches fleeing from cloud to cloud, spilling her blueish light over everything. The stillness of the forest was haunting. The tall tree tops were like the pillars of some mysterious cathedral in whose shadowy recesses the cry of a hunting animal or the swift flight of a bird sounded from time to time. The woodcutter's axe had not yet touched this primeval forest which still retained all its wild, virgin splendor. Immense oaks mingled there with black pines whose spiky skirts trailed the ground, and here and there an outcrop of bramble-covered, mossy rocks thrust up out of the ground. The babbling of a brook could be heard now and then, but the living silence was so wonderfully soothing that Catherine held her breath so as not to disturb it.

She was walking behind Gervais, who strode forward with the heavy, measured tread of the peasant who is sparing of his breath. Sara brought up the rear. Catherine found she had not even stopped to ask herself where Gervais was taking them, or what was to become of her. None of these things seemed important just then. The main thing was to be free and feel safe. Catherine could have gone on walking like this behind Gervais for hours on end. He walked on without a pause, straight through the forest, without even bothering to follow the paths. He seemed to know every tree and stone and stepped boldly out. From time to time a stag, doe or wild boar crossed their path. Once or twice the wild animal stopped fleetingly as if it recognized the old man. Among the forest animals he was like a shepherd in the midst of his flocks.

Catherine was aware of spring in the burgeoning countryside

around her in every fibre of her being, all the more acutely, perhaps, because she herself was expecting a child. There was a quickening of life and growth in the pungent smell of the wet undergrowth, in the faint budding of the black branches overhead and the love calls of beasts calling to their mates in the darkness.

Daybreak found Catherine and her companions standing on the bank of a narrow foaming torrent whose waters rushed between rocky banks overhung with trees. Large grey rocks spaced at regular intervals in the swirling foam formed a ford.

"This is the Suzon!" Gervais said, pointing at the river with his stick. "This is where I shall leave you. When you have crossed it, keep walking due north. About two leagues from here you will reach the Abbey of Saint-Seine, which is a place of asylum. The prior is Messire Jean de Blaisy. He is a good and charitable man and he will receive you hospitably."

This suggestion did not seem to please Catherine very much. She objected that the Abbot of Saint-Seine was the owner of the Château of Mâlain which he had lent to Garin to imprison her in, but Gervais brushed her objection aside.

"I'll wager that Messire Jean had no idea what the Lord Treasurer planned to do with his property. Almost certainly, Garin de Brazey must have borrowed it on some false pretext. You need have no fear of going to Saint-Seine. Even if you were the bitterest foe of his family, Jean de Blaisy would take you in unhesitatingly. In his eyes, any fugitive who comes and kneels on the threshold of his church is sent by the Lord and the Duke himself would not dare to try to force him to hand over a guest. You cannot go on wandering about the highways. You need a safe haven. At Saint-Seine you will be safe. . . ."

Catherine reflected. The long walk had tired her, for they had covered at least two leagues over difficult country. But, little by little, her face brightened. She remembered now that this Jean de Blaisy was a cousin of Ermengarde's and this reassured her. And then Gervais was quite right in saying that she couldn't go on wandering like this for ever. Someone might follow Pâquerette's example and give them away. Garin was rich. He would not grudge a few bags of gold to get his hands on her again. She held out her hand to the old man.

"You are right. I will go to Saint-Seine. But if you see a young man in the village, a young man dressed in green, one of the Duke's horsemen . . ."

"I know," Gervais cut in abruptly. "Pâquerette's lover. I will tell him where you are. He is returning to fetch you, isn't he?"

"Yes. But now I want to thank you. I have nothing to prove my gratitude with now, but later, perhaps, I may be able to . . ."

Gervais interrupted her with a gesture.

"I ask nothing and expect nothing from you. In helping you, I have done nothing more than right the wrong which Pâquerette made me do to you. We are quits now. I wish you all happiness."

Then the old man hastened away the way they had come. Catherine and Sara watched his impressive silhouette vanishing into the trees.

"Let's go," Sara said.

She stepped out onto the rows of stones which just showed above the foaming water. They crossed without mishap. When they had reached the other bank, the two women ate the bread Gervais had given them, drank some water from the river and then prepared to set out upon their journey. Sara cut two stout branches with her knife, and made them into a couple of rough walking sticks one of which she handed to Catherine.

"We still have two leagues to go and the country is rough going," she said. Walking one behind the other, they set off at a slow pace up the sloping valley of the Suzon towards Saint-Seine. The sun was rising, the first real sun for several days. In a little while, the still sodden countryside was bathed in its golden rays.

Several hours later, in a deep fold of the Haute Bourgogne plateau, where a little river ran merrily along, Sara and Catherine came in sight of the grey rooftops of the Abbey of Saint-Seine, the high square tower crowned with scaffolding of the abbey church, and, beyond it, like a clutch of chickens sheltering under a grey and white hen, the brown rooftops of a swarm of little houses where white wisps of smoke could be seen rising in the still air.

"We've arrived," Sara cried. "Thank heavens! I'm exhausted!"

They set off down the slope towards the Abbey, keeping their eyes fixed on the tower where the workmen were just coming to the end of their day's work. The bells were pealing out, summoning the monks to their devotions, their high, solemn notes clearly audible on the quiet air. In spite of a short rest around midday, Catherine was so exhausted she could hardly feel her feet as they moved mechanically beneath her, except where the holes in her shoes—lent by Pâquerette—had chafed and blistered the tender skin. But her fear of Garin was stronger than any pain or discomfort. She was almost running, despite her weariness, as they descended the hill towards the Abbey, eager for the safety of those high walls and a little straw to lie on.

Half an hour later, the two fugitives collapsed rather than knelt before the iron-clad, black oak doors to the Abbey. The village women stared suspiciously at the two fugitives with their clothes rent and torn by the forest brambles, and their grimy haggard faces. They had soon collected a crowd which followed them through the village, staring curiously. Some little boys started picking up stones to throw. Catherine was aware of the danger threatening them both. Vagabonds were unpopular in this rich little township, with its well stocked hen runs and well kept gardens. And Sara, with her blue-black hair and swarthy complexion, was not a sight to inspire confidence. The fear which had lain dormant in her ever since her abduction suddenly gathered strength inside her like a storm. She huddled closer to Sara, lowering her head to avoid the stone which was already being aimed in their direction. They were trapped between the peasants who were crowding in round them now and the Abbey's closed gates at which they gazed with agonized eyes. Sara thought she saw a monk's shaven head through one of the little tower windows. Throwing a protective arm round Catherine's shoulders, she called out hoarsely:

"Shelter . . . for the love of God!"

Another stone fell, but now the great gate was slowly beginning to swing open. The austere figure of a black-robed monk appeared, scapular over his shoulders. The third stone thrown at the two women rolled at his feet. He pushed it aside with his sandalled foot and cast a severe look at the small boys and housewives. Then he went up to Sara and Catherine, still clinging to each other in their terror.

"Enter!" he said solemnly. "There is shelter for you here."

But this last experience had proved too much for Catherine. They had to carry her to the monks' guest house, quite unconscious.

CHAPTER EIGHT

The Attack

Jean de Blaisy, Abbot of Saint-Seine, was just as Gervais had described him: a man of boundless charity. The two women had asked for refuge in his monastery and he gave it to them without question. But when he learnt that one of the two women admitted to the guest house, the part of the Abbey set aside for pilgrims and the care of the sick, wished to speak to him, he was somewhat astonished. Despite his tonsure and his habit of coarse black frieze, he had never entirely succeeded in ridding himself of a slight disdain for people from a lower social order, or paupers, humbly though he might wash their feet on Maundy Thursday as he knelt in the dust before them. However, since the woman claimed acquaintance with his cousin, Ermengarde de Châteauvilain, he ordered her to be taken to the church the following morning where he would talk to her after saying Mass.

As the Mass came to an end, Catherine stood with her back to one of the gravestones ranged along the wall, waiting patiently. When she saw the great nobleman-monk approaching, an imposing figure in a severe, black habit from which emerged his narrow head with its crown of grey hair and the profile of a bird of prey, she sank to her knees. But she did not bow her head. The Abbot stood before her with his hands thrust into his sleeves, gazing thoughtfully at the small face framed between its heavy golden plaits.

"You asked to speak to me," he said. "Here I am."

"Reverend Father," Catherine said, "I owe you my life. You opened the monastery gates yesterday to two desperate, fleeing women. And now I must ask you, in your cousin's name, to continue to give us your protection."

Jean de Blaisy's thin lips stretched in a sceptical smile. There was something incongruous about this peasant wench in her ragged clothes claiming acquaintance with one of the greatest ladies in the province, even if she did express herself uncommonly well and pretty though she might be.

"You know Madame de Châteauvilain? You astonish me!"

"She is my friend . . . my closest friend. Reverend Father, you have not asked me my name nor where I come from. My name is Catherine de Brazey and I was a lady-in-waiting to the late Duchess Marguerite. That was where I met Ermengarde. The reason you see me like this now, a fugitive and dressed in rags, is that I have just escaped from the dreadful prison where my husband put me . . . the tower of your château at Mâlain."

The Abbot frowned. He bent and raised Catherine to her feet. Then, observing that some of the village women who had come to hear Mass were gazing inquisitively in their direction, he led her towards the sacristy.

"Come. We can talk privately in here."

As they entered the little room with its smell of incense, holy water and starched linen, he motioned her to a stool while he himself took a seat on a high-backed bench and signed to the young novices, who were busy putting away the church ornaments, to leave the room.

133

"Tell me your story. But first, why were you imprisoned at Mâlain?"

Slowly, and choosing her words carefully, so that he should not think her mad, Catherine related her story. Chin on hand, the Abbot heard her through without interruption. The story was incredible and fantastic, but the woman who was telling it had a light of sincerity in her violet eyes which carried conviction.

"I don't know what to do now," Catherine said, when she had come to the end of her account. "As a wife, my duty is to stay with my husband and obey him. But if I go back to him, I shall be committing suicide. He will simply shut me up in a deeper, darker dungeon from which I shall never be able to escape. The Duke alone . . ."

The Abbot swiftly laid his dry hand on Catherine's and interrupted her:

"Say no more, child. You must understand that I cannot in any way sanction your adulterous relationship with the Duke. I must confess that your case is a hard one for a priest to pronounce judgment on. Your husband has every legal and religious claim over you and, if he demands your return, I shall not be able to refuse. Yet, on the other hand, you say that your life is in danger, and you have asked for sanctuary here. . . ."

He stood up and began pacing slowly to and fro across the white flagged floor. Catherine watched this monotonous to-ing and fro-ing with anxious eyes.

"Do not hand me over to him, Father! I beg you! If you have any pity for an unhappy woman, do not let Garin have me back again! Remember that I am expecting a child and that he wants to kill the child. . . ."

"I know! . . . Listen, this is not a decision I can make in a few minutes. I shall have to think it over and examine the various possible solutions to this difficult problem in peace and quiet. I shall let you know my decision. Meanwhile, you may remain here in peace. I shall give orders that you and your servant are to be separated from the sick in our guest house and lodged in a more suitable room."

"But, Father . . ." Catherine began, feeling far from reassured.

But he stopped her with a gesture, and made the sign of the Cross over her head.

"Go in peace, my child. You are in God's hands, and those Hands cannot falter."

It was impossible to continue the conversation. Catherine did not try, but when she rejoined Sara, she was more anxious than she appeared. If the Abbot decided that her rightful place was

134

with her husband, nothing, she was certain, could save her from a fate worse than death itself. But could a priest put asunder what God had united? Could he refuse a husband the right to his lawful wife under the pretext of sanctuary? Catherine was not entirely convinced that he had believed her story. He did not know her and had no way of knowing that she was not one of those corrupt women whose dissolute lives bring shame on their families and occasionally force them to take severe measures. She regretted not having asked him to let her write to Ermengarde for a guarantee of her character. . . .

But it seemed that there was more subtlety behind those austere, monastical features than Catherine would have credited him with, for the following evening the great Abbey gate swung open before a blast of trumpets, and a mounted cavalcade swept into the outer courtyard in a cloud of dust. Foremost among them, mounted on an immense snow-white charger, flourishing a gold-handled whip in her gloved hand, rode a large woman dressed in red and black, who all but broke her neck leaping down from her horse: Ermengarde de Châteauvilain in person!

With screams of joy, the ebullient Countess flung herself into Catherine's arms. She was laughing and crying at once, so much moved that in her excitement she embraced Sara as warmly as Catherine. Then she turned to her friend:

"Little wretch! Where the devil have you been? I've been chewing my nails for weeks, I've been so anxious about you! A pox on you!"

"I would be grateful if you would stop swearing like a trooper when you cross the threshold of my monastery, Ermengarde," the Abbot's quiet, refined voice cut in at this point. He had just arrived on the scene after having learnt of his cousin's tumultuous arrival. "I did not know when I sent that message to you that you would be honoring us with a personal visit. Not that I am not altogether enchanted. . . ."

The Prior's majestic mien did not seem to awe Ermengarde as one might have expected. She laughed in his face:

"Aren't you ashamed of lying like that? A monk like you? It's ridiculous! You know you aren't a bit pleased to see me. I make too much noise, I take up too much room and I disturb your nice, tranquil existence. But this is a serious situation, and I may as well tell you now that your life is going to be disturbed still further before we have finished!"

"And why?" the Abbot inquired with a start.

"Because if you're thinking of handing this poor child over to that brute of a husband of hers, it will have to be over my dead body, my friend," Ermengarde announced, calmly drawing off her riding gauntlets, and taking a huge embroidered silk handkerchief from her purse, she energetically mopped her face.

"Now, have some dinner fetched for us—I'm dying of hunger. And I must talk to Catherine alone."

Thus put in his place by his formidable cousin, Jean de Blaisy could only retire, sighing despairingly. He was almost over the threshold of the door leading from the courtyard to his own lodgings, when Ermengarde called out to him again:

"Don't forget, if Garin de Brazey presents himself at your gates, cousin, you are to close them and refuse him entry!"

"I'm afraid I have no right to do that."

"Well, in that case, you will just have to violate your conscience! Everything necessary must be done, even to arming your Benedictine monks and sustaining a regular siege. Let me remind you that the right of sanctuary is inviolable and not even the King himself can set it aside. And secondly . . . the best way to make a mortal enemy of Philippe of Burgundy would be to hand Madame de Brazey over to her charming husband."

"You are impossible, Ermengarde," the Abbot said sharply, shrugging his shoulders. "A siege, indeed! How you run on!"

What the Abbot had dismissed as one of Ermengarde's fantasies soon began to take on the colors of stern reality. When the ringing of the Angelus brought the monks back from their work in the fields, lining up in pairs beneath the Roman arches of the cloister to intone a hymn to the glory of God, the hour when the monkish gatekeeper clanged shut the massive Abbey gates with a noise like thunder and Ermengarde, Catherine and Sara were on their way to the chapel for evening prayers, a fearsome cavalcade galloped into Saint-Seine and thundered up to the gates of the Abbey itself.

It consisted of a troop of brigands, all armed to the teeth. They carried long lances, massive broadswords and battle axes, and rode on heavy chargers accustomed to carrying a hundred pounds of armor over and above the weight of their riders. The men were an evil-looking lot and clearly belonged to one of those roving bands of robbers whose services were so easily procured at that time if one were well supplied with the necessary écus. . . . Gallows-birds, all of them, knowing no law but the law of plunder and gold, men whose crimes were written in every line of their coarse and brutal faces. Their leather tunics, reinforced with steel plates at vulnerable spots, showed traces of dried blood and scorch marks, and their stout steel helmets were covered with dents, but they were a formidable

and terrifying looking troop and the people of Saint-Seine retreated hastily into their homes as they swept through the town,
barricading themselves in and feverishly entreating God to
spare them from the wrath of these bandits. The men had appeared so suddenly that there had not been time to sound the
alarm and take refuge within the Abbey walls as had been the
custom in former times, the days when the Great Companies
roamed the land, leaving a wake of murder, rape and arson
behind them. The idea of a surprise attack had been a clever
one. The people of Burgundy in general, and Saint-Seine in
particular, had enjoyed such a long period of peace and prosperity thanks to their Duke's wise rule, that they had forgotten
the sure safety route of former days. The peasants hid behind
their narrow windows and peered out at the ferocious troops
clattering by in the twilight.

Two men rode at their head. One of them was dressed in
much the same fashion as the rest of the band, but his arrogant
expression and the gold chain hanging on his breast proclaimed
him to be their leader. The other man was Garin, wearing black
from head to foot as was his habit. With his hood pulled down
over his eyes and a black mantle enveloping him from the neck
down, he rode on without so much as a glance around him. But
what terrified the monk-gatekeeper as the troop rode up towards the Abbey, was the sight of the two prisoners being
dragged along by the two horses in front. The ghastly remains
of what had once been a man and woman hung, chained and
barely alive, from the saddles of Garin and his companion.
They had both been treated with savage cruelty. The woman's
long, blonde hair was streaked with blood and dirt and barely
covered her naked body which was striped with whip marks.
The white hair and beard of the other victim showed that he
was an old man. His long, black robe was tattered and showed
his skinny legs and bare feet. His limbs bore the marks of
branding with hot irons. Long streaks of dried blood traced
strange patterns on the faces of the man and the woman. Their
eyes had been put out. . . .

To the gatekeeper's horror, the dreadful band came to a halt
outside the Abbey gates. He ran as fast as his legs would carry
him to warn the Abbot who was reading evening prayers in the
chapel. The Abbot left the chapel immediately, followed by
Ermengarde, Catherine, Sara and several of the monks.

When they reached the battlements overlooking the main
gates, Ermengarde seized Catherine brusquely and pushed her
behind her out of sight, leaving Jean de Blaisy to go forward
alone. It was almost dark, but some of the brigands carried

137

torches which threw a lurid glow over the riders and their wretched prisoners.

"What do you want?" the Abbot demanded harshly. "What is the meaning of these armed men and this mutilated man and woman?"

"What is the significance of these closed gates, my Lord Abbot?" replied a voice which Catherine recognized with a thrill of terror. Fascination got the better of fear; she craned her neck till she could just glimpse Garin's pale face in the torchlight through the gap between Ermengarde's corpulent form and the merlon on which she was leaning. From there her gaze slid to the two blinded captives who had been allowed to fall to the ground, more dead than alive. She recognized them in spite of the blood smeared over their features, and gave a strangled cry. It was Pâquerette and Gervais! Quick as lightning, Sara clapped a hand over Catherine's mouth and pulled her back with one powerful arm. An eerie silence had fallen over the village and the valley. The Abbot's calm voice sounded resonantly through the quiet air:

"My gates are always closed at sundown," he said. "Are you such a miscreant that you have forgotten the ways of the houses of God?"

"I have not forgotten them. I merely wish to enter."

"For what purpose? Do you seek sanctuary? I find this hard to believe, surrounded as you are by armed men. Men must relinquish their weapons before crossing the threshold to the house of God. If you wish to enter, Garin de Brazey, you may do so . . . alone!"

Brazey's companion spoke next. His voice rasped like a file over Catherine's high-strung nerves.

"Why should you refuse me entry, monk? I am the Bègue de Pérouges!"

"I know," Jean de Blaisy replied tonelessly. "I recognized you. I know the trail of blood you leave wherever you have passed—strangled women, dead children and villages in flames have cried witness against your wrongdoings to Heaven these many years past. You are a pestilent vermin and pestilent vermin do not enter here. Lay aside your arms, cover your head with ashes and ask God's forgiveness. Then, and only then, will you enter here. I recognize your handiwork in those two pitiful wretches you have dragged along with you. If you want me to listen to you, you must first allow my fathers to take care of them."

The other man laughed coarsely in reply.

"You are wasting your pity, monk. Those are two sorcerers

138

and devil-worshippers; and traitors, to boot. They deserve to burn."

But Garin was growing impatient with this discussion. He raised his voice, standing up in his stirrups.

"Enough of this chit-chat, Sir Abbot! I have come to claim my wife, Catherine de Brazey, who has taken refuge in your Abbey. Return her to me and we will pass on our way. I even promise that I will painlessly and swiftly dispatch these two wretches who hid her and brought her here."

"Painlessly?" the Abbot repeated scornfully. "Have you taken leave of your senses, Lord Treasurer? Do you suppose your master will forgive your joining up with that ruffian there? And what right have you to order me about like a servant? You seem to forget who I am. My blood is nobler than yours and I am a man of God, so be on your way. Your wife arrived here in a pitiable state, more dead than alive, as a result of your treatment of her. She has claimed the right of sanctuary which is granted to all unfortunates, whoever they may be, who present themselves at the gate of an Abbey, and I have granted her that right. She will not leave this place except of her own free will."

In spite of the horror and dismay which Pâquerette's and Gervais's terrible fate had aroused in her, Catherine could not help admiring the Prior's haughty countenance. His tall, thin, black shape stood out against the ruddy torchlight glow. He stood at the brink of the abyss where the malignant faces of Garin, Bègue de Pérouges and their followers looked like so many demons spewed forth from hell. He was like some dark angel at the Day of Judgment, confronting the sinners, his great wings outspread as he rejects some and welcomes others.

"I am the Resurrection and the Life!" Sara murmured solemnly, and Catherine realized that her old friend was experiencing much the same reaction as herself. As for Ermengarde, her face radiated pride and joy. She was proud of the Abbot. He spoke with the voice of her ancient and noble family, without anger, but not without arrogance.

"Listen well, Jean de Blaisy," Garin cried, his voice soaring eerily to a high falsetto scream in his fury. "I give you till dawn to reflect. We will pitch camp here and your village will come to no harm if you decide to be reasonable . . . but only till dawn. At dawn, either you open your gates to let my wife through or we shall raze the town to the ground, set fire to the houses and lay siege to your Abbey."

This was more than Ermengarde could bear. She sprang forward and the glare of the torches lent her a fiercely impressive air.

139

"Set fire to a village and besiege an abbey? And who do you suppose will protect you from the wrath of Philippe of Burgundy when he learns of these great deeds? You don't imagine he will leave your house or your château standing, your lands intact or your vile head upon your shoulders, do you? Whoever attacks the Church with fire or sword signs his own death warrant."

Garin gave a loud laugh.

"I might have expected you to be there, Dame Ermengarde. 'Struth, you take great care of your master's amors! There's a fine role for a Châteauvilain—a procuress!"

"No worse than butchery for a de Brazey!" Ermengarde answered coolly. "But I was forgetting—you aren't a *real* de Brazey! A packmule will never make a war-horse!"

Even in the ruddy glare of the torchlight, Garin's face seemed to the watching Catherine to turn green. A dreadful twitch appeared in his scarred cheek. He was about to swear a dreadful oath when Bègue de Pérouges intervened:

"Enough talk! You heard what Brazey said, monk! Either you hand the turtle dove over to us, or there'll be nothing but a heap of smoking ashes left of your town tomorrow, and your monastery will be reduced to a heap of rubble. And I promise you I'll hang you with my own hands from your own Church cross! You have my word for it. Now let us go and pitch camp for the night."

"One moment!" Jean de Blaisy cut in. "I accept your challenge. Tomorrow at dawn I will inform you of my decision. But there is something I must do now. . . ."

He withdrew, murmured something to a monk who had been standing beside him, and after motioning to Ermengarde to remain where she was, started to descend the spiral staircase.

"What is he going to do?" Catherine asked.

Ermengarde looked puzzled. She looked down with a preoccupied frown at the menacing-looking band drawn up on the sloping ground outside the monastery walls. Feeling anxious, no doubt, for her cousin's safety, she called to the leader of the ten men-at-arms who had escorted her on her ride thither the day before. The officer returned a moment later with his men. They were all carrying large crossbows and, at a sign from the Countess, they posted themselves along the battlements, bows drawn back ready to let fly.

"I think I know what my cousin intends to do," she explained to Catherine quite calmly. "I'm just taking a few precautions."

Just then, from below their feet, came the chanting of a religious hymn followed by the creaking of the Abbey gates as they were swung open. With one accord, the three women

140

craned forward over the battlements. None of the men below were looking in their direction. They seemed dumbstruck by the sight which had just met their eyes. Three black-robed monks were coming out of the Abbey chanting *"Libera me de sanguinibus, Deus, Deus salutis mea et exultabit lingua mea justitiam tuam! . . ."* in full-throated chorus. The one in the middle carried a large oaken cross. Behind them, crucifix in hand and mitre on his head, covered from head to foot by a great gold-embroidered cope, walked the Abbot. . . . His appearance was so majestic in the splendor of his ecclesiastical raiment, that, one after another, the brigands began to dismount, as if under the influence of magic. Some of them fell on their knees. Only Garin and Bègue de Pérouges remained in their saddles. But they might have been changed to stone; the Abbot and his cross advanced towards them, and passed close by them without either of them moving at all.

From the top of the wall, Catherine watched, deeply moved, as Jean de Blaisy bent over the pitiful wreckage which had once been a man and a woman and whose sufferings were still not at an end. Now that the monks' chanting and the men's shouts were stilled, their faint groans were audible. The Abbot's thin hand rose and traced the sign of the Cross on their pain-twisted faces. Catherine could see his lips framing the words of absolution and his hand raised in the gesture of pardon through eyes that were misted with tears. Then the Abbot moved away. A man stepped out of the shadows behind him. He wore a leather apron and carried a knife. It was soon over. The blade rose twice, flashed, and plunged in a heart thrust. The moans stopped. The calvary of the little sorceress and the tall old man of the forest was ended.

Without a backward look at the executioner, the Abbot of Saint-Seine made his way slowly back towards the Abbey. The great gates closed behind him. Ermengarde's archers lowered their bows. A great silence fell over the threatened village and the valley in its cloak of darkness. When they got back to their rooms, Catherine was weeping unrestrainedly and great tears rolled down the Countess's cheeks.

"If they had dared to touch a single hair on the Abbot's head," she said grimly, "they wouldn't have lived long enough to boast of it! One of those arrows was destined for Garin and another for his worthy companion!"

For Catherine that night was one of anguish and weeping. She was appalled by the danger which her presence had brought to the village and this Abbey. She even thought, in her despair, of giving herself up when the appointed hour arrived and putting an end to fears and flight once and for all. Garin was certain to win in the end, so what was the point of all this suffering meanwhile? Why should other innocent people be subjected to these dangers? The terrible deaths of Gervais and Pâquerette, tortured, blinded and dragged along like animals, filled her with horror and remorse. Pâquerette had betrayed her, it was true, but before that she had taken her in and cared for her. Jealousy might have led her astray, but she had not merited so cruel a punishment. Catherine did not want to see the houses of Saint-Seine in flames. She was determined that blood must not be shed for her sake; she was going to her husband. To tell the truth, she had been so bruised and shattered by recent events, that existence held very little charm for her any more.

Ermengarde, however, was keeping a watchful eye on her. The Countess sensed what was passing through the young woman's mind and she stuck to her like a shadow. When Catherine at last begged her to let her go, she lost her temper.

"My dear, you are no longer the only thing at issue in this business. In fact, I hope you won't be offended if I say that you are of only secondary importance now. If Garin had presented himself at the Abbey gates quite peaceably, asked to speak to my cousin and politely asked for his wife back, Jean could not have refused to let him see you at least, and this interview would have decided what happened next. But instead of that Garin comes armed to the teeth, in the company of a notorious bandit, roaring threats and insults. That's what we cannot tolerate. Our honor is at stake. One doesn't lightly threaten a Blaisy, any more than a Châteauvilain."

"But what's going to happen now?" Catherine moaned, tears running down her face.

"To be perfectly honest, I don't know. We'll have to wait and see. The monastery walls are solid enough to withstand a siege. And I did not observe anything in the nature of a siege engine out there. No battering-rams, or *trébuchets,* and certainly not a single tower on wheels. In principal, therefore, we are quite safe as long as the gates hold. The problem is, how to defend the villagers against the fury of these devils. . . ."

"The only possible solution is for me to go. . . ."

"Do stop saying the same thing over and over again," Ermengarde said wearily. "I've told you that you are to remain here; even if I have to lock you up myself. Let the Abbot do as he thinks fit. You saw how well he handled the situation earlier on. Anyway, there will be plenty of time for you to discuss things with Garin at dawn . . . but from the battlements. Until then, you had better stay quiet. I take it that neither of us will be able to sleep a wink tonight, so we may as well do the sensible thing and go along to the chapel to pray. My intuition

142

tells me that giving yourself up to Garin would make no difference anyway—these people have smelled blood!"

These arguments were unanswerable, so Catherine bowed her head and followed Ermengarde. As they directed their steps towards the Abbey's huge and still unfinished church, they saw that the place was seething with activity. Great fires had been lit in the outer courtyard to heat up massive iron pots into which relays of monks were emptying jars of oil and melting pitch. They were bringing all the pitchforks and scythes out of the barns, and hammers and sharp-edged tools from the workshops. Jean de Blaisy came and went in the midst of all this activity, his robe tucked into his belt, revealing high boots and golden spurs. Before taking orders, he had been initiated into one of the orders of chivalry. The Abbot of Saint-Seine was a different man! The blood of the warrior race from which he was descended was stirred to action by the threat of attack. If Bègue de Pérouges and Garin de Brazey dared to attack the house of God with fire and sword, they would be met by fire and sword! The man of prayer had been transformed into a man of war, and his monks, attracted, no doubt, by the prospect of a violent and dangerous interruption to their everyday lives of work and meditation, joined in with enthusiasm. There was not one of those doughty Burgundians dedicated to the service of the Lord who did not feel the soul of a Knight Templar stirring within him . . . the courtyard was full of shaven heads and black robes which had been tucked up like the Abbot's, displaying muscular legs and large feet which the wearing of sandals had made broad and flat. After Matins—for Jean de Blaisy did not intend God to be forgotten in the excitement—the Abbot summoned an impromptu council of war at which he informed the various dignitaries of the monastery of the remaining precautions to be taken. Naturally, however, the three women were not present.

Catherine knelt in the chapel beside Ermengarde who was praying fervently with her head in her hands, and tried without success to turn her thoughts towards God. She was tormented by an insurmountable fear of what was about to happen. The vague noises and sounds which reached her through the thick church walls only intensified her terror. She knew that the Abbey could be defended, that its walls were solid and that Bègue de Pérouges would find it difficult to breach them. Jean de Blaisy was a resolute man and his monks were brave and courageous. But she couldn't help agonizing over the fate of the luckless villagers! She sensed the terror that must have struck them when they realized that they were defenseless against the bloodthirsty robber band. They had seen a sample

143

of their atrocious cruelty in the bloody treatment meted out to Gervais and Pâquerette, and they must be wondering what lay ahead for them after daybreak. And all because of a woman who had run away from her husband. How many of them, as they were murdered by fire or steel, would die cursing her name?

Catherine suddenly felt that she ought to see what the bandits were doing. Suppose they had broken their word and already begun attacking the villagers? One never knew how far people like that could be trusted. She glanced at Ermengarde. The Countess was praying with such fervor and concentration that she seemed oblivious to what was going on around her. She knelt with her head in her hands, seeing nothing. Catherine was able to steal quietly away without her turning around. She began to walk away down the nave, still not taking her eyes off her friend. The church door had been left half open. She slipped through it and observed that the Abbey gates were in darkness, despite the great fires which had been lit here and there in the outer courtyard. The Abbot was still in his own quarters, planning the defense of the Abbey. The monks were busy round the fires attending to the bubbling cauldrons of oil and pitch. Their shapes were thrown into weird relief by the dancing flames. No one paid any attention to her.

Catherine crossed the courtyard rapidly towards the stone steps of the tower and started to climb them. . . . There was no one upon the battlements, but down below in the village square, there was an unusual bustle of activity. The brigands had started several fires going and some of them were sitting round them now, eating and drinking. Catherine could see Garin and Bègue de Pérouges seated by the largest of these fires, deep in conversation. The majority of the robber band, however, were hard at work and when she saw what they were doing, Catherine gave an exclamation of horror.

They had collected a great pile of wooden planks—evidently stolen from the Saint-Seine carpenter—and nails, and with these they were busy nailing up the doors and windows of the village houses so that the occupants would not be able to get out. Others were on their way back from the other end of the village carrying great armfuls of straw and kindling which they stacked outside the houses as their companions finished sealing them up. Catherine's blood ran cold. She knew only too well what would happen next morning when the Abbot refused to surrender her. It only needed a couple of torches to be thrown into these heaps of straw and dry wood, and the whole village would go up in flames in an instant. The unfortunate villagers trapped inside would be burnt alive along with their children, livestock and modest possessions.

Catherine suddenly realized that she could not bear this. If escaping from Garin meant that she had to watch the devastation of this peaceful countryside and listen to the screams of innocent people being sacrificed, she knew she would never be able to sleep peacefully again. Certainly, Ermengarde's arguments were sound. And she might be right in saying that handing Catherine over would not necessarily save the threatened village, but Catherine felt this was a risk she must take. Even if it only meant her dying along with the rest, that was still preferable. At least she would be able to die then without despising herself. Her mind made up, Catherine ran down the narrow stairway. She had noticed a small door near the Abbey stables which led directly out into the fields. It was in a recess in the walls, and not particularly noticeable, so the Abbot might well have overlooked it when he was stationing Ermengarde's men-at-arms at all the entrances to the Abbey. Slipping along in the shadow of the walls so as to escape observation, Catherine hurried towards the stable buildings. She was so bent on self-sacrifice that she did not even feel afraid. What she felt was a sort of exaltation, like that felt by sacrificial victims offered up on the altars of heathen gods. She would die so that others might live. . . .

She groped her way towards the door and found, as she had expected, that it was not guarded, though it was secured by a heavy iron bar held in place by metal loops. It was not going to be an easy job sliding it out. Catherine began trying to lever it out of the sockets. By dragging on its latch with all her strength, so that her hands were chafed and raw, she managed to move it slightly. Slowly, ever so slowly, it began to slide out of its sockets. Her hands were bleeding and her face running with sweat by the time she finally laid the bar on the ground. There was nothing to stop her going out now, and once outside the walls, she would seek out Garin, throw herself at his feet if necessary, and humilate herself to appease his wrath. . . .

She hauled the heavy door towards her. But just then a hand emerged from the shadows and pushed the door sharply back into place.

"It is expressly forbidden for anyone at all to leave the Abbey," said a quiet voice. "By order of Monseigneur."

A monk carrying a large bundle of straw was standing before her. He must have been in the stable looking for the wherewithal to light a new fire while she was struggling with the door. . . . She saw a short, stocky figure in the gloom, topped by a shaven head encircled by a thin band of hair. The monk

145

calmly set down his bundle, picked up the iron bar and slid it back into place. Catherine gazed at him wildly.

"I beg you to let me go out," she implored. "I must go to those people out there. It is I whom they want! Once they have got me back, they will no longer have an excuse to attack the Abbey and the village will be safe! I can't let a thing like that happen. . . ."

But the monk was gently shaking his head. His voice was again mild and reasonable when he spoke:

"What our Abbot does is well done, my sister! And God's ways are inscrutable. If He has ordained that we should all perish tomorrow, and the village, too, then it must be that He has reasons which I cannot attempt to know. I, for my part, have made a vow of obedience, and when Monseigneur the Abbot orders, I humbly obey. Come, my child. . . ."

Picking up the straw under one arm, he took Catherine's arm with his free hand and drew her along with him. It was useless begging and beseeching him—the monk was obdurate. He was leading her towards the fires. Just then Ermengarde came rushing out of the church in a state of great agitation. When she caught sight of Catherine, she ran towards her.

"Where have you been? I've been worried to death. . . ."

"I stopped her just as she was about to leave through the stable door," said the tranquil little monk. "She wanted to go and give herself up. But the Abbot has forbidden anyone to leave, so I have brought her back. May I hand her over to you, now?"

"You may, Father, you may! And I promise you she won't escape from me again."

Ermengarde was in a fury. She refused to listen to a word of explanation from the tearful Catherine, but dragged her along towards the guest house, and locked them both into her room without speaking.

"Now I can relax," she said. "You will remain here!"

Catherine collapsed in a state of exhaustion onto the bed and sobbed inconsolably without in any way melting the heart of her gaoler who sat contemplating her, arms folded, without saying a word.

And so the night wore on.

When dawn broke, silvering the Abbey buildings with pale light, Catherine and Ermengarde left their apartments only to find that the peaceful surroundings of the day before had been completely transformed. All along the battlements, there were monks watching over smoking cauldrons whose stench polluted the clear morning air. Others were busy feeding the huge fires which blazed in the courtyard, or sharpening sickles and scythes on their whetstones. Still others were carrying hewn stones from the chantry of the church. And in the midst of all this activity the Abbot strode to and fro, hands behind his back, like a general inspecting his troops.

When the women appeared, he went straight over to them. "You ought to go back into the church," he said to them. "You will be safer there. I must go up onto the battlements now, to see what our attackers are doing."

"I shall go with you!" Catherine cried. "There is no longer any point in my hiding myself. And if you won't let me give myself up, at least let me speak to my husband. I might even be able to make him change his mind."

Jean de Blaisy shook his head with a sceptical smile.

"I doubt if you will succeed. If he were alone, you might have a chance ... but I know Bègue de Pérouges. He and his men have got wind of the sack of a rich Abbey. The pretext seems a good enough one to them—you will simply be wasting your breath."

"I prefer to waste it, nevertheless."

"As you wish. Come along then. . . ."

As on the previous evening, the three of them, for Ermengarde had no intention of letting Catherine out of her sight (Sara was helping the apothecary brother make dressings and poultices in the monastery kitchen), went up to the battlements and glanced around at the village from where they could hear sounds of jingling armor and oaths.

The red sun now showing above the curve of the hillside where the Abbey buildings stood, revealed the preparations made by Bègue de Pérouges's men. They had finished their devilish night's work—all the doors were nailed up and the houses half hidden by piles of straw and firewood. Some of the bandits were standing beside the houses holding blazing torches. Their positions left no doubt as to their intentions. The rest of them were grouped round a mammoth wooden beam which they had found, Heaven knew where. Garin and his acolyte were on horseback. They were making their way slowly towards the closed Abbey gates. The Lord Treasurer wore armor over his black clothes and it was hard to say which of the two—he or Bègue de Pérouges—cut the more sinister figure. He glanced up at the battlement, saw the Abbot standing there and smiled.

"Well, my Lord Abbot, what is your reply?" he asked calmly. "Are you going to give me back my wife, or do you want a fight? As you see, we have taken a few wise precautions!"

Before Jean de Blaisy could answer, Catherine stepped for-

147

ward. She slipped between the Abbot and the battlements and cried out:

"For God's sake, stop this cruel game, Garin! Haven't you shed enough blood? Why should all these innocent people die because of our disputes? Doesn't it occur to you how hateful and unjust all this is?"

"I was wondering," Garin said with a sarcastic grin, "how long it would be before you showed yourself. If there is anyone to blame over this business, it is you and not me. I'm your husband and it is your duty to follow me instead of fleeing. . . ."

"You know perfectly well why I've run away from you. You know that I do it to save my own life and my child's, and protect my own freedom. If you hadn't treated me so cruelly, I should never have left you . . . but all is not yet lost. I do not ask anything for myself, but will you give me your word that if I return to you, you will spare this town and this monastery?"

Before Garin could answer, Bègue had come forward.

"Come out first," he growled, "and then we'll see. . . . I don't much like having my time wasted. . . ."

The Abbot pulled Catherine back to safety.

"You are wasting your time and trouble," he said. "They want to attack, and you would only perish without saving a soul. Don't you understand. . . ?"

Catherine turned to Ermengarde in despair and saw, to her amazement, that the Countess was smiling beatifically. She might not have been present at the scene which had just taken place. She stood with her head thrown back and a delighted expression on the face, apparently listening to something. . . .

"Oh, Ermengarde," Catherine cried reproachfully. "How can you stand there and smile when men are going to die?"

"Listen!" Ermengarde exclaimed, ignoring her question. "Can't you hear anything?"

Catherine strained her ears. A muffled, distant, but unmistakable sound reached her from the plain. It needed sharp ears to hear it, but Catherine heard it quite distinctly.

"I can't hear anything," the Abbot murmured.

"Well, I can! We must play for time, cousin. Parley with them as long as you can!"

The Abbot obeyed without quite knowing why. He stepped up to the battlements again and began to exhort the bandits to spare an innocent village and the Lord's house. But they heard him out with obvious impatience and Catherine realized that words alone would not restrain these men much longer; the desire for blood and looting was too strong. . . .

A furious voice came from below. It was Bègue de Pérouges.

"Enough Paternosters! We haven't come here to listen to a sermon! You won't give up the girl—so we attack!"

Catherine's horrified scream as the first mound of straw and firewood was set alight was drowned in another cry, but this time of triumph, from Ermengarde.

"Look!" she cried, one arm outflung in the direction of Dijon. "We are saved!"

At her cry, everyone, including the bandits, turned round. A large body of armed horsemen rode into view, sweeping down from the plateau towards Saint-Seine. The sun glinted off their armor, helmets and lances. They were led by a knight whose helmet was topped by a crest of white plumes. Almost fainting with joy, Catherine recognized the colors of the pennant fluttering on his lance.

"Jacques . . . Jacques de Roussay! And the ducal guard!"

"They have taken their time!" Ermengarde grumbled from behind her. "It was lucky that I had the bright idea of forwarding the Abbot's letter to that young idiot—I had a feeling something might go wrong!"

Their ordeal at an end, the group standing on the battlements could stand and watch what followed. Bègue de Pérouges was a man of courage, that could not be denied. It never occurred to him to turn tail and flee before the formidable relief force now advancing upon him. His men wheeled round and ranged themselves in battle order. Garin did likewise, drawing his sword. Seeing this, Catherine could not repress a warning cry:

"Don't fight, Garin! If you draw your sword against Monseigneur's guard, you are lost!"

She did not know what obscure feeling of pity prompted her to concern herself over the fate of the man who only desired her extinction. At all events, her pity was quite wasted. Garin merely shrugged haughtily and pricked his spurs, riding full tilt at the newcomers followed by the whole troop.

The struggle was fierce, but short. Roussay's numerical superiority was crushing. In spite of prodigious feats of arms on the part of the bandits, who fought with the desperate courage of men who know they can expect neither pity nor quarter from the enemy, they succumbed one by one to the blows of the Duke's men. The spectators on the Abbey walls watched the ferocious duel which was fought out between Jacques de Roussay and Bègue de Pérouges. Garin, meanwhile, was locked in combat with another horseman, wearing armor like the rest of the troop, but bare-headed. Catherine recognized Landry. . . .

The outcome was decided in a quarter of an hour. Roussay wounded and unhorsed his opponent and without a moment's delay hanged him from the nearest tree. A few minutes later, Garin surrendered, overwhelmed by superior numbers. . . .

While the soldiers of the Duke's guard busied themselves freeing the inhabitants of the village, unsealing their doors and windows, the Abbot gave orders for the Abbey gates to be thrown open, and descended in person to welcome the victors. Catherine did not dare follow. She stayed on the battlements with Ermengarde. Jacques de Roussay was climbing slowly up to the Abbey, his helmet under one arm. A little way off, two soldiers were helping Garin to climb back onto his horse, after tying his hands behind his back. The Lord Treasurer was quite passive. He seemed completely detached from what was going on and did not even glance round towards the monastery. This haughty behavior aroused a wild rage in Catherine. She had been so terrified, so sick, and two innocent people had perished in dreadful agony, but this implacable man did not seem in the least concerned about the evil he had done. A violent hatred seized her, leaving her with a bitter taste in her mouth and making her tremble. . . . If Ermengarde had not been standing silent and motionless beside her, she would have flung herself upon the prisoner and screamed her scorn and hatred at him. She felt a fierce joy at the thought that he had condemned himself, and that he would soon perish from his own criminal folly. She would have liked to flaunt this joy of hers before him. . . .

CHAPTER NINE

Garin's Secret

That same evening Jacques de Roussay left for Dijon, taking his prisoner with him. Garin was the responsibility of the Provost of Burgundy from now on and would be imprisoned as soon as he reached Dijon on charges of high treason, attempts on the security of the State, sacrilege and the attempted murder of his own wife; enough to send him to the scaffold several times over! Jacques de Roussay made no secret of that during his short interview with Catherine. In deciding to attack the Abbey, Garin had considerably aggravated the charges against himself. Landry's original instructions to the Captain of the Guard had merely been to ensure Catherine's safety and confine Garin to his own home.

"Unfortunately, I cannot give you permission to return to your own home just yet, Madame de Brazey," Jacques told Catherine. "As a State prisoner, your husband will have all his property placed under seal. Couldn't you return to your mother's house?"

"She will stay with me," Ermengarde interrupted. "Do you suppose I intend to expose her to the tender attentions of the old fishwives of the Notre-Dame quarter? There will be many who will rejoice at the Lord Treasurer's downfall. I am not certain that Catherine would be completely safe in a bourgeois household, but with me I know she will be!"

Roussay had no objections. He gave Catherine permission to stay in the Châteauvilian mansion. The young captain's attitude towards Catherine had grown oddly distant. His trouble was that he no longer knew quite how to treat her—as his master's mistress, or as a criminal's wife. He confided his perplexities in secret to Ermengarde.

"I don't know which side I'm on any more, Countess. Monseigneur Philippe gave me orders to protect Madame de Brazey and prevent her husband harming her, but he knows nothing about all these recent happenings. He is still in Paris and I cannot help wondering how a man as pious as he is will react to the news of Brazey's attack on the Abbey! He will be outraged, and I fear that his wrath will fall on the young woman as well— he may believe her to be partly responsible, an accomplice even. . . ."

"You must be out of your mind, young man! Have your forgotten the Duke's deep love for Catherine? She and she alone rules his heart!"

Jacques de Roussay scratched his head unceremoniously. He was clearly embarrassed. He looked away awkwardly.

"The thing is . . . I'm not so sure of that any more, either. They say that he was paying court to the beautiful Countess of Salisbury in Paris. You know him as well as I do. He is fickle and passionately fond of women. I find it hard to imagine him being faithful to one woman alone. Dame Catherine is in a very awkward situation, and her looks are not improved by her condition. I am afraid. . . ."

"You are afraid for your own future! You are afraid of setting a foot wrong, isn't that so?" Ermengarde added sarcastically. "Indeed you are somewhat deficient in courage for a military man! Well, I may not be a soldier, but I have plenty of courage for all that: I propose to take Catherine under my roof and my protection. If the Duke objects, I shall know what to say to him! You may do what you like with de Brazey's property, but you will kindly bring Catherine's personal maid, and her Moorish doctor and his two slaves to me, along with all Madame de Brazey's personal possessions ... clothes, jewels and the like. There! And I shall take care of the rest. It shall never be said that a Châteauvilain does not know the meaning of friendship. And if Philippe tries to do any more harm to this poor child than he has already, he will find he has me to reckon with! And I don't believe in mincing my words!"

There was no more to be said; Roussay capitulated. The Countess, as he well knew, was quite capable of carrying out her threats, and treating the Duke like a naughty little boy. As he left Saint-Seine, the young captain thought to himself that he would not like to be in the Duke's shoes if he tried to cross swords with his terrible vassal. For his part, he would rather take on the entire Turkish army than Madame de Châteauvilain in a rage. . . .

Catherine and Ermengarde were to leave the Abbey the following day. Catherine was in much need of a good night's rest and the Countess thought it prudent to avoid returning to Dijon on the heels of Garin in his chains. They were climbing into their litter the next morning after having taken leave of the Abbot when Catherine, to her astonishment, saw Landry coming towards them. Since the end of the fight, she had seen very little of him. He had embraced her affectionately, but cut short her professions of gratitude and retired early to the cell which the Abbot had placed at his disposal. Catherine had attributed his extraordinary pallor and haggard face to the fatigue of the journey and the battle. But today he looked worse still.

"I have come to say farewell to you, Catherine," he said simply.

"Farewell? But, why? I thought you were accompanying us to Dijon."

He shook his head and turned away so that she should not see the tears in his eyes.

"No, I shall not be returning to Dijon. I am leaving the service."

There was a silence while Catherine tried to make sense of what Landry had just said.

"Leaving the Duke's Horse? You must be mad! Are you dissatisfied there? Has someone wronged you, then, or are you tired of serving Monseigneur Philippe?"

Landry shook his head. In spite of all his efforts, two great tears rolled down his brown cheeks. Catherine was thunderstruck. She had never seen him weep before. He always confronted life with such unshakable good humor, and an infectious *joie de vivre*.

152

"I don't want you to be unhappy!" she cried passionately. "Tell me what I can do to help you, now that you have saved my life for me!"

"I shall always be glad I rescued you," Landry said gently. "But there is nothing you can do for me, Catherine. I am going to stay here in this Abbey. I have already asked the Abbot to receive me as a monk and he has agreed. He is a man after my own heart. I shall be proud to obey him."

"You are going to become a monk? *You?*"

Catherine could not have been more surprised if a thunderbolt had fallen from a clear blue sky. Landry, the old, cheerful Landry dressed in the gloomy, dark serge of a Benedictine monk! Landry with his head shaven, kneeling night and day on the cold stone floor of the chapel, tilling the soil and ministering to the poor! Landry, who loved drinking and women and roistering! Landry, who used to scoff at Loyse in the old days when she talked of entering a convent!

"Funny, isn't it?" the young man added, with a wan smile. "But it is the only life I want. You see . . . I loved Pâquerette and I think she loved me, too. I always hoped that one day I might be able to persuade her to change her ways and drop all that silly witchcraft nonsense and make a good woman of her, an honest housewife with a brood of children around her. I meant to take her away from that cursed place. She was a strange creature, but I think we understood each other. Now she's gone. . . ."

Landry's weary, discouraged gesture suddenly overwhelmed Catherine with a crushing sense of guilt. She felt dreadfully ashamed all of a sudden that she herself should still be alive after unwittingly being the cause of so much suffering. Was her own worthless, useless life worth spilling so much blood for? She hung her head.

"It's my fault," she cried, stricken. "It's my fault that she's dead! Oh, Landry, how could I have brought so much misfortune on you, of all people?"

"Hush! You have nothing to blame yourself for. Pâquerette herself was responsible for what happened to her. If she had not committed the unpardonable crime of betraying you to Garin in her jealousy, nothing would have happened. It was right that she should be punished, though not in that barbaric fashion! Now that she is no longer here, I find that I only want peace and solitude. But you still have a long and splendid road ahead of you. . . ."

Catherine's tears stopped abruptly.

"Do you really think so?" she cried fiercely. "What more can I hope for? My husband is going to die, I shall be ruined and you are going to bury yourself away in a monastery all because of me. The man I love despises me. I bring bad luck, I am accursed, accursed. . . . You should shun me. . . ."

She was on the verge of hysteria. Ermengarde sensed this and waved Landry away, while she persuaded the shivering Catherine to climb into the litter.

"Come on, child. Stop tormenting yourself. The boy has had a nasty shock. But he is still young and there is still time for him to change his mind and regain his appetite for life. They don't take their final vows overnight. You may rely on my cousin Jean—if the boy hasn't got a real vocation, he will be able to convince him of the fact later on."

These wise words had a calming effect on Catherine. Ermengarde was right. Landry might not remain in the monastery all his life, but for the time being, it was the best place for him, a great repose where a soul might find itself again and discharge its venom and gall. Unprotestingly, she allowed herself to be borne away.

The great Abbey gates swung open to allow the litter to pass, escorted by Sara, perched on a mule lent by the Abbot, and a few men-at-arms lent by Jacques de Roussay in addition to the men of Ermengarde's own escort. In a little while the two women and their cortège were climbing the road up to the plateau. A gentle sun warmed the scene. Below them, the rooftops of Saint-Seine glittered for a moment beneath their frail plumes of smoke and then they, too, disappeared as the procession reached a bend in the road. The masons were back at work, perched on the scaffolding which surrounded the square tower of the monastery church and whistling gaily, the danger which had threatened them and their homes already forgotten.

That evening they reached Dijon, entering the town through the Guillaume gate. As they passed by the castle, Catherine looked away with a shudder. It was there that Jacques de Roussay had taken his prisoner the day before. Garin was somewhere behind those grim and forbidding walls with their few slit windows and loopholes. Catherine thought to herself with mingled grief and anger that it was the marriage arranged by Philippe which had brought the Lord Treasurer to such a pass.

But Catherine was wrong. Jacques de Roussay had not taken his prisoner to the old bastion which served to guard the fortified walls. Instead, he had escorted him to the Vicomte-Mayeur's prison, whose dark and dreadful dungeons were the foundations of an ancient Roman tower, known as the Tournote, which stood behind Dijon's town hall. This building, christened the Monkey House because of the bas-relief carved

154

above the door which showed a monkey playing with a ball, stood between two seignorial mansions, that of the La Trémoille family on one side and that of the Châteauvilains on the other. Thus, without realizing it, Catherine had come to stay only a stone's throw from the spot where her husband was imprisoned.

She was not long kept in ignorance of this fact. The day after her return, the town criers began patrolling the streets publishing Garin's crimes abroad and announcing his forthcoming trial and judgment by the council presided over by the Vicomte-Mayeur, Philippe Mâchfoing, the Duke's body-servant, counsellor and foster-brother.

This announcement gave Catherine a feeling of bitter satisfaction mingled with frustration. She hated Garin with all her heart, but, try as she might, she could not guess what feelings could have driven him to such mad, desperate actions. Garin had always rejected her so violently that she found it hard to believe that he could be jealous. And yet, how else could one explain his crazy rages after he had learnt that she was pregnant? Catherine recalled the evening when she had gone to his room to seduce him. How could she ever have supposed him indifferent after the way he had lost his head on that occasion? He *was* jealous, demented by jealousy, even . . . and yet he had never made her his own. The enigma which lay at the root of Garin's behavior both exasperated and tormented her.

Towards the end of this first day she saw a little caravan headed by Jacques de Roussay making its way towards the Châteauvilain mansion. It was composed of mules laden with chests and coffers. Perrine, Abou-al-Khayr and his two black slaves were on horseback. The Captain was obeying Ermengarde's orders promptly and the noble dame condescended to thank him.

"What about the house?" she asked. "What are you doing about that?"

"The town clerk is fixing the Vicomte-Mayeur's and the Provost's seals on it. There is no one in it now, and nothing in it can be touched before sentence has been passed. The same applies to the Château de Brazey and all Garin's other possessions."

The young man avoided looking at Catherine as he spoke; she was standing beside Ermengarde, a very upright figure in a black velvet dress—she was already in mourning. He finally took his courage in both hands and turned towards her, looking her straight in the eyes.

"I am terribly sorry, Catherine. . . ." he said.

She shrugged and gave a sad little smile.

"There is nothing you can do, my poor friend. You have already done so much for me. How could I possibly be angry with you? When will the sentence be passed?"

"A week from now. The Duke is still in Paris and Nicolas Rolin is with him. He was a friend of your husband's and might perhaps have come to his assistance. . . ."

Ermengarde shrugged contemptuously.

"I wouldn't count on that! Nicolas Rolin would never help a man who had placed himself in such a position, not even his own brother. Garin has incurred the Duke's displeasure . . . he no longer knows Garin. It's as simple as that."

Jacques de Roussay did not answer. He knew that Ermengarde was speaking the truth and he did not wish to raise false hopes in Catherine. As far as he and the rest of the town were concerned there could be no possible doubt as to the outcome of the trial. It would mean death by execution of the Lord Treasurer, the confiscation of all his property, his name struck from the armorial register, his arms broken and, almost certainly, his house razed to the ground as his predecessor, Keeper of the Ducal Jewels, Philippe Jossequin's had been when he had become implicated in the murder at Montereau bridge and had subsequently been exiled to Dauphine where he died in wretched misery. It certainly did not seem to be a lucky office to hold!

When the Captain had departed, Ermengarde left Catherine with Abou-al-Khayr while Sara went off to help the chambermaids put away her mistress's things. The gipsy had returned to her old post, but this did not mean that Perrine had been relegated to her old position as bath attendant. It had been settled that the girl should share in the care of Catherine's dresses and jewels with Sara.

It was a long time since Catherine and her Arab friend had met. They remained for a moment without speaking. Then the doctor sat down in a large chair while Catherine went across to the fire to warm her cold hands.

"What a mess it all is!" she sighed. "First I almost lost my life through the madness of this man they gave me for a husband, and now here we are, both of us, with nowhere to live and all but regarded as criminals ourselves. If it were not for Ermengarde, I should be out in the street for people to point at, not even daring to go to my mother's house in case I placed her in danger. And all for what?"

"All because of the direst folly that Allah has allowed to insinuate itself into the blood and minds of men—because of love!" Abou-al-Khayr replied calmly, staring fixedly at the tips

156

of his fingers which he kept clasping and unclasping. Catherine whirled round to face him.

"Love? Are you trying to tell me that Garin loved me?"

"Yes, and you will see my point if you stop to think for a moment. Your husband was a man of considerable intelligence and strong character. A man of that stamp does not start behaving like an animal without good reason. He knew he was risking his fortune, his reputation, even his life . . . everything he has in fact lost, or is about to lose. And yet he committed these acts of madness. Love, or at least, jealousy, must be at the bottom of such irrational behavior."

"If Garin loved me," Catherine cried angrily, "he would have made me his wife in the flesh as well as in the sight of God. But he never touched me. In fact, he avoided me. . . ."

"And this is what you can't forgive him! By Mahomet, you are more of a woman than I took you for! You gave yourself to one man without loving him, you are angry with another for not having forced himself upon you . . . and yet all the time it is a third man whom you love. Truly, the sage spoke well when he said that there was more wisdom in the flight of a blind bird than in a woman's brain!" the Moor said bitterly.

Catherine was stung by the contempt in the doctor's voice. Angry tears rose to her eyes.

"It's not *that* I can't forgive!" she cried. "It's his hateful attitude towards me. First he throws me into his master's arms and then he does all he can to humiliate and destroy me. And I don't see why! You seem to have the secret of universal wisdom; tell me why my marriage was never consummated? And yet the man desired me, I have proof of that!"

Abou-al-Khayr shook his head. His smooth forehead was furrowed by anxious lines.

"What wise man can sound the secrets of a man's heart?" he said with a hopeless gesture. "If you want to know the explanation of your husband's behavior, why don't you go and ask him before he takes it with him into the grave? His prison is close by, and I have heard that the jailer, a man called Roussot, though a hard character, is also greedy and gold sings sweetly in his ears."

Catherine did not answer. She was standing by the fire gazing into the flames. The idea of finding herself face to face with Garin again made her shudder. She was afraid that her self-control might not be strong enough to prevent her anger and hatred of him bursting out. The little doctor was right, though. The only way to discover Garin's secret, if he had one and had not simply temporarily lost his reason, would be to ask him what it was. However, she would first have to overcome the

157

repugnance she felt at the notion of seeing him again. And this was her problem, no one else could resolve it for her.

A week later the Court convened by the Vicomte-Mayeur and aldermen foregathered in the Sainte-Chapelle cloister. The town magistrates preferred to assemble there rather than in the Monkey House where the nearness of the courtrooms to the grisly dungeons made the whole business somewhat squalid and meditation difficult. Moreover, the nature of the case before them seemed to require a privacy which would be hard to achieve in the council's small meeting chamber.

Garin's trial did not last long—only a day. He conceded all the charges against him and did not condescend to defend himself. Catherine had refused to appear. Though she bore no love towards her husband, the idea of giving evidence against him was repugnant to her. Ermengarde warmly approved this attitude.

"They can sentence him without your help quite well!" she assured her.

On the evening of the judgment, Jacques de Roussay came in person to inform Catherine of the sentence. Garin de Brazey had been sentenced to be hanged, despite his rank, for the crime of sacrilege which he had committed in attacking the Abbey. He was to be put to the torture before that, and dragged through the mire to the gallows at Morimont. His goods would be confiscated and his house and château razed to the ground. . . .

The two women received this terrible news in complete silence. Catherine gazed straight ahead of her, dry-eyed, seemingly changed to stone. Ermengarde shivered slightly and walked across to the huge fire whose crackling was the only sound in the immense room. Catherine spoke tonelessly:

"When will he be executed?"

"Tomorrow, towards midday. . . ."

The two women fell silent again and Jacques de Roussay fidgeted in his embarrassment. Finally he bowed and asked for permission to retire. Ermengarde motioned to him to leave the room. When the sound of his spurs clattering on the stone floor had died away in the distance, Ermengarde came over to Catherine, who still stood motionless.

"What are you thinking about, Catherine? What is going through your mind?"

The young woman turned slowly to face Ermengarde, the light of decision in her eyes.

"I must see him, Ermengarde. I must see him before . . ."

"Do you think an interview would do any good?"

"Not to him, perhaps, but to me!" Catherine cried. "I want to know! I want to understand! I can't let him slip out of my life without knowing the explanation for all this. I am going to the prison. The jailer can be bribed, so they tell me. He will let me talk to him."

"I'm going with you. . . ."

"I would prefer it if you didn't. You are quite involved enough in this affair already, Ermengarde. Let me go by myself. Sara can come with me and wait for me. . . ."

"Very well, then," Ermengarde said. She went across to a coffer which stood against the wall and took a fat leather purse from it which she handed to Catherine.

"Take this. I imagine you were planning to press one of your jewels into this man's paw, since you have nothing else. That would be a pity. You can pay me back later on."

Catherine accepted the purse gratefully and fastened it to her belt. Then she kissed her friend and went up to her room to collect a dark coat and find Sara.

A few minutes later, the two women, closely muffled in black cloaks, their faces masked, left the Hotel Châteauvilain and walked briskly across to the next-door building. It was quite dark and raining hard which meant that the street was deserted. Catherine entered the courtyard of the town hall followed by Sara. She slipped a gold piece into the hand of the drowsy guard, forcing herself not to look at the iron collar and the instrument for applying the strapado, both of which were permanently attached to the corner of the Hotel de la Trémoille and creaked softly in the wind. The guard awoke instantly at the sight of the gold and willingly escorted the two women to the far end of the courtyard which was enclosed by grim, windowless stone walls, with one small door at one corner.

"I want to see the jailer called Roussot," Catherine said.

A few moments later, Roussot emerged from the little door. He was a man of average height, but so broad as to be almost square, and dressed in stained, torn, leather garments. A filthy bonnet was perched on top of the lank, greasy locks which hung about his face. His long, muscular arms hung lower than most people's. The friendliest eye might have found difficulty in distinguishing the faintest spark of intelligence in his little grey eyes, but the sound of the gold chinking in Catherine's purse made them sparkle like candle flames. He threw the mutton bone he had been gnawing into a corner, wiped his mouth with the back of his hand and inquired obsequiously what he might do to be "of service to Madame."

"I want to see the prisoner who is to die tomorrow alone," she replied.

159

The man frowned and scratched his head, but several ducats glittered in the young woman's hand and Roussot had never seen so much yellow metal in his life. He nodded and picked up the bunch of keys at his belt with one hand while holding out the other for the lovely shiny coins.

"Very well. Follow me. But you mustn't stay too long. A friar will be coming towards daybreak to get him ready to kick the bucket. . . ."

He gave a loud guffaw, but Catherine's frozen face did not move. Leaving Sara to wait for her in the courtyard, she followed the jailer down a steep, damp staircase which spiralled down into the bowels of the earth. A gust of cold, damp, stale-smelling air hit her in the face. She took out her handkerchief and held it over her nose.

"Not all roses down here, eh?" Roussot chuckled.

The staircase plunged down below the foundations of the old Roman tower and the walls were streaked with moisture. They passed several doors fastened by immense padlocks. Catherine's throat tightened with a vague distress.

"Is it much further?" she asked in a strangled voice.

"No, we're almost there now. But we couldn't put an important prisoner like this one in any dungeon. It's the 'crot' for him. . . ."

"The 'crot'?"

"The ditch, if you prefer. Here we are!"

At this point the staircase came to an end. It opened into a sort of muddy cul-de-sac. At the far end there was a tiny door, so low that one could only enter it bent double. Iron bars, three fingers thick, reinforced the blackened, pitted, oak door. Roussot struggled to remove them and pushed open the door which creaked lugubriously. Then he lit a torch he had been carrying and handed it to Catherine.

"There! Now go in . . . but be quick about it! I shall wait on the stairs and come and tap on the door when it is time for you to leave."

Catherine nodded and stooped to go through the door. It was so low that she almost scorched her mask with the torch she was holding. It was like plunging into the unknown, entering this living tomb. Then she stood up and raised her torch to examine her surroundings.

"I am over here," said a calm voice which she recognized with a shiver.

She turned towards the voice and saw Garin. Hardened as she felt towards him, she could not repress a cry of horror. He was sitting at the far end of the filthy hole on a sodden mass of what must have been straw. The ground was covered with

160

stagnant pools of water. He was chained to the wall by an iron collar and belt and for even greater security, his feet and hands were shackled together. He had his back against the wall, almost unable to move. His black doublet was torn and revealed a dirty, ragged undershirt. His cheeks were covered with a grizzled beard; his hair had grown and it was matted with filth. He had lost the black bandage which he used to wear over his eye and Catherine saw his wound for the first time. Instead of an eye, there was a little black hole surrounded by puckered pink skin which contrasted strangely with his white face. Catherine stood looking at him by the light of her torch, too shocked to move. Garin's laugh made her jump.

"Are you having trouble recognizing me? I have no difficulty in knowing you, despite the mask you have covered your pretty face with, my dear Catherine."

His mocking tone reawakened all her anger against him. He was unchanged. Nothing, it seemed, could shake him. He retained that sarcasm of his and that exasperating air of superiority even in the most abject and degrading circumstances.

"Do not worry," she said harshly, "I recognize you, though I must confess that you are somewhat altered, Garin. . . . Who would guess that the rich and arrogant Garin de Brazey would ever be brought so low? What a reversal of events! Only a little while ago, it was I who was chained up in a dungeon as vile as this one, while you stood by and laughed! Now it's my turn to laugh as I look at you, with your hands and feet tied together, unable to hurt a fly. Tomorrow they will drag you through the town and hang you as they should have done long ago. . . ."

She fed her anger with these words, but a long sigh from the prisoner cut her short.

"Don't be vulgar, please," Garin said in a bored voice. "You are behaving like some fat housewife gloating over her husband when two of the town guard bring him in drunk. . . . If that's the best you can do after all I taught you, I must confess myself a failure. I hoped to make a great lady of you. . . . It seems I failed. . . ."

The cold, calculated disdain of these remarks was like a bucket of cold water on Catherine's anger. She was speechless for a moment. It was Garin who took the initiative. He had a faint smile at the corner of his mouth which twisted his scarred cheek. This calm, almost carefree, detachment of his astounded Catherine. She felt she would never succeed in understanding this man and yet, that was what she wished most of all—to understand.

"Did you come to see the state in which our good Duke's men had left me?" he inquired. "Ah, well, now you know. And

161

if I understand you aright, you are satisfied. In that case, my dear, say goodbye and leave me to my meditations. I have not much time left."

"Why, he is sending me away!" Catherine thought to herself. "He is dismissing me as though I were an untouchable or a leper." It was the way this man retained his arrogant manner in spite of his chains and his humiliating circumstances that was so hard to take, but she realized that if she gave rein to her exasperation he would not talk to her. So she went up to him quite calmly and sat down on a large stone which, with Garin's chains and fetters, was all the furniture the dungeon could boast of.

"No," she said in a low voice, as she drove her torch into the muddy ground beside her, "I haven't come to gloat over your sufferings. You have done me great harm and I dislike you for it. I think that is only human. . . . I have come only because I want you to explain. . . ."

"Explain what?"

"Everything! Our ridiculous marriage; the absurdity of our life together. Since we were married I have had the impression that I was living one of those strange, extravagant dreams where nothing is quite what it seems. Sometimes they give you the impression of being solidly real, you think you have got the truth . . . but then they change before your eyes, assuming the most grotesque and incomprehensible shapes. You are about to die, Garin, and I know nothing at all about you. Tell me the truth . . . the truth about yourself! Why was I never your wife in the flesh as well as in name? No . . . don't talk to me about the Duke! I am positive there was more between you than this humiliating transaction you told me of. I know . . . I feel it. There is something else; something I cannot understand; something which is poisoning my life!"

An unexpected emotion made her voice tremble. She looked at Garin. From where she was, all she could see of him was a stony profile, the intact half of his face, all of which seemed to be deep in thought.

"Answer me!" she begged.

"Take off your mask," he said gently. She obeyed and the silk felt suddenly wet as it slipped over her cheeks.

"You are crying!" Garin said, astonished. "Why is that?"

"I . . . I don't know. I can't really explain. . . ."

"It's probably better that you shouldn't. I can imagine your bewilderment—the questions you must have put to yourself. It must have been hard for you to understand this man who spurned your incredible beauty."

162

"I began to think I must displease you," Catherine said in a small, nervous voice.

"No, you didn't, and you were right not to. Because I have longed for you like a madman, like the chained man dying of thirst longs for the dripping pitcher placed near enough for him to see, but too far to reach. I would never have been on the verge of going mad with hate and fury if I hadn't desired you . . . and loved you so much!"

He spoke in an even, monotonous voice which affected Catherine more deeply than she cared to admit.

"Then, why did you keep refusing . . . both me and yourself?"

Garin did not answer at once. He sat for a while, his head bowed on his chest, as if meditating. Then he sat up again with the air of a man who has come to a decision.

"It's an old and rather unhappy tale, but you have a right to hear it. Almost thirty—twenty-eight, to be precise—years ago this month I was a hotheaded sixteen-year-old who thought of nothing but fighting and feats of arms and pretty girls. I was bursting with pride because I was to accompany the Comte de Nevers, the future Duke Jean, on a crusade, as his squire. You are too young to have heard of that mad adventure which attracted a whole army of hotblooded young French, German and even English knights to the Hungarian plains, where King Sigismund had been attacked by the Turkish infidels. Comte Jean and the young Maréchal de Boucicaut commanded this cavalcade of ten thousand men. A more brilliant or more foolhardy expedition I have never seen! The horses' trappings, the equipage was sumptuous; the average age was somewhere between eighteen and thirty and everyone, like myself, was delighted by the whole adventure. When the army left Dijon on 30 April 1396, for the Rhine, one might have thought we were on our way to some gigantic tournament. The cavalcade glittered with gold, silver, steel; silken pennants fluttered in the breeze, and everyone was going on at the tops of their voices about the great exploits they planned to perform, for their own glory and the honor of their ladyloves. I was like the rest. . . ."

"You mean that you . . . were in love?" Catherine asked.

"Yes . . . why not? Her name was Marie de la Chesnel. She was fifteen and blonde like yourself . . . not quite so blonde, perhaps, and surely less beautiful! Thus it was that we set out. I shall spare you the full account of this disastrous expedition, the inevitable outcome of our youth and inexperience. There was no discipline whatsoever. All any of us thought about was covering ourselves with fame and glory, without any regard for the common good—despite the bitter remonstrances of King

Sigismund of Hungary, who was appalled by the follies we were perpetrating. He had an advantage over us in that he knew his enemy, the infidel, whose courage and tenacity in war were both familiar to him. The Turks were commanded by their Sultan, Bayézid, whom they called Ildérim, which means Lightning. And he merited the name, believe me! His spahis and janissaries fell like a thunderbolt on the target he had chosen and, as often as not, took them completely by surprise. We encountered Bayézid Ildérim's troops before Nicopolis—and were completely routed. Not through lack of courage, because the knights of this lunatic army fought like heroes. Never before, perhaps, had such valor been seen under that burning sun. But when the eve of September 28 came, eight thousand Christians had been taken prisoner by the Sultan, three hundred of whom were knights of the oldest and most illustrious houses of France and Burgundy: Jean de Nevers and myself, Henri de Bar, the Counts d'Eu and de la Marche, Enguerrand de Coucy, the Maréchal de Boucicaut—almost everyone who had not been killed. But there were heavy losses on the Turkish side, too. We had killed so many of them that the Sultan was in a towering rage. The majority of the prisoners were massacred on the spot . . . and I have never forgotten the horror of that blood bath. It was only thanks to the protection of Comte Jean that my life was spared and I was sent with him to Brousse, Bayézid's capital. We were shut up in a fortress there to await the arrival of the immense ransoms which the Sultan demanded. We were there for many long months, time enough for my eye, which an arrow had put out, to heal. But the cruel lesson we had undergone had not succeeded in sobering us completely . . . not myself, at any rate. Imprisonment, the inactivity, weighed on me. I searched for ways to amuse myself. We had considerable freedom within the fortress itself and I took advantage of this to try and gain access to the womenfolk of the Bey who commanded the fortress—the impulse of a madman! I was surprised as I was trying to climb over a garden wall, seized, loaded with chains and brought before the Bey. He wanted to have my head cut off on the spot, but Comte Jean was informed of this in time to intercede. After a great deal of argument and persuasion, he prevailed upon them to spare my life, but I was delivered over to the executioner, nevertheless, to pay for the crime of which I had been guilty. When he had finished with me I was alive, but I was no longer a man! They tended my wound in the barbaric fashion used for the men destined to be guardians of the harem: they buried me in sand up to the neck for several days. I all but died of it, but it seems my hour had not yet come. I returned to France and my own people . . . and let Marie de Chesnel marry another man."

Silent, wide-eyed with horror, Catherine stared at her husband as if seeing him for the first time. There was no longer any anger in her, only an immense pity which welled up from the bottom of her heart towards this man whose sufferings she at last fully understood. A heavy silence replaced Garin's strangely calm, slow voice in the cell, broken only by the sound of water dropping from the dripping roof. A lump in her throat, Catherine struggled to find words which were neither foolish nor hurtful, for she sensed in Garin a raw and quivering sensitivity. It was she, however, who first broke the silence, speaking in a voice which was controlled, but unconsciously tinged with respect.

"And . . . did the Duke know of your injury when he ordered you to marry me?"

"Of course," Garin replied, with a bitter smile. "At one time only Duke Jean knew my secret and he swore to keep it. Philippe discovered this secret quite by accident when I was wounded alongside him in an engagement. We were alone, separated from the rest of the escort. He looked after me himself, restored me to consciousness and saved my life by having me carried away as rapidly as possible. And he kept his word . . . but I have ceased to feel any gratitude towards him since the day he took advantage of it to marry you to me. I think it was on our wedding night that I began to hate him, when your wondrous beauty was revealed to me at last. You were wonderful . . . but forbidden, inaccessible to me . . . for ever! And I loved you, I loved you like the madman I all but became. . . ."

His voice grew hoarse and he turned away his head, but in the wavering torch-light Catherine saw a tear, a single tear, roll down his unshaven cheek and lose itself in his beard. Overcome, she fell on her knees beside the shackled captive and gently wiped away the little damp mark on his cheek.

"Garin . . ." she murmured, "why didn't you tell me this before? Why were you silent? Didn't you realize that I would have helped you? If I had known this terrible story earlier, I swear that the Duke would never have touched me; I would never have inflicted this shame, this terrible torture upon you!"

"That would have been a mistake, my sweet. You are made for love and happiness, to give life. With me, your life was at an impasse. . . ."

Catherine's anger had changed its objective. Now it was Philippe she hated . . . for the cold and cruel calculation of which Garin had been the victim. How *could* he have made use of the

165

tragic secret which chance had revealed to him? Her grudge against her husband had completely disappeared.

"I cannot allow you to die," she whispered hurriedly. "We must do something . . . that man, your jailer . . . he loves gold. If we offer him a fortune and a place of refuge he would let you escape. . . . Listen, I have no money, but I have my jewels, all the ones you gave me, even that famous Black Diamond. Any one of those would represent a huge fortune to a man like that. . . ."

"No," Garin interrupted abruptly. "Don't go on! I am grateful for the thought which your heart and sense of justice dictate, but I no longer have any desire to live! Philippe de Mâchefoing and his aldermen rendered me a service when they condemned me to death. You have no idea how weary of life I am. . . ."

Catherine's eyes were fixed on Garin's hands, in their wooden shackles. They gave an impression of extraordinary resignation and fragility.

"Freedom!" she murmured, ". . . freedom is a wonderful thing! You are still young and full of life, and rich if you wanted to be. With what I have saved you could make a new life somewhere else. . . . Far from here, you could start again. . . ."

"What would I do with my freedom? Continue to suffer this delicious and infernal torture of Tantalus which you are for me? Remain this Prometheus bound by his own impotence and eaten alive by the vulture of desire, interminably, until old age brings respite? No, Catherine, I have made my peace with you, or so I trust, and now I shall die happy, believe me!"

She would have gone on trying to persuade him, appalled to think that his end was now so near. It all seemed so monstrously unjust! She genuinely forgot that only a little while before, she herself had undergone still crueller treatment than this at his hands. But there were steps on the stairs and the sound of voices.

"There is someone coming," said Garin, who had heard. "The jailer and doubtless the Father who has come to shrive me. You must go now. Farewell, Catherine. . . . Forgive me for not having made you happy, and remember me sometimes in your prayers. I shall die with your name on my lips."

His scarred face was as rigid as if it had been carved of stone. Tears sprang to Catherine's eyes. She twisted her hands nervously together.

"Is there really nothing I can do for you? . . . Nothing at all? I would give anything to be able to help you. . . ."

A sudden gleam appeared in Garin's one eye.

"Perhaps," he whispered very low. "Listen! I am not afraid of torture or death . . . but the idea of being dragged appals me.

166

To be dragged like a slaughtered animal through the dust, at the feet of the crowd—beneath the filth and spit of a stupid mob . . . yes, that frightens me! If you can spare me that, I shall pray God to bless you. . . ."

"But how?"

The cell door opened and Roussot entered followed by a rope-girdled monk whose hands were hidden in the long sleeves of his habit, his face shadowed by the hood.

"The time has come!" the jailer said to Catherine. "I have left you here too long already. But the good Father will not say anything. Come. . . ."

"One moment more," Garin cried. Then he fixed Catherine with a supplicating look. "Before I finish with this life, I would like to drink one more pint of good Beaune wine . . . the sort that my wine steward, Abou, knows so well how to prepare! Ask this fellow here to let you send me a flagon!"

Roussot gave a great guffaw and slapped his thighs.

"There's a good Burgundian for you! Doesn't want to kick the bucket without one last drink! It's a thing I understand—I like Beaune wine myself!"

"My son," the monk exclaimed, scandalized. "What a thing to worry about when you are about to appear before God's judgment seat. . . ."

"Let's call it a last farewell to the earth which He has made so fair," Garin replied with a smile.

Catherine said nothing. She understood what Garin wanted. She went towards the door with the jailer, but turned back on the threshold. She saw that her husband's eyes were still fixed upon her with an expression of such love and despair in them that a sob broke from her.

"Farewell, Garin!" she whispered, with tears in her eyes. The answer of the man in chains reached her from the depths of the cave.

"Farewell, Catherine. . . ."

She ran headlong out of the cell towards the stairs. On the bottom step she turned and faced the jailer.

"How much do you want for giving him this last request?" she asked.

The man did not hesitate. Greed sparkled in his dull eyes.

"Ten gold ducats!"

"And you swear he will have his wine? Take care you do not cheat me!"

"I swear I'll give it to him, on my eternal soul!"

"Very well. Here—take the gold. A woman, the one who is waiting in the courtyard, will return with the wine in a few minutes."

167

Ten gold pieces changed hands. Then Catherine hurried up the slippery stairway. She rejoined Sara who was pacing up and down in the courtyard outside.

"Come!" was all she said.

As soon as she returned to Ermengarde's house, she sent for Abou-al-Khayr and told him of Garin's last request.

"He has asked for some Beaune wine, but it is poison he wants so that he may escape the humiliation of being dragged through the streets on the sledge. Can you give him some?"

The Moorish doctor listened to her without moving a muscle. Then he nodded.

"I understand," he said. "Bring me the flagon of wine. I shall only need it for a moment."

Sara went to fetch the wine and gave it to the Arab. He retired to his room, but returned in a moment carrying the pewter mug which Sara had given him. He put this into Catherine's hands.

"Here! This is what you asked for. Have it taken to him at once."

Catherine stared at the dark red liquid in the cup with a mixture of horror and fascination.

"And . . . he won't suffer?" she asked uncertainly.

Abou-al-Khayr shook his head and smiled sadly.

"He will fall asleep . . . and never wake up. Half the wine in this flagon would be enough. Now, go!"

Sara took the cup from Catherine's hands with a brusque movement.

"Give it to me!" she said. "You should not touch these things."

Hiding the pewter mug under her black cape, the gipsy vanished down the staircase. Catherine and the doctor remained there looking at each other. After a moment, Abou went up to the young woman and touched her eyes with a slender fingertip.

"You have been weeping," he observed. "And the tears have washed away the bitterness in your heart. You will find calm and peace again . . . one day."

"I don't believe it," Catherine cried. "How can I ever forget all this? It is all so terrible . . . so hideously unjust!"

Abou-al-Khayr shrugged and went towards the door, pausing before he left the room.

"Time heals grief, appeases anger and smothers hate; the past will then be as if it had never existed."

At dawn on 6 April 1424, Catherine, who had passed the night in prayer, took up her position by a narrow window overlooking the street. The sky was gray and overcast and a fine rain hung over the town like a veil. In spite of the bad weather,

168

and the earliness of the hour, a crowd was already gathering outside the Monkey House, eager for the bloody spectacle they had been promised. Catherine's prayers had helped her greatly. In them she found a comfort and serenity which had deserted her for a long time. She had implored God's mercy for the man whose secret had been revealed to her at last; a tragic secret and one which held a wealth of terrible suffering and shame! She knew that she would now be able to think of him with a kind of tenderness. In opening his heart to her at last, Garin had won her affection, too. Her only anxiety now was: had the jailer fulfilled his side of the bargain?

A sudden stir in the crowd drew her attention. A picket of the Provost's bowmen with their double-headed axes on their shoulders and their faces hidden by steel helmets streaming with rain, were making their way towards the Monkey House. They acted as escort to an ageing, but still vigorous and powerful looking man whom Catherine recognized with a shudder. It was Joseph Blaigny, the executioner. . . . He had come to take charge of the condemned man. . . .

When the sinister little party disappeared into the Monkey House, Catherine's heart began pounding apprehensively under her black wool bodice. She had a sudden fear of seeing Garin emerge from the building between a guard of bowmen—alive! A massive, white carthorse had already stopped in front of the building, dragging a sort of rough wooden grid behind it. This was the sledge to which the condemned man was to be tied and dragged through the town, and its appearance was greeted by a murmur of satisfaction from the crowd. . . .

Several minutes, which seemed like an eternity to Catherine, elapsed. She sensed rather than saw that Ermengarde and Sara had arrived to keep her company. From without, a murmur of astonishment, quickly changing to a growl of anger, made itself heard.

Jean Blaigny had just reappeared, carrying a long pale body, quite naked except for a ragged cloth knotted around the loins. He flung the inert body down upon the sledge. It was Garin, and Catherine had to bite her hand to stop herself from crying out loud.

"He is quite dead," said Sara from beside her. It was only a corpse which the executioner was so carefully lashing to the sledge and the mob were not deceived. It was this that called forth their anger and disappointment. There was nothing exciting in seeing a dead body being hanged. . . .

The three women crossed themselves slowly. Then Sara started.

"Oh! Look!" she cried, pointing towards the entrance to the

Monkey House. Two bowmen had just come out carrying a large lifeless body which Catherine recognized to her astonishment as being that of Roussot, the jailer. It came to her in a flash what must have happened. Roussot had given the poisoned wine to Garin as he promised, but, in his greed, he had not been able to resist tasting it himself. He had paid dearly for his gluttony.

"He is dead, too," Catherine said.

She heard Abou-al-Khayr somewhere behind her saying quietly:

"It is better this way. Now we know he cannot talk."

But Catherine was not listening. She was watching Joseph Blaigny. The executioner had finished lashing the body to the sledge. Now he seized the horse's bridle in one hand and struck the animal with his whip. The horse moved forward, the crowd parting to make way for it. As the sledge jolted along through the greasy mud of the road, the long, pale body was splashed and spotted with mud. The head and feet hung down on either side.

Suddenly the rain came pouring down and the outlines and colors grew blurred and indistinct. Catherine stood watching through a mist of tears as the white corpse of the man whom a princely whim had joined to her and whom death had released at last from his hopeless love was carried away from her amidst the jeers and insults of the mob.

Part II

JEHANNE

1428

CHAPTER TEN

Jean Van Eyck's Mission

It was autumn and the old trees whose branches overhung the black canal water were spangled with crimson and gold. The sunlight lingered caressingly upon the pointed rooftops and painted gables of the town of Bruges. But it was chilly despite the sun, and all the windows were closed. Every chimney had its waving plume of smoke, the pale gray whorls dissolving as they floated up to meet the clouds sailing across a pale blue sky. A biting wind sent the leaves fluttering down from the trees, scattering them on the dark water. Soon the silence of winter would have closed in. . . .

A fire had been lit in Catherine's house, as in all other dwellings; it leaped and flamed up cheerfully in the high stone fireplace in the spacious room where Catherine and her painter were sitting. Catherine had been sitting for Jean Van Eyck for over two hours now, and she was beginning to feel tired. She had pins and needles in her arms and legs. Without realizing it, her expression had grown forced and the painter noticed.

"Why didn't you tell me you were tired?" he asked, with a smile which lent great charm to his thin face.

"Because you were painting away so hard I felt I couldn't interrupt, Maître Jean. Are you satisfied?"

"More than satisfied. You are the queen of models. . . . That's enough for today. One more sitting and it will be quite finished."

The artist flung his brush into a large green and white faience vase which contained some twenty or more already and stepped back to look at what he had done.

Then his gray-blue eyes, as probing as a surgeon's, returned

171

from the tall poplar wood panel on which he was painting her portrait to the sitter herself.

He was painting her as a madonna and she sat on a high chair placed upon a tapestry covered dais. She was dressed in a magnificent flowing gown of purple velvet, caught under the bosom by a gold belt, which spread out around her feet and hid the steps up to the throne. She wore no jewels in her modest, pointed decolletage, but a narrow gold fillet studded with amethysts and pearls held back the sumptuous mass of golden hair which hung loose about her shoulders. She held a sort of sceptre, in the shape of a finely wrought lily, in both hands.

Van Eyck breathed a great sigh of contentment.

"I wonder if I shall ever weary of painting you, Catherine. . . . If I'm not mistaken, this must be the third painting I have done of you. But what painter could ever grow tired of such incomparable beauty?"

Catherine gave a sigh in answer to his own. She descended the steps of her throne, laid the gold lily on a table and went over to a dresser on which stood a collection of multicolored Venetian glass goblets and a tall flagon of glass speckled with gold. She filled two goblets with Spanish wine, and gave one of them to the painter while she took a sip of the other with an indulgent smile curving her lips.

"Now, Jean, don't start that again. . . . In one moment you will be telling me that I am unique in the world and that you love me passionately. And I will make my usual answer . . . so what's the point?"

Jean Van Eyck shrugged. Then he drained his glass at one swallow and put it back on the table.

"I always hope one of these days you may give me a different answer. It's three years now, Catherine, since the Duke made me his court painter; three years that I've been able to see you living at his side, that I've admired and loved you. Three years is a long time, you know. . . ."

Catherine took off the golden fillet round her head with a tired gesture and threw it down on the table next to the gold lily as carelessly as if it had been a thing of no value whatsoever.

"I know . . . for it is three years now that I have been living this lap-dog existence with Philippe, a pretty toy to be dressed and bejeweled. . . . The most beautiful lady of the West! That is the name which he, whom they call the Greak Duke of the West, has been pleased to bestow on me. Three years! . . . Truly, Jean, there is no woman more lonely than I. . . ."

She smiled sadly at the painter. He was a man of about thirty with a face which was intelligent, but gave the impression of coldness and reserve. He had a long, straight nose, thin, compressed lips, eyebrows so fair as to be almost invisible and slightly protuberant eyes; all of which added up to a countenance more statesmanlike than artistic. And yet there was no greater artist alive! The only painter to equal him had been his own brother, Hubert, who died two years ago at Ghent. . . . Few people realized that this tall, cold, distant man hid a burning flame, a passionate love of beauty and a deeply sensual nature beneath that shrewd glance and caustic wit. But Catherine was one of those few. . . . Ever since he had first met her, Van Eyck had been pursuing her with a passion at once devout and ardent . . . and strangely patient, too. There was nothing Van Eyck could not accept from this incomparably beautiful woman. She might trample on his heart if she wished. Everything was permitted to her because she was beautiful, and sometimes Catherine was tempted to yield to this obstinate, patient love of his. But she was weary of love. . . .

Four years had passed since Garin's death, but each of those years was still as fresh in her memory as if she had lived it just yesterday. Catherine remembered her departure from Dijon a few days after Garin's execution only too vividly! In order to protect her from the curiosity of the townspeople, which could only have distressed the young widow of the former Lord Treasurer, Ermengarde decided to take her friend away as soon as possible. They left the town together, accompanied by Sara, the very day a gang of builders started to tear down the magnificent mansion in the rue de la Parcheminerie which had been the outward, dazzling sign of Garin's wealth. From the end of the street, Catherine saw the demolition men begin to tear down the weather-vanes in the form of gilded dolphins which decorated the roof of the house. She turned her head away and tightened her lips to prevent them trembling. She wanted to turn over that page in her life as quickly as possible, particularly as that last, despairing glance of her husband's still haunted her. If they had not both been marked down as victims of a cruel fate, what sort of life together would they have had? They might have been happy. . . .

Catherine left nothing behind in Dijon except regrets. Her mother and uncle had left the rue du Griffon for Marsannay where they planned to live permanently from now on. Uncle Mathieu was rich enough to live off his farms and vineyards and no longer wanted to live "at the bottom of a stinking hole" as he put it. Loyse was in the convent du Tart and Landry at Saint-Seine. As for Ermengarde, the Dowager Duchess's death had been a cruel blow and she had decided to retire to her demesne of Châteauvilain.

"I shall bring up your child there," she told Catherine. "It must receive an education befitting its ducal blood. We shall make a knight or accomplished lady of it. . . ."

The thought of this child to which she was about to give birth did not afford Catherine much pleasure, but it seemed to give Ermengarde great satisfaction. The Countess was a frustrated grandmother and the idea of having a baby to spoil and cherish delighted her, perhaps because she did not have many people left to bestow her love upon. Her husband remained at Philippe's side, leading a somewhat riotous existence for a man of his age. "He will never wake up to the fact that he is no longer a young man and that women are the most exhausting pastime in the world!" the Countess was wont to declare philosophically. His infidelities had no power to trouble her. Love had long since withered away between Ermengarde and her lawful wedded lord; and her son was away fighting in Jean de Luxembourg's armies and she rarely saw him. He was a great swordsman. "It's in his blood," Ermengarde would say. Catherine's child would be a welcome distraction in the tedium of rural life, for Ermengarde had made up her mind to remain at Châteauvilain from now on, cultivating her estates and keeping an eye on her peasants.

It was behind the stout walls of the Châteauvilain fortress, so like their mistress in the feeling of security and strength which emanated from them, that Catherine found the quiet, peaceful existence of which she was sorely in need. The feudal castle whose grey walls were reflected in the calm waters of the Aujon was a tranquil haven for her and she spent long evenings there watching the sun sink over the treetops. It was there, one morning in August, after a long night of pain and travail, that Catherine gave birth to a son whom the castle chaplain immediately baptized Philippe like his father. . . . Ermengarde was quite beside herself with joy as she watched the wet-nurse, chosen by herself from a thousand candidates, suckling the newborn infant. She was certainly happier than Catherine who felt no great maternal love herself. She had not wanted Philippe's child. Such love as she felt for him was more physical than anything else. He was attractive to her, he knew how to make her veins run fire and his love-making brought her great happiness, but she was not besotted with him; she had never been consumed by the fever of love and passion she felt for Arnaud, and she did not miss him when he was not there.

When he came to Châteauvilain, however, a month or so after the birth of her child, she had been very happy. Philippe had a magnetic charm and, when she was with him, Catherine had no difficulty persuading herself that he could fill her life.

174

He had thrown himself at her feet to beg her forgiveness for not having come sooner. He had vowed that he loved her more than ever and had proved it to her passionately that very night. Catherine had felt herself come to life again in his arms. The deep, passionate responses which he knew how to awaken in her revived her appetite for life, her coquetry, and she found herself wanting to be beautiful again.

He did not hide from her that he planned to remarry: a marriage of convenience, if ever there was one. In November he was to marry the Countess Bonne d'Artois, who was much older than himself and the widow of his own uncle, the Count de Nevers, who had been killed at Agincourt. Bonne was gentle, timid, self-effacing and sickly, but as her alliance was essential to Burgundy, Philippe was setting his own inclinations aside in marrying her.

"You have nothing to be jealous of," he assured Catherine. "I love and shall always love you alone. From now on you will never leave my side; you shall be Maid-of-Honor to the Duchess if you wish. . . ." Catherine refused from pride more than from concern for the proprieties. She had no intention of serving a woman by day whose husband she annexed by night. She pleaded to be allowed to remain a little longer with Ermengarde and Philippe agreed. On 30 November 1424, he married Bonne de Nevers at Moulins-Engilbert, but a few days later he was posting urgently back to snatch a few quick kisses from his mistress and beg her to join him again. She liked the country life as well as Ermengarde's reassuring presence and the company of the child, which, as time went on, she was beginning to grow fond of. But the days of the new Duchess of Burgundy were numbered. She died less than a year later, on 17 September 1425, leaving Philippe once more a widower and once again without a legitimate heir. It was then that he snatched Catherine away from her calm retreat, almost by force, and made her his declared favorite, the dazzling and all-powerful star round which his Court, the most brilliant in Europe, revolved.

He had given back to her, a hundred times over, all that the magistrates had taken from her at the time of Garin's trial. She became Countess de Brazey so that the little Philippe might have a title. She soon acquired a château at Chenôve, outside Dijon, and a small palace at Bruges. And besides this, there were estates, jewels, ravishing gowns and Philippe's unwavering love. He remained prostrated before this beauty of hers which he knew so well how to enhance and exalt in tournaments and feasts.

Loved, adulated, adored and spoiled, Catherine should by rights have been happy, but she was not. When four years had gone by and she lay awake in the silence of certain solitary nights in her brocade-hung chamber and questioned her heart, she found nothing there but silence. She was surrounded by love, for many men were in love with her, so much so, sometimes, that they were ready to brave Philippe's jealousy and declare themselves to her, but she felt nothing for any of them. Some of them had even fought and killed each other, in the hope of a look or smile from her, but she could only pity them, and pity had never turned to love. When she was in Philippe's arms, she often felt nothing but indifference in the midst of his most passionate embraces. She no longer responded as she had done in the early days of their love to the artful caresses which he lavished upon her as passionately as ever.

One man alone might have succeeded in awakening the sleeping heart of the beautiful Comtesse, but she forbade herself even to think of him. He was far away, married, inaccessible, lost to her for ever, that Arnaud whose very name had the power to waken a painful echo in her soul. . . .

Jean Van Eyck had refrained from interrupting the young woman's reverie. She stood by the fireside staring at the flames through the ruby glass of her goblet. Her attitude was so graceful that the painter was tempted to take up his brushes again and begin another portrait. He smiled to himself as he reflected that the "Virgin with Glass of Wine" might receive somewhat doubtful acclaim. But he did not like it when Catherine eluded him like this; of late it was becoming something of a habit.

He was about to speak when a servant entered, wearing the purple and silver livery which Catherine had retained. He advanced noiselessly across the shining mosaic floor where golden stars alternated with blue chimera and informed Catherine that Messire de Saint-Rémy was without and begged to be received by her. Catherine jumped as though the footman's measured tones had woken her from a dream and ordered him to bring the visitor to her. Van Eyck sighed:

"Now we shall have to sit through an hour of the latest Court gossip. I can't stand that ridiculous chatterbox. I've a good mind to leave now."

"No, please don't go," Catherine implored him. "He doesn't dare pay court to me when there is someone else here."

"He, too!" the painter sighed. "I sometimes wonder, my dear, if there is a single man worthy of the name throughout Flanders and Burgundy together who is not more or less in love with you. Very well, I shall remain."

Saint-Rémy had already entered the room, elegant and richly dressed as usual, his face lit by a wide smile. For the occasion

176

of this visit, the arbiter of Burgundian taste had chosen to wear the colors of autumn. The autumn-leaf-colored velvet of his knee-length gown was slashed in several places and sported immense sleeves lined with brocade patterned with gold and crimson leaves. His tight hose were a brave scarlet, and the velvet hat which matched his costume was ornamented with fine gold leaves like those massed around the hilt of the dagger passed through his very low belt. His shoes ended in immense scarlet points which gave him a rather curious walk like a duck's. He brought with him a whiff of the sharp air outside and the cosy peace of the great chamber was shattered.

Saint-Rémy was in ecstasies over Catherine's looks and prodigal in his admiration of the unfinished painting. He examined the gold ornaments displayed on the dressers with the eye of a connoisseur, danced and spun round the room and finally collapsed into a chair where his hostess handed him a cup of wine. He cast a look full of sympathy at Van Eyck.

"Well, Messire-ambassador," he cried. "I hear you are about to leave us once more for the great highways! Faith, I envy you heading for sunny climates and leaving us poor northerners to plunge into the gloom of winter."

"What, Van Eyck? Are you leaving us?" Catherine exclaimed in astonishment. "You never told me."

The painter had gone very red and was casting reproachful looks at the visitor.

"I was on the point of doing so," he said in a surly voice, "when Messire Saint-Rémy appeared on the scene. . . ."

The young councillor was now as red-faced as the painter. His gaze went uneasily from Catherine to Van Eyck and then back again.

"If I understand aright," he stammered, "I have blundered again."

Catherine interrupted him unceremoniously. She went over to Van Eyck, the folds of her sweeping, purple gown fanning out behind her as she moved, and placed herself squarely in front of him so that he had to look her in the eyes.

"Where are you going, Jean? You have talked too much, both of you, not to have aroused my curiosity. Am I not supposed to know about your new mission, then? For you are going on a mission for the Duke, are you not?"

It was not the first time that Philippe of Burgundy had made use of his favorite painter's talent for diplomacy. Van Eyck's artistic sensibility made him particularly suitable for the more delicate type of mission. He shrugged.

"Yes, he is sending me as legate. I would have preferred him to tell you the news himself, but still, sooner or later you will

177

have to know. The Duke is sending me to Portugal. I am to open negotiations there with King John with a view to the eventual marriage between the Infanta Isabel and. . . ."

". . . between the Infanta Isabel and the Duke of Burgundy! Come, come, my friend, you cannot imagine that I don't know the Duke must marry again if he is to produce an heir? I have been expecting this news for a long time. It has not taken me by surprise. Why so many precautions, then?"

"I was afraid you might be upset. The Prince's love for you is immense and I know this marriage is only a political one. The Infanta is over thirty and, though they say she is beautiful, they say the same about all princesses. . . ."

"Now, now," Catherine interrupted again, laughing. "There you go again, still apologizing! There's no need to cudgel your brains for excuses. I know Monseigneur's feelings better than you do . . . and my own. You have not upset me in the least. Let's talk about more important things—when will you finish my portrait if you are going in this mission?"

"I am not leaving till the end of the month, so I shall have plenty of time."

The news that Saint-Rémy had blurted out had, in fact, affected her more than she cared to admit, because it meant that her life must undergo a radical change. She had always known, ever since the death of Philippe's second wife, that a day would come when he would have to choose a new Duchess. The Duke's power had never stopped growing. He succeeded in all his enterprises and his territories kept expanding. He had recently concluded a war to his own advantage with Holland; a war waged against his unruly cousin, the beautiful Jacqueline de Luxembourg, a heroine of romance. The defeated Countess had been forced to make Philippe her heir. Moreover, the Comte de Namur, whose possessions Philippe would inherit on his death, was seriously ill. Such widespread possessions needed not merely a ruler, but an assured succession; the bastards which Philippe had had by various mistresses could not hope to succeed him.

Catherine had always known that another woman must someday share the throne with Philippe and she had long ago come to a solemn decision . . . that when this day came, she would retire, give up her position. During the past three years, Philippe's love had made her a real uncrowned queen, mistress and Morning Star of his Court. Her pride rebelled from the thought of being reduced to the role of mistress—even favorite —again. The time of decision had arrived, but what was it to be? The wisest course would probably be to return to Burgundy, and first to Châteauvilain. It was two years since she had

178

last seen her son, whom Ermengarde was rearing with tender care and her usual vigor. She was beginning to miss the child.

"What are you thinking about?" Saint-Rémy asked. "Your thoughts are miles away, I can see. Here is Van Eyck trying to take his leave of you and you won't even listen."

She excused herself with a smile.

"Forgive me. Till tomorrow, then, Jean. Let me finish this painting as soon as possible for I can see you will be busy. . . ."

The painter did not answer. He nodded sadly. The slight edge in Catherine's voice had not been lost on him. He bent very low over the hand she held out to him.

"Why must *I* be entrusted with this mission . . . when I would give my life to spare a single tear? What irony!"

"Come now. Go off to Portugal and don't worry. Paint a beautiful picture of the Infanta and carry out your mission as well as you can. I assure you, I am not upset by this news. I shall leave the Court without regret . . . for I am weary of this life. And, when you return, you will know where to find me. We shall always be friends."

Regretfully, he let fall the delicate hand he had been holding pressed between his own, and left without a word. Jean de Saint-Rémy watched him go with a smile. He had not moved from his chair.

"If that man's not wildly in love with you, I'll eat my hat! But I suppose it was inevitable that a painter should fall under the spell of your beauty. . . . Don't look at me like that, my dear. I know what you're thinking—that this Saint-Rémy, bringer of bad tidings, should at least have the decency to leave before Van Eyck. No, no, don't try to deny it—it's only natural. If I have been so inept as to remain, however, it is because I have something to say to you . . . something which cannot wait."

"Are you leaving, too?"

"No, of course not. Only I have learnt to be wary of your sudden decisions. I sense that you are on the verge of making one now and I don't want to have to go to the ends of the earth to find you this time. You are the most elusive unpredictable woman I know . . . and the most adorable!"

"For heaven's sake, Jean," Catherine said in an exasperated tone. "I have no wish to hear any madrigals today. Don't talk to me about my beauty and charm . . . please! You cannot imagine how tired I am of always hearing the same thing. If it isn't you it's Van Eyck, if it isn't Van Eyck, it's Roussay, Hughes de Lannoy, Toulongeon . . . even Maître Nicolas Rolin has taken to paying lengthy visits here of late and boring me to distraction."

"No doubt he's trying to make up to himself for the austere

life he leads with his pious spouse, Guigonne de Salins. He doesn't have a very amusing life, that Chancellor of ours. But I didn't come here to talk about him, but about myself. . . ."

"A fascinating topic," Catherine teased him.

"Oh . . . I don't know about fascinating! But interesting, I grant you. Well, then . . ." Jean de Saint-Rémy had risen to his feet. Now he unfolded his long, thin person and planted himself in front of Catherine. "Well, then, my name is Jean Lefebvre de Saint-Rémy. I am thirty-two, rich, in good health. I own considerable lands, I am quite blue-blooded enough . . . and I love you as much as a Saint-Rémy can love anyone. Will you marry me? You are a widow yourself and, therefore, free."

". . . and unemployed at the present moment?" Catherine finished with a mocking smile. "My dearest Jean, you are a darling and I am deeply touched by your proposal. You said to yourself: she is going to be alone, I will offer her my name, a serious position, an honorable husband. . . . Am I not right? I always knew you were my friend. . . ."

"Why must you always talk to me about friendship when I keep telling you at the top of my voice that I love you . . . ?"

"And that's just why I shall never marry you. If you love me, you would be too unhappy. It would not be fair of me to give you my hand alone, and I cannot do more than like you . . . very much. That isn't enough!"

An expression of genuine regret appeared on the young man's candid face. Even his dazzling plumage appeared to go limp and dull.

"I love you enough to be satisfied with that," he said hoarsely. "Of course, I could not hope to replace the Duke. You love him and . . ."

Catherine interrupted him brutally:

"You know very well I don't love him! You are too close a friend to think that. I have never been able to find a satisfactory word for the feelings I have towards him. I cannot love any more, Jean, even if I would . . . and you know that, too!"

A silence fell. Night was closing in outside, gradually invading the large room whose painted beams were already shrouded in darkness. The only light came from the glowing fire against which Catherine's silhouette stood out blackly. Saint-Rémy stepped back into the shadows. He had the impression that a ghost had just passed between himself and this marvelous woman to whom he had never succeeded in coming very close. Saint-Rémy had never forgotten the joust beneath the walls of Arras, or the knight in Royal arms who had excited this cool young woman almost to madness. He murmured:

"I see. It is he, then? After all these years, you still haven't managed to forget Mont . . ."

"Hush!" Catherine interrupted. "I don't want to hear his name mentioned."

She was shaking like a leaf and there was such distress in the huge violet eyes that Saint-Rémy was overcome with pity.

"I'm sorry," she murmured. "I'm nervous. . . . You would do better to leave me alone, now, my friend. You talk to me of love and all I can do is talk nonsense. . . . Come again soon. . . ."

She held out a cold hand which the young man carried to his lips for an instant. He seemed so anxious and perturbed that she smiled gently at him, touched that this idle, carefree young man should genuinely suffer on her account.

"Come back one day when I'm not feeling so nervous," she said. "I'll even let you tell me that you love me again."

"And propose to you?"

"Why not? . . . If you don't mind being refused. Goodnight, my friend."

When he had gone, Catherine heaved a sigh of relief. At last she was alone! The shadows which filled the large room were soothing. She liked the half-darkness. She went across to one of the tall pointed windows and pushed open one of the colored glass panes which bore the arms she had adopted—a chimera azure on a field argent surmounted by a Countess's coronet. The sharp, moist air outside was cool on her face and stirred her loosened hair. The black canal water flowed past below, reflecting the lights of the neighboring houses like a mirror before it vanished under the dark arch of a little bridge. The wind was rising and scattering the fallen leaves. On a nearby rampart, a sentinel called out, momentarily drowning the faint music of a lute being played in one of the buildings across the canal. Everything was so peaceful that Catherine would have liked to stay there at the window for a long while, listening to the noises of the town dying away as night closed in. But it was growing late, and Philippe was coming to sup with her that night. She closed the window regretfully just as the door opened and Sara came in carrying a twelve-branch candelabra which lit up her dark, inscrutable face. There was something solemn about the gypsy woman's manner, and her brows were knitted below the high, starched lace cap which covered her head. She put the candelabra on a carved wooden chest and then, taking one of the lighted candles from it, proceeded round the room lighting all the rest.

There was something mechanical and strained about her movements which struck Catherine.

181

"What's the matter?" she asked. "You're acting very oddly tonight."

Sara turned towards her. Catherine noticed that her face was drawn and anxious.

"A messenger has just arrived from Châteauvilain," she said in a colorless voice. "The child is ill. The Countess Ermengarde wants you to go to her. . . ."

She said nothing more, made no comment. . . . She simply stood there, looking at Catherine, waiting. . . . The young woman had gone pale. It had never occurred to her that anything could happen to little Philippe. Ermengarde's letters were one long paean to his health, beauty and intelligence. But Catherine knew her friend well enough to be sure that if she sent for her now, it must mean the child was . . . seriously ill. A lump rose in her throat. She suddenly realized how great a distance lay between herself and her child, and a wave of remorse swept over her. She didn't reproach herself for having left him with Ermengarde, because Ermengarde adored him and she could hardly have left him in better hands. In fact, it had been to please the doting Countess that she had originally decided to leave him there. . . . What she reproached herself for was for never having loved him enough. He was flesh of her flesh and yet she could go for long months without seeing him. Her eyes met Sara's.

"We will leave at dawn," she said, "as soon as the town gates are opened. Tiercelin will see to the house. Go and prepare our traveling chests. . . ."

"Perrine is seeing to them now. . . ."

"Good. We shall need the best horses and three armed attendants. That should be enough. We will stop as little as possible en route. Not much luggage, then. If I need anything more, I can send for it. . . ."

Catherine's voice was calm and cold and her commands precise. Sara looked in vain for some trace of emotion on that beautiful, impassive face. Court life had taught the young woman the trick of disguising her emotions and controlling her features whatever emotional storms might be brewing within.

"And . . . this evening?" Sara asked.

"The Duke is coming. I will tell him I am leaving. Have the table set up in here and then come and help me dress."

In Catherine's room, a ravishing setting of pale pink Genoese velvet where all the furniture was of solid silver, Perrine and two other maids were bustling about preparing the baggage. But a "deshabille" of white satin embroidered with seed pearls was laid out on the bed in readiness for Catherine to wear that evening. Philippe liked to see Catherine dressed in white and,

182

on the rare occasions which he was able to spend alone with her, he strictly forbade her to wear the formal Court dress. When he visited her Catherine always wore simple dresses and her hair loose about her shoulders.

Leaving her women to their task, she went into her dressing-room where a bath had been filled and stepped into it hurriedly. Guessing that her nerves were on edge, Sara had left some verbena leaves to soak in the water. Catherine relaxed for a moment in the gentle warmth of the bath, forcing herself not to think about the sick child. She felt weary, but oddly lucid. It was strange that she should have to leave Philippe the very day when she had first learnt of their impending separation. It was as if destiny had suddenly stepped in and chosen her next move for her. It was time to go. She would stay for a while at Châteauvilain and try to decide what to do with her life. . . .

She stepped out of the bath and Sara enveloped her in a huge square of fine Frisian cloth and rubbed her down energetically. But when the gypsy woman brought the chest where the rare perfumes Catherine used were kept, she stopped her with a gesture.

"No . . . not tonight, I have a headache," she said.

Sara did not insist, but her eyes lingered for a moment on the young woman as she let her towel drop to the floor.

"Dress me," she said.

While Sara went off to fetch her satin dress, Catherine stood for a moment before her mirror without even looking at herself. The sight of her own beauty no longer brought her the pleasure it once had. Philippe's insatiable desire told her, more accurately than any mirror, that she was more beautiful than ever. Motherhood had rounded out her figure and removed any last traces of immaturity. Her waist, so narrow that Philippe could encircle it with his two hands, was still that of a girl, but her hips were rounder and her breasts fuller, swelling proudly below the infinitely pure and graceful line of her neck and shoulders. The texture of her golden skin was finer and her flesh firmer than it had ever been and Catherine was well aware of its power over the mightiest prince of the West. Philippe was the same ardent lover he had always been in her arms . . . but nowadays all this left Catherine singularly unmoved.

Sara slipped the dress over her head without a word. It fell in long, supple, pearly folds about her body and the cold touch of the satin on her bare skin made Catherine shiver. She was so pale that Sara murmured:

"Shall I send a message to the Palace to tell him you are not well?"

Catherine shook her head.

183

"No, don't worry. I must see him tonight. Anyway, it is too late—there he is."

At that moment there was the sound of a quick step outside and a masculine voice calling a cheerful greeting to the maids next door. The bathroom door burst open as Philippe strode in impatiently.

"Off with you, Sara . . . so I can kiss her at my leisure! Three days without you, my love. . . . Three days listening to the complaints of the aldermen of Brussels! An eternity of boredom!"

As Sara left the room after a hasty curtsey, the Duke came to Catherine and seized her in his arms, covering her with hungry kisses.

"My heart . . . my life . . . my queen . . . my golden-haired enchantress . . . my indispensable love," he murmured in a tender litany while his lips roved from the young woman's eyes to her breast, which the generous decolletage of her dress all but revealed. "Each time I see you, you seem to be more beautiful . . . so beautiful it makes my heart ache sometimes. . . ."

Catherine struggled a little in Philippe's arms, half-suffocating in their passionate embrace. He seemed extraordinarily gay and more amorous than ever. He began to unfasten her dress, but Catherine pushed him gently away.

"No, Philippe . . . not now."

"Oh! Why? I was in such a fever to see you, my darling, that you must forgive me if I seem too impatient. But you know too well what an effect you have upon me to object to that! Catherine . . . my sweet Catherine, you have never refused me before. Are you feeling ill? You are very pale. . . ."

He held her away from him to see her better and then suddenly drew her against him anxiously, holding her pretty face in his hands to make her look at him. Two tears suddenly rolled down Catherine's cheeks and she closed her eyes.

"You are weeping!" Philippe cried in dismay. "But what is the matter? My beloved . . . my heart . . . I have never seen you weep."

In his emotion he seemed to be on the point of following suit. His thin lips trembled against her temple.

"I have to go," she murmured. "Ermengarde has sent for me. . . . The child is ill."

"Seriously?"

"I don't know . . . but I am afraid so. Ermengarde would not send for me otherwise. I am suddenly afraid, Philippe . . . our happy times together are over."

He cradled her tenderly in his arms, then led her towards the bed where he forced her to sit down while he himself sat on the Persian rug at her feet.

184

"Don't talk nonsense," he said tenderly, clasping both her hands between his own. "The child may be ill, but that does not mean his life is in danger. You know that Ermengarde looks after him as if he were her own. I can understand your anxiety, but I am desolated that you should be leaving me. When are you going?"

"At dawn. . . ."

"Very well. I will order an armed escort to be waiting here before then. . . . Yes, yes, I insist. It is a long way and the roads grow more and more dangerous with the coming of winter. I should not be easy otherwise. But . . . don't stay away too long, I beg you. I shall be counting the days. . . ."

Catherine looked away and tried to free her hands, but Philippe held them fast.

"I may have to stay in Burgundy longer than you expect. In fact, I may never come back to Flanders," she said slowly.

"What? But . . . why?"

She leant towards him and stroked the thin face whose proud, delicate features she had grown to love after a fashion.

"Philippe," she murmured softly, "the moment has come for us to be frank with each other. You must marry again . . . and the time has come. Now . . . now, don't get excited. I know you have sent Van Eyck to Portugal, though it was not he who told me so. I don't blame you—you must give your subjects an heir. But . . . I would just prefer to go away myself. After this life we have shared, I don't want . . . a secret existence and a hidden liaison. We have loved each other in the open, in broad daylight; I don't think I could settle for a twilight, clandestine affair."

Philippe gripped her shoulders roughly and knelt above her on the bed, looking down at her.

"Be quiet! Not another word! I shall never condemn you to a clandestine existence. I love you now as I have never loved you and while I may be forced to marry, it is not to heap humiliations on you. I am the Duke of Burgundy and I shall make sure that you keep the rank I have given you."

"That is impossible . . . here, at least. I can live in Burgundy. . . . You do not go there often, but you can go there alone. . . ."

The arrival of Sara to announce that their supper was ready put an end to the conversation. Philippe gave Catherine his hand to lead her to the table. The meal was spread out on a table before the fire in the large reception room and three valets served them. Philippe and Catherine spoke very little in front of the servants. The Duke was thoughtful. A deep furrow had appeared between his grey eyes and when he looked at Catherine, she saw the pleading in his eyes. He did not touch the dishes which were set before him. . . . As the esquire trenchant made ready to cut the game pâté, Philippe suddenly leapt to his feet, pushing back the table so violently that it overturned and crashed to the floor with a noise like thunder. Catherine gave a cry of alarm. Philippe motioned the servants to the door with one gesture of his outflung arm.

"Out, all of you," he cried.

They obeyed, not daring to stop to pick up the platters and gold dishes whose contents were scattered about the floor. The Duke's grey eyes had gone almost black and his face was distorted in a sort of spasm.

"Philippe!" Catherine cried.

"Don't be afraid, I won't hurt you. . . ."

He came across to her and swung her up in his arms as easily as if she had weighed next to nothing and carried her swiftly into the bedroom. His face was streaming with tears. . . . He set her down, but did not loosen his hold of her. Instead, he held her tightly to him.

"Listen . . ." he murmured breathlessly, "and don't ever forget what I am about to say: I love you more than anything, more than my life, or my soul's salvation . . . and more than my estates. If you asked me to, I would abdicate tomorrow in order to keep you! After all, what do I want with an heir? I will tell Van Eyck to stay . . . I won't get married after all. I don't want to lose you, do you hear? I will never agree to lose you! If you insist, I will let you leave tomorrow, but first, you must swear you will return. . . ."

"Philippe," Catherine moaned, "I have to see my child, our child!"

"No matter! Swear that you will return, whatever happens, as soon as you are reassured. Swear it, or I give you my word as a knight and gentleman that you will never leave this town. I would sooner imprison you first. . . ."

He was no longer master of himself. His thin, hard fingers bruised her as he crushed her beneath him. His breath fanned hot on the lips of his distracted captive and great tears rolled from his eyes onto her face. She had never seen him in such a state. He was shaking all over and suddenly she was reminded of Garin on the one occasion when desire had dominated him. Garin had had the same look of agonized desire, the same air of supplicating urgency about him.

"Swear, Catherine. Swear that you will return," he whispered, half imperious, half pleading. "Or tell me that you have never loved me. . . ."

Catherine felt Philippe's heart beating wildly against her breast. She was suddenly weary and full of pity, and perhaps, without knowing it, she was still moved by the passion of this great prince who became nothing more than a man desperately in love when he was with her. She capitulated.

"I swear," she murmured, ". . . I will return as soon as the child is well again. . . ."

Her words had an immediate effect; she felt him slowly relax. His gratitude distressed her. He knelt before her and kissed her hands and feet.

"No, Philippe," she begged. "Please, get up."

He did so, embracing her once more and kissing her on the lips. The passion of his kiss aroused her gradually, and she felt her willpower melting and her last shreds of resistance crumbling. Philippe seemed suddenly to have rediscovered the magic power which had kept Catherine chained to him for so long.

Late that night as Philippe slept at length, appeased, with his head on her breast, she lay staring wide-eyed into the darkness of her room lit only by the guttering fire. She was in that half-conscious state which frees the spirit and allows it to pierce the veil of the future. Philippe had never made love to her before as he had that night. His desire for her seemed insatiable. Of all their hours of love, these had been the most passionate and beautiful. Why was it, then, that Catherine had a presentiment that they were also the last, even though she had sworn to return?

Her cheek rested upon Philippe's short, blond hair. She turned her head slightly to look at him. He was sleeping like a child, with the slightly sulky expression of a little boy scolded which touched her more than the marks left by the fury of his passion on his hard features. Very softly, so as not to wake him, she touched his temple with her lips at the spot where a little pulse throbbed through the delicate skin. Then, despite herself, she wept a little because she felt that she had never loved him as much as she did just then.

Feeling her stir, Philippe clasped her still closer in his arms. Catherine stopped moving for fear of waking him. It would soon be dawn and she would have to waken him and send him away. But for how long?

Catherine felt confusedly that she no longer belonged to this man or this place. She was already embarked along the road which led to her child and her old friend . . .

CHAPTER ELEVEN

The Monk at Beuvray

When, after a long and exhausting journey, Catherine and her escort finally came in view of the towers of Châteauvilain, she was seized by a sombre presentiment. In the little village tucked into a bend of the river Aujon at the foot of the castle mount, the church bells were tolling a funeral knell and the mournful sounds rang out solemnly through the cold air. Up above, on the mound, the castle rose steeply out of the mist, its redoubtable towers crowned by black wooden hoardings whose pointed slate pepper-pot roofs glistened with moisture. Catherine searched automatically for the scarlet Châteauvilain banner which usually hung above the keep, but there was only a black banner flapping limply from its pole high up on the battlements.

She spurred her horse down the steep path. Although the day was well advanced, the fortress seemed strangely silent. The drawbridge was raised and there was no one to be seen on the watch towers. . . . She turned to the leader of the escort which Philippe had provided, a young, almost beardless lieutenant who blushed furiously whenever she looked at him, and ordered him to sound the horn to announce their arrival. She felt feverish, uneasy. The sinister atmosphere surrounding the little village on the high plains of the Marne was beginning to affect her.

The young lieutenant complied. One of the men-at-arms rode on and raised the horn hanging at his belt to his lips. A plaintive, long-drawn out call rose through the misty valley air and finally, at the third repeat, a helmeted head appeared on the battlements. Catherine shivered in her heavy rain-sodden cape and looked around for Sara who rode a little way behind. The journey had seemed endless. They had frequently had to fight off attacks by wandering bandits or even bands of starving peasants who had been driven out of their sacked villages and forced to take to brigandry in order to survive. And the latter were all the more cruel in that they were driven by hunger rather than the hope of gain. Catherine had found herself regretting that her usual escort, Jacques de Roussay, should be immobilized by a leg broken in a joust. The young soldier who replaced him was clearly not equal to the task. His responsibility preyed on him and the slightest mishap would send him into a panic. His voice was steady enough, however, as he demanded that the gates be opened for the Comtesse de Brazey.

"Coming!" a voice cried from the top of the tower.

The delay seemed interminable to Catherine. She leant forward on her white horse which pawed the ground impatiently, her eyes riveted on the gigantic slab of wood which made up the drawbridge. At last it began to descend, infinitely slowly, creaking horribly . . . and revealing the high ogival gate carved with the arms of the Châteauvilain family. Through the portcullis, which was being raised simultaneously, the bowmen could be seen running to take up their positions inside the gateway, hurriedly fastening their helmets and buckling on their weapons. The bridge fell into place and soon the massive planks were drumming with horses' hooves. Catherine rode ahead through the gateway and emerged in the court in front of the massive keep. She bypassed the door into the feudal tower and headed for the main building with its elegant flamboyant windows. A woman swathed in black from head to foot had just appeared on the threshold and stood there waiting. It was possibly because this woman stood leaning on a stick that Catherine did not at first recognize Ermengarde.

She leapt from her saddle, unable to take her eyes off this black-clothed silhouette slowly advancing towards her. The plump Ermengarde had grown so thin that her black velvet dress sagged loosely around her. Her face was ashen pale under hair which had grown quite white and her eyes were red and swollen with weeping. Catherine ran to her friend and seized her by the shoulders, appalled by what she saw and even more by what she guessed.

"Ermengarde! My God . . . What is it? Philippe?"

With a strangled sob, the old woman fell into Catherine's arms and wept piteously, her face resting on her young friend's shoulder. This sign of weakness in the once indomitable Countess told Catherine all she needed to know—her worst fears had been realized.

"Ah, he is . . . ?" was all she said.

She could not finish. The dreadful word would not pass her lips. Ermengarde merely nodded affirmatively. . . . Sara and the soldiers standing at the foot of the steps gazed petrified at these two women weeping in each other's arms, for Catherine's aching heart had at last given way to a fit of convulsive sobbing which shook her whole body. After the first shock of the news had worn off, Sara dismounted hurriedly and ran towards the two women, whom she gently separated. Then she slipped an arm round each of them and led them into the building.

"Come . . . you mustn't stay out here. It is cold and damp. . . ."

A deep silence hung about the château. Servants dressed in black glided about like shadows, not daring to look up. Ever since little Philippe's death the day before, Ermengarde's furious grief had filled the ancient building with alarm and dread. That very morning the chaplain had been forced to tear the Countess away from the child's bedside in order to proceed with laying out the body. . . . Such grief as this made Catherine feel a little ashamed. She felt rather as though she were moving through a thick layer of cotton-wool which muffled her consciousness and prevented her grief from making itself properly felt as yet.

"What happened?" she asked in a colorless voice which seemed to come from a stranger, it was so unfamiliar.

Ermengarde, whom Sara had forced to sit down, raised a piteous, grief-stricken face towards her, eyes red-rimmed from weeping.

"A dreadful fever . . ." she faltered. "Some peasants have died in the village from drinking the water from a poisoned well. The child drank some, too, returning from a walk with his tutor. He was thirsty and he stopped at the mill and asked for a drink. . . . The next day he was delirious—that was when I sent for you. The castle apothecary did what he could . . . and I did not even have the satisfaction of hanging the miller," Ermengarde added, so savagely that Catherine shivered. ". . . He died the same evening from that accursed well-water of his. . . . How can you ever forgive me? You entrusted him to me . . . and now he is dead . . . my little Philippe, my handsome boy . . . dead!"

The Countess buried her head in her shaking hands and began to sob again, so piteously that Catherine leant across and put her arms round the old woman's shoulders.

"Ermengarde! . . . Please stop torturing yourself! You have nothing to blame yourself for. . . . You were the best of mothers to him, far better than I! Yes, indeed, far better than I was. . . ."

Her eyes began filling and she was about to burst into tears again when the chaplain tiptoed into the room to announce that everything was ready and the child laid out in the chapel. For an instant, something of the old Ermengarde seemed to come back. The Countess stood up and took Catherine's hand.

"Come . . . come and see him," she said.

She strode out of the room, followed by Catherine and Sara,

and after descending a narrow stone staircase, hurried along a wide vaulted gallery, one side of which was pierced all the way along by flamboyant gothic windows bearing the Châteauvilain family arms. The door at the far end of the gallery led into the chapel. Catherine gave a startled exclamation as she entered. The sanctuary was not large: a fan-vaulted nave supported on massive, grey stone, Roman pillars. In the center, the child lay upon a catafalque covered in black and gold, dressed in a sumptuous costume of blue velvet. At his feet, his mother's arms lay beside the Duke of Burgundy's blazon crossed by a red bar sinister. Four men-at-arms in shining armor stood, leaning on their halberds, one at each corner of the catafalque, motionless as statues. A forest of thick, yellow wax candles cast a festive blaze of light over the little chapel with its small windows. The old walls were almost hidden by banners and black velvet hangings.

The magnificence of the scene astonished Catherine, who turned a startled face towards her friend. Ermengarde flushed abruptly and raised her head in a movement full of unconscious arrogance.

"He had the blood of princes in his veins!" she said hoarsely.

Without a word, Catherine went to kneel beside the body. She felt a sort of awe and hardly dared look at the child's body, distressed to see how strikingly he resembled his father. It was so long since she had last seen him that she scarcely recognized him. He seemed so tall in his last sleep, his little hands crossed upon his breast! His features were haughty already and his short blond hair was exactly like Philippe's. . . . He could not have been any other man's son and Catherine's grief was aggravated by a vague feeling of jealousy. It was as though the little Philippe had deliberately turned his back on his mother, detaching himself from her in order to turn towards the man who had given him life. . . . A piercing stab of remorse and sorrow struck the young woman's heart: regret for all the time she had lost. She must have been mad to deprive herself of him and him of herself! And now death had robbed her of him for eternity. . . . Bitterly she reproached herself for her indifference, for her coldness. . . . Suddenly, the already loosening bonds of flesh and blood hurt almost too much to be borne! She would have liked to seize the little body in her arms and warm it back to life with her own life. . . . She would have given her own life then to see little Philippe open his eyes and smile at her. But it was at Ermengarde he must have smiled for the last time.

Stricken by a grief whose fangs were beginning to pierce keenly for the first time, Catherine buried her face in her hands and wept a long while at the feet of her dead child. The little boy, on his sumptuous, pointless bed, already seemed to belong to another world.

Catherine remained all the next night praying in the chapel, oblivious of the fatigue of her long journey. Neither Sara's and Ermengarde's gentle protests nor the advice of the chaplain, alarmed by her extreme pallor, could tear her away from the child's side.

"I must stay with him as long as I can," she cried bitterly. "I regret so much all those years when I didn't see him. . . ."

Ermengarde didn't insist, sensing what her friend must be feeling. She joined her in her vigil. At daybreak the child was buried in great pomp before the entire village, all dressed in mourning for the occasion. Then, when the stone which sealed the entrance to the Châteauvilain family vault had been rolled back into place over the body of the little ducal bastard, Catherine and Ermengarde were left facing each other . . . two bereaved women mourning the same loss. In tacit agreement, they had refused food that night and retired into the Countess's room together. They sat for a long while in silence, each in a tall, carved oak chair either side of the fireplace. They cut strange figures in their black weeds, as they sat gazing into the flames. One might have thought they were mother and daughter united in their grief. . . . Neither one dared break the silence first, fearing that the least remark might wound her companion. . . . Finally, however, Ermengarde rallied herself. She looked towards Catherine.

"And what now?" she asked.

These little words seemed to break the evil spell which bound her to silence. Catherine stood up abruptly and then ran and flung herself down beside her friend and with a sob, hid her face in the black folds of her dress.

"I have nothing left, Ermengarde," she sobbed. "No husband, no child, no love. . . . I only have you! Keep me here, let me stay with you. My life is empty . . . empty! I want to stay with you and my child's burial place from now on. Let me stay here. . . ."

Ermengarde took off the tall, black head-dress which was being crushed against her lap and stroked the young woman's golden plaits. A faint, gentle smile stole into her grief-ravaged face.

"Of course, you may stay here, Catherine. . . . Nothing would give me greater pleasure than to keep you here with me for ever. You know, I love you as if you were my own daughter. But it is you, of your own accord, who will leave this place; for you are far from the stage I have reached—of being ready to shut myself up in the depths of an old fortress for the rest of my days."

The snow began falling three days after Philippe's funeral. It fell so heavily that the life of the little town of Châteauvilain almost came to a standstill. The castle itself, on whose keep the black banner had been joined by a scarlet one, seemed to be slumbering in its proud isolation. And within its walls, the lives of the two stricken women slipped monotonously by, each day like the one before. Each morning they would hear Mass in the chapel and then repair to one of the chambers where they passed the whole day in embroidery and needlework. One day a week, Tuesday, some of her peasants would climb the castle mound to bring their grievances before their feudal lord. Then Ermengarde would take her seat on the seignorial bench in the great hall and spend long hours examining and settling arguments about a badly built wall, or a path which cut across a valuable field. Sometimes she would untangle a disagreement over an inheritance, or authorize a marriage or punish an adulterous wife. Ermengarde's justice was impartial, swift and vigorous, but imbued with a deep wisdom which Catherine, who was allowed to attend these sessions, deeply admired. Gradually, the sessions became a source of real interest and distraction to her.

At Christmas, a messenger arrived from the Duke with a letter and a magnificently illuminated Book of Hours in a gold and ivory cover which was Philippe's gift to Catherine. It was by no means the first letter to reach Châteauvilain. Shortly after the child's death, Philippe of Burgundy had written to his mistress expressing all the sorrow he felt at this senseless, cruel bereavement. He had found words of infinite tenderness to soften the mother's grief a little and, had it not been for the prospect of his forthcoming marriage, Catherine would have gone back to him at once. But she did not feel brave enough in her afflicted state to return and endure the inquisitive glances of the courtiers who would be waiting to see her reactions at finding herself no longer the center of interest, and the malice of the women who had secretly hated her for so long.

The new letter was as tender as the first, but reading between the endearments, Catherine felt Philippe's imperious desire to have her return to him. She could not be mistaken; in reminding her of her promise to him on their last night together, Philippe was addressing an order to her.

"It certainly sounds like one," Ermengarde said, when Catherine showed her the letter. "What will you do? Obey it?"

Catherine shook her head.

"I don't think so. I have no wish to do so. The Infanta will be

193

arriving in a few months and I would only have to leave again. So what's the use?"

"He loves you, you know that very well. He can't do without you. . . . He has even written it," Ermengarde said, pointing to a line with her finger.

"He writes that. . . . Oh, of course! But he can do without me. You can't know so little of Philippe as to believe that I alone have been able to satisfy his inexhaustible sensuality these past three years! Many women must have shared, and will always share, his favors with me. He loves me, I know, and I believe he has never stopped desiring me, as much or even more now than before. But there are other women, and the Infanta has a reputation for beauty, they say. She will turn his thoughts away from me."

Ermengarde took Catherine's two hands between her own.

"Seriously, my love, what sort of life do you envisage for yourself? What do you want? What do you hope for? I cannot believe that a young . . . and very beautiful woman like yourself has no other ambition than to spend her days with an old woman buried away in a gloomy castle. I can understand your refusing the humiliating role of official mistress alongside the reigning Duchess. But why not change your life? There must be many others who would gladly lead you to the altar."

"I believe so," Catherine said with a melancholy smile. "Only I have no desire to be led there by any of them."

"What will you tell the Duke?"

"Nothing! . . . For the simple reason that I don't know what to tell him. If my old friend, Abou-al-Khayr, were here he would doubtless come up with a superb quotation from some poet or philosopher to describe my current state of mind. I am convinced that he has one for every condition of the soul. . . . But he is far away. . . ."

The little Moorish doctor had, in fact, set out for Granada shortly after Garin's death in spite of Ermengarde's repeated offers of hospitality. His master, the Sultan Mohammed VIII, embroiled in endless civil wars, had finally sent for his principal friend and adviser. It had been with real regret that Abou-al-Khayr took his leave of Catherine, of whom he had grown genuinely fond.

"If you should find yourself with nowhere to go or nothing to do one of these days, come and join me. Lemon and almond trees grow wild in the garden of my little house beside the Génil river and the air is fragrant with roses most of the year. You would be my sister and I could teach you the wisdom of Islam. . . ."

Now, when her life seemed to be heading for an impasse,

Catherine recalled these friendly words and the recollection made her smile.

"That must be the solution . . . to join Abou-al-Khayr and learn about another way of life!"

"You must be out of your mind!" Ermengarde snorted. "Before getting to Granada, you would have to travel through many foreign lands—by the time you arrived you would have been raped twenty times over and no doubt killed as many times!"

"Once would be enough," Catherine replied. "But you are right. Let us wait here and see what happens. Perhaps destiny will do me the favor of sending a sign."

Despite Philippe's gift, however, and his love letter, Christmas was a terribly sad time for the two women. Together they distributed gifts to the peasants and townspeople and received their greetings in return. Together, too, they passed long hours in the chapel between the crêche, which Ermengarde installed there every year following the example of St. Francis of Assisi, and the grave of little Philippe. The countryside was buried under snow. Every day, as she got up and glanced through the window, Catherine began to despair—it seemed as though the sun would never return. Everything was cold and dark and she felt her heart beginning to freeze up little by little.

But the earth was at work under the snow and winter was soon to give way to the spring . . . and one March day a monk mounted upon a grey mule climbed the steep little path which led up to the drawbridge of Châteauvilain. The first green shoots were beginning to appear on the rich brown earth and the first buds were burgeoning on the bare trees.

When challenged by the guard, the newcomer asked whether Mme. de Brazey still resided at the Château and, when he was told she did, asked to be taken to her.

"Mme. de Brazey knows me well—tell her it is Brother Étienne Charlot."

Catherine sent for him to be brought to her room. She was alone; Ermengarde had gone to the stables to see about a mare in foal. This visit, which brought back the past, delighted her. She had not seen the monk from Saint Beuvray since the banishment which had been passed upon him and Odette de Champdivers. The former favorite of Charles VI had died, so Catherine learnt, soon after the birth of her son, soon after her arrival in Dauphiné. The hardships and privations she had suffered in prison had shattered her delicate constitution. Her mother, Marie de Champdivers, had followed her to the grave soon after, dead of a broken heart. Catherine had been deeply affected by these deaths, following so soon after each other, and she had always imagined that Brother Étienne must have passed on to the next world too. But when he entered the room, she saw that he had scarcely changed at all. His crown of grey hair was now almost white, but his face was as round as ever and his eyes as sparkling.

"Brother Étienne!" Catherine cried, going towards him with outstretched hands. "I never expected to see you again in this world!"

"In truth, I did nearly leave it, Madame, for I was very ill after my spell in prison. But the care of my brother monks and the pure air of Morvan restored me to health, thanks be to God!"

Catherine made her visitor sit down beside her on the long, canopied, wooden bench which stood to one side of the fireplace. Then she sent for some refreshments and ordered a room to be prepared for the traveler.

"Do not go to so much trouble for me," said the monk, embarrassed by this welcome. "When you know why I have come, you may not be so anxious for me to stay. I have come to . . . ask you a favor."

"I don't know what I can do for you, Brother Étienne, but you are none the less welcome for that. First eat and then you shall tell me why you have come. . . ."

As he tackled the cold boar with relish, Brother Étienne quaffed a good flagon of Beaune wine and then he explained. Since October 12 of the preceding year, the English had been besieging Orleans and it was about the desperate situation of that great city that the monk wished to speak. Despite the fact that the English and Burgundian besiegers had not succeeded in blockading the town entirely, and it was still possible to enter by the north-west, the position of the people of Orleans was so desperate that they had sent Xaintrailles to the Duke of Burgundy to ask him to take the town in trust . . . but his troops continued to besiege the town.

"The Duke is only too prone to forget that he is a French prince," the monk said severely. "They say he is thinking of founding an Order of Chivalry . . . yet he must know that the siege of Orleans is violating one of the principal laws of chivalry. It is a violation of feudal law to attack a town whose prince is held captive, and the Duke of Burgundy knows that well, particularly since the town was already paying tribute to avoid being attacked."

"I know that!" said Catherine, who remembered reproaching Philippe for his overly English sympathies more than once.

As for Ermengarde, she had been seething with rage ever since the start of the siege. As far as the Countess was concerned, Philippe was no longer worthy to wear the golden spurs of chivalry.

"But what can I do?" the young woman added.

Brother Étienne's face was illuminated by a look of ardent entreaty. He leant over and took Catherine's hands and held them so tightly they were bruised.

"Madame . . . there isn't a man or woman in this country who does not know about Monseigneur Philippe's great love for you. You must go to him and beg him to withdraw his troops from Orleans. You cannot imagine what this town means to King Charles. If Orleans falls, France and the King are doomed. The Englishman who reigns in Paris will have the whole country at his feet. There will be nothing left for those who have sworn fealty to the King to live for—the efforts of Yolande d'Aragon will have been in vain, and much blood will have been spilt quite uselessly."

The monk paused a moment, then added very softly:

"And so many chevaliers have devoted themselves body and soul to the defense of the noble city! Orleans has destroyed its magnificent suburbs, Orleans fights with a desperate but admirable faith, prepared to die unless a miracle happens. You can be this miracle, Madame! There are prophetic voices everywhere declaring that a woman alone will deliver Orleans. Think . . . Captain de Montsalvy is fighting in the town with a handful of other courageous knights!"

Arnaud's name, flung at her like that without any warning, struck Catherine like a whip. Her heart stopped and she flushed to the roots of her hair, then, as the blood flowed back to her heart, she was left white and trembling.

"Brother Étienne," she said in a colorless voice, "it is unworthy of you and the cloth you wear to rewaken an impossible dream in a heart which only aspires to forget. I am a widow, my brother, and I have lost my child and though it is true I once begged you to help that same Captain de Montsalvy, there is nothing more I can do for him now. If his wife's prayers are useless to help him, what can a stranger like myself accomplish?"

"His wife?" the monk asked, astonished. "What wife?"

Was the monk mad? Catherine looked directly at him, asking herself whether he could have lost his memory, or was mocking her.

"The last time I heard word of Captain de Montsalvy," she said slowly, faltering as she pronounced the name which did not come easily to her, "was several years ago. He was about to wed Demoiselle Isabelle de Séverac, the maréchal's daughter and . . ."

"Isabelle de Séverac is dead, Madame . . . two months before her marriage! And Messire Arnaud, who was not too eager to surrender his freedom, so rumor has it, has not found anyone to replace her."

"What?"

Catherine's hands were trembling as they gripped the arms of her chair. A sudden desire to weep tightened her heart and misted her eyes. She was bewildered. . . . She had refused for so long to let herself think of the man whose very name made her swoon with tenderness, and had so resolutely driven his beloved image from her thoughts as part of an impossible dream! And now, all of a sudden, quite unexpectedly, she heard that he was free—as free as herself! It was enough to make one lose one's reason!

"My brother," she said sadly, "why did you not come to me sooner? Why did you not tell me this? Why have you allowed me to think he was lost to me all these years?"

"But how could I know you were ignorant of the fact?" the monk cried in dismay. "In spite of the war, news is carried from Charles' Court to the Duke's . . . and may I remind you that my sentence of banishment prevented me coming to you. My prior has finally managed to have the sentence lifted . . . and here I am. Will you go and intercede with the Duke for Orleans?"

Catherine's eyes were shining like stars. Brother Étienne sensed that she was far away, lost in that old dream which she had discovered again with such joy.

"Madame . . ." he reproached her gently. "You are not listening. Will you go to Philippe?"

She returned to earth with a bump and flashed him a smile so brilliant that the monk was overcome. This sad lacklustre woman was being transformed before his eyes. It was as though she had thrown off a heavy black cloak which hid the brightness within her; in a few moments, Catherine was transfigured. She shook her head.

"No, my brother! I shall never go back to Philippe of Burgundy. Cease asking me to—I cannot! Though you did not realize it, you have brought me the sign that I was waiting for. It is finished!"

"But, Madame! . . . And Orleans?"

"Orleans? I am going there . . . I shall leave tomorrow for the besieged city. You say it is still possible to enter the town— well, I will enter it, and die there, if need be."

"Your death cannot help the city, Madame," the monk said severely. "She has no need of another corpse to bury beneath her ruins. She needs to be liberated from the Burgundians."

"I begged the Duke to withdraw his troops before, in October," she said. "He did not do so. Why should he change his mind now? The Duke is about to remarry; my power over him is at an end. All I can do for you is write to the Duke and tell him that I am going to enter the besieged city and that if he cares whether I live or die, he will withdraw his men. . . . That might be of some help to you . . . perhaps not! But I can do no more."

She stood up, quivering with joy and excitement, eager to begin her journey. She walked rapidly across to the door, the fur-bordered train of her black dress swirling out behind her.

"Go on with your meal, brother," she said. "I have some arrangements to make. . . ."

She raced to the stairs to meet Ermengarde who was just then coming up. Unable to contain herself a moment longer, Catherine seized her friend by the shoulders and planted two smacking kisses on her cheeks.

"Ermengarde, kiss me! I am leaving!"

"Leaving? Where for?"

"For Orleans . . . to die, if need be! I've never been so happy!"

Before the astounded Countess could utter a word, Catherine had rushed down the staircase on her way to find Sara and tell her to prepare her baggage as soon as possible. Her heart leapt in her breast and if it hadn't been for a last, lingering respect for the proprieties, she would have sung with joy. She knew, with a deep certainty, what she must do now—find Arnaud at all costs, declare her love to him one last time and shut herself up with him in the ruins of the last bastion of French royalty. Orleans would be the giant tomb, on a scale with the immensity of her love, where this love of hers would at length find rest. . . .

Catherine did not know, nor did Brother Étienne, that on that very day a young, eighteen-year-old girl from Lorraine, wearing a boy's costume of rough, black cloth, had knelt before Charles VII in the great hall of the Château de Chinon and declared:

"Sweet Dauphin, I am called Joan the Maid, and I have come to help you and your Kingdom. And the King of Heaven ordains, through me, that you shall be consecrated and crowned king at Rheims. . . ."

That day was 8 March 1429.

At dawn the next morning, six riders galloped full tilt across the drawbridge of Châteauvilain. A black-clad form, standing on one of the gate-towers, watched them as they clattered off down the castle mound and, after crossing the Aujon by the old stone Roman bridge, disappeared at length into the valley mists. When the last hoofbeat had died away, Ermengarde de Châteauvilain went to the chapel to pray. Her heart was heavy and sorrowful, for she did not know whether she would ever see Catherine again. It was such a mad adventure the young woman had charged into so blithely! Not that the Countess disapproved of that! She knew that in Catherine's place she would have done just the same. There was nothing left for her to do but wait and hope and implore Heaven to grant Catherine the happiness that always seemed to elude her.

Meanwhile, Catherine, at the head of her little troop, was covering the first of the seventy or so leagues to Orleans. For this long ride she had decided to wear men's clothes and she congratulated herself on the choice, for she had never felt so comfortable. Tight black hose outlined her long legs which were encased in soft boots as high as the knee. A short, black doublet bordered with astrakhan, and a riding cloak completed her outfit, together with a little hood which hid everything but her pale, oval face. A dagger with a handle of chased steel was thrust through the leather belt which matched her big gauntlets. Catherine had grown a little thinner during these long months of unhappiness and despair, and this severe, masculine costume made her look like the scion of some noble house.

Sara, whose opulent curves were ill-suited to the slate blue costume that had been allotted to her, was not so comfortable. But she was not the woman to vex herself unduly over her appearance and she took a keen pleasure in riding through the countryside again in the fresh air. Brother Étienne followed, telling his beads after the fashion of a man who has long been accustomed to let his mount take its head. The band was completed by three men-at-arms whom Ermengarde had forced her friend to take as an escort. They had been riding all day across the monotonous plains of the Châtillonais, interspersed by seemingly endless belts of forest. That night they entered the double city of Châtillon. Catherine turned her back resolutely on the massive castle of the Dukes of Burgundy where the mere mention of her name would have caused her to be warmly received by the châtelain. Instead, she decided to pass the night at the Hostelry of Saint Nicolas. The gesture was symbolic. Now that she had disobeyed Philippe and gone over to his enemies, she wished nothing more to do with his castles. She was tired by the day's riding and slept like a log, waking up the next morning relaxed and full of energy and excitement she had not known for a long time.

The second day of the journey was much like the first. The countryside was cut into by deep valleys from time to time which alleviated the monotony of the ride. To Catherine, devoured with impatience to see the ramparts of Orleans on the horizon, their pace seemed mortally slow, but they could not afford to go any faster without endangering the horses. Twelve to fifteen leagues a day was the most the horses could go if they were to reach the journey's end without flagging. They spent that night at a pilgrims' guest house and the soldiers spent most of the evening cleaning and sharpening their weapons. They would be out of the Burgundian country the next day and the risk of attack was much more serious. But Catherine did not care a fig for risks like that. Only one thing mattered now— to find Arnaud.

The countryside was swamped by torrential rain when the little band set off again on the third day of their journey. Floods of water poured down upon the earth, blurring the outlines of everything around them and soaking the six riders to the skin.

"We shall have to halt, Catherine," Sara announced towards midday.

"Halt where?" Catherine asked nervously. "We are no longer on sure ground and even the guest houses may conceal a trap. We have barely a league to go before we reach Coulanges-la-Vineuse. We can halt there."

"Coulanges is unsafe," one of the escort objected. "An Armagnac bandit, Jacques de Pouilly, whom they call Fortépice, has occupied the castle there. We would do better to go on to Auxerre."

"Auxerre is no more enticing," Catherine interrupted decisively. "Anyway, there is nothing about us which might appeal to a brigand. In weather like this your Fortépice will be sitting in front of a roaring fire in the great hall playing chess with one of his men. Is there a monastery at Coulanges?"

"Yes, but. . . ."

"Well, that's where we shall stop, without entering the town. We shall not move from there till daybreak when we set out again. Come now, men, surely you are not afraid! If you are, the best thing for you would be to turn round and head straight back to Burgundy while it is still near. . . ."

"Madame, Madame. . . ." Brother Étienne reproached her. "It takes great courage to travel through enemy territory. These men are only doing their duty in warning you of the dangers."

Catherine shrugged and spurred her horse forward at a more

rapid pace. Presently the knoll of Coulanges-la-Vineuse, crowned by its castle, showed up grey behind a curtain of rain. As they drew nearer, however, Catherine began to feel vaguely uneasy. The countryside, which must once have been fertile and smiling, was strangely gloomy. The peaceful, protected lands of Burgundy were behind them. Here, the black earth looked scorched and showed nothing but an occasional fragment of twisted wood which might once have been the stem of a vine. From time to time they passed a ruined house which had been reduced to a mound of cold ashes or, worse still, a body hanging from the branch of a tree, slowly putrefying in the rain. . . . As they passed by one of the few houses still left standing, Catherine and Sara covered their eyes in horror: straddling the barn door like a sinister, pale cross was the naked corpse of a woman with long black hair; she had been crucified and disembowelled.

"My God," Catherine murmured, appalled. ". . . Where are we now?"

The soldier who had previously urged her to change her route now spoke up again:

"I told you that this Fortépice was a brigand, Madame, but I did not realize he went as far as this! See those ruined buildings ahead! That is the monastery where you hoped to spend the night. He must have set fire to it, the wretch! We must flee, Madame, while there is still time. It is possible that Fortépice and his men have stayed inside their castle as you suggested because of the weather, but it would be foolish to tempt fate. Do you see that path on the left which leads into the forest? Let us take that. About two leagues from here, we should reach the town of Courson where we can find shelter for the night. I am not sure about the château there, for I don't know who holds it now. . . ."

Catherine was appalled by the grisly sight she had just seen and made no objection. She allowed the man to take her horse by the bridle and lead it towards the trail which ran deep into the forest. The path wound between thick scrubs whose tangled branches rose up like walls. Occasionally, a grey boulder created a little contrast. The deeper into the forest they went, the narrower the trail became and the branches joining up overhead made it into a tunnel which gradually became darker and darker. There was nothing to be heard except the horses' hooves and the flight of an occasional bird. And then, suddenly, came the attack. . . .

A band of armed men rushed onto the path, dropping down from trees and springing out from behind a wall of rocks. Some of them seized the horses' bridles while others leapt up and caught hold of their riders, forcing them out of their saddles and down onto the ground. In the twinkling of an eye, Catherine and her companions found themselves trussed like chickens and unceremoniously flung down on the muddy track. The men who had ambushed them were a sturdy, but ragged looking lot whose faces were covered by cloth masks which left only their eyes showing. Their weapons were of good quality, however, and well looked after. One of the men, the only one wearing a breastplate of steel plaques over his hide jerkin, a long sword and knight's spurs, detached himself from the rest and came over to inspect the prisoners.

"Not much of a catch," one of the brigands growled. "A lean-pursed lot. Better hang them all straight away!"

"The horses and weapons are of good quality," the man who appeared to be their leader interrupted drily. "And those decisions are up to me."

He stooped his tall, thin frame a little for a closer look at his prisoners. Then he suddenly burst out laughing, removing the filthy rag over his face as he did so. Catherine noticed with some surprise that he was much younger than she would have imagined—not more than twenty-two or three. But all the marks of precocious vice were already written there on that lean face with its slack lips and eyes sparkling with greed and rapacity.

"This brilliant cavalcade boasts but three men," he cried "The remainder is composed of a monk and, God help me, two women!"

"Two women!" cried the other brigand in amazement, craning forward for a better look. "Ah, *she* is a woman, that's obvious, but I would have sworn the other was a boy!"

By way of an answer, the chieftain drew his dagger and slashed a hole in Catherine's doublet as she lay there quivering with rage, exposing one breast.

"With a boy like that around, one could dispense with women," he exclaimed jovially. "But she is too skinny for me. I like them plump and juicy. The other one would suit me better."

"Swine!" Catherine cried, spluttering with rage. "You will pay for this insolence! I would have you know that I am the Comtesse de Brazey and Monseigneur the Duke of Burgundy will make you regret this attack . . . and this insult!"

"I thumb my nose at the mighty Duke of Burgundy, my beauty! And I would have you know this—beside that prince of traitors I, Fortépice, consider myself a veritable angel! You may say what you like about my manners, but now I must allow myself one more insult to see whether or not you are lying."

He reached out and snatched off the hood covering Catherine's head, neck and shoulders so that the thick golden plaits which she had bound close to her head were revealed, gleaming softly in the grey, rainy light. Fortépice gazed at them for an instant, thoughtfully, then he spoke:

"The Comtesse de Brazey, Philippe of Burgundy's beautiful mistress, is reputed to have the most magnificent hair in the world. I'll be hanged if this isn't it!"

"Don't worry," Catherine said drily, "you'll be hanged all right."

"Not too soon, I trust. Well, the catch is better than I hoped. I'll wager the Duke will show himself a right generous prince in order to get you back again, my beauty. Meanwhile, I shall have the pleasure of offering you the hospitality of my château at Coulanges until the ransom arrives. The food is bad but the wine is excellent. The latter compensates for the former. As for the rest. . . . By the way, who is that handsome dame with the black eyes who looks at me as though I were Satan personified?"

"My companion," Catherine answered haughtily.

"Then she shall accompany you," said Fortépice with sudden gallantry. He smiled and his smile alarmed Catherine much more than his earlier bullying tone. He turned to his lieutenant and commanded him:

"Tranchemer, have the two women and the monk hoisted and tied into their saddles. We are taking them back with us. I need a chaplain, as it happens, and the monk will do me very well. As for the rest. . . ."

The gesture which accompanied these last words was so gruesomely explicit that Catherine cried out:

"You can't kill these men! They are in my service and they are brave soldiers and faithful followers. I *forbid* you to touch them! You will get money for them, too. . . ."

"A likely story!" Fortépice exclaimed. "I have no use for extra mouths to feed. Do as I say, men!"

"Murderous brute!" Catherine shrieked desperately. "If you do this thing, I swear to you I'll . . ."

Fortépice sighed deeply and frowned.

"Oh . . . she makes too much noise, that silly woman! I don't like noisy people. Shut her up, Tranchemer."

Though she screamed and struggled, Tranchemer finally succeeded in gagging her tightly with the filthy rag he wore as a mask. The gag half smothered her and reduced her to helpless silence. She was forced to look on, wide-eyed with horror, as two of the bandit's followers fell upon the three soldiers and coolly slit their throats. Blood spurted out copiously, drenching the path and mingling with the water in the muddy puddles. The trampled mud of the path turned red. The three victims died without uttering a sound. . . .

Rapidly, the bandits untied them, then removed their armor and weapons and stripped them naked.

"What shall we do with them?" Tranchemer asked.

"There's a field at the end of the path. Take them there. The crows will see to the rest. . . ."

While the men carried out their grisly instructions under Tranchemer's supervision, Fortépice climbed on to one of his victim's horses and rode out ahead of the troop towards Coulanges.

"We had been hunting all day without success," he cried, glancing at Sara. "But this makes up for all our lost time!"

The prisoners followed behind, still trussed and tied to their saddles with murder in their hearts. Anger and revolt were already brewing in Catherine's spirit. . . .

CHAPTER TWELVE

The Via Dolorosa

The castle which Fortépice used as his hide-out was crumbling and dilapidated, but still formidable. The keep looked as if it might collapse at any moment, but the walls still held firm and, as far as the robber chieftain was concerned, that was the essential thing. Inside it was indescribably filthy. The squalor began in the courtyard where the livestock were penned into stinking little shacks and the dung was piled almost shoulder high. The living quarters were not much more comfortable. Catherine was given a tiny room high up in one of the corner towers overlooking the Yonne valley. It was crescent-shaped and lit by one ancient, narrow, Roman window, divided down the middle by a thin pillar. The walls were quite bare but for festoons of spiders' webs which trembled in the draughty air, and the floor looked as if it had not been swept for a considerable time. It was covered by a thick layer of dust and an old, rotting layer of straw which no one had bothered to remove or renew. It smelt stale, musty and damp, but the low door, furnished with strong bolts on the outside, had been so recently oiled that it did not even creak.

"Let's not have any complaints," Tranchemer said as he escorted her in. "It is our best room. It even has a fireplace. . . ."

There was a fireplace with a conical hood over it in one corner, but as Catherine pointed out, it did not contain a fire.

"You'll get your fire as soon as we have enough wood," said the lieutenant philosophically. "There is only just enough to cook on at the moment. The men have gone to find some more in the forest. You shall have a fire this evening. . . ."

He went out, leaving the young woman to her thoughts, which were far from cheerful. Her anger of a little while back was gradually being replaced by dark depression and self-disgust. What folly it had been to rush headlong into this dangerous countryside! How long would she have to remain in this sinister place? Fortépice spoke of a ransom. He must be going to send a messenger to Philippe of Burgundy, and Philippe would certainly make haste to free his mistress. But whoever came to free her would merely be gaolers of a different sort; they would almost certainly have been ordered to bring her back to Bruges as soon as possible. Philippe would hardly let her rush off to Orleans, to another man, as soon as he had rescued her from Fortépice. . . . She must try and find some other way of escape before the ransom arrived.

She leant against the little pillar in her window and looked gloomily down at the dizzy drop below her. It must be at least sixty feet to the rock on which the castle was built, and she had no wings. . . . Struck by a sudden thought, Catherine ran over to the bed and tore off the shabby coverlet, revealing a straw-filled mattress in a sorry state of repair, but no blankets or sheets; nothing which she could use to make a rope. . . . She flung herself down on the mattress and fought the tears that threatened to overwhelm her. She must not allow herself to break down and weep, because tears would bring a softening of the will, a sort of dull despair at this moment when she needed all her wits about her. If only they had allowed Sara to remain with her! But Fortépice had escorted the gypsy into his own quarters, making no secret of his intentions towards her. And Brother Étienne had vanished in another direction.

The fatigue of the journey was beginning to tell despite her efforts and Catherine closed her eyes. Wretched though it was, her bed was an invitation to rest and she was too exhausted to resist. She closed her eyes and was about to drop off to sleep when the sound of the door opening woke her up. She sat up again. It was Tranchemer carrying an iron candlestick which showed up his pockmarked face and red, drunkard's nose above a huge grinning mouth. He was carrying some clothes on his arm which he threw down on the foot of the bed.

"Here," he said. "For you! The chief says you won't be needing your men's clothes here. He's sent along the best he has. Quick now! He doesn't like to be kept waiting."

"All right," Catherine sighed. "I'll change. You can go. . . ."

"Oh, no!" Tranchemer exclaimed, his grin widening. "I have to stay here to make sure you change at once and then remove all your boy's clothes . . . and help you, if necessary."

Catherine flushed angrily. Did this oaf imagine she would undress in front of him?

"I won't undress with you in the room!" she cried.

Tranchemer put down the candle and came towards her.

"Excellent," he said calmly. "Then I shall have to help you. I can send for assistance, you know. . . ."

"No, no, all right, I'll change."

She was nervous, not knowing what to make of this odd demand. The mere idea of the bandit's hands touching her made her feel sick. She unfolded the clothes he had brought. There was a brown velvet dress, slightly moth-eaten, but reasonably clean, a fine linen petticoat and a sort of thick wool surcoat to go over them.

"Turn round!" she commanded, without much hope of being obeyed. Tranchemer remained just as he was, staring at her with undisguised curiosity. In a sudden fury, she tore off her men's clothes and flung on the petticoat so quickly that her white body flashed before the bandit for no longer than a second or two. But it was long enough for Tranchemer, who let out a sigh gusty enough to bring the roof down.

"By the Pope's intestines!" he groaned. "And we've been forbidden to touch you! The chief must be mad to prefer your servant-woman!"

"Where is she?" Catherine asked agitatedly as she finished lacing up her bodice. Her hands were damp and clumsy. She would gladly have slapped this oaf who stood there staring at her like a half-wit. Tranchemer burst out laughing.

"Where, but in the chief's bed, by God! He doesn't believe in wasting his time! When a girl takes his fancy, it's into bed with her straight away! . . . Let's hope he's in a good mood!"

"What does his mood have to do with it?" Catherine asked coldly. Tranchemer gave a witless grin which exasperated Catherine still further.

"Damme! If he's in a good mood, he'll pass her on to us when he's finished with her. Fine women don't come our way too often in these hard times. Round here they're all as skinny as alley cats. . . . A woman like her, now, that's a real treat!"

Tranchemer's jocular tone was the last straw. Catherine lost her temper. She saw red.

"You go and find that Fortépice of yours," she shouted. "Go and find him and bring him here at once!"

Tranchemer's eyes popped.

"What? Disturb him now? Not on your life! He'd have me skinned alive!"

Catherine ran across to the window and pointed at it with a hand which shook with rage.

"Damn your skin! It won't be worth much if you have to go and tell that cut-throat I'm dead, will it? If you don't go and fetch him at once, I promise you I'll jump straight through this window."

"Are you crazy? What's it to you if someone has a bit of fun with your maid?"

"Mind your own business and do what I tell you. Otherwise...."

She was beginning to climb up on the windowsill. Tranchemer hesitated. He was tempted to reach out and knock her unconscious to keep the silly woman quiet, but Satan alone knew what she'd get up to when she came round again! Anyway, the whole problem was becoming too complex for the lieutenant's simple mind to grasp. One thing he did know, and that was that he could not afford to let a rich prize like this one get spoiled or damaged in any way. Fortépice was counting on making a fortune out of her. If anything happened to this she-devil Tranchemer knew that Fortépice would flay his hide off strip by strip, a favorite trick of his when someone really annoyed him. On the whole, it would be less risky to disturb him in the midst of his pleasures.

"You stay quiet!" he commanded roughly. "I'm going, but don't blame me for the consequences!"

As Catherine slowly swung her feet back onto the ground, Tranchemer went out of the room, shutting the door carefully behind him. When she found herself alone again, Catherine wiped the sweat off her forehead. For a moment she thought she was going out of her mind. The thought of her faithful Sara at the mercy of these loathsome brigands was more than she could stomach. She would have flung herself from the tower unhesitatingly for the sole satisfaction of knowing that she had thereby placed Tranchemer in an impossible situation. Now, however, she must concentrate on getting all her wits about her for an imminent encounter with Fortépice.

He arrived a few minutes later with the surly expression of a dog whose bone has been snatched away. He wore nothing but his tight hose and an open-necked shirt which was torn in several places.

"What do you want?" he barked from the threshold. "If you can't keep quiet, we'll have to put you in irons!"

He looked far younger in this state of undress than in his previous warlike trappings. Catherine realized that she was not afraid of him any more. She felt quite calm and controlled.

"Putting me in irons wouldn't make any difference to what I am about to say," she said coldly. "I've sent for you to tell you to leave Sara alone. I find the idea of your laying your filthy hands on her almost as distasteful as if you were to attack me personally. And Monseigneur Philippe's generosity might suffer in consequence. . . ."

Fortépice glanced at her slyly. He gave a short laugh which sounded more like a whinny.

"Very bold for a prisoner, aren't you? As for your Sara, your request comes a little late. . . . She pleases me greatly, if you want to know, and I have no intention of giving her up. She stays with me."

"I know all about you!" Catherine cried, scarlet with rage. "First you take her and then you let your men have her! Well, I swear to you that you won't touch a penny of my ransom money if those disgusting brutes lay so much as a finger on her! I want to see her, do you hear? I *insist* on seeing her! . . ."

The robber chieftain strode forward and before she could stop him, grabbed her round the waist and pulled her close to him. He was pale with anger.

"That's enough! I won't give her to my men, if that's what you want. But I'm warning you—you had better be quiet if you don't want to follow her into my bed. . . ."

"I'm too thin!"

"I wouldn't be too sure! In your boy's outfit, perhaps, but things look rather different in this dress and I might be tempted to forget that you're an expensive treat. I don't imagine that you're a virgin, so Philippe of Burgundy won't be losing much if I did amuse myself with you. So I warn you—keep quiet!"

He took hold of her by the nape of the neck, forced her flushed, furious face close to his and kissed her hard. His fingers were iron hard and, struggle as she might, Catherine was forced to submit to this loathsome kiss right to the bitter end. When he released her she stumbled and backed away to the bed where she stood, holding on to one of the bedposts.

"*Now* do you understand?" Fortépice said, suddenly quiet. "I advise you to keep quiet!"

"I want you to send Sara to me!" Catherine shrieked, beside herself with rage.

For a moment their eyes met. Catherine's violet eyes were

blazing with such fury the robber felt she might be capable of anything. He shrugged and went over to the door.

"I'll send her to you tomorrow. Till then you'll have to make do with Tranchemer, who'll be bringing your dinner in a few minutes. Good night!"

Catherine slid to her knees beside her bed and leant her forehead against the threadbare coverlet. She was exhausted and her head was beginning to throb with an incipient headache. She had won a partial victory. At least she had the leader's assurance that no one but himself would touch Sara. Anyway, she was too weary now to think straight. She was hungry and sleepy, and when Tranchemer reappeared carrying a platter and a pitcher of wine, she fell upon her meal ravenously. It wasn't much, soup thickened with flour in which several slices of bacon floated, all of it atrociously cooked.

"You aren't generous with your prisoners," she remarked acidly.

"You needn't complain! It's what everyone gets. You even have an extra slice of bacon! You were warned not to expect much in the way of food. Last night the Sire de Courson stole our only cow and our two pigs, so there isn't much to eat tonight. It may be better tomorrow. . . ."

"Why? Are you expecting a consignment of food?"

"Where from? No, we're going to try and steal his goats —the Sire de Courson's, I mean. After all, we've got to live."

The food was abominable, but the wine was surprisingly good. Catherine drank a little too much and soon her head started to swim. It was pitch dark outside and there was nothing left to do but sleep. She flung herself down on the bed fully dressed, pulled the tattered coverlet over her and was soon asleep.

Sara's face bending over her was the first thing that met Catherine's eyes when she opened them the next morning. It was broad daylight and a weak ray of sunshine outlined the black shadow of the central pillar in the window against the dusty floor. Catherine flung her arms spontaneously round the gypsy's neck.

"Sara! . . . At last you've come! I've been so anxious about you! Are you all right?"

Sara smiled faintly and shrugged. Her brown face was drawn. There were deep rings under her eyes, but apart from that, she showed no visible signs of suffering. Her black hair hung down her back in a heavy, shining mane making her look much younger and she wore an old dress of yellow silk brocade

210

whose sleeves were so long they trailed on the ground and which was cut very low in front.

"I'm all right," she said. "But if you mean, how did Fortépice acquit himself—I'd say he behaved much like any other man, no better and no worse. I think his reputation must be a little exaggerated."

In spite of her preoccupied expression, Sara sounded almost gay and Catherine began to wonder whether she hadn't rather enjoyed herself. But she hastily suppressed this uncharitable thought.

"What are your plans now?" Sara asked.

Catherine gazed at her in astonishment. What a silly question!

"My plans? I haven't got any, except to get out of here as soon as I possibly can!"

"Are you sure it wouldn't be better to wait here quietly till your ransom arrives? Fortépice sent one of his men to Flanders last night with a letter from Brother Étienne. I now realize why he wanted a chaplain—not to say Mass or recite Paternosters over the bodies of his deceased companions, but merely because no one in this charming little band knows how to write."

Catherine jumped up with an incredulous expression spread over her face.

"You don't mean it! Wait here for my ransom? You don't imagine that I undertook this mad journey merely to sit locked away in a ruined tower waiting for Philippe to ransom me from an impoverished bandit with sacks of gold? If that were the case, I would have gone straight to Bruges in the first place and saved everyone a lot of trouble. But that's just what I don't want to do. I'm as frightened of Philippe's gold as I am of the bandits, even more so, perhaps, because it's one prison I can't escape from. . . ."

She took Sara by the shoulders and shook her roughly.

"I don't care a damn for Philippe, do you hear!" she cried, her eyes flashing. "I'm going to join Arnaud. *Arnaud!* Do you understand. . . ?"

"You're mad, Catherine. He hates you! All he has ever done is despise you and hurt you!"

"I know, but I love him, you see. And that's all that matters . . . nothing else. I would rather be burned in Orleans than reign at Bruges if I could only clasp Arnaud's hand before I died. Won't you ever understand that I have loved him, and only him, for years and years, now? I want to get out of here and the quicker the better. . . ."

Sara brusquely wrenched herself free.

211

"You're hurting me," she said reproachfully. "I really think you must be out of your mind."

"Well, what's happened to *you?*" Catherine cried, wild with anger. "Have Fortépice's caresses changed you so much overnight? Do you mean to say, Sara, that you can advise me to sit here patiently waiting like a tethered goat till my master comes along and buys me back? You *have* changed! I suppose you just want to make sure Fortépice gets his money."

Catherine was too angry to know what she was saying. Sara recoiled as if she had been struck.

"How can you speak to me like that?" she cried tearfully. "Have we become enemies overnight?"

But resentment made Catherine stubborn. She turned away and went across to the window.

"I'm not your enemy, Sara. But you just don't seem to understand me any more, and that's what I can't understand. Arnaud is the only thing that matters in my life! If I can't have him, there's nothing I want from life."

Sara bowed her head and crossed over to the door. The absurd, brilliant gown she wore seemed to focus the sun's rays. Catherine saw a tear glistening on her cheek.

"I'm not angry with you, because I know you are still suffering. I'll try and find a way to get you out of this place tonight. Till then, stay here and don't make a fuss. . . ."

She went out and Catherine was left alone feeling somewhat ashamed of herself, but only fleetingly. Even Sara's feelings were no longer of any importance. Her whole being yearned towards a single magnetic pole: the hard-eyed, tender-voiced man whom she had never managed to forget. She lived for the moment when she would see him again. . . .

She spent the whole morning standing by the window gazing at the silvery ribbon of the Yonne river glinting in the sunlight and dreaming. Her thoughts were so far away that when Tranchemer appeared with her midday meal, so reminding her of her imprisonment and wretched surroundings, she came back to reality with a shock. The meal consisted of several slices of roast kid, somewhat charred, but delicious. The Sire de Courson's goats, it seemed, had met with a tragic fate the night before!

The afternoon dragged on interminably. Except that she was not suffering physically, Catherine could have believed herself back in that dreadful château at Mâlain, when she had learnt to dread each passing minute for fear of what it might bring. It was hope, rather than fear, which animated Catherine now, but the suspense was almost as cruel. Sara had said that she would be able to escape from Coulanges that night. But how?

She greeted the sunset almost joyfully. A little longer and she would know. . . .

After her supper, brought to her by Tranchemer who made heroic but unsuccessful attempts to draw her into conversation, the hours dragged on again, interminably. The sounds of activity in the château ceased, one by one. Sara still did not appear. At length the only sound to be heard was the heavy, metallic, measured pace of the guards posted on the battlements. It was past midnight and Catherine had given up hope and was about to go to sleep, when the door opened silently and Sara appeared. She was dressed just as she had been that morning, but under one arm she carried a huge bundle of rope. Catherine sprang from her bed.

"I'd given up hope. . . ."

"How little you trust me! I had to wait till Fortépice fell asleep, drugged with wine and . . . well, never mind. . . . But we have no time to lose. This is the only way of escape possible. . . ."

She began unrolling the coils of rope and fastened one end securely to the pillar in the center of the window. The bundle of rope slithered down into the darkness like an uncoiling snake and was soon lost to sight. Sara returned to Catherine who stood watching, speechless, and laid both hands on her shoulders.

"That's the best I can do for you. Are you brave enough to slide down the rope to the ground? I shall watch from here and keep an eye on the rope. Once you have reached the ground, I'll pull it up again and put it back where I found it. If you go round to the eastern side of the château, you will find a track you can follow and which will take you to your love, if that is what you want. . . ."

Catherine fought back the choking misery rising within her.

"It is the destiny you foretold for me a long time ago, Sara, if you remember. But I thought you loved me enough to want to share it with me. Are you letting me go alone? What has this brigand done to you that you should prefer him to me?"

"Nothing . . . and if I could, I would leave with you, but he has taken such a violent liking for me that he has sworn to flay Brother Étienne alive if I try to escape. I don't want the good brother to die for me, so I am staying here. But as soon as we both can escape, I shall seek you out again. Now, go. I would give a lot to be going with you, Catherine, believe me. . . ."

The latter, suddenly overcome with emotion, threw herself into her old friend's arms.

"Yes, of course I believe you! Forgive me, Sara. I think I

213

really have lost my senses since I found out where *he* was and where I could find him. . . ."

"Well, now, you must try your luck! Here are three silver coins I managed to steal from Fortépice's doublet. When you reach the great Loire river, which you are bound to come to if you keep walking westwards, you may be able to hire a boatman to take you as far as Orleans. . . ."

But Catherine refused the silver pieces with a brusque gesture.

"No, Sara. When Fortépice finds you have stolen them, he will kill you. . . ."

Sara began to laugh silently. She seemed to have regained all her former gaiety.

"I don't think so! I'll tell him . . . I'll just tell him that you are a witch and have the power to vanish into thin air. And I'll say the only reason I didn't mention it before was that I was afraid of you."

"Why didn't you tell him that when we first arrived?" Catherine sighed.

"His reaction certainly wouldn't have been the same. He is terribly credulous and superstitious. If I had told him sooner, he would have built a great pile of wood as fast as he could at the foot of the castle walls and left you on it tied hand and foot in the hope that in a day or two his stocks of firewood would have been magically replenished! But we can't go on talking here all night. There's no time to lose! I must go back to him in case he wakes up. That's the most immediate danger. . . ."

Roughly she pulled Catherine towards her and kissed her on the forehead.

"May God be with you, my little one," she murmured in a voice trembling with emotion, "and guide you safely to your beloved. . . ."

Then she went over to the window to see if there was anything stirring outside. Catherine, meanwhile, hurriedly tore a wide piece off the hem of her trailing dress so as to be able to move more freely.

"If only you had been able to get me a man's costume," she sighed.

"Fortépice knew what he was doing when he took ours. It's hard to imagine my running very far in this ridiculous torrent of yellow satin," Sara said, flapping her trailing sleeves. "But with that shabby dress and woollen surcoat, you should be warm and you won't attract attention. I did manage to get one of your possessions back, though—here! . . ." and she handed her the steel-handled dagger which Catherine had been carry-

214

ing when she left Châteauvilain. Catherine took it joyfully and slipped it, still warm where Sara had been holding it, into her bodice. Then the two women embraced tenderly.

"Hurry up and come and join me," said Catherine, forcing a smile. "You know I'm quite lost without you."

"We'll find each other again," Sara promised. "I'm certain of that."

The empty space opening below her set Catherine's heart beating fearfully. As a child she had practiced shinning up and down ropes dozens of times in the back streets of Paris, but then it had just been a game. Would she still be able to do it now, when her safety depended on it? It was pitch dark outside and Catherine forced herself to stop thinking and worrying. She wasn't even going to think about the gulf below her which she had stared at so often during the day. She crossed herself hurriedly, murmured a short prayer, put one leg over the sill and twined her legs round the rope. Sara's frightened face was the last thing she saw before closing her eyes. Luckily, there was not much wind and the rope hung almost motionless. She clung on tightly to the coarsely twisted hemp and, as she swung down and out into the night, her body suddenly seemed as heavy as lead. Then she twisted the rope round her right leg and began sliding rapidly down towards the foot of the tower. . . . It was going more smoothly than she had expected. She found the movements she thought she had forgotten returning to her instinctively. Down she went, smoothly, almost easily, except for her hands which were scorched by the coarse rope. But there was no stopping now. She opened her eyes to see where she had got to. The tower window was already far away above her head, a dim square of light in the night in which Sara's dark silhouette stood out. Catherine felt as if she were living in a nightmare. The peril of her position, swinging between heaven and earth, was brought home to her much more forcibly now that she had her eyes open. If she let go she would certainly break her neck on the rocks at the foot of the castle walls. Sara's voice reached her, a faint, anxious thread of sound:

"Don't lose heart! How is it going?"

"All right!" Catherine called out faintly. Her hands were smarting painfully, but she began to hurry her descent, spurred on by the fear that she might not hold out till she reached the bottom. She felt as if her shoulder muscles were being dragged out by the roots. There was a moment when her heart and breathing stopped and she thought she would have to let go. Fear swelled inside her like a gathering storm, the naked, primitive terror of a little girl lost in the dark. She concentrated on the thought of Arnaud, clinging to his memory with all her might, but the physical strain was too great for her. Every movement was an agony. She began to shake all over; her heart thumped and her limbs grew heavy under the pressure of an immense, irresistible weariness. The pain in her chafed hands was a torture. She was too exhausted . . . she let go!

Her fall was brief. Luckily for Catherine, the foot of the wall was not far below. Except for a sharp bump which stunned her for a second, she was none the worse. The rocks here were covered with a mat of brambles which covered her with scratches, but served to soften the shock of hitting the ground. She picked herself up feeling stiff and shaken and then, remembering Sara waiting anxiously up there, she tugged three times at the rope which was instantly hauled out of sight. Catherine saw Sara leave the window. A moment later she was once more alone in total darkness. . . .

Catherine had spent so much time studying the lie of the land from her window that she had a very clear mental picture of it now. Groping her way along the wall which surrounded the old fortress, she made her way round it as Sara had advised until she came to the path down which she hurried as fast as she could go. Her eyes were growing accustomed to the dark and she managed to find her way along without much trouble. Some way farther on, however, she stopped for a moment, looking about her uncertainly. A great screen of trees rose up, dark and impenetrable, looking as solid as a wall. How was she going to find the path which led to the main highway from here? Catherine's troubled heart sent up an ardent prayer. She *must* find the path, she really must. . . .

As if in answer to her silent entreaty, the clouds massed thickly above the little valley parted slightly so that a faint beam of silvery light shone through, just bright enough to light up the narrow breach in this wall of vegetation. She raced towards it without even pausing to look back at the black bulk of the château. Sara had given her good advice. By cutting across the fields she had avoided the village and the risk of chance encounters. It would be impossible to see her now in the safety of this woodland path, even assuming one of the sentinels had had sharp enough eyes to pick out her slender silhouette.

Once under cover of the trees, Catherine stopped to get back her breath and allow her wildly beating heart to calm down a little. She stretched and felt her spirits returning, despite her aching back and raw, blistered palms. . . . Thank God she had not lost her dagger in the fall. All things considered, it had gone very well. And she was free. . . !

She set off bravely, following the path as best she could. It was a rough track which the woodmen must have cleared while they were felling trees and it grew wider the farther she went along it. Catherine had decided to walk all night and then find a shelter where she could sleep a little. Food was the great problem. Where could she find anything to eat in this devastated countryside? She doubted whether even the money Sara had given her would be of any use. Still, it was no use crossing her bridges before she came to them, she decided sensibly. For the moment, Catherine decided, the most important thing was to put as much distance between herself and Fortépice as possible. She walked all that night, guided more by instinct than anything else, crossing woods and fields dotted here and there with lakes and rivers, trying to keep going in the same direction. At daybreak, from the wood where she was standing, she caught sight of a great town whose jagged rooftops rose up out of the morning mist. A massive castle rose beetling above them, a formidable and clearly well defended building. Catherine hesitated for a moment before striking out in that direction. In her present plight a strong fortress spelt danger and she had no wish to fall once more into hands greedy for princely ransom. But she was tired after this long journey and she had to find bread somewhere. The township appeared to be well defended, still prosperous. . . . Just then a peasant appeared, walking along a dirt track, an axe over one shoulder. He looked friendly enough and she went up to him.

"That town," she said. "What is it called?"

The man looked at her in astonishment. She realized that she must look strange in her ragged velvet gown and shabby surcoat. The peasant was shabbily dressed, too, but his homespun clothes were clean and well cared for.

"Where are you from?" he asked slowly. "That town over there is Toucy and the château you see over there belongs to the Bishop of Auxerre. Is that where you are going?"

She shook her head and added:

"All I want is some bread. I'm hungry and I have a long journey ahead of me. . . ."

The man hesitated for a moment. Catherine felt his eyes upon her, trying to make out what sort of woman she was. But it was a clear, candid look he turned on her and she decided to trust him.

"I was imprisoned in the château at Coulanges," she said quickly. "I managed to escape and I am on my way to Orleans."

Before she had even finished speaking, the man took her hand and began to lead her away.

217

"Come," he said. "Don't be afraid. Just follow me!"

He led her back in the direction from which he had come with long, rapid strides. As they skirted the wood, Catherine saw the chimney of a little brown cottage huddled against the sombre, woodland landscape. The man quickened his step, as if in a hurry to get home. He pushed open the door of solid, rough-hewn planks. A blonde girl who was standing over a cooking-pot on the hearth straightened up in surprise at the sight of Catherine.

"I found her walking through the woods, Magdelaine," the man explained. "She has escaped from Fortépice. She's hungry ... so I brought her here!"

"You did right!"

Without another word, the girl pulled out a stool, took a bowl from a chest and filled it with a ladle of turnip soup. Then she cut some slices of brown, crusty bread. She set all this before Catherine.

"Eat," she said simply. "Then you can sleep a little. There is no need to talk. You must be tired. . . ."

The simplicity and generosity of her welcome brought tears to Catherine's eyes. She looked at the girl. Magdelaine had a round, fresh face which radiated kindness.

"You don't even know who I am . . . but you open your doors to me."

"You have escaped from Fortépice," the man said in a voice vibrating with controlled anger. "And you are on your way to Orleans. That is all we need to know. Now eat and sleep."

Catherine was too weary and hungry to argue. She faltered her thanks, ate the soup and bread and then stretched out gratefully on the mattress placed in a corner which must have been Magdelaine's bed. She fell asleep at once.

When she woke, dusk was falling. The peasant had come home and was sitting before the fire carving an oak branch with a knife. Catherine saw that he was carving a little statue of the Virgin. The girl sat beside him spreading something on some slices of bread. When she saw that she was awake, she smiled at Catherine.

"Are you feeling better?"

"Yes, thank you. You have been so kind! Now I must be off again."

The man looked up from his work and looked at her with the same frank, fearless expression which had struck her that morning.

"Why do you choose to travel by night? Are you in hiding?"

"Pierre," the girl said reproachfully. "You have no right to cross-question her!"

218

"That's all right," Catherine said, smiling. "I'm not hiding; I just want to avoid falling into Fortépice's hands again."

"You need have no fear of him in these parts! It would be better to travel by day, though. Especially if you don't know the countryside. Do you know the way to Orleans?"

Catherine shook her head. Pierre put down his knife and the little woodcarving and came across to her.

"It is easy to find from here. You follow the old Roman road as far as Gien. You will have the Loire itself to guide you from there on. What are you going to do at Orleans?"

"Pierre!" Magdelaine exclaimed. "Her life is no concern of yours."

But Catherine smiled sweetly at him.

"There is no reason why he should not know. I am going there to be with the man I love. He is shut up in the town."

Magdelaine stopped preparing her soup, came over to Catherine and slipped an arm round her waist.

"Come and sit with us," she said. "If you are in love with one of the men who are defending Monseigneur Charles's city, you are one of the family. My betrothed, Colin, is an archer in the army of his brother, The Bastard. Do tell me your lover's name."

"Arnaud," Catherine answered, leaving out the rest. It was better that Magdelaine should believe her to be a simple maiden who loved an archer, like herself. A title would have embarrassed her and possibly made her suspicious. It was hard to believe that a rich noblewoman would be wandering over the countryside in search of a captain! She added:

"And my name is Catherine. . . ."

"You are more welcome than ever," Pierre said amiably. "Stay here tonight! You can leave at dawn. I will accompany you as far as the Roman road."

Catherine was to remember this evening passed in the humble cottage for a long time to come. Their kindliness and simplicity were comforting, and made a welcome pause between the experiences she had just been through and those still to come. They went to bed soon after supper so as not to burn up too much of the candle. Catherine shared Magdelaine's mattress. Pierre's stood in a cubbyhole which led off the cottage's single room. Although she had slept almost all that day, Catherine soon fell asleep again. Her raw hands were no longer hurting so badly. Magdelaine had spread lard over them and bound them with strips of linen.

Pierre woke her at dawn. He had to go to work in the fields and there was no time to lose. She noticed that Magdelaine was already up and about.

"I've been thinking things over during the night," Pierre told her, "and I have decided that you would be more likely to travel safely if you pass yourself off as a pilgrim on your way to the holy Abbey of Saint Benoît. Unfortunately, there is bad as well as good in this country of Puisaye. You are young ... and beautiful. The pilgrim's staff will protect you."

He took a wooden staff with an iron flask attached to it from a cupboard set into the wall and handed it to her.

"An uncle of mine made a pilgrimage to Compostela," he said, laughing. "You will look more authentic with this!"

Meanwhile, Magdelaine draped a thick cloak over Catherine's shoulders, assuring her that she would be better protected like that. Then she handed her a large loaf of bread and a small goat cheese and kissed her.

"May God be with you," she said affectionately, "and help you to find your beloved. If you see Colin, tell him that I am waiting for him and will always wait for him."

Catherine was moved to tears by their generosity and would have tried to refuse their gifts, but she sensed that a refusal would hurt them. Likewise, she dared not offer them the three silver pieces for fear of offending them. She kissed Magdelaine warmly, unable to speak because of the lump in her throat and then joined Pierre who stood waiting for her at the door. She turned back more than once as they walked away to wave a last farewell to the young girl.

Magdelaine watched them set off from the cottage door. . . . Pierre walked in front of her, taking long, even, unhurried strides. She recognized the place where he had met her the previous day. From there, they headed across the fields till they reached a sort of road where large, flat stones laid by the Romans and now green with grass and moss were still to be seen here and there. Beside the road an ancient statue representing the bust of a curly-headed youth was still visible despite the ravages of time and bad weather. Pierre halted here and pointed westwards.

"That is your road! Keep straight on till you reach the big river."

She looked at him gratefully.

"How can I ever thank you and your sister enough?"

"By not forgetting us altogether," he said, shrugging his broad shoulders. "We shall be praying for you. . . ."

As if in a hurry to leave her, he turned back towards the path across the fields, but then, suddenly, he turned and looked at her again.

"After all," he said softly, "one never knows. . . . If you don't find your lover again, I want you to know that you can always

220

return to us. We should be happy, Magdelaine and I . . . I most of all, to have you with us at home. . . ."

Before Catherine had quite understood the meaning of this simple little declaration, Pierre had turned on his heel and was running off across the fields like a hunted man. She stood there a moment watching the burly figure vanish slowly into the misty, gray light. Tears rolled unchecked down her cheeks. She was touched by this shy, awkward love which had sprung up so suddenly, and almost dared not declare itself. It was like a little, friendly flame which would warm her along her travels. Around her, the brightening daylight was beginning to dissipate the morning mists revealing the shape of things around. Behind her, she could see the chimneys smoking gently and a blue banner waving above the castle battlements. The bells were tolling the Angelus, scattering the frail notes across the rich, green countryside. A lark sang somewhere and Catherine's heart surged with a joy as deep, simple and primitive as the vast emptiness of nature all around her. The old road struck on between two little vales. With a fervent prayer of thanks to the Blessed Virgin for having vouchsafed her this moment of joy, Catherine leant upon her staff and set off.

At sunset the following day, Catherine sat among the reeds watching the gray waters of the Loire flow past her feet. She had walked and walked, kept going by a determination stronger than herself, ignoring her weariness and aching feet as she crossed hills, pastureland and forests dotted with an occasional lake, heading for the river which was her best line of approach to the besieged city. At nightfall, she found shelter in an abandoned woodman's hut. She had fallen asleep in spite of the discomfort, after devouring half her bread and cheese and at dawn she had set off once more, heedless of the cramps which attacked her in every limb. Every one of her bones and muscles seemed to have changed into a tiny instrument of torture. Her feet burned so painfully that she had to bathe them time and time again in the ponds she passed along the way. They became covered with blisters which burst so that she had to bind her feet in strips torn from her petticoat. And yet she had gone on and on . . . following that ancient Roman road which seemed to continue uninterruptedly for ever and ever. . . . The peasants she met from time to time along the way greeted her and sometimes touched her pilgrim's staff, asking her to pray for them, but no one stopped her to offer her shelter or food. Her youth and beauty told against her; the simple folk believed they had to do with some great sinner on her way to St. Benoît's tomb to ask forgiveness for her sins. Hundreds of times she had been on the point of falling by the wayside and each time she had somehow managed to make her feet keep on moving. Sometimes, as she passed a wayside cross or a little shrine to the Virgin of the crossroads, she would stop and pray for strength to continue and then shoulder her staff and set off again.

The sight of the great, untamable river made her cry aloud with joy. In spite of her exhaustion, she ran towards it as to a friend, leant over it to drink its waters and bathed her hands and feet. Then she sat herself down beside it to watch the flowing waters which would soon be passing beneath the walls of Orleans and might, perhaps, be taking her there tomorrow. In front of her, the tall, wooden houses and brown roofs of the old town of Gien rose in tiers up the side of a hill. A crumbling old castle, its grim outlines softened by antiquity, did its best to dominate the old city of the Dukes of Orleans, but Catherine was not looking at the castle. At the foot of its walls, just visible between the arches of the still unfinished bridge, a fleet of boats lay waiting, barges, scows and flat-bottomed boats drawn up onto the banks. The sun, a fiery ball, turned the Loire to a river of blood as it sank behind the gray towers of the city. A watchman's horn sounded above the gates, summoning the latecomers within the shelter of the walls. The town was about to close its gates for the night.... Catherine hastily put on her shoes again and then, limping a little, joined the stream of people heading for the drawbridge. The sun had vanished and night was falling fast. Catherine was among the last to enter the high, stone gateway because her sore feet handicapped her. She stopped to ask one of the soldiers of the guard the way to the marketplace. She knew that in most towns, particularly those which stood along a pilgrims' way, a corner of the marketplace was usually set aside to shelter pilgrims for the night. A particular spot between the pillars would be enclosed by a wooden hoarding which gave shelter from the wind and rain.

"Straight ahead and then to the right," the man replied. "Are you going to Fleury, woman?"

"I am."

"God be with you, and Monseigneur St. Benoît, too!"

She thanked him with a nod and turned into a street so narrow that the house gables seemed to be knocking together overhead. As she went along, she finished the remains of Magdelaine's loaf and soon found the marketplace. It was no more than a high, tiled roof perched on tall, wooden columns, but there was a shelter for pilgrims there. As she pushed open the door, she saw that the straw on the floor was new and that there was only one other pilgrim there, an old man asleep in a corner. His face had the stony look that extreme fatigue gives. He opened one eye when she came in, mumbled something, then closed it again and was soon snoring loudly. Catherine was relieved not to have to talk. She settled herself in one corner, pulled a little straw up over her and was soon asleep.

She had no sooner fallen asleep, or so it seemed to her, than she felt someone shaking her. The old bearded pilgrim was bending over her.

"Hey!" he said. "Hey! If you're going to the Abbey it is time to be off."

She opened her eyes, saw that the light was paling above the marketplace and hurried to her feet.

"The night was short," she said, with an apologetic smile.

"It is always short when one is tired. Come, it is time to be on our way."

Catherine shook her head. As a pilgrim, she should by rights continue her journey on foot, but she was too weary to carry on. She trusted that one of Sara's three silver pieces might hire her a boat.

"I do not think I shall be leaving today," she lied. "I have things to do in this city."

"God's wanderers have no business except in the place of their pilgrimage! If you wish to be pardoned, you should only think of the place to which you are going," the old man cried, horrified. "But everyone has a right to do as they please. Peace be with you."

"And with you, too."

The pilgrim went out. Catherine waited a few minutes on the threshold of the shelter. When he had vanished in the opposite direction, she stepped out and threw away her pilgrim's staff because, as the old man had reminded her, pilgrims had no right to any forms of transport save their own two feet. Then she wrapped herself closely in the folds of her coarse mantle, because a fine rain was falling on the town, and went down to the quays.

She did not have much trouble finding a boat. There was a man sitting on the quay, on a pile of folded fishing nets, eating an onion and watching the waters flow by. He was tall and taciturn and seemed oblivious to the rain. When Catherine asked if he knew of a boatman who would take her as far as Châteauneuf, at least, he raised heavy, grayish eyelids.

"Any money?"

She nodded, but the man did not move.

"Let's see! It's easy to say you have the money, you understand, but in these times money is hard to come by. The lands are spoiled and trade is abandoned and the King himself, like

Job, is squatting on his dunghill. Payment in advance nowadays."

Catherine merely took out a silver coin and laid it on the man's grimy palm. He spun it in the air, bit it, examined it closely and his surly face brightened.

"All right," he said. "But no further than Châteauneuf. Beyond that there's too much risk of falling into the hands of those accursed English who are besieging the city and I value my skin."

As he spoke, he ran a flat boat into the water and helped Catherine into it. She sat in the prow, facing downriver. Then the man jumped into the boat himself, so lightly and agilely that the boat scarcely rocked. He picked up a long pole which he plunged into the water and gave a mighty shove. The current flowed swiftly and the boat swept along almost unaided. From where she was sitting, Catherine watched the town unfold before her, followed by flat watermeadows, fringed with reeds still rusty from the winter. The rain wet her face, but it did not worry her, well protected as she was by her thick mantle. Old memories rose up before her, calling up images of bygone days. She saw herself again, fleeing from Paris in revolt with Barnaby, her mother, sister and Sara. . . . How she had enjoyed that first voyage, made so interesting for her by the Cockleshell Man. She seemed to hear his voice still and its deep, slow accents softly reciting the poet's lines:

> "She is crowned the Queen of Cities,
> Wellspring of religion and learning,
> Standing on the River Seine."

But Barnaby was no more, Paris was far off and the city where Catherine was going was a city at bay, a famine-stricken desperate place where she had nothing to hope for but death or, worse still, the cruellest disillusionment. For the first time she began to wonder how Arnaud would receive her; whether he would recognize her! So much time had elapsed since their encounter beneath the walls of Arras!

Catherine forced herself to put aside these morbid fancies, born of excessive weariness and nervous strain. She wanted to make the most of this peaceful interlude as the boat glided along the beautiful river, with its gray banks and yellow sands. . . . Towards sunset the white towers and blue pepperpot roofs of a great château came into view. Its feet were washed by the waters of a large moat fed by the river. Catherine inquired the name of this domain.

"Sully!" the boatman answered. "It belongs to the favorite of

Charles VII, the Sire de la Trémoille. . . ." And, to show the respect which that nobleman inspired in him, he spat into the water with a look of disgust. Catherine did not answer. She had already met Georges de la Trémoille, that turncoat Burgundian who had become the beloved adviser and evil genius of the King of Bourges. He inspired in her a feeling akin to that shown by her guide, but she did not say so. Besides, she had just noticed for the first time that the boat was heading towards the bank as if to tie up.

"Are we stopping here?" she asked, surprised, half turning round.

"I have business here in Sully," the man replied. "Get out."

She stood up to step out onto the flat bank. At the same moment, she received a violent blow on the head and pitched forward head first, unconscious. . . .

When Catherine returned to consciousness, the sky was lit up by the last sunset glow. Darkness was approaching from the east and, towards the west, only a glimmer of light remained, kindling the towers of Sully across the river. She propped herself up on one elbow and found that she was entirely alone. There was no boat to be seen, no boatman; nothing but a flight of curlews winging in arrow formation across the sky overhead. All this dawned on her gradually, because her head ached abominably. She touched it and found a large painful bump. The boatman must have attacked her to rob her! And, in truth, the little she had possessed had gone: the two silver pieces, her dagger and the thick mantle which had protected her so well from the cold night and the rain. For a moment a profound depression seized her. It seemed as though everything were in league to prevent her rejoining Arnaud. Obstacles surged up along the route as if to bar the way, but she soon recovered her spirits again. Though education and circumstances might have made an aristocrat of her, at bottom she still had the unquenchable vitality of a Parisian urchin, accustomed to meeting the direst difficulties head on. She struggled to her feet and clung to the overhanging branches of a willow tree to regain her balance. When the ground had stopped spinning round her, she took a deep breath, pulled the collar of her tattered surcoat higher round her neck and struck away from the bank towards the road which ran along—parallel to the river. She knew that she had only to carry on and that the great Abbey of St. Benoît was only two leagues away. There she would find shelter and sustenance. The boat trip and her good night's sleep had built up her reserves of strength, and had it not been for the fierce pain in her head, she would have felt most lively. She hastened

225

to such effect that barely an hour later she came in sight of the massive monastery buildings and their majestic entrance: a huge Roman gate-tower as strong and beautiful as a fortress, solemn and soaring as a prayer. A faint light glimmered between its massive pillars, throwing the flowers and faces carved in its superb capitals into sharp relief. Catherine saw that a number of pilgrims were sleeping there, huddled one against the other for greater warmth. When she saw her, an old woman signed to her to approach and made room for her.

"The guest house is bursting at the seams," she told her. "So many of us are there who have come to beg Monseigneur St. Benoît to save the good city of Orleans! But it's not too cold here. Come close to me, it's warmer like that. . . ."

Catherine obeyed, fell to her knees and than sank down beside the old woman who generously shared her patched, old cloak with her.

"Have you come far?" she asked curiously.

"From the borders of Burgundy," said Catherine, not daring to reveal that she was a Burgundian.

"You are young for these long journeys! Have you also come to pray at the tomb of the great saint?"

"I am going to Orleans," said Catherine curtly, hoping that the old woman would be put off and leave her alone, but on the contrary, she saw her faded old eyes light up like stars. She leant towards her and murmured:

"Ah . . . you are not the only one! So you too want to be present for the miracle, do you?"

"The miracle?"

"Come, come," the old woman said, winking and nudging her. "Don't pretend you don't know. All the little folk in the Loire valley know that Orleans will be delivered by one whom the Lord has sent, a maid come from Lorraine to Chinon where our gracious King resides. She told him that with God's help, she would kick the English out of France and raise the siege of Orleans."

"It's a fairy story," Catherine remarked with an indulgent smile. The old woman flushed scarlet under her cap.

"A fairy tale? As true as I'm called Bertille-la-dentillière. It's God's truth. There are even people here who saw her, Joan the Maid, that is, when she came to Chinon with six men-at-arms. She wore boy's clothes, but she is young and fresh and as beautiful as an angel with the light of Heaven in her eyes. And to prove it, they say the captains are already awaiting her arrival in Orleans and Monseigneur the Bastard has told his people to be of good cheer, because God was sending them food and help. . . . It seems that the King has sent the Maid to Poitiers so

226

that the bishops and clerics of the land may see her and do honor to her, but soon she will enter Orleans. . . . I know that if I were not so old, I would go straight to the beleaguered city to see her. Only my poor old legs would not take me as far as that and I should die by the wayside. So I prefer to remain here and pray that God may direct her. Our country's guardian angel, that she is!"

It was thus that Catherine heard Joan of Arc mentioned for the first time. She felt no wonder at the news despite the fact that it kept her awake half the night. Irritation, rather, and a flood of jealousy of the "young and beautiful girl" whom the "captains were already awaiting"—those captains of whom Arnaud was one. Would not this Lorraine girl, arriving haloed by her holy mission as well as her own beauty, in all the glory of the arms for which he lived exclusively, surely draw Arnaud de Montsalvy's thoughts and heart after her. She must hurry and get there before this dangerous woman. In the depths of her troubled heart, Catherine began to detest the Soldier Maid.

The next morning she accepted the bread distributed among the pilgrims by the black-robed monks and then, while the others vanished into the great church, she dodged aside and hastened away back to the road before anyone saw her. Old Bertille had told her that there were still nine leagues to go before she reached the capital of the Duchy of Orleans. Nine leagues . . . an infinity!

It was then that the cruellest part of Catherine's penitential journey began, because now anxiety and doubt racked her heart and spirit just as her body itself was reaching the limits of its strength. All went reasonably well during her morning's march, but once past Châteauneuf, the sores on her feet reopened and all her muscles began to ache. Slowly fever insinuated itself into her blood. She leant over a stream to drink and was horrified to see her face reflected there, haggard, drawn, gray with dust and weariness. She looked like a beggar woman and she reflected that Arnaud would never recognize her; he would be more likely to laugh at her! The place was deserted, the spring sheltered by a clump of willows. The weather was quite mild. Catherine hurriedly stripped off her rags and plunged into the water. The cold water made her teeth chatter, but gradually she felt it doing her good. Her feet stopped burning. She rubbed herself clean as well as she could, regretting the gentle soaps that Sara had been so adept at preparing, then she washed her hair which she twisted round her head. As she climbed out of the water, she caught a glimpse of her body in it and this comforted her. Thank heavens, it had not lost any of its splendor or nervous elegance despite the crushing weariness which oppressed her.

Feeling a little revived, she dried herself as well as she could, slipped on her ragged garments again and set off once more. The route ran between the Loire and a dense forest, but as she went on, the rich countryside grew more and more devastated. Large tracts of forest had been burned. Here and there one could see the ruins of a village, a charred tree stump or corpses which had been left to rot. The war was everywhere and its grinning face was more and more in evidence. But Catherine, in her eagerness to reach Orleans, paid little heed to this. She kept straining her eyes in an effort to make out the walls of the city which had come to represent the Promised Land to her. By sunset she had covered six leagues . . . and the blurred outlines of a great city were just visible in the distance, though gray and indistinct. She guessed that this must be Orleans at last and her emotion was so strong that she fell on her knees in the short grass and burst into tears. Then she murmured a short prayer. Night soon hid the city from her; and she stretched out on the ground like a tired animal without even trying to find a spot where she could be under cover. In a deserted spot like this who would ever heed a sleeping beggar woman? She no longer had anything worth stealing on her; she was poorer than the poorest, ragged, hungry, half naked and her feet were bleeding. . . . She slept soundly and woke as the sun's first rays lit up the sky. She rose to her feet as simply as though she had just that moment laid herself down and started off again. A step . . . another step, and yet another. . . . The town seemed to be growing larger in the distance; it seemed to beckon to her. . . . Her fevered eyes saw nothing else and ignored the smoke and flames of sacked and burning houses on the horizon. Had she not been so weary, she would have stretched out her hands in an attempt to seize hold of this mirage which was slowly coming to life before her. Gradually, she began to make out the flat islands tufted with trees, the great bridge destroyed in two places and the fortresses which guarded it at either end. She saw the arrow-like church steeples, the great black streaks of boiling oil and pitch on the walls and the mortars which crowned them. She saw the great waste which the Orleanese themselves had made of their fine suburbs: elegant dwellings reduced to empty shells, the ruins of churches, deserts of heroism punctuated here and there by the small fortresses of wood and earth erected by the besiegers. At last she saw the red standard of the English with its golden leopards planted upon these forts as if challenging the fleur-de-lis whose blue and gold fluttered from the highest tower of the château. . . .

Catherine stopped still, her eyes misted with tears, forgetful of everything—her sufferings, the hunger which gnawed at her belly—except one thing: somewhere behind those walls Arnaud lived, breathed, fought and suffered, too, no doubt, since the town, they said, no longer had any bread to eat. . . .

Then she began slowly and cautiously making her way towards the city, hiding herself wherever possible behind the debris of fallen buildings. A massive bastion, which she later learnt to be that of Saint-Loup, stood between her and the town. She would somehow have to pass by it unobserved and reach the Bourgogne gate, which was still accessible because Suffolk and Talbot's Englishmen were not numerous enough to encircle the martyred city completely. A faraway trumpet call reached Catherine's ears, followed almost at once by a great burst of artillery fire. The mortars on both sides of the bridge disgorged a last volley of stone cannon balls before night put an end to the day's fighting. This was met by culverins and soon after she could hear men's voices shouting and swearing. They must have been attacking the town, because Catherine could see soldiers running about on the ramparts. . . . With infinite precaution, she had managed to pass the Saint-Loup fort unseen and was going towards the gate when she saw a head pop up suddenly out of a stairway which seemed to vanish into the bowels of the earth. Two hands seized her and a moment later she found herself at the bottom of the steps in what looked like a crypt, dimly lit by a guttering tallow candle. Before she could protest, a jovial voice exclaimed:

"Well, my pretty! What's all this? You don't imagine one can walk into Orleans just like that, in broad daylight! You'll have to wait till nightfall!"

Catherine looked round and saw that there were some twenty men and women in almost as wretched a state as herself sitting in attitudes of utter exhaustion on the ground at the foot of the two great pillars which held up the fan-vaulted roof. The roof of the crypt was so high that it was lost in darkness. The smoky candle lit up a charming bas relief of a young boy leaning on a stag which was carved on one of the capitals. . . .

"Who are all these people?" Catherine asked. "Where is this?"

The boy who had dragged her down into the crypt made a grimace which might have been intended for a smile. He was filthy dirty and a bushy black beard hid most of his face, but his eyes were young and his body strong and well built despite its thinness. He shrugged.

"The people of Montaran. The English burned our village yesterday. We're all waiting to enter the city, too. This place is the crypt of the Church of Saint-Aignan which was destroyed by the people of Orleans along with the rest of the neighbor-

229

hood. There is only one thing for you to do now—stay here with us and wait."

He said nothing more, but returned to his observation post at the top of the partly destroyed flight of steps. Examining her neighbors more closely, Catherine saw many grieving faces and tear-stained cheeks among them and some scanty bundles of possessions. They all kept their eyes lowered as if ashamed of their destitution. She dared not speak to them, so she sat down a little way off to wait.

The crypt was chilly and a long shiver ran down her spine. She was sleepy, but had to resist the temptation to fall asleep, because she was afraid that the others might forget her and leave her behind when they finally decided to try and gain entry to the city. As it was, they did not have long to wait: after about an hour the boy reappeared at the foot of the steps, gesturing to everyone down there to get up and follow him.

"Come, hurry, now is the time!"

The refugees got to their feet wordlessly, as passive as sheep trained to follow their leader. One behind the other, they filed out of the crypt and began to make their way across the rubble, bent double to avoid being seen. The night was not very dark and stars glittered coldly high in the sky. Catherine caught sight of the gate between its two towers. . . . In a little while they had reached it. Soon they were standing on the small drawbridge which led to the postern coupled to the great gate. The great drawbridge had been raised. . . . As they passed through a narrow passage let into the ramparts, Catherine almost fainted with happiness. She had arrived at last! Her extraordinary Odyssey was over. She was entering Orleans. . . .

CHAPTER THIRTEEN

In Arnaud's Hands

The Bourgogne gate opened into a narrow street bordered along one side by a monastery and on the other by a row of shuttered houses. There were some men standing in the street, their armor still dusty and blackened from the recent attack. Some of them carried torches which lit up the exit from the passage. Close by, a stew pot bubbled over a fire in an iron cage.

The wind was blowing hard and the flames fluttered wildly in the darkness.

"Some more refugees!" exclaimed a surly voice which immediately set Catherine's heart beating faster. "What are we going to do with them? They're just more mouths to feed. We should send them away. . . ."

"They are the people of Montaran," someone explained. "Their village was burned down yesterday. . . ."

The first speaker said nothing, but Catherine found herself drawn by an irresistible impulse to the spot where he stood. She had not been mistaken; Arnaud de Montsalvy was standing there, only a few feet away.

He stood leaning against the monastery wall irritably inspecting the sorry-looking band which had just entered the town. He was bareheaded and his short, black hair was rough and tousled. There were powder marks on his face and a scar which Catherine had not seen before ran along one cheek. His armor was dented and he seemed a little weary, but Catherine observed with feverish joy that he had not changed. The features were the same, a little more sharply defined, perhaps. His mouth had acquired a bitter line to it. Those eyes of his, which she had so rarely seen softened by tenderness, were as hard as ever and he held his head in just the same old arrogant way. Unshaven and battle-stained as he was, he seemed more beautiful than an archangel to Catherine. After all, wasn't he her dream made flesh?

In her delight at finding him so soon, right there, just the other side of the town gate, she forgot everything else. She was drawn to him irresistibly. . . . Eyes shining and lips parted she stole softly towards him with outstretched hands, like someone in a trance. . . . She looked so rapt, so ecstatic, that her companions stood back in astonishment and let her pass. Arnaud did not see her at once. He was examining his twisted scabbard with a look of intense annoyance. Then suddenly he looked up and saw a ragged woman walking towards him over the round cobblestones, which still shone from the recent rain. Something about her fixed his wandering attention. She seemed barely able to stand up. She had evidently reached the limits of her strength, but her eyes shone with an unearthly brilliance and a magnificent mane of hair streamed like a torrent of gold about her ragged shoulders. She came towards him slowly, slowly, a smile on her lips, holding out trembling hands whose palms were scraped almost raw. He thought for a moment that she must be a hallucination produced by his fatigue. It had been an arduous day's fighting and his arms were weary from wielding the heavy, two-handed sword. He rubbed his eyes hard and took another look. . . . And then, suddenly, he recognized her.

Catherine had stopped, speechless, a little way off and stood devouring him with her eyes. Their eyes met and locked for a moment, while time stood still; Arnaud's opening wider and wider as the moment wore on, expressed astonishment, incredulity, a fierce joy, too, but that was only a fleeting impression. . . . Then, brusquely, he recollected himself. He drew himself up sharply, his face convulsed by a spasm of violent exasperation. With an angry look, he pointed at the young woman and shouted:

"Seize this woman at once!"

Catherine raised her face imploringly to Arnaud's. She wavered, brutally roused from her happy trance. Her hands fell by her sides and the light in her eyes went out. She moaned faintly:

"No! . . . Arnaud! . . ."

But he was blind with rage now. He seized her arm and almost flung her towards the men-at-arms who stood there stupidly, too astonished to move. His voice thundered furiously:

"Are you deaf, or idiots, all of you? I told you to seize this woman!"

"But . . . Messire," a sergeant began.

Arnaud sprang towards him and stood towering above him. His fists were clenched and his whole body taut as a bowstring. His face was scarlet.

"No 'buts', my friend! It's an order! Have you any idea who she is? A Burgundian . . . and the worst of the lot, to boot! She's no pathetic refugee as she would have us believe, but the mistress of Philippe le Bon himself, the fair Catherine de Brazey! It doesn't take much imagination to guess what she has come here for!"

At the mention of Philippe's name, the soldier had clearly taken fright. He was just about to seize Catherine by the wrist when an incredulous, drawling voice made itself heard:

"The fair Catherine *here*? The lady with the golden hair? Who says so?"

It was Xaintrailles. He came striding out of an alley, wearing armor, his red hair flying in the wind. He was as battle-stained as his friend, but his cheerful face had not lost its habitual good-humored expression.

"I say so!" Arnaud declared drily. "Take a look, if you don't believe me!"

The tall, red-headed knight went up to the group of soldiers who had surrounded Catherine and stared at her with undisguised amazement. Then he burst into a roar of laughter.

" 'Struth, so it is! 'Sdeath, fair lady, what errand brings you here? And in that sorry attire, too!"

"She has been sent here to spy for her lover, that's quite obvious," Arnaud muttered angrily. "As for what she's going to do now—that depends on me, my friend. In an hour's time, she will be tied up in a dungeon somewhere to await her trial. Off you go, now. Take her away. . . ."

Xaintrailles had stopped laughing. He was still looking at Catherine. He laid a restraining hand on his friend's arm.

"Don't you think it's a bit unlikely?" he asked, shaking his head. "Why should Philippe of Burgundy send her here, now that he has withdrawn his troops because of his quarrel with Bedford? And in this state! Her clothes are in tatters and her feet are bleeding . . . she can hardly stand up. . . ."

The pitying look in the Captain's eyes gave Catherine back some of her courage. But Arnaud obstinately refused to listen. He shrugged irritably.

"That only proves that she's a better actress than you think. As for the deeper motives of Philippe-the-Devious—I'll get to the bottom of those soon enough! The news that the Maid is coming here must have changed a lot of things at the Court of Bruges. Take this spying female away and put her into prison. I'll find a way to loosen her tongue!"

Xaintrailles did not protest. He knew Arnaud too well. He knew that nothing in the world would ever make him go back on his word, especially in public. Besides, a crowd had begun to gather round the prisoner and threaten her.

"Death to the Burgundian spy!"

In a moment, the cry swelled to a roar. The siege had been going on for many long months now and the people of Orleans, exasperated by their impotence, were ready to snatch eagerly at an opportunity to work off some of their fury and frustration. The soldiers closed in around Catherine, fearing that they might be swept away by sheer force, and headed off the more violent members of the mob with blows from their lances. A handful of mud, thrown with unerring aim, struck Catherine on the breast, but she did not flinch. . . . She stood very straight and erect . . . as if carved from stone. Her whole soul seemed to speak through those eyes which gazed and gazed at Arnaud. The slimy mud slid down her dress, leaving a black smear down the front. Suddenly she burst out laughing . . . a dreadful, strident laugh which did not seem to belong to her and which abruptly silenced the crowd. She laughed and laughed as though she would never stop.

"Take her away!" Arnaud roared. "Take her away, or I will kill her!"

233

The laugh foundered in a sob. The sergeant pushed Catherine forward by the shoulders as a soldier hurriedly lashed her hands together behind her back. She turned her head away. Everything went misty. She shrugged hopelessly and allowed herself to be led away. . . . She no longer cared what happened to her and did not even look up once as they passed through street after street.

She did not notice Xaintrailles step out from behind a fountain as they were crossing a small square, and discreetly take the leader of her escort aside for a moment.

"Put her in a cell," the Captain murmured, "but not in a dungeon and don't put her in irons. Tell the gaoler to try and find her something to eat. She can hardly stand. I've never seen a criminal who looked more like a victim."

The man made a sign that he understood and pocketed the gold piece which Xaintrailles had slipped into his hand. Then he hurriedly rejoined the rest of Catherine's escort.

The Chastelet, where the men were taking Catherine, was the stronghold of Orleans. It commanded the entrance to the great bridge which straddled a sandy island in the river, guarded by the small Saint-Antoine keep, before linking up with the massive stronghold of Tourelles on the opposite bank, one of the English army chief's bases of operations. William Gladsdale, Bailiff of Alençon, was in command there.

At daybreak, Catherine managed to drag herself up as far as the tiny window of her cell and caught a glimpse of the Loire down below, a sight she found vaguely encouraging. Since the time she had reached that great river after her long and exhausting travels, she had grown to look upon it as a friend. When they had flung her into this cell the previous day, she had shown not the slightest emotion. Stunned by fatigue and crushing disappointment, she had collapsed onto the pile of straw which served as a bed and slept the sleep of a hunted animal. She had not even heard the gaoler bring her a pitcher of water and a crust of bread. . . .

It had taken her a moment or two to convince herself, when she woke, that she was not trapped in some bad dream, but as her memories emerged from the mists of sleep, the previous day's events came back to her little by little. She sat on her palliasse with her head in her hands and tried to sort out her situation, but this only left her feeling bitter. She had been living in a sort of hypnotic trance all these last few days, ever since the moment, in fact, when Brother Étienne told her that Arnaud was not married. And now the return to reality left an ashen taste in the mouth. When she thought of Arnaud de

234

Montsalvy, a flush of shame and anger left her crimson to the roots of her hair, but she was even more angry with herself. She must have been mad to think he would take her in his arms merely because she had come to him stripped of all her worldly possessions except her love! Somehow, she had always assumed that he must be waiting for her, merely because he had twice waxed delirious in her arms. She had deliberately forgotten the painful circumstances of their last meeting, when he had found her in Philippe's bed and withered her with a look of crushing scorn and contempt. There were some things a man as hard and inflexible as Arnaud would never forgive and in his eyes Catherine must be doubly guilty and doubly accursed: she was one of the Legoix who had long ago murdered his brother, Michel, and she was the beloved mistress of the Philippe of Burgundy whom he hated as a traitor. No, if there was anyone to blame in all this, it was herself for having sacrificed everything to an impossible dream. She had lost everything, everything. . . . Now she lay in prison, charged with a crime that could incur the death sentence. She had survived a thousand perils, all to no purpose. . . .

Catherine stood up and began to examine her prison. It consisted of a narrow, low-ceilinged cell lit by a small, iron-barred window placed at the far end of a stone tunnel that made it hard to see out. Its entire furniture consisted of her straw bed, the stool on which the gaoler had placed her bread and water the night before and an assortment of chains and rings hanging from the walls. The stone walls were beaded with damp. It was the third time she had been imprisoned and Catherine was hopeful that she would manage to escape this time as she had twice before. It couldn't all end here. . . .

She sat down to eat in the hopes of regaining some of her strength and finally succeeded in crumbling the bread, which was hard and stale and must have been hidden away for some time, because provisions in the town were running out and no new convoys of food were arriving. . . . She dipped it in the water to soften it before eating it and then drained the pitcher to the last drop. She found she felt better, and even managed an inward smile thinking of the magnificent banquets which Philippe enjoyed giving, with their endless courses and exoitic and subtle dishes which she had always found so tedious. The tiniest of those gargantuan pâtés would have been welcome now!

Then she made herself sleep some more so as not to have to think. Her heart was hot with anger against herself and the whole world and she cursed this town she had been so eager to enter from the bottom of her heart. . . .

At nightfall, the low door of her cell opened and the gaoler entered. Four soldiers stood waiting outside, lance in hand.

"Come along, now," said the gaoler, a fat fellow with a round, cheery face which did not at all suggest a prison warder. Catherine looked at him for the first time and was surprised to find that he had blue, honest eyes.

"Where are they taking me?" she asked.

He shrugged his ignorance and pointed to one of the soldiers. "They know. That's all I can tell you. . . ."

Catherine took her place between the soldiers without another word and followed them up a spiral staircase whose massive stone steps had been worn away in the center by the contact of thousands of feet. She soon found herself in a vaulted chamber from which various passages led off, the entrance to each one being closed by a massive, iron grille. One of these swung open, creaking. They went along the corridor and up another shallow flight of steps, at the head of which was a heavy, iron-barred door with a little grille let into it. When the door opened, Catherine found herself in a long, low room with a vaulted ceiling supported by four massive pillars. A long table stood across the far end of the room. There were five men seated at it; another man sat at a small table nearby writing something by candlelight. Torches flamed in their holders round the walls, bare except for a crucifix.

The guards led Catherine to the middle of the room, facing the long table and remained standing around her, their lances resting on the ground, expressionless. Catherine realized that she had been brought before a tribunal. She gave a slight start as she recognized Arnaud among the judges. He sat next to the President of the Tribunal, a man of sixty or so, with a severe, solid face under a crown of gray hair. He wore no arms on this occasion and was dressed in a severely plain green suede doublet. The other judges wore the red, fur-trimmed robes of town aldermen and were all men of mature age. Their faces were gaunt from lack of food and quite expressionless. Arnaud stood up, his eyes steely as he looked at Catherine.

"You have been brought here before Messire Raoul de Gaucourt, the Town Governor, and the other aldermen to answer a charge of collaborating with the enemy."

"What enemy?" Catherine asked quietly. "I have never spoken a word to an Englishman in my life."

Arnaud's fist crashed down on the table.

"Don't play with words! The Burgundians are as much our enemies as Suffolk's men . . . more so, perhaps, because when all is said and done, the invaders are merely doing their duty, whereas your fine lover is throttling his own country to please the English. He sent you here, too, for some reason which we do not as yet know. That is why you have been brought before this tribunal now. . . ."

"Messire," Catherine interrupted with a sigh. "Yesterday was not the first time we had met and you know perfectly well that I was not born a Burgundian, but was forced to become one. Why can't you accept, then, that I might have freely and deliberately turned my back on a party which seemed to me to be acting wrongly? I arrived here stripped of all my worldly possessions, after a gruelling journey which has left its mark upon my limbs. . . ."

Arnaud's fist crashed down again. Catherine was not alarmed. She began to feel that he was forcing his anger and that this aggressive behavior was meant to disguise an inward uncertainty.

"Be quiet!" he cried. "I know better than anyone how little your pretty speeches are to be trusted! You have an artful tongue and great powers of persuasion. . . ."

The Governor of Orleans coughed.

"Messire de Montsalvy," he interrupted courteously. "I fear that you may be letting yourself be influenced by a purely personal resentment. I think it might be better if you would allow these other gentlemen and myself to proceed with the inquiry. When we have found out what we want to know, you may crossquestion the prisoner as much as you like. Incidentally, it seems that we have forgotten to provide the accused with a defense lawyer."

"Begging your pardon, Messire Governor," Catherine interrupted gently. "I have no need of a lawyer. My innocence and good faith should be defense enough. . . . I have not committed any of the crimes which I have been charged with here, and not only that—I had no intention of committing them."

"That still remains to be proved," said the Governor. "But let us begin at the beginning. I want you to answer my questions. You are Catherine de Brazey, are you not, the favorite mistress of the Duke Philippe?"

Gaucourt's voice was deliberate and by no means insulting. Catherine sensed that this man was not her enemy and this gave her a little courage.

"I am Catherine de Brazey, widow of the Lord Treasurer who was executed for high treason, and I no longer have any connection with the Duke."

At this, Arnaud sneered and Catherine had to summon all her self-control to stop herself striking him. She forced herself not to look at him.

"Since when?" he inquired maliciously.

She replied composedly, still looking at the Governor:

"Since I heard of the Duke's forthcoming marriage all the bonds between him and myself have been severed. I have disobeyed his command to return to his Court. You see, Messire, the child we had died five months ago and with his death, the last link between us had gone. I left him. . . ."

"To come here?" Gaucourt said. "A curious choice! And a still more curious mode of travel for a rich and powerful woman such as yourself."

"I was robbed on the way here by a brigand called Fortépice. I managed to escape from his castle when I learnt that he had sent a message to Bruges demanding a great ransom for me. I had to continue as best I could . . . on foot."

"But why come here? What were you looking for?"

Catherine did not answer at once. A slow flush crept up her face and a lump rose in her throat.

She bowed her head and murmured in a low voice:

"I was following . . . an old, old dream . . . but I must have been mad. . . ."

She threw back her head and then, as the hot tears welled into her eyes, she cried vehemently:

"Mad! Yes, mad—like those little children who peer into a well at full moon and try to seize their reflections in their hands and fall to their death. . . ."

Her voice grew hoarse. The Governor examined her with a curiosity not devoid of sympathy. This was not lost on Arnaud. He gave a fierce laugh.

"What did I tell you? She's weaving a spell round us! This woman wants us to believe she was following a dream. The real truth of the matter, gentlemen, is that she takes us for fools. If you want her to talk, you must use different methods. I should be surprised if she is still talking about dreams on the rack."

"I have thought a lot of things about you in my time, Arnaud de Montsalvy," Catherine cried. "But I never thought you were a fool and I begin to regret this now!"

Her last words were drowned in the discussion which had arisen among the judges as to whether or not the prisoner should be put to the torture. Catherine's blood ran cold at the thought! She was already so weakened and exhausted. Heaven only knew what wild avowals torture might not wring from her! She strained her ears anxiously in an effort to hear what the men were saying and discovered that the three aldermen agreed with Arnaud. The Governor was the only one who did not. She heard him say:

"All this is ridiculous, in my opinion. You seem to forget, you

238

people of Orleans, that you sent Messire Xantrailles to Philippe of Burgundy to ask him to take the town under his protection, and that he accepted."

"He accepted, but did not withdraw his troops. It was not until he and his brother-in-law, Bedford, had a disagreement that he did so. It was bad temper and not patriotism which prompted his action. Besides, he must know by now that Heaven has sent us aid and that he need expect nothing more from us. I think, myself, that this woman was sent here for a purpose and I think her secret should be extorted from her. The fate of our town may depend on it," one of the aldermen declared.

The two others applauded their colleague's speech. Arnaud glanced at Gaucourt with a smile.

"You see, Messire, we are four against one. Our decision prevails." He raised his voice. "Executioner! To work!"

Catherine watched in terror as a short, squat man dressed in red and brown stepped out from behind one of the pillars. Another man, identically dressed, but taller, followed. The soldiers fell back to allow them to take hold of Catherine, which they did roughly and unceremoniously. Catherine had only just noticed a part of the room which had escaped her attention before. A horrifying collection of instruments of torture were grouped around a sort of bed whose head and foot were composed of two winches. Long iron brands stood glowing red-hot in a near-by brazier and, a little way off in the shadow, she could just discern the shape of a great wheel bristling with iron spikes.

As Catherine was staring fascinated and appalled at this sinister equipment, a cry of surprise broke from her. The executioner had suddenly and brutally torn off her ragged dress and petticoat. Finding herself suddenly naked before these men whose eyes fastened upon her greedily, she blushed hotly and tried to cover herself with her arms. But the torturers seized her wrists and were about to lash them together when a shouted command stopped them. It was Arnaud.

"Who told you to strip the woman?"

"But, Monseigneur. . . . It's the custom," the man protested.

"I don't give a damn for the custom and I'm not your Seigneur. At least give her back her petticoat!"

If she had not been so frightened, Catherine would have seen that Arnaud had gone as white as a sheet, but she was too concerned with trying to stop herself from screaming with terror as the men dragged her towards the bed of torture. The executioner had more or less covered her with the torn petticoat. Now they stretched her out on the wooden bed. One of them dragged her wrists above her head and tied them to the winch while the other did the same with her ankles. Alderman Lhuillier bent over her and asked:

"Woman, before you are put to the torture, I adjure you to tell us of your own accord why you came to this town. Spare us and spare yourself what must otherwise follow. Why did you come here?"

Catherine's eyes searched desperately for Arnaud, but he was standing out of sight and she could not even tell whether he was still there. She looked at Lhuillier.

"To find the man I loved," she murmured. "But I cannot tell you his name."

"Why?"

"Because you wouldn't believe me!"

She screamed with pain. At a discreet sign from the alderman, the torturer had given the windlass a turn. A wave of pain swept through her. She felt as though her arms and legs were being wrenched off.

"Be reasonable," Lhuillier said softly. "If you want us to believe you, you must at least tell us this man's name. Who is it? Some Burgundian living here in secret, pehraps? Come ... tell us and your sufferings will be at an end."

Scalding tears rolled down Catherine's cheeks. The pain was so great she could hardly speak.

"Ask ... Messire de Montsalvy. He ... should ... be able to ... tell you!"

The alderman paused, but just then two knights strode into the room and walked swiftly across to the rack. In spite of the tears in Catherine's eyes, she recognized one of them as Xaintrailles, but she had never seen the other one before. It was Jean de Dunois, Bastard of Orleans and master of the besieged town. Everyone present made way for him respectfully, because to his noble blood was added a great courage, sterling loyalty and infinite kindness. He glanced at the victim and made a sign.

"Release this woman, executioner. ..."

"Monseigneur," Lhuillier began. "Don't you think... ?"

Quietly but firmly Dunois signed to him to be silent.

"No, my friend. We have better things to do than put a possibly innocent woman to the torture. I bring glad tidings."

Arnaud stepped out from behind a pillar, pale with anger.

"It is _I_, Monseigneur, who ordered the arrest of this woman. _I_ said she was dangerous and it is _I_ whom you offend by countermanding my orders!"

The Bastard gave a smile in which there was much tenderness and Catherine, whom the executioner was helping into a sitting position, observed the extraordinary sweetness of this smile. Dunois laid both hands on Arnaud's shoulders.

"Of course I am not countermanding your orders, Arnaud! How could I? You are my brother-in-arms and I love you as if we were of the same blood. If you consider this woman dangerous, you did quite right in having her arrested, but why put her to the torture? The messenger of Heaven will soon be here. She is about to leave Poitiers where the doctors have confirmed that she is pure and holy, the ladies have attested that she is a virgin and the King has fitted her out with armor to lead the army into battle. She will soon be marching towards Tours. She will rejoin the army at Blois and, shortly after that, she should be here. She will decide the fate of this prisoner when Orleans has been freed. Till then, keep her in prison. Guards, take her away!"

Arnaud bowed his head in defeat. As the torturer helped Catherine put on her dress and get painfully to her feet, she found herself thinking, in the midst of the pain that racked her, that Arnaud must dearly love the Bastard to have submitted so readily to him. She was too weak to walk. The soldiers had to carry her to her cell under the malignant eyes of the city aldermen.

So little notice was taken of Catherine during the days which followed that she began to think that she had been forgotten. No one tried to interrogate her further, or came to see her. She was left in her prison cell and she soon came to regard it as a blessing from heaven that she should have been given a gaoler like hers. Pitoul's character was what might have been expected from his appearance. He was a kindly man and the only reason he was employed in such an unsympathetic job was because his late father-in-law had bequeathed the position to him. Pitoul had three passions in life: his wife, Alison, a massive goodwife with a powerful voice who beat him at least once a week to keep her hand in, good food—in particular the sausages which made the name and fame of the "Golden Sausage" half way up the rue des Hostelleries—and, lastly, tittle-tattle and gossip of all descriptions. The siege had put an end to culinary delights, so Pitoul had to make do with Alison and the occasional gossip. And though he had regarded his new inmate with some suspicion at first, owing to her suspected relationship with the Burgundians, the fact that Monseigneur the Bastard had taken a personal interest had gone a long way towards quieting his fears. He saw no reason why he should not visit her from time to time, particularly now that she was the one and only prisoner in his charge.

241

Pitoul kept Catherine informed of all the news from outside. Hope was rising like a fever in the city where people had been reduced to devouring cats and dogs, and the smallest bowl of flour was worth its weight in gold. Occasionally, some pedlar managed to slip through under cover of night with a supply of food, but what he brought was only a drop in the sea and it was always the rich who profited. The people of Orleans had but one thought—to hold out no matter what might come, till the miraculous Maid should reach them. Day after day at the town hall, Jean de Dunois used to harangue them and exhort them to have courage and patience and there was not a man, woman or child in the town who did not follow reports of Joan's advance with keen anxiety. It was known that she had left Poitiers for Chinon and thence for Tours where the King had founded a military household for her and had a banner made.

"She has been given a squire, two pages, two heralds and a chaplain," Pitoul related, round-eyed. "Just like a great captain. And now she's marching outwards Blois, God preserve her, where the captains are to join forces with her!"

Gradually, in Catherine's tortured mind, a bizarre impression was forming of the peasant girl turned war-leader. Because she hated her without having seen her, because her own fate depended on this girl, she imagined her as a creature of unspeakable cunning, gifted with powers of seduction such that she was able to bewitch men at a distance and those who saw her were instantly captivated and enslaved, even men of high rank like Jean de Dunois. Arnaud would soon fall into the trap as well, just like the rest. Thus, little by little, Catherine began to hold the Maid responsible for all her misfortunes. She was positive that if Arnaud had not been all agog to see her, like the others, he would never have treated her so cruelly. The girl he awaited was a heavenly messenger, a woman so far above all other women that she had banished the last traces of affection he might have felt for Catherine from his mind. Anyway, where he was concerned, Catherine was an evil being, a child of the Devil, someone dangerous and harmful ... and so it was with sorrow mixed with anger that she heard Pitoul's account of the Maid's exploits. She forgave him, however, because he always remembered to bring her a pitcher of water to wash herself in and had also procured an old dress of his wife's for her to wear.

One Tuesday, at the beginning of the last week in April, Pitoul came into Catherine's cell as usual. He was carrying a pitcher of water and a bowl containing some thin broth made of turnips and musty flour. He looked radiant.

"It isn't much of a meal you've got there," he said, as he set

242

the bowl down on the stool, "but many of the soldiers have to fight on less. Anyway, we shall soon be able to eat our bellyfull."

"Why? Have the English gone?"

"Lord, no! But there is a convoy of food waiting at Blois and the Maid is going to escort it here in person. . . ."

He leant towards Catherine and whispered behind his hand as though he feared the walls might be listening:

". . . Tonight the Bastard, Messire de Gaucourt and almost all the captains have set out to meet Joan. Tomorrow she may be here and we shall be saved. . . ."

"They have left?" Catherine cried in astonishment. "But who has been left to guard the city?"

"Why, the aldermen, of course, and some of the captains. They haven't all gone. Messire de Montsalvy is still here, for instance. . . ."

But Catherine was no longer listening. It was more than a month now since she had been locked up in the dungeon and all that time she had had but one thought—to escape and regain her freedom at all costs. Unhappily, this dream seemed almost impossible to realize in such a heavily guarded city, so the news of the departure of most of the military leaders was a capital piece of information. It might be easier to make her escape while they were out of the city. As Pitoul rattled on, she looked at him with a half smile on her face. She had thought of a plan. . . .

Pitoul was in the habit of spending a few minutes with her every evening, partly because she was such a good listener and, also, because he was flattered to have such a grand lady as a prisoner in his charge. On these occasions the worthy Pitoul trusted her completely, not that he had ever been very suspicious of the lovely, golden-haired lady with her soft, sad ways and Catherine was reflecting that it would be a simple matter to knock Pitoul out with her stool, take his clothes and escape under cover of night. But first she would have to be better informed about the uses and customs of the fortress itself. She decided to devote that evening's and the following morning's chat to making Pitoul talk and, at the same time, she could be working out her plan of escape in greater detail so that it would be ready to put into effect the moment an opportunity arose. The important thing was to be out of the city before the Maid arrived. Catherine had not the slightest desire to have to submit to that girl's judgment upon her. . . .

It was child's play getting the information she needed. Pitoul was so overjoyed at the thought of being able to stuff to his heart's content that she did not even have to coax him to talk. In fact, he was hard to stop. Catherine soon knew the exact times that the guards made the rounds of the castle, the names of the gatekeepers, even the watchword. She decided to make her bid to escape on the Thursday and that night, for the first time since she had been imprisoned, she slept soundly.

All the Thursday she was nervous and uneasy. The bursts of artillery fire sounded louder that day than they had before. The English, too, knew of the approach of the girl whom they, for their part, dubbed "The Witch." The din of the bombards and culverins was deafening, but it gladdened Catherine. If this tumult should continue after sunset, it could only assist her plan. . . . She watched the sun set with mingled feelings of hope, fear and impatience. The time for Pitoul's visit was drawing near.

At last, she heard footsteps approaching in the corridor and her heart started to pound wildly. The moment had come. . . . She was just about to reach out and pick up the stool when the door opened, Pitoul came in and stepped aside at once, cap in hand. Catherine stepped back in astonishment as the Alderman Lhuillier came in, followed by two soldiers. He carried a parchment scroll in one hand. His red robe cast a sinister glow over the cell. Catherine stood up instinctively, her eyes fixed on the new arrival's frozen countenance. He glanced at her rapidly, unrolled the parchment and began to read aloud:

"In the absence of Monseigneur Jean d'Orléans and Messire Raoul de Gaucourt, governor of the city of Orleans, we, the aldermen of the city, have condemned to death Dame Catherine de Brazey, convicted of treason and complicity with the enemy. . . ."

"Death?" Catherine cried, appalled. "But . . . I haven't been tried yet!"

Lhuillier went on imperturbably:

"Wherefore we have decided that the said Dame be taken tomorrow at sunset to the Cathedral Church of Sainte-Croix to ask pardon of God for her sins and thence to the Place du Martroy to be hanged by the neck until she is dead. Signed this day at Orleans. . . ."

Catherine was shattered. She no longer listened to him. She had fallen back onto her mattress, hands clasped under her knees, her whole body racked by convulsive trembling. Hanged! . . . She was to be hanged!

"Messire Jean said that my fate would not be decided until after the city had been freed," she said in a faint voice.

"Monseigneur has entrusted the city to our keeping and in his absence it is we who are sole judges of what is good for Orleans," Lhuillier answered drily. "It seems fitting to us that our city should be rid of a corrupting presence like yours before the arrival of the messenger of the Lord. You are a blot of which we fain would rid ourselves."

The alderman's thin lips twisted in an expression of unspeakable disdain. He clearly regarded her as a limb of Satan, too, and Catherine realized that she must expect neither grace nor mercy from these people.

"Are you not afraid to burden your consciences with a murder?" she asked bitterly. "I have told you again and again that I am innocent."

"That is something between God and yourself, woman! A priest will come to see you tomorrow to prepare you to appear before Him."

The alderman coldly rolled up his scroll, slipped it up his loose sleeve and turned on his heel. The door banged heavily behind him and his companions. Catherine found herself alone again in deep darkness. This was the end . . . no one could save her now! A profound despair took hold of her and she flung herself down on her straw mattress and sobbed wildly. She was alone, quite alone in the heart of this uncaring, indifferent fortress! Tomorrow her enemies would be taking her out to her death. . . . Tomorrow! She only had a few hours left to live!

She stayed lying there for a long time. She had stopped crying, but it seemed to her that her soul was already beginning to leave her body. She felt icy cold and shivering. . . . Even if Pitoul returned now, she would have been unable to put her plan into effect. She had heard Lhuillier ordering the guards, as he left, to stay at the door of the cell and not to leave under any pretext whatsoever. There was nothing to be done!

A great tumult could be heard from outside. From the depths of her cell, Catherine heard cries of joy and singing. The town sounded unusually joyful this evening. Catherine reflected bitterly that it was probably her imminent death that they were celebrating. She remembered only too vividly the cries of hate which had followed her the day she was admitted to the Chastelet. Tomorrow it would be worse. They would crowd along the roadside to jeer and insult her and throw mud. . . .

Towards midnight, the cell door opened once again. Catherine started back, thinking that it must be the priest, but it was Arnaud. He stood for a second on the threshold looking at her. Then, very slowly, he pushed the heavy door shut and came forward.

"I have come to say farewell," he said hoarsely.

Arnaud had set his lantern down on the ground and its yellow light threw a gigantic shadow against the wall. Standing, he towered above Catherine and when she looked up at him, she thought she had never seen him look so tall ... or so pale. Or was his chalky pallor and those deep lines at the corners of his mouth due to some trick of the light? He was wearing his plain, green, leather doublet, as on the day of the trial, and was unarmed save for a small dagger thrust through his belt.

Catherine's heart was thumping in her breast. She felt her blood pounding in her temples, but, seeing that he remained standing there, looking at her, speechless, she finally broke the silence belligerently, fiercely.

"So," she said slowly. "Messire de Montsalvy felt he ought to say farewell, did he? What an honor! What an extraordinary mark of esteem from a man of such tender pride! But might I inquire just why you imagined that I *wanted* you to say farewell? Come now, Messire, be honest with yourself! You only came to see what sort of state I was in and how I was preparing to meet my death, didn't you? Well, I'll tell you: I await it joyfully, with a happiness you cannot even imagine, because it will free me from you and people like you. Now you know; you can go!"

The captain shook his head. His handsome face expressed no anger, only a sort of nervousness and uncertainty.

"No ... it wasn't that at all!" he said at last. "I came because I couldn't help myself. Night after night now, I've been fighting against the desire to come here. In the daytime I fight and I can forget you, but the night defeats me ... you are there ... always! You haunt me, you witch!"

She burst out laughing, full of a cruel, sweet joy to find that she still had the power to make him suffer.

"Witch!" she cried. "Is that all you can think of? Truly, I thought you were more intelligent. . . ."

"And I, too," he answered, quietly, refusing to be angered. "And I thought I was stronger, too, but it is years now since you bewitched me and obsessed me and poisoned my life ... I hate and despise you. I've done everything to try and forget you—wine, women. . . . I even came close to marriage. She was beautiful, the demoiselle de Séverac, gentle and pure, and she loved me. But when I was with her, it was you I saw, your hand I was touching, your cheek I was kissing. . . . So I ran away from her, because it was sacrilege to be dreaming of a whore like you with a sweet young maid. Then I returned again and clung to her and implored God to let me love her. . . . But Heaven was deaf to my cries and my desire for you only tortured me more cruelly. Then she died and I was alone again. For a moment, I thought of becoming a monk. . . ."

The idea struck Catherine as so insane, that she burst out laughing again.

"A monk? You? A man of your pride, your ruthlessness?"

"I could have done it, but I loved war too much to be a good servant of God. Pride can be stifled, but not the love of strife! That is something you carry in the blood from birth, something you suck in with your wet-nurse's milk. So I flung myself back into battle in the hope that death might release me from you, but death remained deaf, too."

Catherine had got slowly to her feet. She leant against the wall as if needing its support, but her eyes met Arnaud's proudly with a look as cutting as steel. She smiled contemptuously.

"So you thought, perhaps, she might have some use for me? It was you who forced the aldermen to sentence me in Gaucourt's absence, wasn't it?"

"Yes, it was I. And I don't regret it! You hung over them like an ill omen. They will hang you joyfully. . . ."

"What about you? You will hang me joyfully, too, won't you? You think you'll be free of me then for all eternity, don't you? Is that what you think?"

His voice came thickly:

"Yes . . . I do!"

She laughed in his face: a triumphant, mocking, maddening little laugh. She threw back her head insolently. A wild joy filled her, a bitter, heady exultation. How weak he seemed suddenly, how helpless before her! A hundred, thousand times more pathetic than she, even though she was already brushed by the wing of the Angel of Death!

"You really think that? Do you think my ghost will haunt you less than my memory? That once my body is reduced to dust it will stop haunting you? Poor fool! I shall be a hundred times more formidable once I am dead. You will see me everywhere: behind every woman's face, in all the bodies you embrace—because neither age nor sorrow will be able to touch me. And because your desire will be sharpened by remorse. . . ."

For the first time, a spark of anger flamed in the young man's dark eyes.

"Remorse? Don't be silly. You thoroughly deserve your fate seeing that you only came here to do harm."

"Oh, let's stop lying to each other like this! None of that matters any more to us now that you have disposed of my life. You know very well why I came. You knew from the moment I came towards you at the Bourgogne gate. You knew it in the torture chamber. You know I love you enough to dare anything, risk everything for you; that I have renounced everything

247

and have only one desire left in the world: to find you and die beside you in the ruins of this city."

"Be silent!" he growled.

"No, I won't be silent. I'm not dead yet, and I shall talk as much as I like. I shall say all the things I've been meaning to say all these years. And in the long sleepless nights ahead, you'll hear my voice crying: 'I loved you ... I loved you and you killed me.' ..."

"Will you stop?"

He seized her brutally by the shoulders, shaking her so fiercely that her head rolled like a doll's. She cried out and stumbled. Then he let go of her so suddenly that she fell heavily to the ground. One of her legs was bent up beneath her and the pain shot through her. She tried to struggle up again when he fell upon her, crushing her beneath his weight. The lantern's dim light showed her Arnaud's face close to hers, contorted with fury and desire.

"No, you won't haunt me! You will be dead tomorrow and I shall exorcise you tonight, you witch! I shall tear all your secrets from you. Perhaps, when I've slept with you, I shall realize that you are a woman like the rest. ..."

A fierce, silent, merciless struggle began between them. Catherine fought as if her life depended on it, saving her breath, economizing her strength as much as she could. She was supple and slippery as an eel, but Arnaud was a man in full possession of his strength, whereas she was but a woman weakened by privation and imprisonment. She felt herself weakening slowly and knew she couldn't hold out much longer. Her long hair was getting in her way, coiling round her like a net. Arnaud had seized one of her wrists and forced it behind her back. Now he tried to grab the other. Catherine's strength suddenly collapsed and, at the same moment, Arnaud's mouth swooped on hers so she couldn't breathe. She felt herself going soft, weakening, and knew she was about to swoon. She tried to steel herself, but she was too weak.

Half conscious, she felt him move away from her a little, still holding her wrists behind her back, and start tearing off her clothes. She had closed her eyes so as not to see him, but she heard him breathing hard like a man who has run a long race. His hard fingers hurt as they gripped her wrists and she twisted in an effort to escape the grip, but then he swept her whole body in a long caress and she trembled. He kissed her again and Catherine felt all the old demons awakening inside her, clamoring all the more hungrily for having been stilled so long. She forgot everything, her hate and rancour and imminent death and abandoned herself to him completely. She did not even

248

notice that he had let go of her wrists and that she had instinctively slipped her arms round his neck. He was talking now, in
a hoarse, almost inaudible voice: the voice of a man talking in
his sleep. With his lips close to her face he was murmuring
passionate endearments mingled with insults, only stopping to
cover her with kisses. Eyes closed, lips half open, she said
nothing, allowing herself to be carried away ecstatically. . . .

And the miracle happened, the miracle struck like a spark
from the collision between two beings created for each other
out of all time. Catherine gave herself as she never had before
and, in exchange, knew a joy which effaced everything and gave
her, in one minute, the price of a lifetime. . . .

When the wave of passion rolled back, leaving her spent and
motionless on the ground, Catherine felt Arnaud moving away.
She opened her eyes and saw him stumble towards the door.

"Arnaud," she called.

He turned very slowly, almost regretfully. He opened his
mouth to speak, but no sound came. Then she murmured very
softly:

"You can go now . . . and I can die happy. I know now that
you will never, never forget me."

With a hoarse cry, he pushed the door open and disappeared,
leaving his lantern behind. Catherine heard his footsteps dying
away down the prison corridors. Afraid that the soldiers on
guard might enter and see her, she hurriedly put on her clothes
again. Then she laid herself down and fell asleep. When one of
the guards came in to get the lantern, he found her fast asleep
and stood staring at her, open-mouthed, for a moment.

"Fancy sleeping like that when one is going to be hanged in
a few hours! And she only a woman, too!" he confided to his
companion. "She must be a brave one!"

CHAPTER FOURTEEN

Joan

Arnaud had no idea as he fled from Catherine's cell of the
immense joy he was leaving behind him: a joy which freed her
from herself, from her ugly prison and the dreadful fate which
awaited her to fling her into the midst of a blue heaven of bliss.
She had known such happiness in one short hour that she no

longer feared death. The monk who came to exhort her found a woman who seemed completely detached from everything around her and who paid him very little heed. She had listened to him talking about God with a half-smile playing on her lips which had somewhat scandalized the good monk. Pitoul had come in tears to serve her with the best meal she had seen in months: white bread, fresh meat and wine—a convoy of food had managed to enter the city the day before by water, protected by the Maid in person.

"When I think that she will be making her entry into the city this very evening and you won't be here to see her," the good fellow snuffled. And Catherine found herself comforting her gaoler. The Maid scarcely mattered to her now that she was going to die, because she would die happy.

This strange serenity of hers lasted while they hoisted her up, at about eight that evening, into a sort of cart which was ordinarily used to carry dung. The monk climbed up beside her and the executioner got up behind. An escort of bowmen surrounded the cortège and they set out from the Chastelet. Dressed in a coarse frock, with the noose already round her neck, Catherine let herself sway in time to the rattling, jolting cart. Her wide eyes were like a sleepwalker's. She no longer seemed to belong to this earth.

The cart crossed the poultry fair, empty at this hour, and headed down the great rue des Hostelleries. This bustling street, with its normally thriving inns and richly painted signs, usually presented an animated spectacle to the passers-by, but tonight it was almost empty. The houses were all shuttered and the few passers-by were in such a hurry that they barely heeded the sombre procession. One of the guards growled:

"They'll be at the Bourgogne gate where the Maid is to enter the city. Why couldn't milords the aldermen have had this woman hanged a bit earlier? Then we could have been there, too. . . ."

"We'll just have to be quick about it!" another said.

"Silence, you there!" the sergeant cried.

At that moment, a great hubbub of thousands of voices was heard. It came from the east of the town and sounded like a swarm of giant bees in the silence. Then the bells of Saint-Étienne and Notre-Dame-de-la-Conception began to ring out a joyful carillon, while the cheers and cries grew louder.

"She has entered the city!" one of the archers cried. "God be praised!"

"Amen," the monk echoed automatically. Catherine shrugged. She was beginning to long for this sinister farce to be ended, and oddly, it was no longer Arnaud who occupied

250

her thoughts, but Michel. She found herself seeing again, with appalling clarity, the dreadful journey he had made to the gallows all along the rue Saint-Denis. He had been surrounded by a crowd, whereas she was alone, and there was no couple of children anywhere determined to risk their lives in an attempt to rescue her. She was going to her death in the midst of total indifference with a dozing monk and some heedless soldiers as her sole companions.

The road suddenly widened and opened out into the cathedral precincts. The spires still glimmered in the evening light. Beneath the dark porch, a priest in a black chasuble stood waiting, holding the tall processional cross. Just then the bells of Sainte-Croix pealed out in their turn, loosing a float of insolent jubilation right over the condemned woman's head. She felt herself stiffening with sudden revolt. What right had all these merrymaking, joyful people to force her to die? The instinct of self-preservation suddenly awoke in her, so violently that she shuddered uncontrollably. She began to struggle in her bonds and cried out:

"I don't want to die! I am innocent . . . innocent. . . ."

Her voice was drowned in a deafening tumult. The road alongside the cathedral seemed to burst open suddenly under the pressure of an immense crowd, running and brandishing so many torches that the darkness was banished. In a trice, the place was packed, while windows all round were flung open, disgorging torrents of colored silk and tapestries which hung down into the dust. Catherine's cart was jammed in a sea of humanity which paid not the slightest attention to her. Above the press of heads, Catherine could see a military procession slowly drawing near. A bareheaded rider on a white horse rode at the head of the procession and it was there the crowd pressed closest. Catherine realized that this was Joan the Maid and in the same moment all her resentment melted away. Wide-eyed, hypnotized, she watched the soldier-maid approaching. Joan wore a suit of white armor which shone like silver and covered her from head to foot. With one hand she guided her horse, while in the other she held aloft a great, white silk banner embroidered with the image of the Savior, flanked by angels holding lilies in their hands. The words "Jesu Maria" were written down one side. But all Catherine saw of this dazzling image was the girl's face under the cap of short, boyish brown hair, a clear luminous face with blue, candid eyes. Men and women crowded round her, trying to touch her hand, armor or even her horse's trappings. She smiled gently at them and warned them not to come too close or they would be crushed beneath her horse's hooves. Behind the Maid, Catherine saw Jean

251

d'Orléans, Xaintrailles, Gaucourt and many others whom she recognized. Arnaud alone did not seem to be present.

Suddenly Joan's eyes fell upon her with a look of incredulity. She stopped her horse and turned to Dunois, pointing to the sad, little cortège.

"Sire Bastard, are there hearts in this good city hard enough to send a poor woman to her death at the very moment of their liberation?" she asked in a deep voice which thrilled through Catherine.

Dunois frowned. He had instantly recognized Catherine and was looking about him for someone who seemed to be absent. He shrugged with annoyance.

"I had given commands for this woman to be kept in prison till your arrival, Joan, so that you might dispose of her as you saw fit. She came here a month ago in rags and on the brink of collapse, but one of our captains recognized her as a great lady and none other than the beloved of Philippe of Burgundy. He accuses her of having come here as a spy."

"It isn't true! I only wanted to join the people of this city in their fate and die with them," Catherine cried, so ardently that Joan looked at her more closely. Violet and blue eyes met for a moment and Catherine suddenly felt a new surge of confidence. There was such kindness in Joan's eyes, so much sincerity, that she instantly forgot all her suspicions and as Joan smiled back at her, she found herself shyly smiling, too.

"What is your name?" Joan asked.

"Catherine, noble dame."

Joan's smile this time lit up her whole face and she merrily shook her short-cropped head.

"I am not noble at all, but a simple country girl and I have a little sister called Catherine, too, like one of my dear saints. Since your fate seems to depend upon me, Catherine, you shall be set free. I hope there is someone here prepared to take you in and look after you for my sake. We shall meet again. . . ."

All of a sudden, everyone wanted to take charge of the prisoner. She was untied and taken from the stinking cart and set down on the ground while a cloak was thrown about her shoulders. They seemed to be arguing over her and the very people who had been crying death to her a little while before, were now fighting over the right to give her hospitality. Meanwhile, Joan and her escort had dismounted in front of the cathedral where the girl wanted to pray as she did every evening at sundown. A tall, strapping woman, richly dressed, went up to her.

"Entrust your prisoner to me, Joan," she said. "I am the

mother of treasurer Jacques Boucher who is to have the honor of lodging you in this town. I shall take good care of her."

Joan smiled her thanks. Then she went into the great church still carrying her white banner. Mathilde Boucher laid a hand on Catherine's arm and began to make her way through the crowd which parted before them with a murmur of sympathy. "Come, poor dear. You look as though you could do with a little care and comforting."

Catherine allowed herself to be led away somewhat unwillingly. Her eyes still strained after Joan's white, shining figure as it went into the cathedral porch. Mathilde smiled.

"Come now," she said. "You will soon be seeing her again since she is lodging with us."

Then she allowed herself to be led away obediently by her new protectress. As they passed in front of the Hotel-Dieu, she caught sight of a kneeling figure with huge wings sculpted outside the gate.

"One day," she said softly, "a long time ago, when I was a little girl, a gipsy woman told me that I should meet an angel. Do you think Joan is that angel, Dame Mathilde?"

Mathilde paused for a moment and looked at her guest with sudden liking. A simple impulse of charity was becoming something more like respect.

"I am sure of it," she said solemnly.

The house belonging to Jacques Boucher, treasurer to the King in the city of Orleans, stood near the Regnard gate which faced west. It was a tall, handsome dwelling whose carved gables, fine mullioned windows and slender pepperpot roofs testified to its prosperity. From its upper windows, it commanded a view of most of the English camp. Beyond the moat, between the Loire and the Bannière gate on the nothern side, Salisbury's and then Talbot's and Suffolk's men had built five huge, wooden bastions with towers and defenses, the largest of which was named the Bastille Saint-Laurent. The pennant of John Talbot, Earl of Shrewsbury, floated above it and Dame Mathilde pointed it out to Catherine from the window of her bedroom. Dark though it was, it was quite possible to make out the extent of the English camp and the chains of multi-colored tents strung between the bastions. Beyond, the baked scorched countryside looked as bare as a bald head.

"They aren't much better off than us," Catherine's new friend remarked, pointing to the great bastion. "And it isn't often they have a square meal. Tonight, thanks to Joan, we shall be feasting royally in this besieged city!"

Catherine felt rather as if she had just woken from a bad

dream. The lady's kindness was comforting. She reminded Catherine in more ways than one of her friend, Ermengarde de Châteauvilain. She could not resist telling her so and Dame Mathilde was immensely flattered, the Châteauvilain family being far too distinguished not to be known the length and breadth of France. She was not insensible, either, to the rank of the new guest herself and, quite forgetting that only an hour before the noble lady in question had had a noose round her neck, she took evident pleasure in calling her "my dear Countess."

Thanks to her, Catherine was rediscovering all the joys of civilized life. The numerous servants were busy preparing for a great banquet which the treasurer had planned to give for the Maid, but Mathilde managed to find a couple of maids who hastened to fill a tub of hot water and prepare a room.

Lying back in the scented water, Catherine reflected that she had never known a more pleasurable moment than that. Masses of hot water, scented soap, colognes—all suddenly appeared within reach as if by magic. It was a far cry from the pitcher of cold water which Pitoul brought to her every morning! When she had scrubbed herself down and washed her hair, Catherine felt like a new woman. A chemise of finely pleated lawn, a dress of russet-colored silk—a little large, but she cunningly took it in with a few pins—and Catherine was transformed. While a maid combed out her long hair with many an admiring exclamation, she thought that all her agonies and fears and even the memory of those bad times had been washed away in the tub of water which the maids were just removing. When Mathilde appeared on the threshold, she paused for a moment, thunderstruck at the transformation. In barely an hour the wretched creature on her way to the gibbet had been changed into a very beautiful and elegant young woman. She could not resist stepping forward and embracing her.

"My dear Countess, you look quite ravishing! Now I begin to understand! To tell the truth, I was wondering what madman could have imagined that you were the beloved of the exacting Duke!"

"Well, I am his beloved no longer," Catherine replied with a smile. "I'll tell you all about it. You've been so kind to me, I'd like you to know."

"Don't worry about that. You are very welcome here. Like the Maid, I instantly realized that your whole experience must have been caused by some terrible misunderstanding. Come now, let me introduce you. I can hear the procession arriving."

The sounds of rejoicing in the city did seem to be drawing

254

nearer. Joan must have left the cathedral on the way to her new lodgings. But Catherine refused.

"No, not this evening. I should be embarrassed, but tomorrow I shall throw myself at Joan's feet to thank her!"

Just then, Marguerite Boucher's red, perspiring face appeared in the doorway. She smiled at Catherine whom she had warmly welcomed out of deference to Joan, then she spoke to her mother-in-law:

"Here she is! Please come! I should never dare to go out to meet her alone!"

"When will you get over this terror of a scrap of armor, Margot?" Mathilde chided her. "It isn't a brigand chieftain you are entertaining, but a lovely, sweet, smiling young girl. . . ."

". . . who has been sent straight here from Heaven! As if that weren't twenty times more alarming than all the robber chiefs in the world!"

The two women rushed out, leaving Catherine alone. Joan's procession was approaching and she went over to the window to watch them arrive. The Maid was still on horseback, but she had handed her banner to her squire, Jean d'Aulon, so that she might more easily touch all the hands held out to her and kiss the babies.

The captains had all fallen in behind her, smiling and patient for once. One alone among them looked sombre and rode along staring gloomily at his horse's ears. Catherine recognized Arnaud with a great leap of her heart. He looked like a prisoner being dragged along behind the victor's chariot and Catherine wondered whether he knew yet of her rescue by Joan. Was this lugubrious face of his the result of knowing her to be alive, or was he already stricken by remorse? Memories of the previous night must be torturing him now and she smiled. It was so good to be alive, young, free . . . free to take up that strange conflict which had existed so long now between Captain Montsalvy and herself.

"I shall give you neither rest nor respite," she murmured. A fierce desire for revenge had suddenly taken hold of her. In truth, her feelings towards Arnaud were complex: she loved and hated him at the same time, this man who had sent her so coldly and unhesitatingly to her death and then gone wild with passion in her arms. His gloomy expression and the sorrow stamped all over his face awoke a streak of malicious glee in Catherine. It was his turn now to learn, too, that pride did not solve everything or protect him from everything.

When they had all entered, the house hummed with noise and activity like a hollow shell. Catherine went and lay down on her bed. Tonight or tomorrow she and Arnaud would meet again and Catherine secretly dreaded the encounter. How would he act when he knew her to be alive? To Catherine, Arnaud was an insoluble enigma. Twice, now, she had abandoned herself to him, so gladly and passionately that he surely could not have failed to notice. Why, then, did he pursue her with this implacable hatred—even to the point of delivering her to the torturer and sending her to the gallows? He was afraid of her, that was certain; afraid of the mad desire which she awoke in him and, believing as he did that this attraction was evil, he had tried to rid himself of her in the most effective manner possible.

Catherine tried loyally to put herself in the young man's place. The first time he met her on the route to Flanders he had made no attempt to disguise the fact that he was violently attracted to her. He had not stopped to think, but simply because she was beautiful and he wanted her, he had taken her in his arms and tried to make her his without bothering to find out more about her. But from that instant in which spontaneous attraction had drawn them together, fate had stepped in and taken a malicious pleasure in separating them again. How cruel it was that the one fact he had remembered of the circumstances of his brother's death should be the name of Legoix! There were lots of Legoix in Paris and it was only one of them, cousin Thomas, who had swung the cleaver which had ended Michel's life so brutally. How was it Arnaud had failed to hear about the little Parisian girl's part in the affair? Had no one talked to him about the goldsmith who had been hanged for sheltering his brother, or the heartbroken child who had pitted her frail strength against the mob and begged for the young man's life to be spared? Arnaud lumped Catherine in with all the other Legoix, not even troubling to discriminate between guilty and innocent.

Nevertheless, as she pursued these reflections, her attitude to Arnaud gradually became more sympathetic and she found herself coming up with excuses for him. After all, why should Arnaud trust her? She came from a family on whom he had sworn vengeance and yet when he had met her beneath the walls of Arras, he had forgotten his legitimate vendetta in the love and passion she aroused in him.

And then what had happened? In defiance of the laws of chivalry, Arnaud had been taken and thrown into prison and no sooner had he been released than he had discovered Catherine installed in Philippe's bed—a sight not exactly calculated to give him pleasure. When he had finally caught sight of her that time in Orleans how was he to guess that she had come there to join in his martyrdom after a long and gruelling jour-

256

ney of many days? For a man who had been cooped up in that city for six months, reduced to starvation, anything from Burgundy must inevitably be suspect and, as such, suppressed. . . .

As the time passed, Catherine's thoughts became more and more favorable towards Arnaud. She understood him now. Not only that, she could forgive the implacable hatred he felt for her. Perhaps, in his place, she would have felt the same . . . and perhaps the best thing for Catherine would be to give up. . . . She was beginning to see that she had been dreaming, that there was too much bitterness between them for her and Arnaud ever to be united. He would never be able to believe in the love of a woman whom he so deeply mistrusted. She felt suddenly weary and hopeless. . . .

She had got out of the habit of undressing for bed and was just about to fall asleep when Dame Mathilde appeared again in a state of great agitation.

"Would you believe it? Joan has refused to touch a morsel of our banquet!" she cried. "Monsieur Jean and the captains have made a royal repast, but all Joan would have was a few pieces of bread dipped in water. Her chaplain, Brother Jean Pasquerel, tells me that she rarely eats anything else."

The good woman's voice was so distressed that Catherine could not help smiling.

"Neither you nor I know anything of the Lord's messenger," she said gently. "We have a lot to learn. . . ."

Mathilde Boucher, far from reassured, shook her head solemnly under its towering, double-horned headdress.

"Do you really think she can be just a simple peasant girl? Have you seen how well she sits her horse? What nobility and assurance! Her squire, Messire d'Aulon, tells me that at Tours recently she broke a lance with Monseigneur the Duc d'Alençon and the Duke was quite stunned by her skill. Isn't it amazing?"

The good woman might have rattled on for hours in this vein about Joan's oddities, but Catherine was hardly listening. Her whole attention was strained towards the sound of a male voice, rising from the floor below: a voice at once rough and warm which sent shivers down her spine. When her hostess left her, Catherine felt a heavy weight of sorrow and depression settle over her again. It was so hard to know what to do. Would she ever be brave enough to break away from Arnaud and leave him for ever?

The next morning Catherine woke with a jump at the sound of a voice in the street outside swearing and cursing most dreadfully. She ran to the window after throwing a wrapper hastily about her. Yes, it was Arnaud. He stood there, wearing armor, helmet under one arm, arguing fiercely with treasurer Boucher. They were both shouting so loudly that Catherine did not understand what they were saying at first. Boucher appeared to be barring the captain's way.

"By the Pope's intestines!" Arnaud roared at last, "I swear I will make you let me pass. I thought the whore dead since yesterday and now I learn that she is staying with you as a valued guest! This is a scandal that cannot be borne, even if I have to string the damned witch up with my own hands!"

Boucher was about to reply when another voice—no whit less vigorous than the captain's—joined in the dispute. Catherine saw Joan rush from the house, seize Arnaud by the shoulders and start shaking him like a rat.

"Messire!" she cried. "How dare you take the Lord's name in vain? Let me tell you that you shall not leave this place till you have retracted everything you have said!"

Arnaud could not have been more astonished if a thunderbolt had struck him. The young girl's imperious tone and strong hand appeared to be enough to daunt the most vigorous captain. The Lord's messenger was certainly no milksop! But Arnaud was not the man to be easily intimidated.

"I am Captain de Montsalvy and I wish to enter here to see that justice is done," he cried.

"Were you the King, our master himself, you should not enter against Maître Boucher's wishes. Besides, this is an affair which concerns only the two of you. What I want to make sure of is that you ask pardon of God for the offense you have caused him with these oaths. I shall not be finished with you till then. Come now, on your knees!"

His knees? The Maid had actually dared to order a Montsalvy to his knees? Catherine could hardly believe her ears. Her amazement grew as she saw Arnaud—his color changing from scarlet to chalk white—get to his knees on the cobbles and mumble a short prayer. A little sadly, she reflected that he would no doubt add this humiliation to all his other grievances against her.

When the culprit had finished his prayer, Joan went back into the house and, at the same moment, Xaintrailles appeared accompanied by another captain, somewhat older looking, but massive and formidable in appearance as a fighting bull. At the sight of Arnaud kneeling in prayer in the middle of the street, they stopped in their tracks and burst into great roars of laughter. Arnaud's anger was switched against them.

"I'd like to know just what you think you're doing, standing there laughing like idiots!" he cried furiously. His belligerent

258

manner did not worry the two men in the least and the elder of them only stopped laughing for a moment to remark slyly:

"It looks as if the Maid has given you a good dressing-down, my friend. It looks as if you have found your master at last!"

"I'll wager you find the same, La Hire. No one swears more abominably than you in the whole army and we'll see what Joan has to say when she hears your repertoire. Why I'll even have a wager with you!"

"On what?" the Gascon asked suspiciously.

"About you! I wager a hundred gold écus that she gets you to go to confession!"

La Hire's laughter shook the walls. He wept for joy and slapped his thighs resoundingly. Étienne de Vignolles, nicknamed La Hire (Wrath) for his dreadful temper, had bursts of gaiety almost as overpowering as his celebrated rages.

"Done!" he cried. "You had better start counting out your money now. Get me to confession? Why, the Pope himself would not dare. . . ."

"No, but Joan would. And you will obey her, my lad . . . because it just isn't possible not to, you'll see!"

As he spoke, Arnaud looked up and caught sight of Catherine standing at the window with her golden plaits hanging down over her white chemise. He went pale and looked away. Then he slipped an arm through Xaintrailles's and said:

"Let's be off. Joan can do what she likes with that woman. The best thing she could do would be to send her to the Devil. . . ."

"Joan? Send someone to the Devil? That would surprise me!" La Hire exclaimed. Not knowing anything of the situation, he was genuinely astounded by the suggestion, but Xaintrailles grinned and, as the other two turned on their heels, he smiled up at Catherine and swept her a tiny bow. This smile and bow mollified her a little, but Arnaud's words still hurt. Xaintrailles still seemed to have a slight penchant for her and Catherine thought he might perhaps have some influence with Arnaud. At all events, he would have some inkling of the young man's secret feelings. She promised herself to take him aside and speak to him at the next opportunity.

All that day Catherine watched Joan of Arc going about her daily business. The Maid fascinated and attracted her more than any woman ever had before, so much so that she even forgot Arnaud from time to time and, when his image came to mind, she set herself to banish it again, because of the too precise, physical memories it evoked which embarrassed her in the presence of this tall, devout, simple girl from Lorraine. Joan, however, for all the reverence with which she was

259

treated, was not just a figure out of a stained glass window. She radiated joy, a deep, infectious joy, but when occasion arose, she could let loose a rage as fearsome as any of her captains, as Arnaud had found to his cost. That morning, after Mass said by Jean Pasquerel in Mathilde Boucher's chapel, Joan was visibly devoured by impatience. She burned to launch an attack immediately and was clearly exasperated at being checked by Dunois. The Bastard advised that it would be safer to wait till the main body of the army had arrived from Blois.

But Joan, good Lorraine that she was, was as stubborn as a mule. Catherine listened, aghast, to the tempestuous council of war raging in the great hall from her hiding place with Mathilde behind a door. On the one hand, Joan, backed up by La Hire, Xaintrailles, Illiers and Montsalvy, was all for attacking at once, while on the other, the Bastard, Gaucourt and the Sire de Gamaches urged that they should wait for reinforcements. One thing led to another and a violent quarrel took place between Gamaches and the Maid who, regarding herself as commander-in-chief, would not allow her orders to be disputed. Gamaches lost his temper, called Joan "a common trollop" and announced that he was retiring from his post and narrowly escaped being disemboweled by Arnaud who sprang at him, sword in hand, intent on making him swallow his insults at sword-point. With some difficulty, Dunois managed to prevent the Auvergnat from slaughtering the irascible Picard. He soundly scolded Gamaches, and Joan more gently, and finally managed to persuade them to embrace—which they did under protest.

It was settled that the Bastard and Joan's squire should be sent to Blois to accelerate the army's departure and that Joan should dictate a letter to the English to Jean Pasquerel. Xaintrailles, meanwhile, left the hall and found himself face to face with Catherine.

"Messire," she said gently, "I should like to talk to you! Can you spare me a moment?"

By way of reply, he led her into a window embrasure, first making sure that they were alone in the room.

"What can I do for you, beautiful lady?" he asked pleasantly, grinning broadly.

"I want to thank you, first of all," Catherine said. "My gaoler told me that my treatment in prison was greatly improved thanks to you. I was given food to eat and was not chained up and . . ."

"Not another word! You do not owe me any thanks. I merely did what my conscience dictated. Don't you remember freeing us from prison at Arras?"

Catherine gave a sigh of disappointment.

"Oh, so that was why! And I thought it was because you believed in my innocence! I thought you wanted to make up to me for Messire Arnaud's injustice."

"Perhaps that came into it, too. I never believed in this 'mission' of yours here. You were in far too pitiable a state! Only Arnaud in his blind rage could have been so mistaken. And, since he wouldn't hear a word in your favor, I did what I could."

"You have no idea how grateful I am. If it hadn't been for you, he would have had me torn to pieces by the executioner, quite pitilessly. He hates me, doesn't he?"

Xaintrailles broad face took an expression of unwonted thoughtfulness. He hesitated before answering, no doubt feeling himself to be on thin ice.

"Frankly, I don't know. He appears to hate you, and yet . . ."

". . . And yet?" Catherine echoed hopefully.

"And yet, he behaves oddly. Do you know why he didn't learn of your release until this morning? Because he got as drunk as a Polack last night: miserably drunk. He drank cup after cup and every time he seemed to be toasting an invisible presence. He had to be carried away at dawn, half insensible and crying like a child. He was mumbling something incomprehensible, but I thought I caught the mention of your name. Perhaps he does hate you, but personally I would say he loves you still more!"

A voice reached them from the hall. It was Illiers calling for his wine.

"Coming!" Xaintrailles called back. Then he bent towards her, as Catherine put out a hand to detain him, and asked, very low and fast:

"You still love him, don't you?"

"More than the world! More than my life!" she cried, so passionately that Xaintrailles smiled.

"He's a lucky man—luckier than he knows! Well, listen then, fair Catherine. Arnaud is as obstinate and stubborn as all the mules in France put together, but he has a strangely soft heart beneath that fearsome manner of his. If you love him enough to accept everything and live only for the moment that will bring him back to you, you might have a chance. However obstinate he may be, the day will come when he can no longer struggle against himself and you."

"This morning he wanted me hanged!"

"When he got here, perhaps! But I wish you had seen his face when he heard that you were alive—saved by Joan. Ar-

261

naud's face cannot lie—I could swear that I saw it kindle with joy. . . ."

Xaintrailles said nothing more. He went off, leaving Catherine to her thoughts. His remarks had kindled a little spark of hope, the hope that dies so hard in a loving heart. . . .

While the men drank in the great hall, Joan went back to the women to be helped into her armor. Mathilde, Marguerite and Catherine bustled round her, passing her the various pieces of armor one after another. Catherine knelt at her feet helping her on with her white mailed shoes. She looked up suddenly and asked:

"Why are you putting on your armor, Joan, since you will not be attacking today? I trust you are not going to launch an offensive single-handed!"

Joan laughed.

"Not for lack of wanting to, my dear, but for the moment, all I plan to do is to accompany my messengers as far as the main bridge and get an idea of how things are."

Joan's two heralds, Guyenne and Ambleville, had been charged with the task of delivering her letter to Talbot's camp with all the traditional ceremony of chivalry.

"Joan," Catherine whispered, holding out one of her mail gloves. "I would love to go with you. Ask them to give me some boy's clothes. I could go as your squire."

". . . And my captains would be distracted by this overly pretty squire in their midst," Joan smiled. "They need all their sangfroid and the town has need of them. Go to the ramparts, Catherine, you will see just as much from there."

Catherine sighed, but did not insist. She saw Joan mount her charger along with several other of her captains, among them Arnaud, his armor gleaming somberly. He seemed among the most ardent in the service of the Maid, but strangely, Catherine was not in the least jealous. Joan had a strange power to still the ugly voices which might speak in the depths of one's innermost soul. Besides, Catherine had a feeling that no harm could come to him while he was with Joan. She inspired confidence. . . .

While Joan and her suite were outside the city, Catherine remained on the ramparts watching after them and she did not descend again till they had returned safely. When she reached the house, she saw that Joan's eyes were full of tears. The English had replied to her letter with insults, calling her a whore and a cowherd. But, what was more serious in Joan's eyes, they had taken one of her heralds a prisoner. Ambleville alone had returned. Gladsdale had seized Guyenne and threatened to have him burnt alive.

Arnaud instantly leapt forward.

"Let me go!" he cried. "I will bring him back!"

"No!" Catherine cried, so sharply that everyone turned to look at her. She went crimson with shame and, seeing that Arnaud refused to acknowledge her except by a haughty stare, she slipped behind Dame Mathilde's broad back, wishing the earth would swallow her up. Joan had smiled at her.

"Ambleville must return," she said, turning back to her other herald who was ashen with apprehension. As the poor man's teeth chattered, she nodded at him and slapped him on the shoulder.

"Eh, there, they won't kill you," she cried. "Tell Talbot himself to meet me in single combat outside the city walls. If he can take me, he can have me burned with Guyenne. If I prevail, he must raise the siege and the English must go."

Dunois interrupted here:

"Your plan is generous and noble, Joan, but Talbot would never come. He is a great leader and a good knight and he would never agree to measure arms against a woman. It seems to me that Ambleville need only say that anything done to Guyenne will be repaid in full measure to our English prisoners and anyone else who comes to us to discuss ransoms."

His advice was wise. An hour later, Ambleville returned with Guyenne and Joan went to the cathedral with the entire household to offer up thanks to the Holy Virgin, Catherine among them. She went with Marguerite and Mathilde.

When the Mass was over, and they were on their way home, she could not help noticing that one of the Maid's captains was favoring her with a particularly insistent stare; so insistent that it made her feel a little embarrassed as well as faintly triumphant. It was the first time for a long while that any man had stared at her like that, with a desire that he did not even trouble to hide. It restored her self-confidence a little.

The knight in question was a tall man of about twenty-five. His hair and the short beard framing his hard, arrogant face were blue-black. His dark eyes glowed like coals and his thin, red lips were like a gash across his pale face. He made Catherine shiver and she whispered to Mathilde:

"Who is that knight with the sullen face?"

The old lady threw a quick glance at him, frowned and quickened her steps a little.

"A Breton, of the noble house of Laval. His name is Gilles de Rais. They say he is fabulously rich, and brave, too, but savage. He was brought up by his grandfather, a formidable old robber, Jean de Craon, who recognized no law but his own. The whole town is talking about this young man's prodigal existence

—and his brutality. He is lodged at the "Moor's Head" with Agnes Grosvilain, who doesn't know whether to praise his liberality or bemoan his excesses. They say he seduces young girls ... and even boys! I don't like him at all and I don't advise you to attract his attention. ..."

Despite Mathilde's advice, Catherine found it hard to shake off the curiously disturbing memory of the Sire de Rais's lingering glances and they still remained with her late that night. Long after everyone was asleep, Catherine lay tossing and turning in her bed. She could hear the snores of Jean d'Aulon, sleeping outside the door of the room where Joan and Marguerite Boucher were asleep. That was one of the Maid's habits: every night a woman shared her bed. Her two pages, young Raymond and the naughty Louis de Coutes, known as Imerguet, slept in the corridor, but, despite all these reassuring presences, Catherine could not get rid of a vague feeling of anxiety. Around midnight, she suddenly heard a suspicious sound below her open window: a prolonged scratching noise as if someone was scrabbling at the wall.

She jumped up and ran to the window and craned her head out cautiously, taking care not to be seen. She just stifled a cry of astonishment: a man was down there, slowly but surely clawing his way up the wall, smooth and precarious though it was. He seemed endowed with a feline agility, and was unmistakably making progress. He would doubtless soon have reached Catherine's window had not another masculine figure suddenly materialized out of the shadows and flung itself upon the climber. The latter gave a smothered cry, feeling himself seized around the ankles, lost his balance and crashed to the ground. The newcomer fell upon him heavily. A savage struggle followed and Catherine did not know whether to keep silent or call for help. Her eyes were gradually becoming accustomed to the darkness and she could see that the two men were of roughly equal height and strength. First one seemed to be getting the upper hand, then the other, but since they were both wearing dark clothes it was impossible to tell one from the other. She could hear them breathing and panting like bellows. Suddenly she was terrified to see the gleam of a dagger and one of the combatants gave a cry of pain. She was about to cry out when a window opened on the top floor and a man in a nightgown, carrying a candle, leant out. Catherine recognized Jean Boucher. He held his candle high, looking up and down the street to see what was happening.

"Ho, there!" he cried. "What's going on?"

This new turn of events seemed to be more than the two combatants had bargained for. They broke apart as if by tacit

264

agreement and ran away, one towards the river and the Notre-Dame tower and the other towards the Bannière gate. There was the sound of hurrying footsteps and then silence. Maître Boucher shrugged and went back in. The light vanished. Catherine went back to bed thoughtfully. She was sure she had recognized the black beard of the Sire de Rais, but who was the other?

She was still mulling over the problem a few minutes later, when she suddenly sat bolt upright in bed again, her heart thumping wildly. That noise . . . the noise had begun again. She strained her ears and eyes gazing towards the window. She held her breath, listening to the faint scratching sounds drawing nearer and nearer to her window. She was bathed in a cold sweat and her hand clutched nervously at her chemise. Was it the same man returning . . . or the other? She was too terrified to move.

As a head appeared at the window, she opened her mouth to scream, but the sound died in her throat. A dark shape clambered over the sill and dropped into the room noiselessly as a cat. The nearness of danger brought her back to herself. She slid to the foot of the bed and started to make for the safety of the door, but the rustle of her long nightgown must have alerted the intruder. He leapt towards her and seized her round the waist.

Catherine felt herself crushed against a powerful body with hard muscles under a leather jerkin. The man was breathing hard and she recognized the faint smell of his breath as his mouth closed over hers. Her fear instantly vanished and she gave herself up.

"Arnaud!" she sighed. "You've come back!"

He did not answer. A strange frenzy seemed to have seized him. Wordlessly, roughly, he tore off her nightgown, his hands searching greedily for the softness of her skin. Catherine yielded herself to the slow, overwhelming crescendo of passion which surged through her like a tidal wave. Half wild with desire she clung to him, returning kiss for kiss. The dark room began to spin and she felt herself stumble, but just then he swept her up in his arms and flung her on the bed. The night closed over the two lovers, a night disturbed only by sighs and sometimes a soft moan.

When Arnaud got up, many long minutes later, he still had not uttered a single word. He had taken her with clenched teeth, with a sort of desperate frenzy. Catherine could not tell, in his arms, which was the slave of the other, so much were they both driven on by this violent delight they found together.

When she sensed that he was leaving her, she stretched out

her arms to try to keep him, but they met nothing but emptiness. She sat up just in time to see his shape at the window and, a moment later, he was gone. She fell back against the pillows again. He might leave her now. Her cup of happiness was brimming over. Tomorrow would bring another day and she would see him again. There was no longer any question of running away, or burying herself in Burgundy. Xaintrailles was right, but perhaps the battle would not last as long as he thought. Arnaud already seemed close to surrender. Catherine spent the rest of the night building delicious dream castles, each one more rapturous than the last.

But the next morning, as the Captains arrived to take their orders from Joan, Catherine, who stood watching from the top of the stairs, admiring their gleaming armor and colored pennants, noticed two things: first, that Gilles de Rais had a new-looking scratch right across one cheek, while Arnaud de Montsalvy sported a rich, black eye, a detail which had escaped her the night before. And he barely looked at her; he turned away at once, frowning a little, and, from then on, took good care not to look towards the stairs.

The marks on the Captains' faces had not escaped Joan's sharp eyes. Letting her blue gaze travel from one to the other, she remarked, half in jest, half in earnest:

"It would be better for God and the Dauphin, Messires, if you spent your nights in bed."

The two culprits hung their heads like guilty schoolboys, but Arnaud's shamefaced air was no consolation to Catherine. She just couldn't understand him. Why adopt this remote, even rude attitude to her after the passionate moments of the night before? Was he ashamed? And, moreover, could this fierce hunger he felt for her really be called love?

Catherine was to retain a strange, blurred, but dazzling memory of those last days of the siege of Orleans, a memory dominated by the tall, blue-eyed girl who managed her horse like a man, led the attack with all the fire and vigor of a seasoned captain and then was able to summon the tenderness of a mother and movements of infinite gentleness to comfort the wounded and dying; the girl who one minute would be weeping humbly as she confessed her sins to Jean Pasquerel, and the next, would be threatening to "lop the fellow's head off!" if the Bastard allowed the English reinforcements through. Great, tender Joan, whose ardent heart had never learned to compromise!

On the evening of 4 May Catherine saw the relief army and convoy of food led by Dunois entering the city, a fitting end to this day in which the Maid had recaptured the Bastille Saint-Loup from the English and opened up the road to Burgundy. She saw Joan praying, prostrate, in the cathedral on Ascension Day before crossing the Loire on the sixth, capturing the remains of the Augustine monastery which the English had made into a redoubt and launching an attack against the Tournelles fort on the seventh, in the course of which she was struck in the shoulder by an arrow which she pulled out herself. After the wound had been dressed, she returned to the attack. Before sunset the body of William Gladsdale, the man who had insulted her, fell from the walls into the moat. From the height of the city walls Catherine kept a constant vigil during the pitched battle of Sunday, 8 May which finally freed the valiant city. She saw Talbot collect together the remains of his army, strike camp and leave Orleans once and for all. Loyal to the last, the captive prince's city had never wavered from its role as last guard-post of the kingdom. . . .

During all this time, however, Catherine never managed to approach Arnaud. From time to time she would catch sight of his black armor and the sparrowhawk crest on his helmet during the battle, laying about him with his battle-axe as unwearyingly as a woodchopper cutting wood, but she never got closer to him. At night, when darkness put an end to the day's fighting, he would vanish, no doubt overpowered by fatigue. Night after night Catherine waited in vain, listening for a sound outside her window . . . none came. And on those rare occasions when she found herself in his presence in Jean Boucher's house, she had the disagreeable impression that she might just as well have been transparent. Arnaud stared right through her as if she had been made of glass. . . . She had tried to bar his way one evening just as he was leaving the house, but he had evaded her with devilish cunning and she had been too offended to try again. He had become remote and distant again and this determination to ignore her had reawakened all Catherine's doubts and fears. Where he was concerned she was almost paralyzed with shyness.

Several times, after learning from a maid that he lodged at the "Écu Saint Georges," she had sworn to go and meet him there and demand an explanation, but when the moment came for putting her scheme into effect, she was seized by a sudden terror. With this extraordinary, capricious man, what guarantee was there that he would not throw her out into the street in front of all the other people in the inn?

While she, in common with the other townspeople, assisted at the open-air Mass which was celebrated on the ramparts facing the fleeing English army, she was suddenly overtaken by despair; the town was free now and she no longer had an excuse to stay on with the Bouchers. She would have to decide soon. But what? Where could she go where she would be near Arnaud? Joan's task was not finished. Catherine had often heard the Maid declare that she would have to escort Charles VII to Rheims to be crowned and so put an end to the disputes which had raged around him for so many years. And the captains, Arnaud among them, would follow Joan. It was this departure, which Catherine felt to be imminent, which dismayed her so, because she did not know what she could do.

When Joan returned home to rest after the Mass, Catherine followed her into the room to help her make herself comfortable. They were left alone together for a moment while Mathilde and Marguerite bustled off to attend to the last details of a great banquet for the city notables, and Catherine decided to make use of this opportunity to speak to her. As she helped Joan divest herself of the different pieces of armor, she asked humbly:....

"Joan! The city is freed now and you will soon be leaving to complete your task. I want to go with you. I could do whatever you wanted: look after your clothes and lodging, for instance...."

Joan looked at her in astonishment, her candid eyes seeming to bore right through into Catherine's innermost heart. She smiled, but shook her head.

"I would like you to stay with me, my dear Catherine, but I could not let you do it. Where I am going is not the place for you. I am a peasant girl used to hard work and a rough life, whereas you are a fine lady, and delicate and frail despite the sufferings you have endured."

"I? I am a girl of the people, Joan, quite as much, if not more so, than you," Catherine cried with a suggestion of pride and defiance which brought a smile to her lips.

"True, I remember you telling me now, and you are right to be proud of it, but there is another thing, Catherine: you are much too beautiful and seductive to live in the midst of an army. My soldiers are no angels, nor are their captains, and you would awaken their worst instincts, inflame quarrels and jealousies."

"I would dress like a man and cut my hair like you!"

"That would make no difference. You would still be every inch a woman, even under a monk's robe. No, Catherine, these men must face long hard campaigns and I have to make sure that nothing undermines their unity or confidence. The sweet Dauphin and the Lord God have great need of them. It would be better for you to return home till the war is over."

"Return home? To Burgundy?" Catherine cried, horrified. "To my old, sinful life? Joan, you know quite well what my life there was like. You can't send me back there, not you!"

Joan reflected for a moment. Catherine held out the half red, half green doublet in the colors of Orleans which Dunois had just presented to her. When she had finished tying the laces, Joan laid a kindly hand on her shoulder.

"You are right," she said. "If you don't feel strong enough to resist your old habits it would be better not to return, but what else can I do for you, Catherine? A convent? There is too much life in you to suit you for the cloisters. Ah, I have an idea. Why not go to Madame Yolande?"

"But . . . I don't know her."

"That doesn't matter if I send you there. Go to the Queen of the Four Kingdoms. I will give you a letter to her. You will find help and protection and you can wait for the final victory there . . . as well as the return of the man whom you *really* want to follow, much more than me!"

Catherine was stunned that her secret should have been so readily discovered. She collapsed onto a stool and stared round-eyed at Joan.

"How did you guess?" she asked.

"Not difficult," Joan smiled. "Your eyes give everything away. But a time of patient waiting has come for you, as a time for battle has come for the men—each to his appropriate role. Go to join my Queen and pray for our success in battle."

She realized that nothing would change Joan's mind now and she did not try to stop her as she got up to go. Perhaps this was the best solution. Brother Étienne had spoken to her so often about Yolande, the King's mother-in-law, that Catherine felt she already knew her. And the main thing, after all, was to remain in the same camp as Arnaud since she couldn't follow him.

While the maids tidied the room, she waited for a moment to help them, but the sounds of revelry in the house were growing louder. Through the windows, opened wide to the May sunshine, Catherine could see the city notables and their elaborately dressed wives hurrying towards the Regnier gate and Jean Boucher's lavish hospitality. Catherine, for her part, had no wish to join in the festivities, though she knew Arnaud was to be present. She felt she would prefer to slip away for a while and join the humbler townspeople who were already dancing in the squares of the city where barrels of wine had been broached. All the city gates were wide open and there was free access to the neighboring countryside for the first time in seven months. She left word with one of the maids that she was

269

taking a short walk and slipped out of the house, after throwing a shawl round her head. She headed towards the cathedral. Something seemed to compel her towards the Bourgogne gate where she had arrived that evening so long ago, exhausted, but full of hope. She wanted to see it again. The streets were full of people. People called out to each other and fought for possession of the soldiers—Scots, Gascons and Spaniards as well as French—who had made up the army which liberated the town. The air was bubbling with excitement and joy.

When she came in sight of the Bourgogne gate, she saw a ceaseless stream of men, women and children going and coming through the massive, stone arch. With a half-smile on her lips Catherine stood for a moment gazing at this procession of cheerful, radiant-looking people. Suddenly her gaze sharpened. A bizarre-looking couple had just crossed over the bridge: a tall, dark woman draped in an extraordinary patched and tattered garment with a ragged shawl over her shoulders and a stout stick to lean on, and a little monk in a ragged habit, who walked with his head thrown back and a look of ecstatic joy on his rubicund face. It was Sara and Brother Étienne.

A great wave of delight swept through her and she ran towards them as fast as her legs would carry her. Crying and laughing at the same time she threw herself into Sara's arms. . . .

CHAPTER FIFTEEN

Queen Yolande's Tapestry

On Friday, 13 May, at the precise moment when Joan of Arc was paying homage to her King on the road to Tours, Catherine, Sara and Brother Étienne reached Loches where Queen Yolande, mother-in-law to Charles VII, was to be found. They had left Orleans at dawn the previous day, seen off by the entire household with many tears and mutual promises to meet again. It had been a short matter for Sara and the little monk to win over Dame Mathilde, who professed herself enchanted by this oddly assorted pair, whose one point in common seemed to be their affection for Catherine. As for Catherine herself, finding Sara again had been like a favorable sign from Heaven. With her old friend at her side, nothing ill could befall her.

The gypsy and the monk were in a somewhat bedraggled state on reaching Orleans. With the one difference that they had had better weather, their journey from Coulanges-la-Vineuse had been carried out under almost as hazardous conditions as Catherine's, but they both seemed to cherish particularly pleasing recollections of the way in which they had given Fortépice the slip.

"We were doubly lucky," Sara had recounted to the assembled household. "After Fortépice's magnificent coup with the Sire de Courson's goats, there was much galloping to and fro between the two strongholds every night. Sometimes one of Fortépice's horses would be stolen, another time the Sire de Courson's hens, but come what might, the mutual plundering went on night after night. It all came to a head with a regular battle in which de Courson had the worst of it. To crown it all, the next day Fortépice managed to get his hands on a group of merchants from Auxerre who were returning from Geneva laden with goods of every description. Fortépice was so delighted he ordered a great banquet for himself and his men—or rather, a great drinking session, for the entire band was dead drunk, Fortépice included, by sunset. No one even thought of lowering the portcullis and raising the bridge, still less of manning the watch towers. Naturally, we made the most of our chance, Brother Étienne and I, and walked quietly out without meeting a living soul. We were even able to steal horses thinking that they would make our journey to Orleans less arduous, but we were unlucky there: at our first halt, a ruined abbey, we had our horses stolen while we were asleep. We had to finish our journey on foot."

"I didn't mind at all," Brother Étienne added softly. "I've done so much walking in my life, but Sara had got out of the habit!"

Dame Mathilde set about welcoming the two travelers, urging them to treat the house as their own, but it was Joan's presence in the place which agitated Sara. The first time she saw the Maid, she almost went into a trance. She fell to her knees with staring eyes, trembling all over, unable to utter a word. When much later, Catherine persuaded her to get up, she was still shaking and her face was ashen.

"My God! What's wrong?" Catherine asked anxiously. "You make me feel quite frightened!"

Sara seemed to wake out of a dream. She looked at Catherine with the absent expression of someone waking too suddenly.

"Frightened?" she echoed softly. "It's her you should be

271

frightened for, Catherine! In that one moment I saw so much glory and suffering around her that I lost my head!"

"What did you see? Tell me!"

Sara shook her head sadly.

"A glittering crown and flames . . . high, red flames! But I could have been mistaken; I'm so tired. . . .''

Catherine had tried to laugh at the strange vision, telling herself that Sara was dreaming and that fatigue had given her hallucinations, but she had been alarmed despite herself. So much so that when she met Xaintrailles in the courtyard, she had pointed at Joan, who was mounting her horse, and said:

"You must take care of her, Messire. She comes first!"

The red-headed Captain had smiled with his usual confidence.

"Never fear, fair Catherine! No one, least of all the English, is going to snatch her away in the midst of her followers!"

But despite his reassurance, Catherine was not entirely convinced. Her dark forebodings followed her on the long journey across Sologne and did not go till the bristling towers of Loches rose up on the horizon. She knew Joan would soon be going there, and Arnaud with her. He was still her constant thought.

As she passed through the Royal gate, she saw Brother Étienne spur in his mule a little and have a whispered consultation with the sergeant of the guard who had run out to meet him. Then he straightened up in the saddle with a smile and beckoned to his two companions to come forward.

"The Queen is waiting for us," was all he said as he started to climb the hill. "Come!"

"How can she be expecting us?" Catherine cried, astonished. "Did you warn her of our arrival?"

"I sent a messenger on ahead from Orleans, as I often do," the little monk replied calmly. "Rest assured that Her Majesty already knows everything about you and that she will receive you in full knowledge of your mission. Come!"

When Catherine curtseyed before Yolande d'Anjou she felt more nervous than she had for a long time. The woman whom they called the Queen of the Four Kingdoms had just celebrated her fiftieth birthday, but no one would have guessed it. She was tall and slim, straight as a sword blade, and she carried her striking little head with its delicate, meditative profile, with superb assurance. Her beauty, with pale ivory skin stretched across perfect bones, was such as to defy the ravages of time. Yolande was regal in the poise of her elegant body, the expression of her dark eyes, in the nervous beauty of her hands and the firm line of her mouth.

There remained little of the girl of the mountains, Violanta d'Aragon, raised and bred in hardy Saragossa, who had knelt in awe and wonderment one December morning in 1400 beside the handsome duc Louis d'Anjou in the Church of Saint-Trophime d'Arles, save the unconquerable energy, the matchless courage and an acute intelligence. In every other respect she was a Frenchwoman from head to toe, wisest and greatest of Frenchwomen. She had been left a widow at thirty-seven and, broken-hearted by her bereavement, had turned her back resolutely on love and the other pleasures of a woman's existence to concentrate on being the guardian angel of a poor kingdom, mutilated and auctioned by its own ruler. Ysabeau la Bavaroise hated Yolande, not so much because she was, as Juvenal des Ursines described her "the prettiest woman in the land", but because this pretty woman had outwitted her. It was Yolande who had decided on the marriage of the little Prince Charles to her own daughter, Maria, Yolande who, when the little prince whom his mother had rejected became Dauphin of France, resolutely refused to send him back to the indignant Queen. Ysabeau never forgot the letter which Yolande had written to her on that occasion.

"A woman with a lover has no need of a child. I have not raised and fed this one to see him murdered like his brothers, or sent mad like his father, or turned into an Englishman like you. I keep him! Come and take him if you dare!"

Ysabeau had never dared and, for years, fighting against impossible odds, Yolande had kept the kingdom together. It was she again who, hearing from her son, Duke René de Bar, of a visit he had received from a strange peasant girl from Domrémy, had smoothed the way for Joan and had her brought to court.

Catherine had heard all this from Brother Étienne, for many years the Queen's secret agent.

And if awe and respect left Catherine almost breathless as she appeared before her, it was precisely because she had had the opportunity to gauge what a great and noble lady Queen Yolande was. Her legs were trembling so much that her deep curtsey ended with her falling to her knees and she remained there, kneeling on the shining marble floor, hardly daring to breathe. Such profound humility was not displeasing to Yolande, who smiled and put aside the great tapestry at which she had been working and came forward to raise Catherine up.

"It is a long time now since Brother Étienne first spoke to me of you, Madame de Brazey! I know what a faithful and loyal friend you were to poor Odette de Champdivers. I know that both she and Brother Étienne owed their lives to you and that she would never have died in such wretched circumstances if

273

you had not been even worse off at that point yourself! And I know that your heart has always been with us and that you have gone through terrible ordeals to be with us. You are welcome."

The Queen's contralto voice had kept a slight Spanish accent which added to its charm. Catherine kissed the Queen's hand respectfully and thanked Yolande for her welcome, protesting that henceforth her one wish would be to serve her in any way possible.

"A queen always has need of a faithful lady-in-waiting," Yolande said. "And a royal court always has need of a pretty woman. You shall be one of my ladies, my dear, and I shall have the chancellor draw up your brevet. Meanwhile, I entrust you to the care of Madame de Gaucourt, who will see that you are properly looked after. I will now talk to Brother Étienne alone for a moment."

For a great lady, Madame de Gaucourt was agonizingly shy. She seemed to go in perpetual terror of something or someone, but most of all of her husband. She seemed hardly able to breathe freely in the presence of the governor of Orleans. Of much the same age as the Queen Yolande, she was small, silent and so quick-moving that she reminded one irresistibly of a mouse. But when she was not tongue-tied by shyness, she was full of wise advice, knew the Court like the back of her hand and had no equal in running a house, even a Royal one.

In no time at all Catherine and Sara were accommodated with lodgings in the center of the city with an adequate staff and even with the clothes of which they were both in sore need. Madame de Gaucourt's thoughtfulness even extended to sending round a purse of gold that evening to the new lady-in-waiting by the palace treasurer. At the same time a messenger was leaping into his saddle en route to Châteauvilain with a letter to Ermengarde from Catherine. In her letter, Catherine had asked her friend, to whom she had entrusted all her jewels and most of her possessions, to send it all on to her unless she would rather bring it in person.

The house which Catherine had been given was on the small side, consisting only of four rooms, but it was newly decorated and very attractive. It had belonged to a former governor of the castle who had stopped living there when his wife died. It was generally used to accommodate passing guests. Two valets took care of the place and when Catherine moved in she thought that it seemed ideal. It stood half way between the collegiate Church of Saint-Ours and the formidable square keep which guarded the southern flank of the Royal city, and its narrow windows looked out over the Indre valley, whose sunny slopes extended as far as the eye could see. While Sara went down to the kitchen to see to their dinner, Catherine made a slow and careful toilette in order to be ready to receive Madame de Gaucourt who was returning to see her later that evening.

She arrived after the Angelus, as hurried and flustered as ever, but this time she was not alone; a splendid creature, dressed with immense taste and lavishness, accompanied her and, when Catherine saw them enter, she thought she had never seen a more beautiful red-head. She had a magnificent complexion and a red, sensual mouth and she wore a heavy dress of green and gold Venetian brocade whose color set off her hazel eyes and whose daring neckline exposed a magnificent bosom. Her darkly flaming hair was largely hidden by a fantastic headdress of the same material, so tall that she had to bend almost double to pass through the door. Her heavily painted face might well have done without this embellishment, because it was smooth and full. Its triangular shape was vaguely reminiscent of a beautiful cat and Catherine thought with amusement that she and Madame de Gaucourt made a curious pair: the cat and the mouse!

Meanwhile, the lovely red-head had flung her arms round her neck with every sign of extravagant joy and was embracing her warmly.

"My dear! How lovely to see you here! After all these months when no one seemed to know what had become of you. My husband and I were in such a state about you! And they say the Duke Philippe is inconsolable!"

Catherine grimaced. The last person she wanted to talk about at Loches was Philippe! But Madame de Gaucourt, blushing fiercely, rushed to her rescue.

"It is quite true that Madame de la Trémoille and our Grand Chamberlain have often talked about you."

"Well, of course! The rose of Burgundy, the Queen of Bruges had vanished. I don't imagine there is a civilized court in Europe which wasn't wondering what had become of you!"

The beautiful Madame de la Trémoille flung herself down in a tall chair and began talking about this and that while Catherine, somewhat recovered from her surprise, watched her between half-closed eyes with a polite smile on her lips.

She had met fat Georges de la Trémoille before at Philippe's court, but it was the first time she had seen his wife, though certainly not the first time she had heard her spoken of, because the lady in question had lived the most notorious existence imaginable! So this was the famous Catherine de l'Isle-Bouchard! The story of her life was a novel in itself!

Widowed soon after her marriage to a great Burgundian lord, Hughes de Châlon, her voluptuous beauty had soon seduced the enigmatic Pierre de Giac, then the favorite of Charles VII, who was said to have sold his right hand to the devil. For love of the fair Catherine, Giac murdered his first wife, Jeanne de Naillac, in peculiarly horrible circumstances: after forcing her to drink poison, he tied the unhappy woman, who was about to give birth at any moment, to her horse and sent it careering off about the countryside until his victim had given up the ghost. Then he had her buried on the spot and coolly returned to marry his ladylove. But he had to reckon with La Trémoille, who also coveted the wealthy widow and did not rest till he had Giac convicted of treason. He was arrested one night by order of Queen Yolande, tried, convicted, sewn up in a leather sack and thrown into the Auron. Three weeks later, Catherine de Giac married La Trémoille.

Since then, the couple had led the most lavish and dissolute life imaginable. The husband, a man of insatiable ambition, had the tastes of a satrap and his wife had a fiery temper. Between the two of them, they added up to a sort of living curiosity which was none the less formidable for that.

Catherine maintained a smiling reserve during the remainder of the Dame de la Trémoille's visit. She was beginning to realize that it would be as difficult to steer her way through Charles VII's court as it had been at Philippe of Burgundy's—more difficult still, perhaps, since here she would not be helped by either the love of its master or the loyal friendship of Ermengarde de Châteauvilain. She must be prudent, but nonetheless, she accepted her visitor's offers of assistance.

"I shall present you to the King myself tomorrow. Yes, yes, I insist! I shall lend you a suitable dress, too, because you would never have enough time to see to your wardrobe by then."

Catherine thanked her politely and the two visitors left soon after, advising her to have a good night's sleep. Madame de Gaucourt seemed to be in a hurry to leave and Catherine did not detain her.

"If I were you," Sara said, when they had left, "I would beware of the beautiful copper-nob! She smiles and her words are honeyed, but her eyes are cold and calculating. You can be certain that if she doesn't get what she wants from you she will become your worst enemy."

"What do you think she wants from me, then?"

"How should I know? We've only just arrived. But I shall try to find out everything I can about La Trémoille."

Catherine turned towards her as she undressed for bed.

"There is something much more important than that which you can find out for me," she said. "I want to know where Captain Montsalvy is lodged."

Sara did not hesitate.

"When he is not on duty with the King, he lodges in the town near the Cordeliers gate, in a house belonging to a rich tanner which has a figure of St. Crépin carved above the door."

As Catherine stared at her open-mouthed, she went on with a laugh:

"It's the first thing I asked our valets about, because I knew it would be the first thing you would want to know."

Catherine was already beginning to lace up her bodice again, a little flushed about the cheeks, when Sara snatched at the laces firmly and took them away.

"You are not going there this evening! He won't be back till tomorrow with the King and you are not going to wander about the streets for the sole pleasure of gazing at a closed door, even if it does have a figure of St. Crépin carved above it! Go to bed now. I will bring you a light supper and then you must go to sleep. You must look beautiful and rested for tomorrow."

Suiting actions to words, Sara finished undressing her mistress in a twinkling, wrapped her in a long pleated gown and tucked her up in bed as unceremoniously as if she had still been a fifteen-year-old schoolgirl. Then she came and stood before her, hands on hips, smiling at her teasingly.

"Have to drop these gypsy habits of yours, my pretty! We've become a lady again, now—a proper lady! And you mustn't forget Madame the Queen, either, who isn't likely to approve of her ladies-in-waiting traipsing about the streets after dark."

The dress which Madame de la Trémoille sent round the next morning was really very handsome and Catherine could not help giving a shiver of pleasure as she touched the magnificent material. It was a long time since her fingers had caressed a real Milanese brocade, although to tell the truth, she wasn't so excited by the color. It showed a flight of fantastic birds, principally eagles, in blue and crimson against a background of cloth-of-gold. Catherine found it a little gaudy for her own taste, but it was undeniably gay and luxurious-looking.

"How do I look?" she asked Sara. "You don't think I look a little like a dye-shop sign?"

Sara shook her head, frowning at her consideringly.

"Anything looks good on you. It's a little bright, but it's pretty."

In spite of Sara's approval, Catherine took the precaution of filling in the deep neckline of the dress with a little pleated lawn fichu, because it was cut so low it threatened to expose her breasts completely at any moment. An inner voice whispered that Queen Yolande might not appreciate a generous display of flesh. The sound of a distant trumpet interrupted her contemplation of herself in the mirror. She hurriedly crammed the matching headdress on her head, pinning it a little haphazardly, and rushed to the door.

"I can hear the procession," she cried to Sara. "I must go to the château now."

The sound was coming closer now, announcing the approach of the King, Joan and their numerous escort. Catherine joined the circle of ladies around the Queen just as the foremost heralds passed through the Royal gate. She went and stood next to Madame de Gaucourt. Feeling a little self-conscious, she could not help noticing the Queen's slightly amused smile, the whispered comments of the other ladies and La Trémoille's dazzling smile. That lady was looking very elegant in white and tawny satin. Long familiarity with Court life and its inquisitive manners had trained Catherine to deal with embarrassing situations and she remained composed under their scrutiny. Then the brilliant procession drew near and Catherine forgot everything else. She saw Joan and the King riding side by side, but what really interested her was that other suit of armor just visible behind the Maid, a black steel suit with a helmet topped by a sparrow-hawk crest. The mere sight of it made her heart beat faster. Arnaud seemed thoroughly integrated into Joan's suite these days. He rode close behind her and next to him Catherine recognized Xaintrailles, La Hire and Jean d'Aulon.

The King did not interest Catherine at all. She was even a little disappointed in him. He was thin, pale and frail, with a morose face, all downward lines, a drooping nose and protruding colorless eyes. He seemed to bear the burden of an eternal discontent on his narrow shoulders. His velvet robes looked too big for him and his immense, floppy-brimmed hat dwarfed him. Behind him rode a massive nobleman, fantastically attired in crimson and gold, with a complicated headdress somewhat resembling a turbun. At first, Catherine took him to be a Moslem. With his dark beard, broad face and unctuous gestures, and above all, his showy magnificence, he could easily have been taken for some sultan. But seeing the Dame de la Trémoille flinging herself into his stubby arms, Catherine realized that he must be in fact her lord and master, Georges de la Trémoille. He had grown so much fatter since she last saw him at Philippe's court that she would hardly have recognized him! If anything, he seemed more vain and sinister than ever! A fitting silky tom to the beautiful red-headed cat!

While the assembled people were entering the château for the cold collation which had been prepared for them, Catherine suddenly felt a hand pull her back and, turning round, found herself face to face with a glowering Arnaud. He pointed accusingly at her dress.

"Where did you get that?" he asked rudely, without even condescending to greet her.

"What has that got to do with you, I'd like to know?" she snapped back. "Or have you become clothes conscious now that you have a woman as a leader?" Then she added with a mocking smile: "Don't tell me that Joan's entourage spend all their time talking clothes!"

Arnaud shrugged and flushed slightly.

"I'm not interested in your opinions. Answer me! Where does that dress come from?"

Catherine was sorely tempted to send him packing, but there was something in the Captain's aggressive voice which brooked no argument.

"Madame de la Trémoille sent it round to me this morning so that I might be suitably dressed for the King's arrival. All that I have at the moment are my everyday clothes. . . ."

"Which would have been a hundred times more suitable as it turns out! The whole court knows this dress—Madame de la Trémoille has worn it many times and it is made in her colors. Making you wear it is the same thing as publicly enrolling you among the supporters of La Trémoille. 'Pon my word, it's practically a livery you're wearing! And what do you suppose the Queen Yolande thinks of it? Or didn't you know that La Trémoille is her deadliest enemy and that there isn't one of the King's well-wishers who doesn't wish he'd smother in his own fat for the bad advice he gives the King? And furthermore, he is a mortal enemy of Constable Richemont and therefore of Joan's. You are richly compromised!"

Catherine flushed hotly, furious at having allowed herself to fall into this trap which had only succeeded in making her suspect again in Arnaud's eyes.

"I didn't know anything about all that," she said simply. "How could I have known? I only arrived yesterday and I didn't know anything about this Court!"

"Well, you will soon realize that it is exactly the same as your great friend, the Duke Philippe's! The same intrigues, lies, same rapacities and the same sharp claws beneath the velvet gloves. Go and take that dress off if you want to keep Yolande's respect."

He was already turning to follow Xaintrailles, but Catherine stopped him, laying a timid hand on his arm.

"Arnaud," she murmured, gazing at him with eyes shining with tenderness. "Yours is the only respect I care about. Have you really made up your mind to hate me all your life?"

For the very first time in the history of their stormy relationship, Arnaud did not lose his temper, but he turned his head away, possibly to escape the soft bewitchment of those lovely, imploring eyes. Then, gently, he detached himself from her hand.

"I don't even know whether I love you or hate you, Catherine. How can you talk to me of respect?"

Catherine's eyes followed him for a moment as he walked off towards the royal apartments. His normally firm walk seemed strangely hesitant. Resolved to do everything which could please him, she raced home and tore off the compromising dress while she explained the situation to Sara.

"I thought as much," Sara said. "I thought the red-head was too charming to be true. You'll have to make do with a plain black velvet dress this evening. It's the best we can do at the moment."

"A homespun dress would be better than this gaudy finery," Catherine cried angrily, throwing the garment aside. "Have it taken back . . . and don't bother to thank them. . . ."

As soon as she was ready she went back to the château. As the Queen saw her approach, she gave her a long approving look.

"You have changed your dress, Madame de Brazey?" she asked gently.

"Yes, Madame," Catherine said, dropping a deep curtsey. "I beg Your Majesty's pardon for absenting myself without permission, but . . . I didn't like the dress I was wearing and I have had it returned to its owner."

Yolande held out her hand to her and then added, very softly:

"I didn't like it either. Thank you for changing it! And now let us go to the church, where Joan is already awaiting us."

As the ladies formed up to escort the Queen to the church, Catherine received the Dame de la Trémoille's angry stare full in the face, but if Arnaud were pleased with her, she little cared what new enemies she might make.

That very evening a great banquet took place in the King's apartments. The whole Court was invited, but Catherine was granted permission to remain at home. Her status as a new arrival and her need to organize her home and wardrobe temporarily excused her from joining in Court life, but her real reason for absenting herself was that Arnaud, for a private reason, had also declined to attend. As for the Maid, she had retired to her lodgings, which were, as usual, in the house of the city notable with the most irreproachable wife. No doubt Arnaud wished to imitate the girl he now thought of as his leader.

But Catherine found she could not settle down at home. The night was loud with sounds of revelry from the château: shouting, music of the viols, women's laughter, none of them sounds which found an echo in her heart. She stood for a long moment looking out of the window, watching the moon rise over the shining rooftops of Loches. The sleeping town offered a picture of peace and calm which contrasted strikingly with the lights streaming from the château windows. In the town all was silent, except for an occasional owl hooting on the misty banks of the Indre. . . . Catherine turned and looked towards the towers either side of the Cordeliers gate. Something seemed to be drawing her towards them like a magnet. The night was so mild! She would never get to sleep! She knew all about the heated discussions which had taken place at the château between Joan and Yolande on the one hand, and the King, La Trémoille and the Chancellor Regnault de Chartres, Archbishop of Rheims, on the other, over the question of Charles's coronation. Joan and the Queen were for pressing on and capturing the city of Rheims at once, while the King's entourage insisted on the danger of traveling through countryside which was still under enemy occupation. If Joan won the day, as Catherine hoped she would, Arnaud would soon be off again, so there was no point in wasting the little precious time remaining to her.

Without saying a word to Sara, who was asleep in a corner, she slipped on a cape and went out. As she headed towards the Royal gate and from there into the commercial city itself, Catherine was not even wondering what she should say when she saw Arnaud again. What was the point? Her heart could dictate the right words when the moment came. She could think of nothing but her painful longing to see him again.

The lanes and alleys of Loches and particularly the slope which joined the Royal gate to the Cordeliers, were completely deserted. Sounds of distant revelry still reached there, and the tramp of the guard making its rounds of the walls of the royal city. Catherine flew, rather than ran, down the hill towards the house with the St. Crépin figure above the door. The tanner's house where Arnaud was lodged stood in the shadow of the massive square tower in which the gate was set. A faint glow

281

from beneath the round arch announced the presence of the guard. Beyond, came the murmur of the river.

The neighborhood was silent, but beyond the gate the lights of an inn blazed in the night, the merrymaking there seemed almost as lively as at the château and Catherine took care not to step into the pools of light which the windows cast on the uneven cobbles outside as she passed by. She stood back in the shadow of one of the angles of the tower and tried to imagine what was happening behind the windows of Arnaud's house. A little light showed at one of the first floor windows and it drew her irresistibly towards it. She crept slowly towards the door where a huge bronze ring which served as a knocker gleamed faintly, but just as she was about to put out her hand to seize it, she fell back again and flattened herself against the wall. She could hear people talking just behind the door and, a moment later, it opened. There was a rustle of silk, then a woman's voice.

"I'll come back tomorrow, don't worry . . ." whispered a feminine voice which Catherine was sure she recognized.

Another voice, a man's this time, murmured something which the young woman did not catch, but the light of a candle lit up the form of a tall, elegant woman wearing a purple silk cape. Catherine's curiosity was too much for her. She craned her head forward to catch a glimpse of the woman's face. She wore a mask of the same silk as her mantle over the upper half of her face, but her hood had slipped back a little revealing some locks of red hair, and those sensual red lips were unmistakably those of Catherine de la Trémoille.

Biting back an exclamation of anger and dismay, Catherine fled back into the shadow again, trying to stifle her wildly beating heart with both hands. A sharp unbearable pain flashed through her, more agonizing than anything she had ever known. It was her first experience of that raging jealousy which gives one the desire to scream and bite all at once!

The Dame de la Trémoille's nonchalant silhouette had long since vanished into the shadowy street by the time Catherine stirred again. In a blinding flash, everything was made brutally plain. So that was why Arnaud had not attended the King's feast! Her husband would have to stay with Charles VII, so he might receive his mistress without fear. And Arnaud's fury at finding her wearing one of his mistress's dresses took on a different color. Why should he care whether the woman he had despised for so long wore the colors of one faction or the other? All he minded about was that the fair La Trémoile's finery should not appear on another back.

The house in front of her was silent again and the light at the

282

window had been put out. The noise from the inn was increasing, however, and the hubbub from within suggested that there must be some soldiers and their girls in there celebrating the victory at Orleans, but nothing mattered to Catherine any more. She no longer bothered to conceal herself, but stepped heedlessly out of her hiding place, her temples pounding and her head swimming. All she could think of was her urgent need to get home and bury her head in Sara's lap till she had wept away all her tears. Vague plans were already forming in her mind—tomorrow she would ask leave of Yolande to leave the Court and go and join Ermengarde again. This life at Loches, decidedly, had nothing more to offer her.

She took a few uncertain steps out into the middle of the street. Just then the inn door burst open and two drunkards reeled out into the night, clutching each other for support. Hopelessly drunk though they were, they were not so drunk that a feminine silhouette did not attract their attention.

"A . . . a girl!" one of them exclaimed, seizing her round the waist while he pulled back her hood with his free hand. "And . . . a beauty! Look, Flambard!"

The other gave a hoarse grunt which might have passed for admiration. Clearly he was a lad who didn't like wasting time, for he flung both arms round Catherine and tried to kiss her. The smell of his wine-fouled breath made her feel violently sick. In despair, she gave way to instinct and screamed with all her might:

"Arnaud! . . . Help!"

In surprise, her two attackers paused for a moment. Catherine was about to cry out again when a window opened in the house and a black form sprang down into the street below, sword in hand. The struggle did not last long. Two thrusts and a parry and Arnaud de Montsalvy had put the soldiers to flight. Their balance miraculously restored, the two men raced away along the ramparts. Arnaud sheathed his sword with a shrug and came over to Catherine who had been watching, faint with terror, flattened against the wall of the house. A moonbeam lit up her pale face.

"I thought I recognized your voice," the Captain remarked calmly. "Would you mind telling me what you are doing here at this time of night?"

Catherine would rather have died than admit that she had intended to visit him.

"I'm going for a walk," she said defiantly, but with a slight tremble in her voice which robbed it of its conviction. "I suppose that's allowed? I . . . I wanted to see Joan."

"Really? Here? Didn't anyone tell you that she was living on

283

the other side of the town? And shouldn't you be at the King's banquet?"

"Why should I be there if you aren't? Although it's true that you have excellent reasons for staying away."

She bit her lip, raging inwardly with herself for having spoken so freely, but it was too late to go back. She saw the young man's teeth gleam in the darkness and heard him laugh.

"Excellent reasons? I'd like to know what they are!" His disdainful, slightly mocking tone when talking to her stung Catherine to a fury. She suddenly forgot all her good resolutions.

"Red-headed reasons!" she hissed at him furiously. "And don't try to lie to me, Arnaud de Montsalvy. I saw them leaving the house a few minutes ago, those reasons of yours. And I suddenly realized why it was that you didn't like me wearing Madame de la Trém . . ."

Arnaud's hand clapped roughly over her mouth effectively stopped her talking and breathing.

"No names, please! It's always dangerous! Come, I'll take you back home."

He was already drawing her along with him, but Catherine freed herself with a brusque movement.

"I'm quite capable of walking along by myself and I don't need you to take me home. Go back to your love affairs and don't worry about me."

"Love affairs, love affairs? Really this grotesque story of yours is too ridiculous! I can't prevent that woman forcing herself upon me at all hours of the day and night and even bribing my servants to let her in."

"I suppose you'll try to tell me that she isn't your mistress?"

"Of course not! Who do you take me for? Do you think I'm the sort of man to be content with someone else's leavings? You should know me well enough to know by now that that sort of woman hasn't a chance with me. Now, come!"

Catherine looked doubtfully up at his tall, dark silhouette. She longed to believe him, but the image of the tall woman in the purple cape haunted her.

"Swear to me that you don't love her," she asked in such a little-girlish voice that it wrung a reluctant laugh from the captain.

"I don't see that my private affairs concern you, but I suppose I shall have to give you an answer to have some peace and quiet—I swear I don't love her."

"Whom do you love then?"

The reply came curtly, but after a slight hesitation.

"No one! And now that's enough!"

Slowly, side by side, they climbed the hill towards the gate into the Royal city, walking in unison, each one sunk in their private thoughts. Catherine, however, was struggling against an imperious desire to fill this silence which had fallen between them. Her love raged all the fiercer at feeling him to be so near and so distant all at once. She summoned up all her courage and murmured, without looking at him:

"When will you realize that I love you, Arnaud? That I have never loved anyone else? Haven't you felt, during those two nights we spent together, that I belonged to you body and soul and that you could do anything with me?"

She did not dare turn towards him, but, sneaking a sidelong glance at him, she saw a stony profile and eyes which stared straight ahead.

"I would be grateful not to be reminded of those two occasions when I behaved in a manner of which I am ashamed."

"Well, I'm not. We were both honest then, and I'm not ashamed to have given myself to you. In fact, I'm glad and if you want to know, it was only in the hopes of another night like that that I came to see you tonight. I've given up everything for you—honors, fortune, love. I've accepted misery, suffering, even death, in the sole hope of finding you once more . . . and yet you refuse to see it."

She slipped an arm round Arnaud's neck and pressed against him, distracted with love, and longing to communicate this fever which possessed her to him, to his blood. He tried hard to push her away with hands which secretly asked nothing better than to hold her and embrace her. She stood on tiptoe trying to reach his lips with her own, but he turned his head away in sudden anger and pushed her away so roughly that she bruised herself against the wall.

"I've told you over and over again to leave me alone," he hissed between clenched teeth. "Yes, twice I've lost my head, twice I allowed my desire for you to carry me away, but I've reproached myself for it . . . as if for a crime . . . a crime, do you hear, towards my brother's spirit! You seem all too ready to forget that. I had a brother, remember . . . a brother I adored . . . whom your people killed, slaughtered as they would never have slaughtered an animal in the abattoir."

The Captain's voice broke in a sudden, strangled sob.

"You don't know what he was like, my brother Michel," he went on in a grieving voice which cut Catherine to the quick. "The Archangel himself was not more beautiful or valiant or courteous. To the little marveling peasant lad I was then, just a dirty little clodhopper, he was more than a brother: the pure, shining image of all I admired. He was chivalry, faith, youth, the honor of our house personified. When I saw him pass

285

through the village on his great white horse with his hair shining in the sun, I felt my whole heart leap out towards him. I loved him more than anything in the world. He was . . . he was Michel, that is to say, unique. You can't understand. . . ."

"Yes, I do," Catherine said gently. "I saw him. I . . ."

These simple words, innocent though they were, were enough to bring Arnaud's fury to boiling point. He thrust Catherine back against the wall and brought his anger-contorted face close to hers.

"What did you see? What your people did to him? A bleeding, mangled wreck of humanity on which your butchers flung themselves like famished wolves. He sought refuge in the cellar of one of your accursed Legoix and he was betrayed and murdered, torn to pieces. . . . Ah, you saw him, you say! Did you see the dreadful thing which my uncle and I went to cut down one night at Montfaucon? A headless body strung up by the armpits in rusty chains. The head was thrust into a leather bag hanging by his side . . . a head, that abominable black mess! And you dare to speak of your love! You don't understand that when you say that word I feel like strangling you! If you weren't a woman, I'd have done it long ago. . . ."

"If you didn't succeed, it wasn't for lack of trying," Catherine cried. "You did all you could to hand me over to the executioner. . . ."

"And I don't regret it. I would do it again tomorrow if the occasion arose."

Scalding tears rose to Catherine's eyes and spilled over her cheeks.

"Don't wait, then. Kill me now. You have a sword—it wouldn't take a minute! It would be better than your injustice. Why won't you hear what I have to say about your brother's death? I swear that . . ."

A sudden din rising up within the royal city interrupted her. There were cries and sounds of running feet from beyond the gate and a great red glow lit up the sky above the walls. Arnaud let go of Catherine.

"What's happening?" she asked.

"It looks like a fire. Come and see. . . ."

With one accord they began to run, passing through the gate and heading towards the place where the cries came from. Catherine saw great tongues of fire licking out from the shattered windows of a house and stumbled.

"But . . . it's *my* house!" she cried faintly. "It's my house on fire!"

"What did you say?" Arnaud cried, seizing her hand. "Is that where you live?"

"Yes, and Sara, too ... my God! Sara! Sara! She was asleep when I left...."

She began to run towards the burning house like a mad thing. Built of wood like most of the neighboring buildings, it was flaming like a dry log. The street was full of people already forming into a chain with leather buckets full of water, but this measure was hardly effective and screams and cries could be heard from within the blazing building.

"My God!" Catherine moaned, wringing her hands in despair. "Sara is trapped in there! She'll be killed!"

Tears started from her eyes. At that moment she forgot everything but her old friend's mortal danger. How could Sara escape from that brazier? Catherine saw a disheveled figure silhouetted blackly against the dancing flames appealing for help.

"I'll try and get her out," Arnaud said curtly. "Don't move!"

He swiftly unbuckled his sword-belt, tore off his doublet and chemise so that he was left in nothing but his tight hose, which would not be so inflammable. Catherine watched wide-eyed as he raced towards the blazing house and then, after throwing a bucket of water over himself, plunged into the clouds of smoke billowing out of the doorway. The crowd fell silent and Catherine, on her knees, was praying with all her might.

The fire roared ferociously under the still intact roof. One could hear woodwork crackling and beams and furniture crashing down. What seemed like an eternity to Catherine passed. There were no more cries to be heard from inside.

The roof was starting to break up in a shower of sparks. Just then Arnaud rushed out of the building carrying an inert body in his arms. A triumphant shout greeted his success. Catherine stood up and ran towards him.

"You are alive! Thank God!"

He was safe and sound and laughing like a child at the success of his adventure. Sara lay in his arms unconscious. There were a few scratches on his brown skin and his hair had been slightly scorched, but otherwise he was intact. He placed Sara on a bench and the women crowded round her. At the same moment, people came running up from the château. Catherine recognized Madame de Gaucourt running as fast as her legs would carry her, holding up her skirts with both hands and a pack of valets at her heels. She informed Catherine that Queen Yolande had sent her and wanted Catherine and her servants to be escorted to the château.

"You really are unlucky, my dear," she sighed, mopping her brow, "One might think the furies were after you!"

Arnaud came up at that point.

"Where are you thinking of lodging Madame de Brazey?" he asked the Queen's housekeeper.

"In the little room in the tower next to Madame Yolande's own rooms. The Queen wants to keep Madame de Brazey under her eye."

The young man nodded in approval, but his frown remained. While Madame de Gaucourt bent over the prostrate Sara he took Catherine aside.

"Tomorrow," he said solemnly, "you must ask Queen Yolande to send you to her daughter, Queen Marie, at Bourges. And stay there."

"You're still trying to get rid of me!" Catherine protested. These simple words were enough to infuriate Arnaud who seized her by her shoulders and shook her like a rat.

"I'm beginning to think you must be half-witted! I want you to be safe and as long as you remain here your life is in danger. Do you know what I found under the stairs of your house? Wisps of straw and three torches which must have been thrown among them. There are people at Loches who want to harm you and who tried to grill you alive in your house, Catherine. Listen, did you send that dress back to its rightful owner?"

"Immediately!"

"Then we need look no further! That woman never forgives the slightest wound to her pride. If you had agreed to become her disciple she would have exploited your beauty and grace to her own ends, but you rejected her and this immediately made you a dangerous enemy. You are much more beautiful than she and the King has already noticed you. If you were to gain any influence over Charles, La Trémoille's power would be threatened. Do as I say: go and bury yourself for a while among the pious ladies with whom Marie likes to surround herself."

"It's ridiculous!" Catherine protested. "Anyway . . . if I am in danger, you will be rid of me all the sooner!"

She expected a sarcastic jibe, but all he did was shake his head.

"Don't be a fool! I have to leave soon. Joan managed to get them to agree to start the march towards Rheims by attacking the towns of Meung, Beaugency and Jargeau where the English are entrenched. Then, if her plan is followed, we will strike into Champagne to open up the road to Charles's coronation at swordpoint. I won't be able to look after you, so go to Bourges."

She looked down, pouting like a sulky child, and refused to meet his eyes.

"You aren't being very logical," she observed. "Only a moment ago you were saying that you would gladly strangle me with your own hands. Why don't you leave me to my fate? My life doesn't interest me too much at the moment. . . ."

Her voice had a little catch in it which was so touching and tragic that Arnaud was moved in spite of himself. She was sitting on a mounting block, hands clasped around her knees, staring absently as her house went up in flames. She pushed back a long, stray lock of blonde hair with a weary gesture. Then she turned to Arnaud and tried to smile, but all that she could manage was a pathetic little grimace.

"Don't worry about me any more, Messire de Montsalvy. I realize I obsess you now, but it won't last long."

Before she could finish, he snatched her up in his arms and lifted up her chin with one hand.

"I haven't the right to love you, Catherine, because the souls of my ancestors would rise up and condemn me, but I do have the right to make sure you are safe and well. Tomorrow the fighting starts again. I shall fight better if I am easy about you. Tell me that you will go to Bourges tomorrow—tell me! I must know."

She bowed her head in defeat, inwardly praying that this marvelous moment in his arms might go on for ever. As she looked up at him, with the glow of the fire lighting up her magnificent eyes, the young man succumbed to the impulse which had been tormenting him. He kissed her, long and passionately. . . . Then letting go of her almost as suddenly as he had seized her, he ran off as fast as his legs would carry him. . . .

Catherine made as if to follow him, her cheeks aflame, but just then there was a satisfied exclamation from Madame de Gaucourt which told her that Sara had regained consciousness. She went over to kiss her old friend and when the valets had lifted her onto an improvised stretcher, she followed the little procession on its way back to the château. Her mind was in complete chaos. How was she to reconcile Arnaud's words and his evident desire to get rid of her with that kiss he had just given her? It was hard not to believe he must love her as much as she loved him, but how was she ever to explain to him that she had never been his enemy when every time she tried to lance this great abscess of misunderstanding, he either ran away or ordered her to be silent?

CHAPTER SIXTEEN

To See Arnaud Again

Queen Yolande had freely consented to allow Catherine to go to her daughter in Bourges, but she set off without much enthusiasm. She had no wish to become one of the "pious ladies" of Marie's entourage, but nevertheless she felt a distinct pleasure in obeying Arnaud's wishes. Joan's army had left Loches the evening before on its way to Jargeau which the Maid planned to wrest from the English. Catherine had stood for a long time looking out of the window after the departing troops and, most particularly, at the advance guard where La Hire, Xaintrailles and Montsalvy all rode and it wasn't till long after the last gaily colored pennant and gleaming suit of mail had vanished in the June dust that she stopped straining her eyes after a certain sparrow-hawk crest atop a black steel helmet.

Bourges, which she had always pictured to herself as a dreary sort of convent town, came as a pleasant surprise. Not even the rich Flemish cities of Philippe the Good could rival the magnificence of the capital of the Duchy of Berry which was now, perforce, the capital of free France. The Duke Jean de Berry, great-uncle of the weak Charles VII, had been the first and one of the most lavish patrons of the arts in France. When she found herself in front of the imposing gates to this immense palace, Catherine thought that neither Bruges nor Dijon had anything to compare with this splendor. In truth, the "King of Bourges" was not so much to be pitied—it must be sweet to reign over this fine city with its great private mansions grouped around the lacy stonework of the cathedral.

Marie d'Anjou, however, could not be said to live up to the beauty of the town, or even to one's picture of a daughter of Yolande d'Aragon. Plain, with a long charmless face and soft but unremarkable eyes, and none too bright withal, the twenty-five-year-old Queen seemed to have been designed for the express purpose of giving birth to dozens of children. She had acquitted herself in this task conscientiously: four children had already been born at the palace in Bourges. One of these had died at birth, but another was already on the way.

Queen Marie received Catherine graciously and instantly forgot all about her. She was sent to swell the ranks of the Queen's ladies-in-waiting. She was provided with a huge room with a fine view and so began the rather dreary existence which was the rule when the Queen was alone in Bourges: morning Mass, charitable visits, improving readings, caring for the children and occasionally, as a relaxation, some business connected with the Duchy to attend to.

"If I have to stay here much longer," Catherine confided to Sara, "I shall either end up in a convent or throw myself into the nearest lake. I have never been so bored. . . ."

She was, however, suitably equipped now to appear at any court anywhere. Ermengarde de Châteauvilain had sent on her clothes, jewels and a large sum of money to her under heavy guard as well as a long letter giving the latest news from Burgundy. Catherine learned that her mother and uncle were both in good health and that their estate at Marsannay was prospering, but that the Duke had seized back the château of Chenôve which he had given to Catherine. Ermengarde had had a letter from the Duke which had put her in a very awkward position. He asked the Comtesse de Châteauvilain to intercede with Catherine on his behalf and try to make her see reason and return to Bruges as soon as possible.

"The best thing would be to let him think I am dead," Catherine said, folding up the letter. "That way Ermengarde will not be bothered by him."

"I don't agree," Sara said. "You never know what may happen. You might want to return to Burgundy. It would be foolish to burn your bridges behind you. All Dame Ermengarde need say is that she has no news of you yet and doesn't know what has become of you. Your parents know nothing, so they can't betray you. Silence is the best safeguard. . . ."

Her advice seemed wise. Catherine, not without many inward groans, settled down to the monotonous life at Court, putting up as best she could with Queen Marie's interminable embroidery sessions. The Queen was quite capable of bending her long nose over a piece of tapestry or embroidery for long hours at a stretch and she was a past mistress of this particular art. Catherine resigned herself and stitched away while her thoughts followed Joan's army on its campaign. Through messengers sent by the King, she learnt of the victories of Jargeau, Meung, Beaugency and Patay where the Maid slew two thousand English with the loss of only three French; then of the departure for Rheims across the dangerous country of Champagne. They were on their way to the Coronation and Catherine, naïvely, had expected Queen Marie to join her husband

291

for the occasion, but, alas, Madame Marie was quite content with meeting her husband briefly at Gien, leaving most of her ladies, Catherine included, at Bourges.

"My pregnancy makes such a long journey unthinkable," she confided to her industriously stitching circle of ladies. "We shall content ourselves with praying for my lord's success in battle and a glorious coronation."

"Our one chance of seeing a coronation!" sighed Marguerite de Culant who, together with Catherine, was working on a banner for King Charles. "And a chance to dance for once!"

She was a lively, amusing young girl with dark hair and the only one of Marie's ladies with whom Catherine had struck up an intimate relationship. She and the young girl had ended up installing themselves side by side and passing the time as best they could chatting and gossiping and discussing the news from the army.

"Bah!" Catherine exclaimed. "The King will return with his entourage for the winter and then I'm sure we shall have feasts and dances. . . ."

Marguerite stared at her in genuine amazement, her slender face quite round between her coiled plaits.

"Lord, dear! Who gave you that idea? Of course the King will return, but he won't stay at Bourges! He has his Court at Mehun while the Queen prefers Bourges because it's better for the children. We shall stay here, too, and see nothing of the feasts at Mehun!"

Catherine was beginning to think that Arnaud had played a nasty trick on her in sending her to Queen Marie. Presumably he wanted a bit of elbow room. She was beginning to suspect that such a display of solicitude for her safety only boiled down to his perpetual desire to get rid of her. As her nimble fingers wove the gold thread in and out of the blue silk banner, forming the seven lilies of the Royal arms, her imagination roved far afield and her thoughts grew more and more bitter. How could she be sure that Arnaud had not been lying when he swore that Madame de la Trémoille meant nothing to him? That lady had not had the air of someone being ejected from the house where Catherine had come across her leaving the St. Crépin house. And Arnaud's anxiety to keep her in a safe place was much more likely to stem from a secret desire to get rid of a dangerous rival to the woman he loved.

These ideas tormented Catherine so much that she finally had to mention them in conversation with Marguerite, though only casually and in the most off-hand manner possible.

"I heard at Loches that Messire de Montsalvy and the Dame

de la Trémoille were very close," she mentioned in the most nonchalant fashion. The girl burst out laughing.

"Ah, that would surprise me! Messire de Montsalvy can't stand either of the La Trémoilles! Anyway, my parents would never have considered him as a possible husband for me if there were any truth in the story."

Catherine's blood ran cold in her veins. She hid her hands under the embroidery so that Marguerite could not see how they shook.

"A marriage?" she said with a forced little laugh. "Allow me to congratulate you! You must be wildly in love. Your fiancé is very handsome. . . ."

"Hush!" Marguerite cried as she threaded a needle with a length of silk. "Nothing has been settled yet and that's how I want it. Messire Arnaud is handsome as you say, but very brutal, too, so they tell me. Anyway, I don't love him."

The young girl's positive tone comforted Catherine a little. She had almost thought her heart was going to stop beating, but, if Marguerite didn't love Arnaud . . .

"Does he love you?"

"Him? He doesn't love anyone except himself. Anyway, if you really want to know, Dame Catherine, I love someone else. I'm only telling you because I like you and you are my friend. It's a secret. You won't tell a soul, will you?"

"Of course not! Don't worry!"

She could breathe again, but she had been badly frightened. If the Culants were determined upon this marriage it might still take place. She felt an urgent desire to see Arnaud again. Would he never return from that accursed Coronation? But the weeks passed without any sign of Arnaud.

When autumn came, Catherine saw Joan again and scarcely recognized her, she seemed so sad and crestfallen. The victorious Soldier Maid of Orleans had become a thin anxious child. After the unparalleled splendor of the Coronation, where she had wept for joy; after the thrill of seeing the English-held villages fall before her advancing army like hoarfrost in May sunshine, the Maid had finally become enmeshed in La Trémoille's tortuous designs. Because she had been wounded in one shoulder by an arbalest shot she had been forced to leave Paris and retreat up the Loire "for wintering" and the army had drawn their angel along with them like a captive in golden chains.

"They tell me I should rest," she confided bitterly to Catherine. "But I wanted to see Paris from close to. We should have gone on and pressed for victory. God wished it so. . . ."

"But La Trémoille didn't!" Catherine said sarcastically. "He hates you and is jealous of you, Joan. Why does the King listen to that arrogant pot-belly?"

"I don't know. . . ."

Catherine could not resist asking the question on the tip of her tongue. She had looked in vain for the Knight of the silver sparrow-hawk when the army entered Bourges.

"Messire de Montsalvy is all right, isn't he?" she asked anxiously.

Joan's face brightened in a smile.

"He is well. I left him at Compiègne, which the Sire de Flavy holds for the King. Flavy is a good soldier, but as reliable as a wild beast. Messire de Montsalvy is responsible for keeping an eye on him . . . discreetly. His heart is loyal and true and I have every confidence in him. . . ."

Such a compliment from Joan filled Catherine with joy. It even helped to soften the blow of not seeing Arnaud again. While Joan tried to stifle her impatience with sorties and attacks on Saint-Pierre-le-Moutiers which she took, and Charité-sur-Loire where the brigand, Perrinet Gressard, held her in check, Catherine returned to her life of prayer and eternal embroidery.

Only once, at Christmas, did she attend a real feast and have an opportunity to contemplate the splendors of Mehun-sur-Yèvre where the Duke Jean had assembled a fantastic collection of jewels, tapestries, rare books, works of art, intaglios, paintings and sculptures. The château itself was a jewel: an airy building of white stone dug from the green waters of the Auron. It was there that the King, with due solemnity, conferred patents of nobility upon Joan of Arc and her parents and heirs in perpetuity, together with arms depicting a sword crowned with gold and flanked by lilies on a field azure. But these fripperies were no comfort to the girl whom everyone now called Joan of the Lilies. She did not stay for long at Mehun, but went back to Bourges where she was lodged with a woman of spotless reputation, Marguerite la Touroulde. Queen Marie, whom the King did not want to see too much of, did likewise with her train of ladies, Catherine and Marguerite among them. For once she was glad to return to the monotonous existence which used to annoy her so. She had not liked the enigmatic glances of La Trémoille which had come her way during the ceremony of ennoblement, and his wife's green eyes were not more reassuring.

Winter passed. Spring returned with its frail greenery, and with it the time for battle again. Joan was bursting with impatience to be off and, hearing that Philippe of Burgundy was

294

besieging Compiègne, she set off one morning at dawn with a handful of men.

One evening towards the end of May, Catherine was entrusted by Queen Marie with the task of escorting a cartload of furs to her furriers to be cleaned, mended and made ready for the following winter. The Queen was a frugal woman and took great care of her clothes. Catherine set off on horseback with the wagon.

Maître Jacques Coeur's house and shop stood on the corner of the rue des Armuriers and the rue d'Auron. Catherine had often visited the Coeurs to whom Marguerite de Culant had first introduced her. They were young, kind and helpful and their house, enlivened by a brood of five children, was one of the liveliest in Bourges. Catherine liked going there and enjoyed playing with the children, chatting to the gentle Macée Coeur or admiring the fine furs which Jacques procured with so much difficulty owing to the dangers of the roads.

Once she had performed her task, she was expecting to spend the evening with her friends who would certainly ask her to stay and sup with them. Catherine ambled along on her horse in the last evening glow, looking forward to eating under the great elm in the Coeur garden where the scent of roses and honeysuckle perfumed the air.

Where could Arnaud be at that moment? Was he still safe behind the walls of Compiègne or had Joan managed to take the town and open up the route to Picardy to her soldiers? Nothing evil could befall her men where the Maid was. She took luck and divine protection with her wherever she went.

Lost in these thoughts, Catherine did not notice what was going on around her. She failed to hear a horse galloping up and did not wake from her reverie till the horse had overtaken her and wheeled round barring her path. Its rider wore a suit of bloodstained armor so thick with grey dust that his face and armor were indistinguishable. Only his hair showed red and Catherine recognized Xaintrailles with a shock of surprise. She held out her hands to him with a smile, but the Captain merely said abruptly:

"They told me at the palace I should find you here."

His broad, normally cheerful face was drawn and haggard. Catherine sensed that something was wrong.

"What's wrong, Messire? You have some terrible news for me, I feel it. Is it Arnaud?"

"He is gravely wounded . . . and asks for you! And Joan . . . has been taken prisoner by the Burgundians! I have to take you back with me."

295

Seeing that Catherine had halted, the valets had followed suit. She sat motionless as if turned to stone while her horse pawed the ground impatiently.

One of the servants came up timidly and plucked at her long riding habit.

"Dame . . . what should we do?"

She looked at the man as if seeing him for the first time. Then she shuddered from head to foot and seemed to come to her senses again. She waved a hand vaguely.

"Go on without me! Make my apologies to Maître Coeur and ask him to carry on without me!"

Then she turned a pale, stricken face to Xaintrailles.

"Tell me the truth! He's dead, isn't he?"

"No . . . he's asking for you! But if you don't hurry, he may not be alive when we get there. . . ."

Catherine closed her eyes in agony. A sob rose in her throat. Destiny had struck them—Arnaud was dying. How could such a thing happen? It was absurd—Arnaud was as indestructible as the earth itself. And then, where was Joan? Ah, yes . . . Xaintrailles had said something about Joan! Yes . . . That she had been taken prisoner. Another absurdity! The Maid a prisoner! Who could possibly capture the Lord's messenger?

"Catherine!" Xaintrailles cried harshly. "We must return home and get ready. Time is pressing!"

She nodded. Yes, of course, she must hurry! Hurry! There was not a minute to lose. She turned her horse's head towards the palace whose tiled turrets were glimmering in the last red sunset glow. The sky was darkening overhead.

"I will follow you," she said simply.

An hour later Catherine, Sara and Xaintrailles left Bourges, only a moment before the gates were closed for the night. A visit to the washhouse, clean clothes and a square meal, had dispelled the Captain's fatigue as if by magic. But his face, now that the layer of dust had been washed away, still wore its tragic mask. He rode with set jaws, and anger smoldered in the depths of his brown eyes. He had imagined, in his innocence, that the news he brought would have plunged the Court into dismay and anxiety. But as the three riders took the road north sounds of lutes and viols followed them in cruel mockery. The King and his inseparable La Trémoille had arrived unexpectedly after the hunt. A supper and dance had been hastily improvised for them. . . .

"They're dancing," Xaintrailles growled furiously with a murderous glance at the lighted windows of the palace. "They are dancing while others die and the safety of the kingdom is endangered. May the Devil take them!"

Yolande of Aragon, who was spending two days with her daughter, had been the only one to see them off. Wordlessly she had slipped a heavy purse into the Captain's hands. Then, observing his look of astonishment, she said:

"Do the impossible!"

She left without a backward glance.

The three travelers rode on for many hours without exchanging a word. Xaintrailles nursed his anger, while Catherine brooded over her own sorrow. She and Sara were once more dressed in men's costume because it was more practical for long journeys and Catherine carried a heavy casket on her saddle pommel into which she had put a large quantity of gold and some of her more precious jewels, among them the famous black diamond which she had never had the courage to dispose of. Gold is a powerful weapon in times of war, as Catherine was well aware.

In a few quick words Xaintrailles had outlined to her the events which had taken place on 24 May beneath the walls of Compiègne. He described how Joan, during a sortie into la Venette's camp, had gone too far afield and had then sought to beat a retreat from Jean de Luxembourg's army towards Compiègne. But on reaching the city she had found the gates closed and the bridge lowered. She had been captured with her squire, Jean d'Aulon. . . .

"But who gave the order for the bridge to be raised?" Catherine asked.

"Guillaume de Flavy! Swine . . . traitor! It was while he was trying to force him to lower the bridge that Arnaud was wounded. He did not take part in the sortie itself because Joan had expressly commanded him to inspect the reserve forces, so when he attacked Flavy he was not wearing armor. The two men fought and Flavy gained the upper hand. Arnaud fell, pierced through. He just had time to see that swine Lionel de Vendôme—whom he unfortunately spared that time at Arras —wrench Joan from her saddle. Then he became unconscious. . . ."

Catherine was thinking about all this as she spurred her horse on. The wind buffeted her face and made her feel better. She felt no hunger, thirst or weariness, nothing but a burning anxiety to get there before the worst could happen. All she had to console herself with was the thought—a radiant one, however—that he had asked for *her!* He had sent Xaintrailles to find her, and her alone!

What could this last deathbed appeal mean, except that he

was at last going to let his love speak out? Catherine implored God, from the depths of her misery, to allow her to arrive in time to catch the dying man's last look and breath.

"At least grant me that, Lord, at least let me have that moment to remember!" she whispered. "After that I would be ready to die. . . ."

It was a terrible, gruelling ride. They galloped till the horses were ready to drop. They stopped for an hour, just time enough to bolt down a crust of bread and cup of wine and dash some cold water over their faces, while Xaintrailles busied himself procuring new mounts for them, paying handsomely for them, his sole stipulation being that they should be sturdy animals. He himself ate in the saddle. He seemed to be made of solid steel. Apparently nothing affected this incredibly brave man. Catherine was tormented by weariness and cramps but nothing in the world would have made her admit it. She gritted her teeth to stop herself crying out as the saddle chafed her sore legs and jarred her aching back. Sara said nothing either. She too struggled on, knowing full well that Catherine's whole life and happiness hung from the faint flicker of life left in Arnaud de Montsalvy's stricken body. And Sara did not even dare think what would happen if the injured man should have given up the ghost before they arrived. Catherine had already suffered so much, for him and by him, that she could not even bring herself to contemplate the immensity of pain which this new tragedy would inflict upon her. Could Catherine survive such a blow? . . .

On the evening of the third day the three exhausted travelers finally rode into the vast forest of Guise, which covered the whole country from Compiègne to Villers-Cotterêts.

"We are nearly there," said Xaintrailles. "Only three short leagues to go! The Burgundians and the English are encamped to the north, beyond the Oise. We can enter the town from the south quite easily. This forest screens more than half the town."

Catherine signed to him that she understood. It had become painful to her even to speak. She seemed to see things through a mist and simply let herself be carried along, passively, kept going by an instinct even stronger than her deathly exhaustion. Behind her, Sara had fallen asleep on her horse and they had had to tie her to her saddle to prevent her from continually falling off.

Those last three leagues seemed interminable to Catherine. Trees gave way to more trees without so much as the suggestion of a town. And there was something nightmarish about this ride through the night through endless trees! . . . When at last the forest thinned out and the stark outline of Compiègne came

298

in sight, Xaintrailles went forward alone to the moat to signal to the watch for he did not know whether or not the enemy might have seized the town in his absence.

"If that proves to be the case," he told the two women, "you must flee at once and take refuge in the forest."

"Never!" Catherine cried. "Where you go, I go!"

He had great difficulty even in persuading her to let him go forward alone to reconnoitre, but the town still held firm and soon a little postern gate opened before them and the three travelers entered on foot, leading their horses by the reins. A soldier waited on the other side carrying a torch. Xaintrailles spoke to him anxiously.

"Do you know if Captain Montsalvy is still alive?"

"He was alive and conscious at sunset, Messire, but I don't know whether he is now."

Xaintrailles helped the two women to remount without speaking. Without his assistance Catherine could never have managed. Her legs buckled and refused to obey her. Xaintrailles swung her up in his arms and bodily replaced her in the saddle, followed by poor Sara, who was almost unconscious with fatigue.

"Arnaud is in the Saint Corneille monastery being looked after by the monks," he whispered. "For God's sake don't forget that you are supposed to be a boy! The Benedictines are strict about not allowing women into their monasteries. Try to make your servant see sense, too, if she's capable of getting anything into her head by now."

Soon the high stone arch of the Abbey door appeared before them in the gray dawn light. Xaintrailles went up to the entrance and exchanged a few words with the monk gatekeeper, whose suspicious face had appeared at the grille.

"Thank heavens," he whispered to Catherine as the monk began opening the door, "Arnaud is still alive! It seems he's asleep."

As she followed Xaintrailles through the Abbey cloisters, Catherine sent up a fervent prayer of thanks to the Power which had heard her entreaties and allowed her to see Arnaud again—alive. Hope and confidence were slowly returning to her—perhaps all was not lost, perhaps he would live ... and perhaps tomorrow she would find happiness at last. ...

Arnaud lay stretched out on a little bed in one of the cells. He lay on his back with his eyes shut. A monk sat beside him on a stool, telling his beads. A yellow wax candle burning in a crude iron holder standing on a table was the only light in the place. Apart from a crucifix hanging on the wall and a Missal on a bench, it was all the furniture in the narrow room in which Xaintrailles and Catherine now found themselves. As they entered, the monk stood up.

"How is he?" Xaintrailles whispered.

The monk made a vague gesture and shrugged.

"Not much better! He is in great pain, but he has regained consciousness. The nights are bad. He breathes with difficulty. . . ."

The panting breath came and went in the injured man's breast as noisily as a bellows. He was pale as wax and two deep gray shadows ran from his nostrils down to the corners of his mouth. His hands roamed about pathetically over the coverlet. Catherine was too overcome to speak. She sank on her knees by the bed and pushed back a stray black lock which had stuck to his damp forehead with a gentle hand. She heard Xaintrailles explaining to the monk:

"This is the person he asked me to fetch. Would you mind leaving us for a moment, Father?"

Catherine heard light, sandaled footsteps moving away and the creak of the closing door. Arnaud opened his eyes. They moved about vaguely for a moment and then settled on his friend. Their expression cleared.

"Jean!" he breathed. "You came back! Is . . ."

"Yes," Xaintrailles murmured. "She is here. See. . . ."

An expression of intense joy spread over Arnaud's ravaged face. He turned his head painfully and saw Catherine bending towards him.'

"You came. Thank you. . . ."

"Don't thank me!" Catherine stammered in a voice so hoarse she scarcely recognized it. "You must have known I would come! I'd go to the ends of the earth for you, Arnaud. . . ."

"It isn't for me! I am dying . . . but others still live!"

The joy lighting up the young man's face vanished as suddenly as if it had been extinguished. He looked away from her and his features began to regain the sinister rigidity of a moment before. His lips moved, but the sound that came out of them was so faint that Catherine had to lean closer to hear what he was saying.

"Listen carefully . . . because I can't talk much. Philippe . . . of Burgundy . . . has captured Joan! She is Jean de Luxembourg's prisoner, which is the same thing. You must go to him . . . at his camp . . . and ask him to set Joan free."

Catherine thought she must have misheard him.

"*I* must go to the Duke? *I*? Arnaud, you can't want me to do that!"

"Yes . . . you must! You are the only person who can win . . . this war. He loves you!"

"No!" The sound which broke from Catherine was almost a scream. Ashamed of herself, she lowered her voice and began again more softly. "No, Arnaud ... you mustn't believe that! He no longer loves me. He is as proud as Lucifer and he would never forgive me for running away. He has taken back all the lands he gave me ... I have been banished. Besides, he is married ... and no longer thinks of me."

Arnaud's face darkened with anger and he made a convulsive effort to raise himself in the bed, but he fell back again with a groan. Now it was Xaintrailles who answered tonelessly.

"You are wrong, Catherine. Your hold over him is as great as ever. As you say, he is married. He wed the Infanta Isabel with great pomp and rejoicing at Bruges in January this year, but the most lavish of these wedding feasts was dedicated to the creation of a new order of chivalry, a fabulously wealthy one which will be a real monument to his pride. Do you know what it is called, Catherine?"

She shook her head quickly, not looking at him, sensing that once again her past was about to rise up and trap her. Xaintrailles' voice seemed to come from a long way away.

"The Order of the Golden Fleece. No one can be in any doubt as to why he chose that name. The people of Bruges are unanimous that he would never have chosen it if he were not still mourning the loss of a mistress with incomparably beautiful golden hair. It is an act of homage, Catherine, and all the more striking for being made so public. You could not ask for a more unmistakable declaration of love. Your power over him is intact and the confiscation of your properties is merely the action of a frustrated man who secretly desires nothing better than to see you return."

Catherine, still kneeling beside the bed, gave the impression of not understanding what he was saying. Her feverishly glittering eyes were riveted on Arnaud's face, searching it desperately for some denial, or hint of disagreement with what his friend was saying. But, no! He listened attentively to Xaintrailles, watching his lips as he spoke ... he did not even look at her once, not even when Xaintrailles had finished and Catherine timidly touched his hand.

"You must ... go!" he panted. "It's our last chance!"

Crushed by grief and disappointment, Catherine laid her tear-stained cheek on his great, burning hand.

"Arnaud," she beseeched, "don't ask that of me ... not *you!*

His black eyes slid towards her and trapped her in their burning gaze. He was panting and every word he uttered seemed to cause him immense pain.

301

"I do ask it of you . . . because you are the only one . . . whom Philippe will listen to . . . and because Joan . . . is more important to France . . . than you . . . or me!"

A sudden revulsion seized her making her oblivious to everything: the place where she was, even the most elementary precautions.

"But I love you!" she cried in agony. "I love you enough to die for you and yet you ask me to go back to Philippe! Oh, I know you despise me, but I thought perhaps you loved me just a little . . . a very little!"

Arnaud closed his eyes. His face seemed to shrink under the weight of an infinite weariness and his voice was no more than a whisper.

"None of that matters . . . Joan . . . Joan . . . nothing else!"

A sudden spasm of pain tore through him and he jerked back and a pinkish froth appeared at the corners of his lips. Xaintrailles laid a hand on Catherine's shoulder.

"Come!" he whispered. "He is too tired now! You must leave him to rest. And you should rest yourself. . . ."

Catherine's head jerked up suddenly and she flashed him a look of burning resentment.

"You knew all along why he had sent for me, didn't you? You knew and yet you didn't tell me! You deceived me brutally. . . ."

"No, I didn't deceive you. I merely said he had asked for you and you didn't question me further. You must see, Catherine, that for us, her brothers-in-arms, Joan is more important than anything else, as Arnaud said. She represents the salvation of this country and her capture by the Burgundians is a disaster of incalculable consequences. It is imperative, *imperative*, do you hear, that someone goes to Philippe of Burgundy and reminds him that he is, first and foremost, a French Prince . . . do you understand—FRENCH! It is high time he remembered this! They say that the English are already clamoring for Joan to be handed over to them and this is something which must be avoided at all costs. . . ."

"And you were saying a little while ago that he loved me," Catherine moaned, unable to concentrate on anything but her own problems.

"And I still say so! But he loves his country more! He would sell his own sister to Philippe to save Joan! I do understand what a sacrifice we are asking of you, Catherine . . . I really do . . . but if you really love Arnaud as much as you say, you *must* try to save Joan!"

"What makes you think that Philippe would listen to me or that I would succeed?"

302

"If he doesn't listen to you, he won't listen to anyone! But we can't afford to neglect such an important chance!"

Catherine gave a deep sigh. She could see the Captain's point of view and, in truth, there was much to be said for it. In their place, doubtless, she would have acted in the same way. She made one last attempt to persuade him.

"The Duke is a chivalrous knight. He would never hand over the Maid to the English. . . ."

"I wish I were sure of that. Anyway, if he is a chivalrous knight . . . you are the incarnation of chivalry itself! You . . . the Golden Fleece!"

The phrase struck Catherine and she shivered. She seemed to hear Philippe's voice saying it a long time ago, when they were lovers. It was true he often called her "my golden fleece" and that he had loved her passionately. . . . How could one blame these loyal companions of Joan of Arc's from placing their last hopes on her? It was inevitable! She bowed her head.

"I will do as you ask," she whispered. "Where is the Duke?"

"I'll show you. Come and see if you are not too weary."

Weary? She was weary unto death. She would gladly have lain down there, in the cloister, on the earth already redolent with the scents of summer, and waited till her heart-beats stopped and she fell into an everlasting slumber, but she followed Xaintrailles up into the monastery bell tower. The Captain pointed through one of the slit windows past the shining ribbon of the Oise still rosy in the early morning sun. Beyond stood wooden bastions like the ones Catherine had seen at Orleans, and rows of tents.

Opposite the bridge over the river, towering above the rest like an oak in the midst of a forest of lesser trees, an immense pavilion of purple and gold silk shone in the pearly light. Catherine recognized the banner of Philippe the Good floating from the tent pole.

"Margny Camp," Xaintrailles said. "That is where you will have to go, but first you must rest and regain your strength. You will have need of it."

CHAPTER SEVENTEEN

The Golden Fleece

Catherine did not set out for the Burgundian camp till sunset. She had to wait till nightfall and, with it, the unofficial truce which allowed both sides to rest till morning, before she ventured into the enemy camp. Towards evening she climbed into the saddle and passed through the gate before crossing the bridge across the river. One of Xaintrailles' squires, carrying the white banner of parley, preceded her. . . .

Catherine sat passively and allowed her horse to carry her on, its hooves clattering over the heavy planks of the bridge. She felt heavy-hearted and light-headed, much as she had done on that terrible day in Orleans when she had climbed into the tumbril to go to the gallows: a feeling as though nothing mattered any more. She did not allow herself to think of how Philippe would receive her or of what he would say to her. She was resolved to attempt the impossible to save Joan or at least have her put to ransom. Her plans went no farther than that.

All those eyes staring at her from the battlements felt like a solid weight on her back! Among them Xaintrailles, the fat, bestial Flavy whom she had glimpsed as she was about to mount, and all the other soldiers ranged along the battlements. She felt as though she were trapped between two walls of men, both implacable: Joan's followers and Philippe's, which included the English. And cruellest of all, Arnaud himself, struggling for life in the depths of a monastery—it was a trap from which she had not the strength to escape.

Once they had crossed the bridge, the squire raised his banner. She heard him give her name to the first archer who appeared and say that she was a Burgundian lady who wished to speak to the Duke Philippe. The archer went to look for an officer who dispatched a sergeant towards the Duke's immense, sumptuous tent, now crimson in the light of the setting sun. Catherine waited passively, prepared for anything. She did not let herself even think of Arnaud, because the thought hurt like a reopened wound. . . .

The sergeant soon returned, running as fast as he could go. He seemed quite beside himself with excitement.

"Messire Golden Fleece, the Burgundian King-at-Arms, is on his way to greet you, Madame!" he cried. "When he heard who it was, he was determined to receive you in person!"

The name "Golden Fleece" brought a bitter smile to her lips. Must they keep on throwing it in her face like this? But then her attention was drawn to a fantastic apparition which had just issued from the Duke's pavilion, and was now galloping towards her at full speed. Over his armor, the man wore a dazzling silken tunic embroidered with the escutcheons of all the Burgundian possessions, and over this a massive gold and enamel necklet as large as a neckpiece, from the center of which hung a miniature golden sheep looped about the belly. A plumed bonnet completed this rich apparel. As soon as he drew near to Catherine, he leapt off his horse and ran towards her, both hands outstretched.

"Catherine! . . . Dear Catherine! I never expected to see you again!"

With astonishment mingled with joy, Catherine recognized her old friend, Jean Lefebvre de Saint-Rémy, and spontaneously stretched out her hands.

"Jean! How happy I am to see you again! But, how handsome you are looking!"

Almost without realizing it, she had dropped into the teasing, familiar tone they had always used towards each other, and this was salutary to her. She pulled herself together and regained all her customary self-control. Meanwhile, Saint-Rémy was pirouetting about in front of her with the simpering expression of a fashionplate. Then he swept her a low bow.

"You see before you, my dear, the new King-at-Arms, Golden Fleece, unanimously elected by the Burgundian College of Heralds. I have become an important person. What do you think of me?"

"Magnificent! But, Jean, it is the Duke I came to see. Do you think he will consent to see me?"

The smile vanished from Saint-Rémy's face.

"He is waiting for you. But I must warn you that he is not in a good temper. He has been waiting for you for such a long time now, after all! What happened to you? And how do you come to be here looking like this? Oh, don't worry, you are as beautiful as ever, but you have grown much thinner . . . and you seem weary. . . ."

"Ah, I am, my friend. Weary of everything, believe me!"

The new King-at-Arms shook his head mournfully and took her horse by the bridle.

"I trust Monseigneur Philippe will know how to put the

305

sparkle back in your eyes. Our Court is a duller place since you went away."

"You have a duchess. . . ."

"She is elegant, accomplished, and undeniably beautiful. But she is a bit stately for my taste. But come! Here I am chatting away while Monseigneur awaits. It would be foolish to provoke him further."

A moment later Catherine leapt from her horse outside the entrance to the Duke's tent, where two of the Duke's personal guard were on watch. She looked about for Jacques de Roussay's white plume, but the young Captain was nowhere to be seen. Saint-Rémy, grown a little nervous all of a sudden, preceded her into the pavilion of crimson velvet and cloth-of-gold. A second later, she found herself face to face with Philippe the Good.

Catherine's first impression, on seeing the Duke again, was that he had aged. His features looked sharper and more solemn. But that might have been a trick of the light cast by the flickering torches placed round the tent. He was standing, very stiff and upright, beside a table upon which lay a massive ivory gospel. His hand was placed upon the book in a haughty pose which came to him naturally enough but which had more than a suggestion of pomp and arrogance about it. He was in full armor with a massive gold collar about his neck studded with gems. The same golden sheep hung like a pendant from this necklace as from the King-at-Arms's.

Catherine did not bow her head, but she slowly bent one knee before him, instinctively reverting to the old feudal salute for the man whom she wished only to regard as a sovereign for the moment. Besides, the man's clothes she was wearing would have made a curtsey ridiculous. But then, with a very feminine gesture, she threw back the black hood covering her head and revealed the plaited gold treasure of her hair. Philippe, meanwhile, had not so much as blinked. His gray eyes remained fixed on Catherine's face without the trace of a smile to soften their steely expression. It was he, however, who broke the silence.

"So you are here at last, Madame? I really had given up hope of seeing you again. In fact, I believed you dead. I confess, I am astonished at your impudence! You disappear for two years . . . or very nearly . . . and then you suddenly reappear out of the blue and demand an audience as though nothing unusual had occurred, and you had not forfeited such a favor by your misbehavior!"

As he spoke, Philippe's voice rose a little. Catherine sensed that he was struggling to control his anger and decided to speak out boldly:

"Why grant it to me if I don't deserve it?"

"To see whether I should recognize you: to see if you were still at all like my memory of you. Thank Heavens, you are not! You are greatly altered. Madame, and not to your advantage!"

Philippe's brutality, his lack of the most elementary politeness, did not impress Catherine in the least. She had long ago lost the power to frighten or intimidate her—even assuming he had ever had it! On the contrary, his rudeness helped to affirm her self-control and she permitted herself a slight smile.

"You surely don't think I have come here to ask you to do duty for a mirror, Monseigneur? These last two years have been peaceful, even profitable ones for you, but for me they have been years of misery and suffering."

"Who asked you to suffer?"

"No one! And you mustn't think I regret them! I may have suffered, but I have also stopped despising myself!"

The flash of anger in Philippe's eyes told Catherine that she had gone too far and that if she were to continue in this vein, the success of her mission would be seriously imperiled. She had nothing to reproach Philippe with, after all, and she had come to ask a great favor of him. She stepped back.

"Forgive me! I spoke hastily. I only meant that since you were getting married, I no longer had a place beside you. I heard that you were married . . . happily, I trust?"

"Very!"

"I'm glad. Then my prayers for your happiness have been answered. . . ."

A heavy silence fell between them, broken only by a yawn from one of the greyhounds lying by the door. Catherine could not think what to say next and was casting about for a suitable remark, when suddenly, Philippe abandoned his hieratic pose, flung down his large, black felt hat adorned with a heron's feather and ruby clasp, and seized Catherine by the wrist.

"Enough of civilities and beating about the bush! Surely I have a right to some sort of explanation! I've been waiting for one, for two years, *two* years, do you hear? Why did you leave me?"

His familiar tone dissolved her awkwardness as if by magic. Catherine felt herself on firm ground again.

"I've told you: because you were getting married again. I am too proud to take second place and after the life we had shared together, I didn't want to become the laughing-stock of the Court."

A look of genuine surprise spread over Philippe's face.

"A laughing-stock? Did I cut such a sorry figure in your eyes that you could not trust me to maintain you in the rank and style to which I had raised you? You, the woman who still mourned the loss of our son?"

Catherine would not let herself be softened by the memory of the child.

"Oh, I have no doubt you planned to marry me off . . . for the second time! Whom had you picked out to be my sham husband this time, as a successor to poor Garin whose terrible misfortune you exploited so heartlessly? Saint-Rémy? Lannoy, Toulongeon? Which of your lords was prepared to marry your mistress to please you . . . and then keep his eyes piously shut to what happened afterwards?"

"No one! I could never share you with anyone. I would have made you a duchess, an independent princess . . . you might have chosen whichever of my lands you pleased. You knew very well that I loved you more than anything in the world . . . as if I hadn't proved it to you time and time again! Only a little while ago, too! Do you know what this is?"

He snatched off his heavy gold chain and held it under Catherine's nose.

"Do you know?"

"Yes," she answered softly. "The Golden Fleece; the order you created in honor of your marriage."

"My *marriage?* Whom do you think I was thinking of when I called it by that name? Was it not you who let loose the most magnificent of all golden fleeces? Was it not you whom I called my golden fleece?"

He flung the jewel angrily into a corner of the tent and, with a sudden movement, reached up and deftly unloosed her hair. Her thick, shining tresses cascaded over her black suede costume, miraculously restoring all her former splendor. Then he led her towards a great Venetian mirror which decorated one wall of the tent.

"Look! It is you who possess the real Golden Fleece!"

But he didn't leave her enough time to look at herself. Instead, he pulled her into a passionate embrace, crushing her against him regardless of how his steel breast-plate might bruise her.

"Catherine . . . I still love you . . . I have never forgotten you. . . ."

"It will be easier for you now . . . now that I have changed so much!"

"No . . . of course you haven't altered! I only said that because I've been seething with frustration for almost two years now! You are as beautiful as ever—a little thinner, perhaps, but it makes your eyes look all the larger and your waist all the narrower. Catherine . . . my love! I've called upon you so many times, my sweet, beautiful, irreplaceable. . . ."

He unfastened the collar of her leather jerkin and buried his face in the soft hollow at the base of her throat. Bent backwards and imprisoned by his strong arms, Catherine felt herself weakening. The old attraction which had kept her attached to this strange, charming man for so long was beginning to exert itself again all the more powerfully. In a few seconds he would lift her up in his arms and carry her across to the great, gold-hung bed shining softly in the shadowy recesses of the tent and she would not be strong enough to resist him . . . and then suddenly, in a flash, she had a vision of Arnaud dying, stretched out on the narrow little bed in his cell, Arnaud, to whom she belonged body and soul. What did those old sensual pleasures matter compared with the fullness of love he alone could arouse in her? Their fierce passion, cruel and devoid of tenderness as it was, had more value and savor than all Philippe's caresses. Catherine's body stiffened in revolt. Gently but firmly she pushed the Duke away.

"Not now! Let me go."

He released her at once and stepped back, frowning.

"Why? Why did you come here if not to take up the thread of our old love again?"

Catherine hesitated for a moment. Was the best moment to choose the one in which she had just repulsed him? No matter, she had to see the thing through now.

"I came to ask a favor of you," she said calmly.

"A favor?"

Suddenly he burst out laughing, a spontaneous roar of laughter which left him weak and spent and forced him to sit down in an ebony armchair. He laughed and laughed till he was gasping for breath. Catherine was growing annoyed.

"I don't see what's so funny!" she said rather sharply.

"Funny?" His laughter stopped abruptly and he got up and came across to her.

"My angel, your naïveté is only matched by your ingenuousness. I really might have guessed that you still had a favor up your sleeve to ask me. It's a positive mania with you. Who is it you want to save now?"

"Joan of Arc!"

The name fell between them like a cannon ball. Philippe's smiling face closed up instantly and, as if he were suddenly afraid, he moved away from Catherine, placing the table like a rampart between them.

"No!" was all he said.

Catherine hid her trembling hands behind her back so he should not see them. In that moment she knew Philippe had passed out of her power. The passionate lover had been absorbed into the rigidly autocratic figure of the Duke of Burgundy. She smiled wanly.

"I expressed myself badly. I came to ask you to fix ransom for the Maid as you are bound to according to the rules of war. Whatever the price, it is accepted in advance."

"The laws of war do not apply to the children of the Devil. The girl is a witch, not a knight!"

"What nonsense! Joan a witch? She is loyalty, purity, courage and piety incarnate! There is no one more honest or true! You don't know her. . . !"

"But you do, it seems."

"I owe her my life and I intend to repay my debt. They say you are planning to hand her over to the English . . . but I refused to believe it."

"Why, may I ask?"

"Because it would be unworthy of you . . . unworthy of this Order of Chivalry you are so proud of!" Catherine cried, pointing towards the magnificent necklace glowing softly on the richly patterned carpet. ". . . and also, because it would bring you bad luck. She really is . . . a messenger from Heaven!"

"Nonsense!" the Duke stepped out from behind the table and began pacing up and down the huge tent without even glancing at Catherine. "I have seen this girl, if you must know. When Lionel de Vendôme captured her and handed her over to his leader, Jean de Luxembourg, I decided that I must see her and I went to the château of Beaulieu where Luxembourg has imprisoned her. I found her an overweening, bumptious person, stiff with arrogance. Instead of humbling herself before me, she did nothing but reproach me. . . ."

"And haven't you ever reproached yourself? Do you always behave as a loyal vassal of the French crown?"

Philippe stopped short and glared at Catherine. Two red spots appeared in his pale cheeks and his eyes flamed with injured pride.

"Vassal? What do you mean? I am a hundred times richer and more powerful than that marionette of a Charles who calls himself King of France. I refuse to pay him homage; I refuse to accept him as my sovereign. Henceforth, Burgundy will be free and independent . . . a great kingdom which could one day become the nucleus of an empire. I shall build up an empire like Charlemagne's around it . . . and all the people on earth will bow before my throne and my crown."

Now it was Catherine's turn to laugh, with an edge of scorn which Philippe noticed, and which silenced him at once.

"Who will bestow this crown upon you? Which cathedral will you go to to be crowned? To Westminster, I suppose, as behooves a loyal ally of the English invaders, because Rheims is already booked. Charles VII is already the legitimate king of France, both by divine right and the sacraments. Neither you nor the young puppet who rules in Paris can ever undo that. He is the King. The KING!"

"I will never accept the murderer of my father as King!"

"Come, come! I know you too well. If Charles made it worth your while, offered you half his kingdom, perhaps, and enough land to satisfy your ambition, you would give him your hand in homage. Do you really think I'm such a fool I hadn't noticed the artful—oh, very artful!—double game you've been playing for the last two years? One can't build an empire on treachery, Philippe . . . and the empire of Burgundy will never see the light!"

"Enough!"

He shouted the word, while his hand closed convulsively round the hilt of his dagger. Catherine saw the murderous glint in his eyes, but it did not frighten her. She had gone beyond fear, and her flashing eyes met his calmly. She defied him! It was he who capitulated. His gaze faltered and dropped.

"What has happened to us?" he asked hoarsely. "Here we are fighting like enemies!"

"You have only to say the word to bring us together again! Agree to put Joan to ransom and I ask nothing more of you. If you do that, I shall come back to you!"

Philippe could not begin to guess at the world of self-sacrifice and abnegation summed up in those few words of hers, but they silenced him for a moment. Finally . . . he murmured:

"No . . . I cannot accept, not even at that price, inestimable as it is for me. In my treaty with the English there is a clause stipulating that any prisoners I may take in this war be handed over to them to dispose of as they see fit. This girl has endangered Burgundy. I cannot permit her to be set free to endanger us further."

"At least, promise not to hand her over to the English."

"Impossible. Besides, she is Luxembourg's prisoner, not mine. It is for him to decide."

"That is your last word?"

"My last word. No other is possible. . . ."

"Not even . . . to me?"

"Not even to you. If you were in my place, you would understand."

Slowly she turned and went over to the velvet-draped entrance to the tent. She realized that the game was irremediably lost, and for a reason she was powerless to prevail against—fear! Philippe was afraid ... primitively, abjectly afraid of this strange girl who seemed literally to have fallen from Heaven to snatch the French kingdom out of its misery, and this fear dominated any other feelings he might have. Catherine knew it was useless to ask him what had really happened during his interview with the Maid, because he would rather have his tongue cut off than confess the truth. He had doubtless had the worst of it, but though she might understand the motives of the powerful Duke of Burgundy, that did not prevent her from raging inwardly. The bitter taste of disappointment and anger filled her mouth and she wanted to spit.

She stretched out a hand to part the heavy draperies and then turned back once more, a frail, slim, upright figure on the threshold of this sumptuous, but fragile palace. She stared at him, cold-eyed.

"Understand? I suppose that man called Pilate also expected people to understand him. If you don't surrender Joan, I shall never forgive you! Adieu!"

She went out without turning back once, deaf to the sound of her name which she thought she heard ringing from the depths of the tent. This time, the bridges really had been burned. . . . She would never see this man again, because he had refused her the one thing that really mattered to her. Outside she found her horse and squire waiting, as well as Saint-Rémy who ran up to her excitedly.

"Well, Catherine, are you coming back to us?"

She shook her head and held out her hand to him.

"No, Jean, I am afraid not. . . . In fact, I think that you will be obliged to forget that you ever met me."

"What? Has Monseigneur the Duke refused to forgive you? I don't believe it!"

"No, it is *I* who would not forgive him! Adieu, Jean . . . . I shan't forget you. You have always been a faithful friend. . . ."

The young man's long face reddened with sudden emotion. He gripped her slender fingers hard.

"And so I shall remain. I don't know what you and Monseigneur have quarreled about, and I remain his loyal servant, but nothing can stop me being your friend."

Catherine was touched and her eyes misted with tears. She stood up on tiptoe and dropped a swift kiss on the King-at-Arms's cheek.

"Thank you! I shall remember that. And now, farewell ... farewell, Sir Golden Fleece!"

Before he could stop her, she leapt into the saddle and spurred her horse towards the bridge. It was dark now, but the camp was lit by a mass of torches which cast a fantastic pattern of flickering shadows and lit up the strange machinery of war standing at rest for the night. Fiery braziers stood along the walls of the town like a crown of flames. Catherine and the squire were soon out of sight and Saint-Rémy hastily and furtively dashed a tear from his eye with his sumptuously embroidered sleeve.

When she entered the town gate Catherine found Xaintrailles waiting there with an armed troop. The men's jaws dropped when they realized that the messenger who had ridden out a few hours ago was a mere woman, as her floating hair proclaimed her. The Captain silenced them with a curt gesture. He helped Catherine down and noticed her flushed cheeks.

"You must have had a heated discussion," he murmured. "You look as though you had taken part in a hard fight."

"More heated than you imagine. You were right about the Duke, Messire Xaintrailles. . . . But I'm afraid I failed."

"No hope?"

"None at all. He is afraid. . . ."

Still holding the horse by its bridle, Xaintrailles slipped his hand through her arm and led her away. They walked along in silence for a moment, then the Captain spoke between clenched teeth:

"I might have guessed it. Nothing in the world would ever make him surrender her. *"Te Deum"* which Bedford ordered to be sung at Paris proves how terrified they are of her! We must think of something else. . . ."

But Catherine had just realized that they were walking away from the Saint Corneille Abbey towards the old château of Charles V, whose triangular mass stood out blackly against the night. She stopped in her tracks.

"Where are you taking me? I want to go back to Arnaud. . . ."

"It would be useless. He is unconscious and you can't stay in a Benedictine monastery. I have had a room prepared for you in a rich widow's house and your maid is already waiting for you there. Tomorrow morning you can come for the latest news before returning to Bourges . . . ."

"Returning to Bourges? Are you mad? Why do you think I came here? For the dubious pleasure of making a lifelong enemy out of Philippe of Burgundy? As long as Arnaud remains here, here I stay and nothing on earth will budge me. Do you hear? Nothing!"

313

"Very well," he said, half smiling. "There's no need to shout! You'll wake up the whole neighborhood. You can stay, since that's what you want, but you must promise not to go to the monastery without me. I don't want the good monks scandalized. Anyway, the siege is going to be fiercer and I shall need all my men. It would have been awkward for me to supply you with an armed escort. Come now, Catherine, stop looking at me like that! Haven't you realized yet, after all this time, that I'm on your side? Look, here is your house. Go in and rest; you must be very tired."

"But . . . Arnaud?"

"Arnaud is not going to die tonight! The prior who is looking after him is beginning to feel hopeful. He says that by rights he should have been dead long ago and that this obstinate will to survive is a good sign. He is going to try a new treatment, but he is as silent as a carp about the details of it. . . ."

Catherine was not completely convinced and she flashed the ginger-haired Auvergnat a suspicious glance, but he seemed strangely relaxed this evening. The worried frown had disappeared from between his brows. Feeling a little reassured, Catherine went into the house obediently while he held the door open for her. She found Sara waiting for her on the stairs, smiling. . . .

"Come," the gipsy said. "They have made your bed ready for you; nothing like those horrible monks' beds. You will sleep well here. . . ."

While he did not seem greatly improved the next day, Arnaud had lost his frighteningly cadaverous appearance. He was still pale, but his skin had lost the greenish tinge of the previous day and his hands no longer plucked at the covers. He listened without a single interruption to Catherine's account of her interview with Philippe. He seemed so remote, so indifferent to what she was saying that she felt that he must have written her off once again.

"I did all I could!" she protested. "I swear I did, but there are things which no one can overcome. . . ."

"Don't be afraid to say what they are, Catherine," Xaintrailles interposed. "The Duke is afraid of Joan, so much so that his fear is greater than his love for you!"

"I didn't expect him to be as frightened as that," Arnaud said. "You need not reproach yourself, Catherine. I'm sure you did what you could. Now . . . Jean is going to have you escorted back to Bourges. . . ."

Xaintrailles grimaced and leant forward over his friend's bed so that no one could possibly hear what he was saying.

"That's what I had planned to do, but she won't hear of it. She wants to stay."

"What for?" the wounded man asked irritably. He seemed about to lose his temper and Catherine decided she would do better to plead her own cause.

"To help you! I'm sure you don't mean to leave things as they are. Surely, you are going to try everything possible to free Joan, aren't you? Well then, let me stay and help . . . at least let me do that. . . ."

Her eyes glistened with tears as she seized Arnaud's hands in hers and clung to them.

"I hate to admit I've failèd! I would do anything possible to help. I have the means: a fortune in gold and jewels!"

"And how do you suppose you are going to lay your hands on them now?" Xaintrailles asked mockingly.

"Wait and see!"

Obeying some obscure presentiment, Catherine had brought her casket of gold and jewels with her. She had forgotten to mention it to Xaintrailles before. Now she went and picked it up and carried it to the bed. She opened it and showed it to the two men. . . . In the dim light, the mass of gold and flashing stones was such a concentration of brilliance that they both gasped admiringly.

" 'Sblood!" Xaintrailles grumbled. "When I think that we traveled with that all the way from Bourges! If anyone had got wind of that we'd have had our throats cut before you could say 'knife'!"

Arnaud struggled up painfully into a sitting position. His thin hand plunged into the mass of jewels scattered over the bed and picked up the amethyst collar which Garin had presented to Catherine on their engagement.

"I remember this . . ." he said slowly. "You were wearing it . . . at Arras."

Happy that he should remember it, she felt in the bottom of the casket and took out a little leather bag. A moment later, the huge black diamond was sparkling on the palm of her hand.

"And I was wearing that at Amiens the time you challenged the Duke," she said softly. A faint smile curled the sick man's lips.

"Do you think I don't remember? Or that I didn't see you? Indeed . . . you outshone all the other women in that black dress! And you say you want to sacrifice these jewels for a cause which isn't even yours?"

"To prove that I want to help you," Catherine amended. "And to make sure you respect me a little. I realized a long time ago that there was no hope for anything between us, that

315

there could be no other bond between us, except perhaps death. At least leave me that."

She spoke so passionately that the ironic glint faded from Arnaud's eyes. They lingered on her for a moment, but the look in them was inscrutable. Finally he sighed:

"You really are a strange girl, Catherine! I really think . . . I won't ever understand you! Stay if you wish. At such a price, it would be churlish of me to try to prevent you."

The effort of talking so much was beginning to tell upon him and he fell back upon the pillows, haggard with exhaustion, but Catherine was too happy to feel alarmed. Brusquely, she snatched up the jewels, put them back in the casket and placed it in Xaintrailles' arms, while he gaped at her in astonishment.

"Keep that, Messire Jean! . . . and look for a moneylender in the town who will buy it off you. There must still be someone here who would take them."

"There is indeed, but you seem to forget we are still under siege. They wouldn't pay us anything like a fair price. Gold is useful, but these jewels are worth a king's ransom! It would be ridiculous to let them go for a song!"

Just then the prior entered the cell, carrying a tray with bandages, lint and various pots and jars with which to dress the injured man's wound. With one last look at Arnaud, Catherine left with Xaintrailles and they went out into the street. On the Abbey threshold they parted: Xaintrailles to go to the ramparts to fight and Catherine to her lodgings.

"I think it would be better if you looked after the fighting fund until further notice," said Xaintrailles. "I don't see myself fighting off Burgundians with a fortune tucked under one arm. Keep it well hidden!"

"Never fear! Good Luck, Messire!"

She was already hurrying away when he called after her:

"Catherine!"

"Yes?"

He gave a rueful smile and grimaced comically:

"We're a precious pair, Montsalvy and I! I don't think it even occurred to us to thank you!"

She smiled back at him, happy to see the real friendliness in the brown eyes of Arnaud's great friend. From now on, she felt, she could rely implicitly on Xaintrailles. He would back her up as far as he was able. Truly, a friendship beyond price.

"It doesn't matter," she said sweetly. "My debt to you is much greater!"

A passing cart separated them. Members of the citizen's army were hauling cartloads of stone cannon balls for the

316

bombards and firewood and jars of oil to the ramparts. The muffled roar of English and Burgundian cannon was already audible beyond the river. It was now mid-morning and the enemy had clearly decided that the time was ripe to attack.

While the men ran to the walls, the woman continued about their daily tasks as though nothing out of the ordinary were happening. They were used to the agitation and tumult of war. Soon they would go to join their menfolk with everything necessary to tend the wounded: wine and oil to wash the wounds with, torn strips of linen for bandages and shrouds for the dead. Catherine decided to join them since she had nothing else to do. She went home, placed the casket in a safe place, changed her man's clothes for a blue woollen dress Sara had bought for her and then joined the other women going towards the ramparts.

Once the tide had turned, Arnaud made rapid strides towards recovery. Luckily, the Captain was blessed with a remarkably vigorous constitution. By summer, he was able to leave his bed in the monastery and by the beginning of August, he was back at his place on the ramparts with the rest of the defending army. Compiègne still held out, so stubbornly that Philippe of Burgundy had left in discouragement for Lièges where his presence was urgently needed, leaving the field to Jean de Luxembourg.

Contrary to what Xaintrailles had predicted at the time of Joan's highly suspect capture by the English, Guillaume de Flavy had continued the defense of the town with remarkable courage and obstinacy. A rumor circulated among the captains that, in lowering the drawbridge too hastily, Flavy had sought to propitiate the hatred his relative, Regnault de Chartres, Chancellor-Archbishop of Rheims, felt towards Joan, a cousinly gesture. . . . Unfortunately, the situation was growing more serious daily. In spite of the forest, Compiègne was now completely blockaded. Luxembourg held Royal-Lieu and the road to Verberie, while a great fort under the command of the Sires de Créqui and de Brimeu had been erected on the road to Pierrefonds, on the edge of the forest. Provisions were running out, convoys were no longer able to get through. Their only communication with the outside world was through a handful of brave men who smuggled themselves out of the city under cover of darkness and returned the same way.

Catherine spent her days near the city walls in a sort of improvized field station organized by the ladies of the town. She and Sara went there each time an attack began and stayed there helping and tending the wounded till they were ready to

317

drop. At night, exhausted, they collapsed onto their beds and slept like logs in spite of pangs of hunger and the intense heat.

High summer was upon them, adding to the distress of the defending forces. The soldiers, especially the wounded, were persecuted by clouds of flies. A few cases of plague had been reported and to stop the contamination spreading, the corpses were burned and the victims' homes sealed off. The little food that could be procured soon went bad. The only thing which was not scarce, thanks to the nearby river, was water, but this could only be fetched at night when the enemy's fire had ceased.

However, Catherine's chief distress was not physical in origin. Every day, in her boy's clothes, she went to the Abbey to visit Arnaud and, every day, she felt a little sadder and more discouraged. Not that Arnaud was ever openly disagreeable towards her, but he kept within the limits of punctilious courtesy which dismayed her far more than rudeness would have done. Short of being allowed to tend him herself, she would have liked to be allowed to stay with him for several hours at a time, talking of something else besides the siege and Joan's captivity . . . about himself, for instance, all those long years during which she had not known him; about his childhood. In those few minutes he had spent with her in the cellar on the Pont-au-Change, Michel had started to talk about his childhood so spontaneously and vividly that Catherine was always hoping that Arnaud would confide in her too. But she was beginning to realize that he was not softening towards her in the least. His thoughts roamed past her and focused on the Maid to the utter exclusion of the unhappy woman beside him. As she returned home, where Sara was waiting for her, Catherine often thought that Michel's body lay between them like an eternal obstacle. She seemed unable to find a way of convincing Arnaud that she was not guilty of his death. She had nothing but her word! He would never believe her—he never had before! His current treatment of Catherine was visibly based on the fact that you cannot absolutely reject a woman who is prepared to sacrifice her life and fortune to help you. But for that, she was convinced he would have cast her aside quite ruthlessly.

News of Joan came via a Spanish spy. She had tried to escape from Beaulieu and had then been taken to Beaurevoir where Jean de Luxembourg had his headquarters. A second attempt to escape had nearly proved fatal. She had jumped from a tower and been picked up half dead in the moat.

There could be no hope of rescuing Joan while the siege continued. The enemy blockade was growing tighter and it was becoming more and more difficult to get through. It was all they could do to get a messenger through to the Maréchal de

Boussac, who commanded the Normandy countryside. The town had reached its last gasp; famine and disease were cutting great swathes in the ranks of the brave defenders and, if help did not arrive speedily, the city would be forced to surrender.

"Trapped here like hungry rats in a hole!" Arnaud raged. "While Joan is a prisoner of the Burgundians and the King does nothing to try to rescue her!"

"You can be sure that La Trémoille is there keeping an eye on him!" Xaintrailles sneered. "He is sworn to the destruction of the Maid."

Finally, on the last day of October, help arrived. A convoy of food managed to get through and spirits rallied at once. At the same time, Maréchal de Boussac's forces attacked the Anglo-Burgundian army in the rear. In spite of Luxembourg and Huntington's fierce resistance, the strongholds fell, one after another. Boussac forced a way through and entered the city. Then a single massive sortie on the part of Boussac and his men shattered the enemy's resistance. Everyone tensed themselves in expectation of a heavy counterattack the following day, but when the day dawned, it revealed a desert where the enemy camp had been: they had vanished without a single drum beat or trumpet call. Compiègne was saved ... and Arnaud's complete recovery coincided with it, but he was already raging to be off, impatient and eager to go in search of Joan and try to rescue her from the enemy. He, Xaintrailles and Catherine were already working out a plan of campaign when terrible news reached them, reducing their fine schemes to ashes: Jean de Luxembourg had accepted the English offers. He had sold them his prisoner for ten thousand écus. Joan of Arc was now in the hands of the enemy, but no one knew yet what was to become of her or even where she was at that moment.

The evening they heard the news, the three of them were gathered together in Catherine's house. After a long silence, Xaintrailles cried:

"We must separate!"

"Separate?" Catherine exclaimed in alarm. "But that's impossible! You promised ..."

"That you should help us to save her? I still promise you that, but at the moment we don't know where she is or where they are taking her. Until we have found that out, we can do nothing."

"To England no doubt," Arnaud said.

"That's possible. And in that case, Catherine, as a Burgundian, could be very useful to us. I don't imagine the gossip from Bruges reaches that far. We could pass ourselves off as her

319

servants. Meanwhile, we shall have to start searching. Catherine, I shall escort you to the Convent of the Bernardines de Louviers whose Abbess is a cousin of mine. La Hire commands the town, which is not far from Rouen, one of the principal English strongholds, or from the sea. When we are certain of her whereabouts, we shall contact you. Now, now . . . you mustn't cry. It's the best plan for the moment. Until then, you would only be in our way and . . ."

Arnaud's sarcastic voice cut short this discussion.

"That's enough! She must know that soldiers can't have her trailing about with them! We shall go and get her when we need her and that's an end of it!"

In spite of Xaintrailles' encouragement, Catherine had difficulty suppressing her tears. How eagerly Arnaud seized on the slightest pretext to be rid of her! It was hopeless! He really did hate her and doubtless would continue to do so all his life. She looked away so he should not see the tears in her eyes.

"Very well," she said sadly, "I will go to this convent."

CHAPTER EIGHTEEN

Rouen

Winter had wrapped its shroud of snow and ice about the little town of Louviers, bringing all activity there—commercial as well as military—to a standstill. The two arms of the Eure river, under their cloudy, white carapace, imprisoned and immobilized tanneries, stone quarries and windmills—all those, at least, which had not been destroyed in the war. As for the soldiers, they had once more been plunged into the customary hibernation period which the onset of winter brought with it every year. Thick snow muffled the fields and roads. Once outside the city walls, one sank in it up to the knees. Spring, nevertheless, was not far off: February was almost ended.

During the three months she had been living with the Bernardines, Catherine had conformed to the rigid rules of convent life without too much difficulty. Mother Marie-Beatrice, Xaintrailles' cousin, had received her with kindness. She was oddly like her tall, red-headed cousin and the resemblance disarmed Catherine. She and Sara lived in a large room somewhat more luxuriously furnished than the nuns' cells, but they made it a point of honor to join in the community life as far as possible.

The long sessions in the chapel which had been so irksome to Catherine as a young girl had now become necessary, even welcome, to her. She had the feeling that in speaking of Arnaud to God, she was bringing him a little closer and, in truth, she was beginning to think that only Divine Providence could bring them together again. Would he really remember his promise to her to let her help them rescue Joan? She found it hard to believe. Three months had gone by without a word from them and the world outside seemed a long way from the convent where any news, even of the progress of the war, was a rare event. . . .

Louviers, nevertheless, had played an important part in the war. She had been captured and recaptured and for the last few months had been in the hands of La Hire who had seized her in the course of a dazzling Norman campaign during which he had earned the added glory of winning back Château-Gaillard from the English. Now he held Louviers and held her securely. Though the English army was not far off, the fear which the mention of his name inspired throughout the surrounding countryside helped to maintain a state of relative calm wherever his black banner flew.

Every night before going to bed Catherine would spend a long time standing on one of the turrets of the convent, gazing out over the snow-bound countryside. Sometimes she would see horsemen approaching and her heart beat faster for a moment, only to be disappointed again a moment later. They were never the ones she hoped to see. How long must she go on waiting here? Would she have to go forth again, braving a thousand dangers and terrors, in search of the man she loved?

"Do not fret so," Sara said. "Men always forget women when war has them in its grip."

"Arnaud does all he can to stay away from me . . . he will never come to fetch me. . . ."

"The other captain, the red-headed one, will keep his promise to you—I am sure of that. He at least is a good friend of yours. As for the other . . . the reason he is unyielding could be that he is afraid of you and doesn't feel quite sure of himself. . . . Be patient; wait. . . ."

"Wait, wait!" Catherine echoed with a bitter smile. "That's all I ever seem to do: wait and pray. . . ."

"When you are praying, your time is never wasted, Catherine. . . ."

One morning, however, as Catherine was leaving church

321

after Mass, a nun came to say that someone wished to speak to her at the grille.

"Who can it be?" Catherine asked, surprised, trying to stifle the hope which had suddenly surged up in her.

"Messire de Vignolles with a monk and another person I have never seen before."

Ah, it couldn't be them! Catherine pulled her blue silk scarf up over her hair, handed her Book of Hours to Sara and went to the convent parlor. As the door opened she almost screamed, the shock was so violent. Arnaud was standing there with Brother Étienne Charlot and La Hire.

"You!" she exclaimed. "You came!"

Gravely, unsmilingly, he bent his tall frame a little.

"I have come to fetch you. Brother Étienne here, has just arrived from Rouen where Joan has been a prisoner since Christmas. He knows a way by which we can enter the city, which will not be easy, because it is held by a large English force."

Catherine was glad to see Brother Étienne again. She had long ago ceased to wonder at the strange way he vanished and reappeared without warning. She knew that Yolande's secret agent could not lead an ordinary life like everyone else. She clasped the little monk's hands affectionately.

"So you know where Joan is?" she asked, not daring to look directly at Arnaud because she was not sure of herself and did not want to let him see how excited she was.

"She is in the château at Rouen, in a cell on the first floor of the Bouvreuil tower overlooking the fields. Five English soldiers guard her day and night: three in the cell itself and two outside the door. On top of that she is chained by the feet to a massive piece of wood. The tower and the château are packed with soldiers because the young king, Henry VI, and his uncle, the Cardinal of Winchester, are both lodged there."

As he spoke, Catherine's heart ached and Arnaud and La Hire's faces darkened.

"In other words, there is no hope," said the Gascon. "It would be a simple matter to kill five men, but it would seem there are many others besides."

Brother Étienne shrugged. His cheery face had lost its sparkle. His brow was furrowed.

"In such a case, cunning often succeeds where force is useless. Joan goes out each day to attend her trial."

His listeners all cried out at once:

"Trial? Who is trying her?"

"Who do you think? The English, of course, but under the guise of a religious trial. She appears before an ecclesiastical

322

tribunal composed almost exclusively of priests who support the English. Most of them come from the University of Paris which is almost entirely on their side. The Bishop of Beauvais, Pierre Cauchon, presides over·it assisted by his friend, Jean d'Estivet, who organized the trial. They say he has promised Warwick that Joan shall be put to death, and I believe he is capable of carrying out his promise."

The name struck Catherine. She saw before her once again the impecunious academic of Caboche's time, and the prelate puffed up with pride and self-importance whom she had met at Dijon. The man who could judge Joan was certainly on a par with those two other personages. She shivered as she recalled the Bishop's cold little eyes. Joan might expect neither pity nor mercy from him.

"And what is the motive of this trial?" La Hire asked haughtily.

"To dishonor the King of France by showing that he owes his crown to a witch and a heretic, and to please the English by handing Joan over to be burnt at the stake," Brother Étienne said quietly.

A moment's silence followed these terrible words and each one echoed solemnly in their hearts and consciences. At last Arnaud sighed.

"Very well. Tell Catherine your plan. . . ."

"Here it is! I have some relations at Rouen. Very interesting relations. My cousin, Jean Son, is a master-mason . . . he is responsible for repairs to the château. They are good people, his family, with a comfortable income . . . and they have won the trust of the occupying army with whom they maintain excellent relations."

"*Friends* of the English?" Catherine exclaimed, appalled.

"Yes, indeed," Brother Étienne went on imperturbably. "As I said, my cousin enjoys the support and esteem of the English, but I didn't say where his own sympathies lie. At bottom he is a faithful subject of the King of France, like all the other citizens of the unfortunate town of Rouen. His connections could prove very useful to us. His wife, Nicole, is a linen-draper. She sells goods to the young King and also to the Duchess of Bedford, who is at present in Rouen. She is an ill-tempered woman, Dame Nicole, but it was thanks to her that the Duchess of Bedford heard that Joan's guards had tried to rape her and they were replaced by others under severe penalties. My cousins would be glad to receive one or two members of their family— refugees from Louviers, for instance. Personally, I visualize a modest young couple . . . a mason and his wife, perhaps."

His bright eyes went from Arnaud to Catherine and then

back to the captain. The word "couple" brought a rosy flush to Catherine's cheeks. Arnaud said nothing. La Hire rubbed his chin and made a hideous grimace as he gave the plan his concentrated attention.

"A good idea!" he exclaimed finally. "That would mean there would be two of us in there!"

"Three, if you please," said Brother Étienne. "I shall of course be returning there myself. I only came to explain the situation and discuss our next move with you. When I heard Mme de Brazey was here, I had an idea."

La Hire was right in thinking that Catherine was agreeable to the scheme. In fact, it made her almost lightheaded with joy. To pass for a while as Arnaud's wife—even if only for purposes of disguise—was a dream such as she had never even dared to entertain. Perhaps this dangerous adventure might bring them closer to each other. Such a disguise would necessarily throw them together a lot and during those moments of intimacy she might find a way of rekindling the flame of passion which he had already succumbed to twice before. To hide her feelings, she asked:

"What has happened to Messire Xaintrailles?"

Arnaud replied with an irritable shrug:

"He has met up with a sort of religious crank, a shepherd from Gévaudan, called Guillaume, who makes prophecies and claims to have been sent by God. Xaintrailles is in ecstasies over him and takes him everywhere with him. He is relying on him to help free Joan. He hopes to join us later ... but I haven't much faith in him."

"Why not?"

"Because one must be completely mad not to see that this shepherd is just such an imposter as that girl from La Rochelle whom Joan advised to 'go and look after your home and children'. I can only suppose that Xaintrailles has gone quite out of his mind," Arnaud concluded.

One day towards the end of March, a little after nones, a pathetic-looking little group passed through the Grand Pont gate and entered the town of Rouen: a man, a woman and a monk. They were all sufficiently dusty and filthy to attract no more than a perfunctory, disdainful glance from the English archers guarding the gate. The guards were all busy playing dice on a barrel top and did not even trouble to inspect the contents of the bundle which the man was carrying on his shoulder and which, presumably, contained all the young couple's worldly possessions. As for the monk, all he appeared to own was his brown serge habit and wooden beads. Their attitude might have been a little different if they had known that the woman carried a fortune's worth of jewels, including a fabulous black diamond sewn into her dirty dress. The rest of this fortune was hidden in the wooden beads knotted at the monk's waist.

Arnaud was unrecognizable. He had not shaved for three days, and was dressed in a dingy smock and baggy hose which hung in wrinkled folds round his lithe, horseman's legs. He wore a shapeless cap pulled down over his head and walked with a stoop to disguise his height. Catherine wore a faded, blue dress, a patched and torn brown cape and her hair pulled back tightly and unflatteringly under a cap which had not been white for a long time.

"Jean Son and his wife live in the rue des Ours," Brother Étienne whispered to them as soon as they had passed the guard post near the Beffroi. "It is not far from here. But for the love of God, my dear friend, try to keep your eyes down when you run across an Englishman and don't run them through with that fierce stare of yours—one can tell you are a soldier a league away!"

Arnaud gave a reluctant grin and flushed.

"I'll do my best, but it is hard, Brother Étienne; the sight of those iron helmets and green tunics of theirs idling about a French city as if they owned the place makes me see red!"

"You must try to ignore them . . . at least for the moment."

An air of misery hung over the ancient capital of the Norman Dukes, which consorted strangely with the magnificence of the town itself. The tall, gabled houses, decorated with fine wood-carvings and elaborately painted signs, and the soaring pinnacles of the church steeples, their Norman towers enriched with flamboyant, gothic carving, looking like queens in elaborately carved crowns, formed a strange setting for the hurrying silhouettes, glum faces and lowered eyes of the inhabitants. There was no joyful din to be heard at the crossroads and the half-empty shops were evidence of the restrictions imposed upon the townsfolk. Silent women queued up outside the baker's, butcher's and tripe sellers, standing up to their ankles in snow in the hope of getting something to eat. Soldiers in green tunics, on the other hand, were to be seen on all sides. In groups of twos and threes they walked up and down the streets of the town keeping a close watch on the townspeople's movements. The most severe penalties had been imposed since the beginning of the trial which was held in the chapel in the château, so terrified were the authorities of some show of force, either in the hope of freeing the prisoner or with a view to

325

assassinating the lofty personages sheltered by the stout walls of the fortress with its seven towers.

When the three companions reached the little shop selling linen, laces and other trifles which was kept by Dame Nicole Son, they found the lady herself attending to the needs of two richly gowned ladies whose pronounced English accents proclaimed them ladies-in-waiting to the Duchess of Bedford. They were poring over the Flanders lace and lengths of fine linen with an avidity which made Catherine smile. Her eye was caught momentarily by a headdress on a wooden dummy standing on the counter—a tall, pointed headdress covered with Mailes lace and enveloped in a cloudy, floating veil. Burgundian fashions seemed to be all the rage in Normandy!

But Dame Nicole, a tall, sallow, skinny woman who wore her gown of fine gray cloth decorated with black astrakhan and a large gold cross with little grace or style, now turned a frosty stare on the three travelers. Brother Étienne judged it advisable to intervene.

"Peace be with you, Dame Nicole!" he said sweetly. "Here are your poor cousins from Louviers . . . in a very sorry state! I daresay you have trouble in recognizing them! They have lost everything. That savage brigand, that accursed Étienne de Vignolles, burned their house to the ground and robbed them of all they possessed. I found them half dead on the wayside. . . ."

"How sad!" Dame Nicole exclaimed with a look of absolute disgust. "Take them through to the kitchen, Brother Étienne. I am very busy!"

The two English ladies, meanwhile, had dropped their lengths of lace and were gazing at the newly arrived couple. They nodded and whispered to each other so pityingly that it was all Catherine could do not to burst out laughing. Feeling, however, that she ought to do something, she dropped a clumsy curtsey and stammered with well-feigned shyness:

"Good day to you, cousin!"

Dame Nicole responded to this with the sort of gesture usually reserved for chasing away flies.

"Later, later! . . . Take them to the kitchen! You're in the way, don't you see?"

They followed the monk to a door in the back of the shop. As they passed by the ladies, one of them rummaged in her purse and took out a gold piece which she dropped into Catherine's hand. She was too astonished to react.

"Poor woman!" the lady cried in English. "Buy yourself a new dress!"

These words were accompanied with such a kindly smile that Catherine could not help feeling touched by her kindness in

326

trying to alleviate another woman's wretchedness. She thanked her with a curtsey and a:

"Thank you, gracious lady! May God bless you!"

But Dame Nicole appeared thoroughly put out by the incident.

"Madame la Comtesse is too kind ... such generosity! Off with you, the lot! Off you go!"

When they reached the huge kitchen, warmed by a great fire crackling in the chimney, they found the place empty and the door into the back courtyard open. The maid must have gone to the well or the poultry run. Arnaud, who had only managed to keep silent with great difficulty since they entered the house, now burst out furiously:

"If it's a case of having to live with that Nicole, I think I'd rather sleep on the quays with the stevedores."

"Hush!" Brother Étienne exclaimed. "You mustn't be misled by appearances. You may change your mind about your hostess later. Ah, here is the maid!"

A sturdy girl carrying two buckets full of water came into the kitchen just then. Finding it full of people, she nearly dropped her load in her astonishment.

"What do you lot want?" she demanded.

Brother Étienne was just about to answer when Dame Nicole appeared from the shop.

"They are some cousins of my husband's who have just come from Louviers and have lost everything they had," she explained, still as surly looking as ever. "We shall have to take them in. Give them something to eat, Margot, and then take them up to the loft. When the master returns he can decide what's to be done with them."

"Thank you for your generosity, good lady," Brother Étienne began, but Dame Nicole interrupted him with a shrug.

"One is either a Christian, or one isn't. We are short of food and there is little or nothing to spare, but I cannot let my husband's relations starve outside in the streets. Now come with me, Brother, I want to talk to you. . . ."

He followed her without haste, leaving Arnaud and Catherine behind with the maid who was looking them over with some curiosity. She evidently found nothing strange about them, because she turned away to fill a couple of bowls with soup. Then she cut a large piece of black bread and pushed it all in front of them.

"So you've come from Louviers?"

"Yes," Catherine said, plunging her spoon into the thick appetizing soup. "From Louviers. . . ."

"I have some cousins there, some tanners ... Guillaume Lerouge. Do you know him?"

Now it was Arnaud's turn to plunge into the fray. He stopped noisily lapping up his soup and looked up at the fat maidservant.

" 'Deed I do! Guillaume Lerouge? I'll say I know him ... poor lad! That bandit, Vignolles, strung 'em up t'other day! Oh, it's sorry times we be living in! It's hard on poor folks like us."

Catherine could hardly believe her ears. Here she was, since her arrival in Rouen, terrified that Arnaud would give them away by lapsing into his natural, lordly ways and now, all of a sudden, he revealed himself even better at the game than she was. Now Margot sighed gustily.

"Aye, so they be! But you won't be too bad done by here. The mistress is a hard one, right enough. She's as hard as they come, that one! But there's plenty to eat. You look a sturdy fellow. Maître Jean will find work for you and your wife will find plenty to do here. The other maid is dead, so there's no shortage of work."

"And I bain't afraid of working, neither," Catherine assured her, while Arnaud, apparently satisfied, finished gobbling up his soup. When he had finished, he mopped up the last drops in his bowl with a piece of bread, then wiped his mouth on his sleeve.

"That's better!" he cried with a look of intense satisfaction. "Good soup, that!" And, all the better to show his appreciation, he let fly a resounding belch.

"Come, now," said the maid. "I'll show you your room, Dame. It's not luxurious and there's no fire in there, but when there's two of you, you bain't be needing fires, eh?"

The attic, crowded under the roof, was shaped something like a truncated pyramid. There were a few pieces of broken furniture scattered about and the place was as cold as the grave, but Margot carried in a couple of mattresses and a good number of woolen coverlets.

"Tomorrow we'll do a bit of tidying up in here," she said. "But the main thing tonight is to keep warm. Rest awhile, now."

When she had gone out, Catherine and Arnaud stood looking at each other for a moment or two. Then Catherine suddenly burst out laughing. Her sides were aching from the effort of containing herself.

"I didn't know you were so talented," she said mockingly, taking care to keep her voice down. " 'Struth, you make a perfect village blockhead! And here I was, afraid you would behave too nicely and give us away!"

"I told you I was brought up like a little peasant, didn't I?" he said with a sudden smile which lit up his whole face. "I think

328

I've always been a peasant at heart, and I think I'm proud of the fact. I'm really not cut out for high society. . . . But, come to that, you were pretty convincing yourself!"

And all of a sudden he burst out laughing, succumbing, like Catherine, to a burst of spontaneous gaiety which temporarily swept away their grievances, discord and bad memories. They laughed like two children who have perpetrated a successful joke, closer together, perhaps, than they had ever been, even during their most passionate moments. They were still laughing when Dame Nicole came in with a parcel under one arm.

"Hist!" she said with a finger on her lips. "They might hear you and for two destitute refugees, it seems to me you are a little too cheerful!"

She was smiling now and Catherine noticed that this smile lent her long, plain face an extraordinary charm. She threw the bundle of clothes down on the bedding and then, quite naturally, dropped a curtsey.

"Messire and Madame, please forgive me for the harsh way I welcomed you down in the shop . . . and for any snubs and bad temper I may be forced to display in the future. I am by no means sure I can trust the servant-girl, or indeed, anyone!"

Feeling greatly relieved, because she had felt ill at ease ever since entering the Son household, Catherine ran across and kissed Dame Nicole, while Arnaud assured her that they were profoundly grateful to her. It was much better to go on as they were before. Now that she had cleared up any possible misunderstandings or ill-will between them, Nicole did not linger for long enough to arouse Margot's suspicions. Water and washing things were fetched for them. When Maître Jean Son returned, they were clean and presentable looking, though humbly dressed as befitted poor relations.

At first sight, the master-mason was no more sympathetic than his wife. He was stout and florid, puffy with fat and pride, and he had a sleepily complacent way of looking vaguely round at things which did not lead one to think very highly of his intelligence. But his "cousins" soon discovered that this air of harmless stupidity hid a clear and lucid brain, remarkable courage and deep, Norman cunning.

"Rest this evening," he advised them sotto voce when the maid had finished serving them their supper. "Tomorrow I will show you our cellar. That is where we shall meet in future to avoid being overheard."

When the curfew sounded, the household met for prayers and then everyone retired to their own rooms. Arnaud and Catherine went up to their attic and the young woman's heart began to beat faster. This cohabitation embarrassed and de-

329

lighted her all at once, for, as it turned out, Margot had only made up one bed for them both. She did not know whether to rejoice or fear some new rebuff, but as soon as he saw what had happened, Arnaud calmly removed one of the mattresses and a coverlet and placed them in a corner of the room. He found a tattered, old curtain tucked in among the odds and ends in the room and carefully hung this up between them by passing it over the beams. She watched him, meanwhile, trying hard not to let her disappointment show in her face. When he had finished, he turned towards her, smiled and bowed as courteously as if he had been in a château instead of this sordid attic.

"Good night," he said pleasantly. "Good night, my dear wife!"

A few minutes later a loud snore informed Catherine that he was sound asleep. It had been a hard day and she would have liked to follow his example, but she was too agitated to sleep. She tossed and turned for hours on her hard mattress. She was angry with Arnaud, with herself, with the whole world. And if only that idiot didn't snore so loudly!

A strange sort of existence began then for the two companions in adventure. All day long, under Nicole's supervision, Catherine worked her fingers to the bone about the house helping Margot cook, wash, iron and clean the house, frequently snubbed and scolded, especially when there were strangers in the house; in short, playing the part of a poor relation to the life. Arnaud, for his part, had entered fully into his mason's role. The fact that he knew how to write had saved him from having to risk his life on scaffoldings and Jean Son, in making him his secretary, had spared him from the risk of arousing the curiosity of the other masons. Seeing that he was the boss's cousin, no one thought it odd that he should be treated a little better than the rest. . . .

But once night had come and Margot was asleep, secret meetings took place in the cellar in which the craft of masonry played little part. It was there that the latest news of the trial was discussed, brought by certain Preaching Friars of the Order of Saint Dominic, who had been attending the sessions regularly since they were first held in secret at the beginning of March. These monks, Brother Isambard de la Pierre and Brother Martin Ladvenu, did all they could to help and advise Joan when they were allowed to go near her. But Cauchon and Warwick kept close watch over their prey and Brother Isambard, who had advised Joan to appeal to the Pope and to the Council of Basle, found himself threatened with being sewn up in a sack and thrown into the Seine by the terrible Bishop of Beauvais. Both of them deeply admired and pitied the Maid.

They retraced, for Jean Son and his friends, each instant of the calvary she was undergoing and recounted her replies, always simple, clear and full of faith, to the subtle traps laid for her by the learned doctors in their eagerness to please the conquerors. Joan defended herself with a skill, intelligence and exact recall of her previous answers which was little short of prodigious, especially when one considered that this eighteen-year-old child did not know how to write or read. She could barely sign her name.

"Everything about the trial is illegal, false and corrupt," Brother Isambard remarked in his beautiful, deep voice. "Cauchon has promised to kill her but first and foremost he wishes to discredit the King of France. And there is nothing he would not stoop to for that!"

They learnt, through him, that Joan had been put to the torture, but that she had remained firm and unmoved by the whips, armed with spikes and lead pellets, with which they had threatened her. Nothing, it seemed, could overthrow her remarkable courage. But as the days passed, it became more and more difficult to reach her. Jean Son, accompanied by Arnaud—who had grown a beard to disguise himself all the better—went to the tower of Bouvreuil, where Joan was imprisoned, on the pretext of wanting to inspect the masonry and make sure that no one had tried to tunnel through it to help the prisoner escape. They had both come back despairing.

"No one can talk to her. She is kept under constant guard and the château is swarming with soldiers. We were searched at least ten times going and coming. It would take a veritable army to attack that fortress," Arnaud said, collapsing onto a stool. "We will never succeed, never!"

The conspirators had thought briefly of trying to bribe the judges with Catherine's jewels, but Brother Isambard had soon dissuaded them.

"It would be useless. It pains me to have to say such a thing of doctors of the Church, but the fact is, they would take your fortune . . . and then betray you. Not one among them would hesitate to have a foot in both camps. Those who were once of good faith, like the Bishop of Avranches, have long ago gone across to the enemy."

"What are we to do then?" Catherine asked.

Maître Jean Son shrugged his fat shoulders and downed a goblet of red wine at a gulp to raise his spirits.

"Wait till the day she is sentenced—because it will enevitably come—and try to do something then. It's our only chance . . . Joan's only chance, may God have mercy upon her!"

When they left the dark, vaulted cellar, a relic of Roman

331

days, and found themselves back in their attic, Arnaud and Catherine found they had nothing to say to each other. The tragic, pitiful shadow of the captive girl rose between them. She united them in a common effort and will to save her from an unjust fate, but at the same time she separated them by the loftiness of her martyrdom. How could one make love, knowing the suffering the young girl was going through only a little way away?

One evening as they were sitting down to supper, there was a knock on one of the shutters. Margot went to open them. A tall man dressed entirely in black entered the room.

"Good evening to all," he said. "Forgive me for disturbing you, but I must see Maître Son."

The man wore a hood which hid a good part of his face, but, at the sight of him, Nicole went pale and shuddered. Catherine leant across to her pseudo-cousin and whispered:

"Who is it?"

"Geoffroy Terrage ... the executioner!" Nicole said tonelessly.

Jean Son rose from the table, without even troubling to hide his expression of contempt, and interposed his vast bulk between the two women and the executioner's black form.

"What do you want?" he demanded rudely.

"I have need of you, Maître Son, straight away. I have been ordered to build a high platform in the Saint-Ouen cemetery by the day after tomorrow, Thursday, 24 May."

"What for?"

Terrage looked away, suddenly embarrassed by all those eyes fixed upon him with unconcealed loathing in them.

"For a fire!" he said curtly. Then, as no one present spoke, their blood turned to ice, he added: "A high enough fire so that the condemned woman can be seen from all around and too high to let me come up behind her, once the fire has been lit, and strangle her discreetly."

In spite of the risk of speaking too plainly, Catherine could not resist saying:

"So far as I know, Joan has not yet been sentenced!"

The executioner shrugged indifferently.

"What do you want me to say? Those are my orders; I merely carry them out. May I rely on you, Maître Son?"

"It will be done," said Son, unable to suppress a tremor in his voice. "Good night."

"Good night."

When he had left, they all stayed frozen to their seats, even Margot who stood staring dully at the door where the man had vanished, with the stew pot in her hands. After a moment, she came and set the pot down on the table and crossed herself hurriedly.

"Poor girl!" she said. "To be burned alive ... 'tis a terrible death!"

Late that evening, after the most silent of their communal suppers was over, the inhabitants of the house in the rue des Ours met in the cellar where they were joined by the Brothers, Isambard and Martin, recently returned from a mission in Louviers. The Dominican and the Benedictine had a solemnity about them which augered ill. Their wrinkled and furrowed faces were shadowed by a deep sorrow.

"No, she has not yet been condemned to death," Brother Isambard replied to Arnaud's question. "But it will not be long now. On Thursday she is to be taken to the Saint-Ouen cemetery to be publicly admonished and adjured to repent her sins and submit herself to the Church as She is represented here, that is to say, to Maître Cauchon. If she refuses, she is to be thrown to the flames ... if she accepts ..."

"If she accepts?" Nicole repeated.

The monk shrugged his thin shoulders under his white robe and black cloak. His emaciated face lengthened:

"Normally she would be sent to a convent under guard to undergo whatever sentence the tribunal saw fit to impose, but I feel that there is a trap there—that Cauchon has something up his sleeve. He has promised Warwick too many times that Joan will die."

While the others weighed up what the monk had said, Maître Son took a parchment scroll from his pocket and spread it out on a barrel. Then he weighted it down with a candlestick and spread out the crackling skin which was brown with age. While the faces of the rest gradually darkened with gloom, he alone seemed strangely contented. His wife noticed this.

"One would almost imagine that you were pleased with what Brother Isambard has just said!"

"More pleased than you think, because I now see a strong possibility of being able to save her. This," he said, pointing to his scroll, "is a very ancient plan of the Abbey of Saint-Ouen, whose upkeep I am also responsible for, and this plan seems to me to be of capital importance. Come and see. ..."

They crowded about him, leaning over his shoulders with eager faces. Jean Son went on talking for a long time in a low voice. ...

CHAPTER NINETEEN

Fire and Water

So as to be sure of stationing herself where Maître Son and Arnaud had arranged for her to be, Catherine went along to the cemetery of the Saint-Ouen Abbey early in the morning. She was to wait on the steps of a half-ruined Calvary opposite the stands prepared for the judges and the little scaffold destined for Joan. A little way off, between the stands and the south door of the Church of Saint-Ouen, stood the sinister pyre which the master-mason had built the day before, piled high with a towering pyramid of faggots. Shortly afterwards, Nicole took her place among a band of housewives in their best finery below one of the wooden galleries which surrounded the enclosure of the dead. This place was known as a charnel house. The cemetery was filling up rapidly, the mild weather and a burning curiosity having induced almost all the citizens of Rouen out of doors. For most of them, this was their first opportunity of seeing Joan of Arc.

Soon Catherine caught sight of Arnaud. Wearing his tight, worn, black costume, he stood with bowed shoulders and head hidden beneath a vast green hood, as near as possible to the scaffold prepared for Joan, just behind the cordon of English archers. With their pikes held horizontally, they formed a solid barrier round the scaffold, but one that it might just be possible for someone as powerful as Arnaud to break through. The other conspirators would be in their appointed places by now, too: Jean Son in the town belfry and Brother Étienne inside the church.

The mason's plan was simplicity itself. He had long ago discovered in some of the old plans of the church an underground passage to the neighboring countryside whose entrance was situated under one of the flagstones of the old Roman crypt. For no very obvious reason, no one had ever mentioned the existence of this passage to anyone, and he was glad of this now. He knew exactly which flag covered the ancient stairway and while his workmen were constructing the cement foundation ordered by the tribunal, he had unsealed the stone under pretext of examining the stone pillars of the crypt and shown

Brother Étienne how it might be raised without too much difficulty. The monk's habit allowed him to enter the church without attracting attention. At this moment he should be praying in the crypt, waiting till Arnaud should bring him the fugitive.

The published orders announced that no one was to move from their places before sentence was passed. Then, two possibilities would present themselves: either Joan submitted to the Church's judgment on her and was handed over to the nuns, or she refused and was handed over to the executioner. In both cases, Catherine was instantly to throw a fit of convulsions, like a woman in extreme hysteria, and Nicole was to increase the general confusion and uproar as much as possible under the guise of coming to her assistance. Meanwhile, Jean Son, posted in the town belfry, whence he would be able to hear the piercing screams of the two women, would instantly ring the two alarm bells, Rouvel and Cache-Ribaud, whose powerful voices had summoned the townspeople to revolt or self-defence throughout the centuries. This unexpected tocsin would help to create enough agitation and tumult for Arnaud, helped by Brother Isambard, stationed not far from Joan's side, to snatch the prisoner from her guards and rush with her into the church. With a man like Cauchon, it was unlikely that the right of asylum would have much force, but it would only be necessary to gain two or three minutes over the pursuers to get Joan safely away into the secret passage. Before the English could trace the entrance to the passage, the Maid and her rescuers would have reached the countryside, and at nightfall would join up with La Hire who was meanwhile to advance as close as possible to the town with a detachment of troops. Once she recovered from her sudden fit, it would be easy for Catherine to rejoin the fugitives a little later. . . .

The cemetery was becoming crowded and the steps against which Catherine was leaning were buried under a sea of people over whose heads she could only just see. Over by the stands, a wave of shining steel bristling with pikes signaled a detachment of soldiers, then the judges' stands filled up with black and white robes against which the episcopal purple stood out sharply. To Catherine, standing at a distance, Cauchon looked gigantic, his plump shoulders sheltered by an ermine cape against which his scarlet face shone somewhat grotesquely. High in the sky, swept by the black and white flight of swallows, the heavy notes of the death knell fell into the air from the church tower like drops of lead. Catherine's heart was seized by a sudden anguish as she saw the executioner and his assistants approaching, followed by a slender silhouette surrounded by a squad of soldiers.

When Joan appeared on the scaffold which had been set up

335

for her, a long murmur ran through the crowd, a murmur in which pity predominated over curiosity.

"What a young, thin little thing!" a woman whispered.

"Poor child," an old, white-bearded man took up. "They must have given her a hard time in prison, those God-damned English!"

"Hush!" a young girl exclaimed. "They might hear you!"

Soon afterwards everyone fell silent. A man dressed in black went and stood before the kneeling Joan, a red-ribboned parchment in his hands. Someone behind Catherine whispered with awed respect:

"It's Maître Guillaume Erard of the Sorbonne. He is going to preach."

At that moment the black-robed doctor's sonorous voice was uplifted in a pompous but emphatic sermon whose theme was: "The branch cannot bear fruit if it is severed from the vine. . . ." But Catherine was not listening; she was looking at Joan, appalled to find her so pale and thin. The Maid seemed almost to float in her black serge, man's clothes. Her long hair framed a face so drawn and hollow that her clear blue eyes seemed to have devoured everything around them, but her courage appeared undaunted.

Below the stands, just behind the cordon of archers, Catherine could see a patch of dark green: Arnaud's hood. She could feel the nervous tension he must be feeling in her own body. Joan's life and his own would depend on his strength and speed when the moment came. Arnaud would be staking his own life when he sprang up to try and free the prisoner. He and Catherine both knew this and that morning, when they had been separated, the young man's frozen mask had slipped . . . oh, just for an instant! . . . and he had taken Catherine's hand, chapped and rough from her household tasks, and pressed it to his lips.

"Don't forget me, if I die. . . ." he had murmured. Catherine had been so moved that she could hardly speak. Tears filled her eyes, but he was already leaving, a ridiculous, touching figure in the black costume which was too tight for his powerful body. All she could do was to bury this moment of tenderness in the warmest corner of her heart. . . .

The preacher's voice rose up, forcing Catherine to listen.

"Oh, House of France!" he thundered. "You had never known a monster till now, but now you stand dishonored for supporting this woman, a sorceress, heretic, superstitious. . . ."

But then Joan's clear voice could be heard, quite calm and icy with scorn.

336

"Don't speak of my King thus!" she cried. "He is a good and true Christian!"

The crowd vibrated to this like a taut bowstring, but it was only a passing moment of drama. Soon Erard's purring voice arose once more and Catherine lost interest. The moment was drawing near; she could feel it. . . .

When it arrived, everything happened so quickly she thought she would lose her head. There was so much agitation between the two stands that it was impossible to tell what was happening. Everyone was shouting at once, Catherine saw a monk thrust a piece of paper and a pen into Joan's hands. She seemed, for once, quite panic-stricken. All round her the crowd seemed about to riot . . . Joan scratched a sign on the paper and they pushed her down off the scaffold. They must be going to take her away, but where to? Catherine saw Arnaud look round in her direction and realized the moment had come. . . . She threw herself into her part. With a piercing shriek which turned the heads of a good part of the crowd, she fell backwards, displaying all the symptoms of a nervous attack. She fell heavily on the steps and hurt herself badly, but this only made her shriek the louder. Nicole's face, distorted by the shrieks that she too, was uttering, appeared before her in the crowd. The tumult became deafening and then the great bells rang out, dominating the din. The crowd roared and swept this way and that. Catherine, prostrate on the ground amid a crowd of people all trying to help her to her feet, saw nothing. A moment later a voice thundered out:

"Arrest that woman whose fits have caused all this commotion!"

Nicole, her eyes wide with terror, vanished, swallowed up by the crowd. A moment later the ungentle grip of an English soldier hauled Catherine to her feet. Then, she saw. . . .

She saw Cauchon, purple with rage, pointing a shaking finger at her. . . . And saw Joan being dragged by soldiers towards the prison, She saw Arnaud struggling still with three English archers with all the frenzy of desperation and she realized that the plan had failed . . . all was lost.

An hour later, bruised and shaken from the blows they had received and loaded with chains, but side by side, Arnaud and Catherine appeared before the Bishop of Beauvais. They stood proudly. The time for stooping and hiding and disguises was past.

"All is lost," Arnaud whispered to Catherine as they crossed the threshold of the keep. "It only remains for us to die bravely . . . for me, at any rate!"

An archer cuffed him to silence and Catherine saw a thin

trickle of blood flowing from his split lip. Now they stood before the massive, oak chair where Cauchon sat, chin on hand, in an attitude which he imagined to be full of dignity, and allowed the Bishop's shifty eyes and ominous silence to weigh upon them.

"Troublemakers!" he barked. "Poor, wretched madmen who thought they could capture the witch, perhaps? What sort of a pass have we reached when mere peasant clods think they have the right to an opinion?"

He seemed tremendously bored by the incident. His gaze was indifferent, blank. He began to bite his fingernails, then he spat, but suddenly his blank stare kindled and came to life. A spark of amazement, incredulity, lit up his eyes. He got out of his chair and ponderously descended the steps of the dais and came over to Catherine who watched him approach with her head held high. He flung out a fat hand and knocked off her bonnet so that her golden ropes of hair were revealed. An ugly smile wrinkled his face.

"I seem to remember telling you that I would never forget you, Dame Catherine, but, 'pon my word, I scarcely expected to be able to prove it to you under such circumstances. I had heard of your exploits, like everyone else in Burgundy, but I did not know what had become of you. So we have become a conspirator, unless I am much mistaken! We are interested in that foul witch who does not even merit the faggots she will cook on! So it is true that whores understand each other! . . .

Arnaud's icy voice cut him short:

"Leave her alone, reverend swine! She had done nothing more than feel sick at the sight of your exploits against another woman. I know that women are your favorite adversaries, but you would do better to pay attention to me. I am worth it."

Cauchon turned towards him and examined him more attentively, but the room was dimly lit. The prelate went over to the chimney, snatched a lighted brand and held it up to Arnaud's face.

"Who are you, then?" he asked curiously. "Your face is not unfamiliar to me . . . but where have I seen you before?"

"Think!" Arnaud said mockingly. "And get it into your head that you have only one opponent to deal with here—me! This woman has nothing to do with what has happened. . . ."

Realizing that Arnaud was trying to save her, Catherine protested passionately. She was determined to share his fate, whatever it might be!

"Thank you for your generosity, but I don't want it. If you are guilty, then I am too. . . ."

"Nonsense!" Arnaud cried angrily. "I acted alone!"

338

The Bishop's doubtful glance went from one to the other. He scented a mystery here somewhere and was determined to clear it up.

"The executioner will soon bring you to agreement," he said with a sly laugh. "If you would give your name, I might see the picture more clearly. Are you, like Mme de Brazey, a turncoat from Burgundy?"

A look of indescribable disgust twisted Arnaud's face.

"Me? A Burgundian? You insult me, Bishop! I have nothing more to lose by telling you my name. At least it will prove that I have nothing in common with this mad woman here. I am called Arnaud de Montsalvy and I am one of King Charles's captains. She is a Burgundian. . . . It was her family who killed my brother in the time of Caboche. Do you still believe that I would let myself be involved with her in anything like this? You must be mad, Bishop. . . ."

Tears sprang from Catherine's eyes. Perhaps Arnaud was only trying to save her, but even so, his scorn was more than she could bear. She cried out in despair:

"Must you reject me still . . . even now? Why won't you let me die with you? Tell me!"

She held out her manacled hands to him. She would have gone down on her knees for a kind word. She was oblivious of the gloomy surroundings and the dangerous man who was listening to them. The only thing that mattered to her now was this man she loved so passionately and desperately and who still rejected her, even at this moment of crisis. Arnaud stiffened and set his jaw, and stared straight ahead of him, refusing to let her appeals soften him.

"Come, Bishop, let's get this farce over with! Release her. I will confess everything I plotted against you."

But Pierre Cauchon burst out laughing. Carried away by mirth, he collapsed back into his chair. With his mouth thrown open showing the few decayed stumps of teeth that remained to him, he laughed and laughed and laughed, while his two prisoners stared at him in astonishment. Then, abruptly, he sobered down, and licked his fat lips like a greedy cat about to devour a succulent mouse. A gleam of hatred lit up his yellow eyes and he came back to his prisoners. His fat hand fell upon Arnaud and seized him by the collar.

"A Montsalvy, eh? Young Michel's brother, I suppose! And you really thought I'd believe your little story? Do you take me for a simpleton, or do you think I've lost my memory? Release her? Your accomplice? . . . Do you think I would, knowing how devoted she and her family have always been to the Montsalvys?"

"Devoted to my family? The Legoix? You must be out of your mind!"

The fat bishop lost his temper. He turned and spluttered angrily, but still intelligibly, at Arnaud:

"I won't have you mocking me! I was one of the leaders of Caboche's riots, greenhorn, and I know better than you that there were Legoix and Legoix! Am I to believe you didn't know what this woman here did for your brother, when she was still but a child? Do you think that I'm too doddering to remember those two young children who kidnapped a prisoner on his way to the gallows at Montfaucon, imperiling their own lives and showing a courage worthy of a better cause, and hid him in a cellar belonging to the girl's father . . . the cellar where he was discovered . . . the cellar of Gaucher Legoix, whom I promptly had strung up from his own goldsmith's sign. Gaucher Legoix! *Her* father!" he screamed, pointing at Catherine with a shaking finger. She was listening to him joyfully, something he would never understand. Almost choking with fury, he went on:

"She . . . Catherine Legoix . . . the little whore who tried to hide your brother in her bed . . . and now you're trying to tell me I should release her, poor fool!"

"Not in my bed!" protested Catherine, indignation giving her back her wits. "In the cellar!"

But Arnaud was not listening to Cauchon. He was looking at her as he had never dared to look at her before. With a beating heart, Catherine timidly returned his look. Arnaud's black eyes burned with all the love and passion she had despaired of ever seeing there. Still looking at her, he murmured:

"You don't know what you have just done for me, Bishop. Otherwise I think you would have thought better of it. Catherine, my love . . . my one and only love . . . can you ever forgive me?"

And they were both far, far away from the sinister keep with its damp walls and the capricious old man choking helplessly in his high-backed chair, gasping for air to fill his sick lungs. His burst of anger had set off a violent attack of emphysema. The breath rattled in his throat as he struggled for air, but he could have died in front of them without Catherine and Arnaud paying him the slightest attention, so lost were they in their private dream. They were making the most of this unforgettable moment in which, quite unexpectedly, all the wasted years of jealousy, rancor and cruelty were set at nought and the obstacles to their love overthrown.

"I have nothing to forgive you," Catherine murmured at last, her great violet eyes glowing with happiness. ". . . Because now, at last, I can tell you that I love you. . . ."

340

By now, the Bishop's apoplectic gasps had attracted the attention of a monk who rushed in to his assistance. Between two fits of coughing, he managed to point at the two prisoners and gasp out:

"To the dungeons . . . with them . . . one dungeon for each . . . in secret!"

As the archers dragged them from the room, they were still gazing at each other. The manacles on their wrists prevented them from touching each other, but the silent exchange of their eyes brought them closer together than any of their embraces had ever done. They both knew for a certainty now that they had been created for each other through all time, each chosen to complement and complete the other and be the whole world to each other. In their happiness, they forgot not only everything which had kept them so long apart, but the death which threatened them both. . . .

Their jailers were so afraid that they might find a way of communicating with each other, that they shut them up in the deepest dungeons in two different towers. Arnaud was chained up in the depths of the Beffroi tower and Catherine in a cell in the Deux Écus tower, thus forming a sort of tragic triangle with the cell in the Bouvreuil tower where the Maid was incarcerated. But although she had never been so cruelly imprisoned—they had lowered her on a rope to the bottom of a stinking hole where no light ever penetrated—Catherine was happier than she had ever been in Philippe's palace, or her dead husband's luxurious mansion. Her love made up for the lack of light and heat and everything else she was deprived of. She was in a state of grace, sustained through her wretchedness by the thought of Arnaud, made unhappy only by the thought of what he too must be suffering. She had but one fear: that she might not see him again before she died, but this fear did not torment her unduly. She knew Pierre Cauchon too well to believe that he would deprive himself of such a choice entertainment as torturing them both in front of each other would provide.

Time went by, however, and nothing happened. No one came, judges, interrogators, even jailers. Catherine had calculated that something like six days must have elapsed, but it was hard to be sure, since she could only work it out by the tramping of the guards overhead, and time meant little at the bottom of this dark, dark hole. No doubt if this entombment had gone on much longer, Catherine would gradually have succumbed to despair, but she did not have time. At length the glare of a torch lit up the foetid hole where she was crouching and a rope swung down with a warder tied to it who then helped to pull her out. She found herself standing in the bright sunlight on the Châtelaine tower, blinking her eyes like a night bird. The soldiers, who appeared to have been waiting for her, started to laugh when they saw her emerge, stumbling awkwardly in her bonds. One of them snatched up a bucket of water and threw it over her.

"Phew!" he cried. "Filthy creature!"

The game appealed to the others. They began to vie with each other to give her a soaking. The cold water took her breath away at first, but the sun was hot and she took a secret pleasure at the thought that each bucketful was washing away the stench of the dungeon. . . . A curt order from the captain of the guard and the men dropped their buckets. As Catherine stood there dripping, she felt her heart suddenly swell and almost burst with joy, for another figure was being led out of the Beffroi tower, tottering and groping before him with chained hands, because the bright sunlight had blinded him. He was filthy and emaciated, but Catherine would have recognized Arnaud in any conditions. They were surrounded by guards and so they could not run to each other, but merely to know that he was still alive was joy enough. . . . Their chains were replaced by ropes and they were propelled forward with the occasional blow from a pike-staff in the direction of the castle drawbridge. The time to die must have come and they were being taken to some town square where their punishment would serve as an example. . . .

When the prisoners and their guards reached the Old Market Square, Catherine began to feel a tremor of fear in spite of the happiness which still buoyed her up. Some ways of dying are peculiarly horrible and Catherine's eyes had fallen on a veritable mountain of faggots and logs, crowned by a grisly looking stake from which chains dangled. Distractedly, her eyes sought Arnaud's. He stood frowning, jaws clenched, looking at the stake as if he too were struggling with the same fear. It occurred to Catherine that he must confront his enemy with just the same look in his eyes in battle. But then, his thoughts flew to her and his eyes turned to her with such a look of love and pity in them that she already felt less frightened. A crowd of ragged men ran to and fro around the mountain of logs, piling them higher and higher under the executioner's instructions. . . .

The square was full of people, most of them English soldiers. The townspeople must have contented themselves with watching from windows, rooftops and the pillars of the old marketplace, because there were at least six or seven hundred soldiers packed into the triangular square, whose apex was marked by the steeple of Saint-Sauveur. Near the faggots stood a small gibbet, but Catherine knew that it was always there and no one was paying any attention to it at that moment.

The soldiers pushed their prisoners forward, but instead of directing them towards the stake, they led them up to two great, purple-hung stands which had been erected in front of the old Crown inn and which were, even now, beginning to fill up with priests and English dignitaries. The bowmen surrounded them so thickly that they were hidden from the crowd, but they were close enough to touch, fleetingly, and Catherine felt all her courage returning. Arnaud murmured, very quickly:

"It is not we who will die there, Catherine. That stake awaits someone else . . . and I hardly dare guess who that person can be. Look at the stands. . . ."

"Silence," growled the sergeant of the guard.

Just then, a party of bishops appeared on the stands. Among them, Catherine recognized Cauchon. They surrounded a massive silhouette dressed in a crimson cassock and ermine cape: the Cardinal of Winchester, and beside him, in full armor, the arrogant Earl of Warwick. These important personages sat down in throne-like chairs and the fat cardinal made a sign. As if awaiting this signal, all the town bells began to toll out a death knell: first Saint-Sauveur, then the Cathedral, Saint-Maclou, Saint-Ouen and all the rest. The mournful notes oppressed Catherine to the depths of her soul. She began to shiver in spite of the hot sun which had dried out her clothes and wet hair. A cart emerged from a nearby street, surrounded by a hundred English pikemen. Chained to the rails of the cart stood a slender, white figure wearing a sort of mitre on her head.

"Joan," Catherine moaned, her voice almost stifled by grief. "My God, it's Joan."

The *Miserere* chanted by the lusty throats of some fifty monks drowned her words, but she turned a horrified glance towards Arnaud.

"Are we going . . . to have to watch this horror?"

He merely nodded in reply, but Catherine saw two great tears roll down his cheeks. She bowed her head and began to weep. Her bound hands hurt her and she wildly regretted that she could not cover her eyes or ears to shut out those bells, the sinister chanting and the coarse laughter of the soldiers. The great tragedy that followed took on the character of an atrocious nightmare for Catherine, culminating in the moment when she saw that slim, white silhouette tied and bound up there on the summit of the huge pyramid of logs. Her tear-filled eyes did not let her see clearly, but she recognized Brother Isambard. He had climbed up beside Joan on the logs and

343

continued to exhort her. Catherine heard her ask for a crucifix and saw the sergeant standing before her stoop and pick up two sticks which he lashed together into a rough cross and held it out to the martyr. The executioner was running round the pyre, now, setting fire to it with a blazing torch. A pall of black smoke rose up, the flames crackled and leapt up towards Heaven. A terrible smell of sulphur and bitumen filled the air. Catherine had reached the limits of her endurance. She doubled up and vomited the little that her stomach contained.

"God!" Arnaud cried, struggling in his bonds. "Catherine! Don't die! You mustn't die!"

Without a word, the English sergeant ran to the inn and fetched a cup of wine from which he forced Catherine to drink a few mouthfuls. She felt a little better. The wine ran through her body like fire, bringing her back to life. She smiled a piteous smile at the sergeant who had come to her aid and saw that he was an ageing man with graying hair and mustache. She saw, too, that his eyes were full of tears beneath his helmet.

"Thank you, friend," came Arnaud's voice beside her.

The soldier shrugged his broad shoulders, dashed his hand angrily over his wet cheeks and growled, with an eye on the stake:

"I don't make war on women! Not like Bishop Cauchon. . . ."

His French was halting and guttural, but the meaning was plain.

Flames had completely enveloped the stake. A cry came from their midst. It was the condemned girl. She cried "Jesus." She was lost to sight now, but Brother Isambard still held out the great processional cross towards her, at the risk of going up in flames himself. The bonfire roared and crackled, belching out clouds of thick, black smoke. Not another sound was heard from its burning heart. Then, suddenly, the executioner beat back the flames and Joan's body appeared. She was dead. The fire had burned her chemise and exposed her girl's body, already charred and streaked with blood. This horror was too much for Catherine. She fainted away. . . .

She opened her eyes as a violent blow struck her. Someone was slapping her face, then something burning coursed down her throat. She coughed and choked and finally sat up, gazing round wide-eyed. The English sergeant who had given her wine to drink during Joan's execution was kneeling in front of her with a bottle in one hand.

"Better?" he asked gently.

"Yes . . . a little . . . thank you. Arnaud! Where is Arnaud?"

She was sitting in a low-ceilinged, bare room on a pile of straw.

344

A small barred window high up let in a little light, but the room did not look much like a prison.

"Your companion? He is next door, under strong guard. I left you here till you regained consciousness. . . ."

"Where are we?"

"The guard-room on the Great Bridge. Our orders are to keep you here till nightfall, under guard. I don't know any more than that. . . . Try to sleep. . . ."

He went out, his nailed boots clattering heavily across the stone floor. Catherine would have liked to detain him, but her hands were still tied together. She fell back on the straw, her eyes full of tears.

"Arnaud! I want to see him!"

"You will see him later. At present, it's forbidden."

She called him back:

"One moment, please! Why were you kind to me just then? You are English, aren't you?"

"Does that seem reason enough for a man to have no pity towards a poor girl?" he asked, with a sad smile. "Look, you, I have a daughter, too. She lives with her mother in a village near Exeter . . . and you look a little like her. When they dragged you out earlier on, I thought it was her I was seeing for a moment and it grieved me. . . ."

He evidently felt he had said enough, because he hurried from the room and shut the door. Catherine heard voices. She was too exhausted even to try and guess why she had been brought to this guard-post. Why hadn't they taken them back to prison since they had to wait here till nightfall? Anyway, she would soon know the answer. She heard the great bell tolling seven and closed her eyes, anxious for a little rest.

Little by little, the room grew dark. She could hear the river lapping below the window. The contours of the room disappeared into shadow. Soon there was no light except for a thin, yellow ray coming under the door. She would have stood up to try and hear what was being said on the other side of the door where voices were still engaged in conversation, but she found she had been chained to the wall. And then, suddenly, soon after, the door opened. Two archers entered, one on either side of a man in a black gown and a square cap. Another man followed and Catherine shrieked with terror as she recognized Geoffroy Terrage, the executioner. He was carrying something white over his arm. One of the archers released Catherine and untied her hands and then forced her to kneel, pushing her down by the shoulders. The black-gowned man coughed, withdrew a scroll from his pocket and read it by the light from the open door:

"By order of the ecclesiastical court of this town of Rouen, the said Pierre and Catherine Son are declared guilty of conspiring with the sorceress, known as the Maid, who was consumed and burnt this day in the Old Market Square of Rouen, and are condemned to be drowned in the Seine by the hand of the executioner till they are dead. . . ."

A sudden fury seized Catherine and she sprang up as though about to fling herself at the man with the scroll.

"Condemned? And who passed sentence upon us? This document has nothing to do with me. I am not Catherine Son, but Catherine de Brazey, and my companion is the noble Lord Arnaud de Montsalvy. . . ."

If she had hoped to impress the judge, she was mistaken. He sighed heavily and looked at the executioner.

"Do your work, Maître Geoffroy . . . Monseigneur the Bishop warned us that these people were not in their right minds and that the demon of pride was rife in them. She also takes herself for a high and mighty lady."

Terrage gave a loud laugh and threw the white garment he was carrying at Catherine.

"Put this on . . . and quick about it, unless you want me to do it for you."

It was a long white chemise. Catherine had the strange impression that she had gone back to the beginning again. Was she really at Rouen, or were these still the walls of Orleans around her? Once again, she was going to her death. But she did not flinch from the idea. . . . She might die . . . but Arnaud would die with her and they would be together for all eternity. What did it matter, then, how she died, by drowning or by hanging, so long as it was not by fire.

She undressed hurriedly, eyes lowered to avoid the men's gaze, and slipped on the chemise, calmly knotting the ribbon round her neck.

"I am ready," she said, so haughtily that the executioners were intimidated.

They led her from the guard-post and then through the city gates. The curfew had sounded and there was no one in the streets. A sharp wind was blowing in from the sea and dark grey clouds raced across the black sky. On the middle of the bridge stood a group of men, lit up by the flickering light of a couple of torches. Catherine perfectly understood Cauchon's ruse. It would have been tricky to condemn and execute two people of their rank, especially knowing of the attachment which had existed for so long between Catherine and Philippe of Burgundy, but this way he had nothing to fear. Who would reproach him for having two, half-crazed clodhoppers thrown

346

into the Seine at night for complicity with Joan of Arc? It was indeed a cunning stroke. . . .

Catherine felt icily calm. She could even look at the black water whose damp smell was borne to her on the wind. So it was all to end here? There was nothing left to hope for, unless it were a better life hereafter. It was really better like this. They would die together, those erstwhile enemies whom a great love now welded indissolubly for all time. That dream, at least, Catherine would have realized. . . .

When she reached the group on the bridge, she saw Arnaud standing there. He had been stripped of all his dirty, torn clothing, except for a strip of cloth about his loins. He was as magnificent in his half-nakedness as an antique statue in a mud pit. He stood watching her approach, smiling. . . . His hands were tied behind his back. A huge, leather sack lay at his feet, open, with three heavy stone weights in it. Beside him, a priest held up a black crucifix.

"You have a minute in which to repent of your sins," said the executioner maliciously.

Then, side by side, they knelt before the priest, like a bride and groom in a chapel, and bowed their heads. The words of absolution came to them like words in a dream. Then the executioner asked:

"Have you a last request?"

It was Arnaud who answered, looking at Catherine.

"Untie me, so that I can hold her in my arms. That way, death will come easier to us both."

Geoffroy Terrage consulted the black-robed man. The executioner seemed like a man devoured by an inner torment. The judge shrugged indifferently.

"Do what they wish. . . ."

A blow from a dagger and Arnaud's bonds fell. Then he took Catherine in his arms, held her close and covered her face with kisses.

"It won't be long, you'll see," he said tenderly. "Once, when I was a boy, I nearly drowned in a lake back home. . . . I lost consciousness. . . . It doesn't hurt. . . . Don't be afraid."

"I'm not afraid of pain with you, Arnaud! I just wish I had had a little more time to tell you how much I loved you. . . ."

"But we shall have all the time in the world, my sweet . . . all eternity, an eternity for us both alone."

Someone sniffed behind them. Then an anonymous voice asked, a little hoarsely:

"Are you ready?"

"We are ready. You may proceed," said Arnaud, with his lips against Catherine's hair.

They looked only at each other and did not see the executioner drop the weights into the sack. Still entwined in each other's arms, they were laid down on the sack and then total darkness enveloped them. The priest's voice murmuring the prayers for the dying reached them from a long way off. Catherine suddenly felt very warm. She trembled a little, a nervous reflex, and Arnaud calmed her with a kiss. Then she felt herself being lifted up by many hands.

"Do not be afraid," Arnaud murmured, close to her lips. "I love you...."

They fell through what seemed like aeons of space. Then, there was a loud splash and a cold shock hit them. The heavily weighted sack was filling up. The waters closed over it. . . . It was all over, ended. Catherine clasped Arnaud to her and thought that she was taking her love with her. He was there, pressed close against her, one with her, flesh of her flesh. He drank in her breath, this breath which was already failing. Blinding red lights flashed across her closed lids. She could not breathe. The icy water was beginning to invade the thick, leather sack like a monstrous, slimy beast. Catherine tried to murmur once more:

"I love you...."

But she had no breath left. She plunged into a huge, black chasm, freed at last from pain and fear and the desire of men, alone in death with the man she loved. . . .

"I began to think I would never get that cursed sack open!" Jean Son's voice came sleepily through the darkness. "It was so heavy! Luckily, my knife cuts like a razor."

Still only half conscious, Catherine was astonished to hear the voices of the living around her. Something sharp and scented reached her nostrils and made her open her eyes.

It was dark and cold and a great star blazed high in the sky. . . . But it was so cold! Catherine's teeth started to chatter.

"We'll have to take that soaking chemise off her," said another voice. "There are some dry clothes on the barge."

Then she realized that she was not dreaming and that she had been saved. Just then, a dark form bent over her and she heard Arnaud's voice and felt his hands undressing her and enveloping her in something soft and warm.

"How can I ever thank you, Jean? You worked a miracle getting us out of the river like that! It seems almost incredible!" he was saying.

"Not at all, not at all," Jean Son said, laughing. "I have enough connections among the English to keep track of what was happening. I knew what was going to happen to you, so I slipped into the water under the bridge, just where they usually throw the people in. Mind you, I was a bit nervous. . . . It's a long time since I last had a swim. But I was lucky enough to hit the sack first go and slit it right down from one end to the other. It's at the bottom of the river now, and both of you are alive and well, which is the main thing. Now, we must hurry! You must get as far as possible from here by daybreak. The boat is solid enough. It has a rod, money and food aboard. . . . You need only head towards Pont-de-l'Arche, then Louviers. I leave you now! Good luck!"

"Thank you again," Arnaud murmured.

Catherine struggled up weakly. She was sitting in a boat. In the darkness, she felt Arnaud's arms around her, strong and protective. On the shore, a rotund silhouette was fast disappearing from view.

"Are we really safe?"

She felt him smile in the darkness and felt his lips on her eyelids.

"Yes, indeed! Safe, free . . . it's marvelous!"

"Dying together . . . that was marvelous, too!"

Arnaud's laugh, his old, gay, strong laugh, rang out softly in her ear.

"One would almost think you were sorry!"

"A little bit. . . ." Catherine sighed. "It was beautiful. . . ! What are we going to do now?"

"Live . . . and be happy! We have so much lost time to make up for."

He stood up and Catherine saw his powerful silhouette against the night. He pushed the boat out into the current, then looked for the pole and with a mighty push, thrust the boat downstream. Something white flashed past them with a shrill scream, then dived into the black water.

"What's that?" Catherine asked.

"A gull. Fishing. I'll teach you to fish, too, when we get to Montsalvy."

"Montsalvy?"

"Of course. That's where I'm taking you. . . . To my home, your home, our home. . . . I haven't forgotten that I have a score to settle with Cauchon, but first we must build our own happiness. We have had to wait too long for it."

A great joy overtook Catherine. She lay down in the bottom of the boat, tranquil and happy, and let herself drift with it, downstream. For the first time in her life she was able to savor the joy of no longer having to decide for herself, or letting a stronger, but gentle force carry her along with it. She no longer regretted that union beyond the grave. At the end of this dark, watery road, a life together awaited them. . . . Life with the only man she had ever loved. All was well!

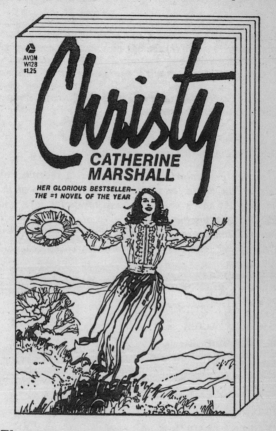